SHARED VENGEANCE

SHARED VENGEANCE

BILL BLIZZARD

SHARED VENGEANCE

XYRA Publishing

ISBN: 978-0-578-33608-4

Cover Design: Rich Denham
Cover photograph courtesy of NBC News

For Pat, Parul and Marcie
and
The Millions of Women Who Are
Still Forced to Navigate a Man's World

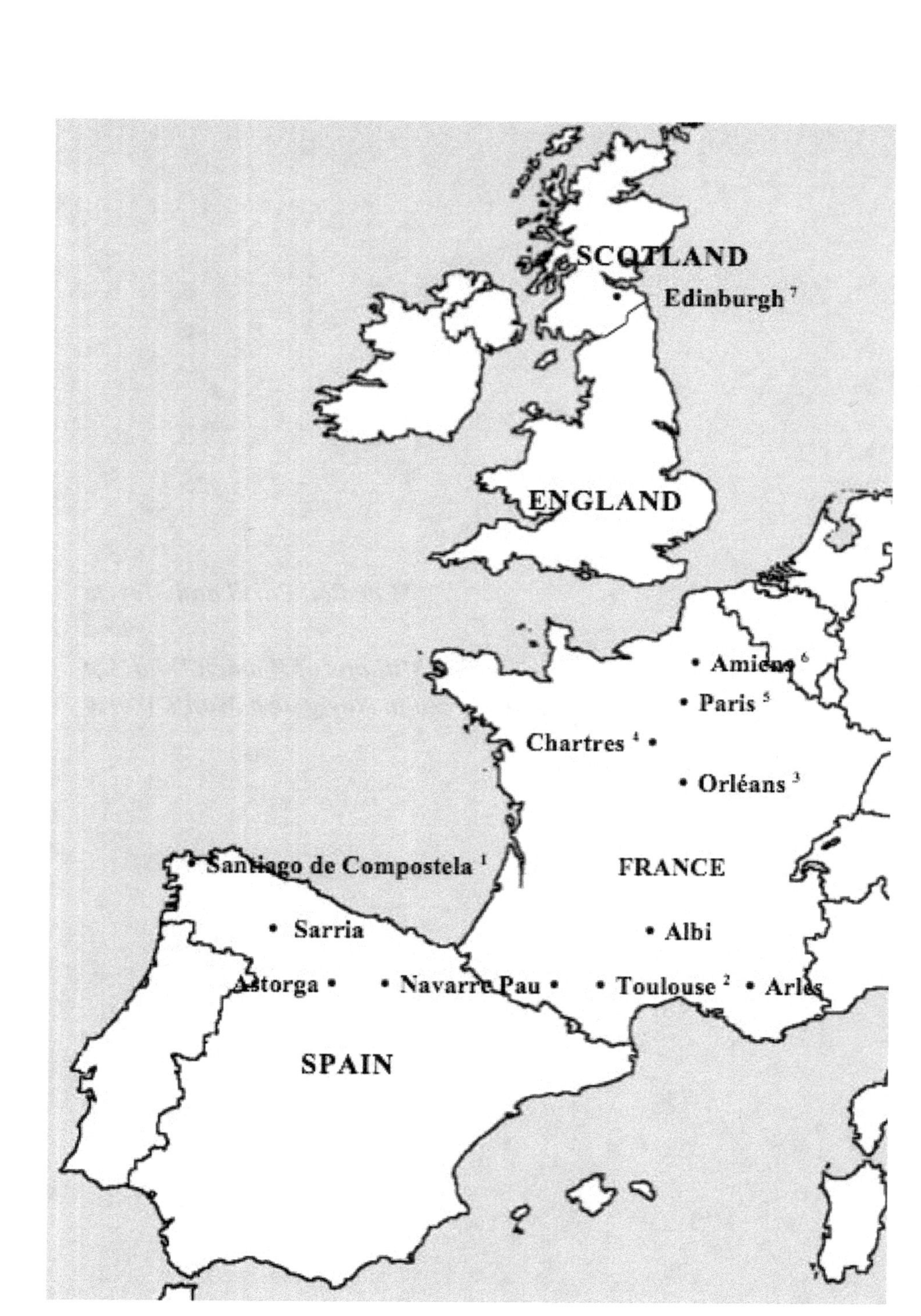
SCOTLAND
Edinburgh [7]
ENGLAND
Amiens [6]
Paris [5]
Chartres [4]
Orléans [3]
Santiago de Compostela [1]
FRANCE
Sarria
Albi
Astorga
Navarre
Pau
Toulouse [2]
Arles
SPAIN

ACKNOWLEDGEMENTS

SHARED VENGEANCE draws on the mystical, European sites described by Tim Wallace-Murphy and Marilyn Hopkins in *Rosslyn, Guardian of Secrets of the Holy Grail* [1] as shown and numbered on the facing page. These sites set the stage and informed the sequential path from Santiago de Compostela in north-western Spain to Edinburgh, Scotland for Renee Gaston and other characters in this book.

The late Tim Wallace-Murphy was a scholar, notable author and lecturer "on the Knights Templar, Rosslyn Chapel and the Sinclairs (founders of Rosslyn)."

Marilyn Hopkins, "gifted with a natural dowsing ability," spent many years "studying various forms of Christianity and esoteric spirituality." She has lectured on these subjects extensively.

In this work the authors "... pay tribute to Trevor Ravenscroft, whose insight and thinking pervades our own."

In keeping with their tribute to Trevor Ravenscroft, I am grateful for their ideas, identified traditions and observations in this fascinating field of study.

My thanks also go to Kathy, Keith, Martha, Nancy, Teresa, and Jim – friends all – whose early reading, criticism and encouragement meant so much to me. And a special thank you goes to my wife, Pat, whose love, intelligence and strength were my inspiration for this book.

FACT

WASHINGTON, DC - FEBRUARY 4, 2020

The first two decades of this century have seen the predictable clawing back of the social progress made in the United States during the thirty-five years that followed the mid-1960s. Save a smattering of both northern and southern states, in no place has this been more evident than the District of Columbia. And perhaps nothing has been more regressive and demeaning than the attack on women. This was clearly demonstrated by the 2016 GOP presidential candidate who bragged to *Access Hollywood's* Co-Anchor Billy Bush about his celebrity and sexual dominance over women in general and Bush's prior co-anchor specifically. Nancy O'Dell's response:

> Politics aside, I'm saddened that these comments still exist in our society at all. When I heard the comments yesterday, it was disappointing to hear such objectification of women. The conversation needs to change because no female, no person, should be the subject of such crass comments, whether or not cameras are rolling. … I feel I must speak out with the hope that as a society we will always strive to be better.[2]

Tuesday, February 4, 2020 once again underscored this continuing problem in a society whose stated goal is "life, liberty and the pursuit of happiness." On this date, the former president awarded the Presidential Medal of Freedom to Rush Limbaugh during his third State of the Union address.

At its close, the Speaker of the US House of Representatives, Nancy Pelosi, stood and calmly ripped the former president's speech in half.

Women are finally fighting back. Since the election of 2016, #MeToo has focused a bright light on sexual harassment and sexual assault. On October 29, 2018, *New York Times* article reported, "#MeToo Brought Down 201 Powerful Men. Nearly Half of Their Replacements Are Women." Jeffery Epstein and Harvey Weinstein among many others have been convicted of physical attacks, while it seems verbal attacks are not only protected by the first amendment but awarded with a now tarnished medal.

According to the White House, "The Presidential Medal of Freedom was established in 1963 by President John F. Kennedy and is the nation's highest civilian honor. It's awarded by the president to those who have made exceptional contributions to the security of national interests of America, to world peace, or to cultural or other significant public or private endeavors."

Critics responded on social media to denounce the former president's decision immediately following the award. Many comments were aimed at Limbaugh's verbal attack on a co-ed law student, whom he called a "slut" and "prostitute" after her Congressional testimony supporting women's health in the Affordable Care Act.

Since then, the global impacts of climate change and Covid 19 and attacks on minorities, voting rights, and the U.S. Constitution have gained equal attention to sexual harassment and this regressive stance on women's rights. This novel is set in 2012 to capture a moment in history and tell a fictional story that still needs to be told.

And with growing tension surrounding *Roe v Wade* it needs to be told now more than ever.

PREFACE

JERUSALEM – C. 1000 BCE

King David unified the Northern Kingdom of Israel and the Southern Kingdom of Judah approximately 1,000 years before the Common Era. Succeeding him, his son, Solomon, built the First Temple in Jerusalem, 'King Solomon's Temple.'

By the time the oral stories of the Kingdoms of Israel and Judah were first written (c. 900 BCE) a belief in a single god was emerging. The pairing of gods and goddesses, however, still remained in the minds of the Israelites. These early stories were later expanded to become the Jewish epic known as the Torah.

Asherah was the consort (or wife) of the god of the Israelites, Yahweh (YHWH), or Elohim (El) depending on how the word is used in biblical text. Asherah's statue stood at the altar of Yahweh, within King Solomon's Temple. King Solomon made offerings to her. Asherah continued to be seen as a goddess for about 350 years after Solomon's death.

Two tragic events bookend the history of the Jewish people. The first is the Israelites' bondage by their Egyptian oppressors. Their faith in their God led to Passover and their Exodus in c. 1250 BCE. The second is the holocaust of Jewish extermination beginning with the construction of Dachau Concentration Camp in 1933 through VE Day in 1945. You are likely familiar with both.

At least three other times in Jewish history were similarly devastating.

- **c. 625 BCE:** King Josiah ascended to the throne at the age of eight following the murder of his father, King Amon. As he grew, the prophets invested a great deal in him. His faithfulness to their traditions was seen as a sign of hope after the evil of the past two kings – his father and grandfather. At age twenty-six, King Josiah began to reconstruct the First Temple. In doing so he purportedly discovered a book written by Moses himself. It was substantially the book of Deuteronomy – meaning "the Second Law".

King Josiah and his High Priest, Jeremiah, initiated a great transformation in the way people worshipped with Deuteronomy. This included removing Asherah from places of worship and solidifying monotheism.

"And you shall tear down their altars, smash their monuments, burn their asherim [poles related to the worship of Asherah] with fire, cut down the graven images of their gods, and destroy their name from that place." Torah, Deuteronomy (Devarim) 12:3.

As dramatic as they were, these reforms did not bring about God's favor. In 609 BCE, Egyptian Pharaoh Neco went north to join the Assyrians. King Josiah refused to let him pass and intercepted him on the plains of Megiddo. Josiah was killed. This battle and his death combined to be such a tragic moment in Jewish history it gave rise to the mythological battle of Armageddon, which would take place at the end of times.

- **596 BCE:** Within thirteen years, the Babylonians had defeated the Assyrians and had become the most dominant military power in that part of the world. Nebuchadnezzar II, the commanding general of the Babylonians, swept through Judah and conquered Jerusalem in 596 BCE after a two-year siege. A puppet ruler, Zedekiah, but still a member of the royal House of David, was set on the Jewish throne. Ten years later, a Jewish rebellion caused the Babylonians to recapture Judah. This Davidic king was forced to watch as all of his sons were killed. Then his eyes were plucked out. Solomon's Temple was destroyed. Almost all of the Jewish people were exiled to Babylon and held for forty-eight years in a period known as the 'Babylonian Captivity'. Their captivity ended in 538 BCE. Upon their return to Jerusalem the construction of the Second Temple began.

- **66 CE:** The Roman Empire dominated most of the known western world and ruthlessly oppressed the Jewish people. Led by the Zealots, Judah revolted against Rome in year 66 of the Common Era. Roman legions occupied Jerusalem, razed the city, sacked and plundered the Temple and killed hundreds of thousands of people of Jewish faith over the next seven years. The final stronghold at Masada was overrun in the year 73 CE.

* * *

The Deuteronomists described Canaan, roughly the area of modern day Israel, as having been taken by war after the Exodus of the Israelites from Egypt. As they crossed the Jordan River, the Israelites "… utterly destroyed all of the city [of Jericho], both man and woman, young and old, ox and sheep and donkey, with the edge of the sword" *(Joshua 6:21)* in the name of a vengeful and jealous god – a god who, according to the author(s), demanded to be worshipped alone. The prophets tried to soften this in later writings by making love central to the meaning of God, by making the poor visible, and by demanding justice. However, the God portrayed in this early part of the Jewish epic begs the following question.

If the worship of Asherah, the consort of Yahweh and Mother Goddess of the Kingdoms of Judah and Israel – the tree goddess, Mother Nature herself – had continued, would the world be different today?

It is in this context that the story of **SHARED VENGEANCE** is told.

CHAPTER 1

PARIS, FRANCE - JULY 3, 2012

The commotion from her fellow passengers went unnoticed as Renee Gaston concentrated on what she would tell her fiancé. She had spent four lonely weeks in Europe. She now nervously waited for her return flight. Yesterday, her world was upended, her vision for the future shattered.

The serenity of May commencement came to an abrupt end the week before she left her Jesuit University for Paris. Catholic Bishops had rejected President Obama's proposal for birth control coverage in the Affordable Care Act. Their coordinated attack resulted in forty-three plaintiffs filing a dozen lawsuits against his administration.

Renee's first international journalism assignment waited for her in Europe. Gerard trusted her ability. She was eager to get to it. She was now leaving a campus and country in turmoil. A week after the lawsuits were filed the Bishops lost the high moral ground as the media began to see their attack as more political than religious.

In the distance, she could hear her boss, Professor Howard Gerard, ranting about recent events, "If last February wasn't bad enough with Fluke's Congressional testimony and the Vatican's reprimand of the Leadership Conference of Women Religious in April, we now have to deal with the bishops lighting their hair on fire and the press getting involved."

Don't even get me started, she thought as she closed the door of her Georgetown University office and headed to the airport.

Stan Parker and Renee were engaged to be married after her graduation. She could hardly wait. Her future was set. It would have been perfect had her life unfolded as she had envisioned. It did not.

Should I tell Gerard what happened to me? How? I've done my time in Spain for him and in a few hours, I'll be back with Stan. He'll help me figure out this nightmare, Renee thought as she sat quietly, her eyes now closing to dream of the moment.

"Renee," Sebastian's quietly strained voice came from the seat behind her. It frightened her back into the reality of where she was. She turned toward the man from her youth she once loved, but now despised.

Her life had progressed from their shared days at a Jesuit high school, but Sebastian Phillipe's had not. His grew darker and regressed into a life obsessed with what he distorted to be the will of God.

"How did you get in here?" Renee demanded.

He pulled his ticket from his jacket's pocket.

Wearing a stunning ruby ring inlaid with a gold Maltese cross, his outstretched hand pulled back to his lips and gestured for her to remain quiet. The ring's symbol was curiously familiar to Renee from her days as a young girl. She could not remember why. She now knew it symbolized the misplaced piety of some who wore it.

"Are you going on this flight?" she anxiously asked.

"No. I had to see you before you left France," he said as if obsessed about her and her departure. "I will try to get a refund later."

She turned in her seat and looked away.

He whispered to the back of her head. "Renee, before you left France, I had to tell you the Colonel asked me to follow you to Chartres and I did. I shouldn't be telling you this, but I hope it will in some way make up for my past mistakes. I know the man you spoke to and what he likely told you. The Colonel and members of the Order believe this man and his brother will tear down the Church and crucify our Lord once more. They must be stopped by any means necessary. I've come here to warn you that you are involved in a struggle that is way over your head. What you must be thinking is dangerous, Renee. You must abandon the idea."

An amplified announcement interrupted his dire warning. "Flight 4176 to John F. Kennedy International Airport is now ready for boarding."

"You must be careful," Sebastian insisted. "If you do not believe me, call your father."

She angrily stood and turned to see his sullen face. "My father? What has my father got to do with you? With Chartres?"

He rounded the row of seats and looked through the rage in her eyes to the soul of a girl he still loved. He did not answer. He attempted a smile. His eyes teared knowing what he had to do. His voice cracked as he said goodbye and picked up her daypack from the seat next to the one she had just occupied.

At Georgetown, the daypack contained class notes and an occasional book or two. Now, it contained a few items for the flight home, her journal, a final report for Gerard, as well as a few papers and photographs she was given, but did not want. The daypack also contained a small listening device Sebastian placed in a side pocket as he helped her slide her arms through the straps.

Renee checked in at the gate visibly shaken by his prophecy and unaware he would exchange his ticket for the same flight that departed the next day.

As she entered the jetway she turned back to see Sebastian lingering. He waved and mouthed the words "be careful."

* * *

"Hello, Papa. … Yes, Renee. … Yes, I'm here in New York. … Yes, fine, safe flight, no problem. … Yes, I know it's late. Papa, stop talking and listen.

"Right before I boarded the plane Sebastian accosted me. His words were frightening if not threatening. He told me the Colonel asked him to follow me there! He told me to be careful and what I was doing was dangerous. He told me if I did not believe him, I should call you. Do you know the Colonel? Do you know what he's talking about?"

"I'll take care of Sebastian. Trust me. Things will be fine," Jacques said. "I'll confront him when he gets home."

Renee's father, Jacques Gaston, tried to conceal his emotions as he explained recent events. He told her about the two men who paid him a visit just hours before her flight, but said he knew nothing about the Colonel. He seemed tense and anxious to a daughter who knew him well.

"Please don't. Leave him to me," she said afraid of what he might do.

WASHINGTON, DC - THE SAME EVENING

Jacques' end of the conversation went on for ten minutes leaving Renee just enough time to clear customs and get to her connecting one-hour hop to DC. *It's great to be home. It feels safe,* she thought as Sebastian's warning and her father's confirmation intensified what she'd recently learned. *Stan will know what to do.*

Renee left the secure area of Washington National and wove her way through the advancing passengers to the main terminal. Stan waited to greet her. Throwing herself into his arms she whispered, "My God, I've missed you. It's so great to be home! There's so much I have to tell you. I really don't know where to begin. But you know what? We really don't need to get into all of that right now. You're off work tomorrow, right? It can wait 'til then."

"Okay … I guess. Hungry?"

"No. No thanks, I had dinner on the plane. I just need to get some sleep, but somehow I need to force myself to stay awake for a few hours to get back on Washington time."

"Want to head back to my place and watch TV or something?"

"Sure, what's the something you had in mind?" she asked.

"Oh, I don't know. We could play scrabble or maybe some cards," he teased.

A ten minute drive south and they were in the heart of Old Town Alexandria at Stan's retreat. His education and work as an architect provided him with an appreciation for the many one-to two-hundred year old homes surrounding him. The classic colonials with brick walls and slate roofs were terribly attractive to him, but steam heating, multiple levels, small rooms, and heavily laden classic trim all combined to make them seem more like he was at work rather than a quiet refuge to call home. His inherited wealth provided him with the ability to express the other side of his personality – a contemporary condominium with a floor to ceiling glass-walled great room and a spectacular vista to Oronoco Bay Park, the Potomac River and the city beyond. Renee loved being there.

Multiple colored fireworks prematurely lit the darkening sky above the Potomac as home enthusiasts got a jump on the next day's festivities. *The burst of lights are so beautiful,* Renee thought as she gestured to Stan in the direction of the terrace.

"Go ahead. I'll join you in a minute," Stan encouraged. A prepared plate of cheeses and grapes awaited him in the refrigerator together with a chilled bottle of Cristal to welcome her home. In the distance, she could see his hands carried something not yet discernible. As he approached, she opened the door with a joyful smile and eyes that reflected starbursts above.

"Here you go. Care for a glass of champagne?" Stan said pouring a flute of Renee's favorite. "Welcome home, Renee."

The cool evening breeze off the Potomac was a needed relief to the intense heat and humidity of Washington in early July. Little was said. It was unnecessary. As the dusk of the evening sky slowly turned to a star-filled night of exploding fireworks, simply standing there, breathing in unison in the still and quiet of each other's embrace, captured their souls.

* * *

Renee awoke to the smell of bacon and to the early morning sunrise streaming through the balcony doors. Stretching, she smiled, remembering Stan's tenderness.

"Hey, Renee, is that you stirring? Come on out. Coffee's brewed and I'm getting ready to start a couple of omelets – goat cheese, caramelized scallions and chives – sound good?" asked the gourmet cook.

Renee rubbed the sleep from her eyes and took a moment for herself. She walked into the kitchen, kissed him on the cheek and managed a shy and quiet, "Good morning, dear. Last night was wonderful."

"For me too, Renee. Just a preview of our lives together."

"Yes, I know. When I was with my parents last month, I told them about our future plans. They are so excited for us. Next June is such a long time away, but I guess it is best we wait, right?" Renee asked with a sense of mixed emotions.

"I think so. It'll be here before you know it. Renee, last evening at the airport it seemed like you needed to tell me something about your trip?"

"Yes, I do, but just give me a little more time to sort all of this out," Renee said hoping to find the courage to discuss all she had been through. She knew time was a luxury she did not have.

"Okay, but I'm here."

"For now, just let me say this. The past four weeks have been life changing. It opened up a whole new way of thinking about how our culture grew out of a patriarchal set of values from thousands of years ago. I never thought about it much until now, but I'll ask you the question that has been rattling around in my head. Is there a connection between a society that worships a warrior god and one that spends lots of money on war and the preparation for war?"

"I suppose so, but why do…?" Stan began.

"Or more to the point," Renee interrupted, "like you implied on our first date, is there a connection between a society that has rejected the Mother Goddess and one that spends so little to save the planet, disparages women, denies its citizens universal health care, and allows its children to live in poverty, while it squanders money preparing for war?"

"Wow, that's pretty heady stuff for this time of the morning, Renee. That will need a lot of discussion. Sounds like your work for Gerard had a big impact," Stan said.

"Yeah, that's what I have been trying to tell you. It did; that and a couple of people I met while I was away. We can do this later, Stan. Meanwhile, why don't I turn on some music and enjoy the holiday?" Renee asked as she inserted a CD.

She picked up a copy of the *Washington Post* from the coffee table, "Says here they're expecting about 450,000 people on the Mall tonight to watch the fireworks."

"I know. If it's all the same to you, Renee, I think we can see them just fine from the park across the street. I'd really rather not go downtown today."

"Sounds like a plan. A holiday with my man," Renee announced, lifting herself onto the kitchen counter. She thought about the last four months and how her life had changed since that bitter cold evening last February. She smiled and said, "The past four months have been wonderful."

CHAPTER 2

WASHINGTON, DC - FOUR MONTHS EARLIER

Renee's eyes drifted from the window and scanned the room of the Federal Style home-turned-restaurant.

Outside, the streetlights captured the beauty of the snow laden evergreen branches of distant trees. Closer, the gently falling snow seemed to ease the bitter cold night air.

Inside, the marble clad fireplace of the nineteenth-century home warmed the chill of the room; maps of L'Enfant's vision for the city and Currier and Ives prints adorned its walls. This ambiance and the crisp linens, vintage china dinnerware, crystal goblets and silver flatware combined to not only provide an elegant shelter from the cold, but also took Renee to a time when Georgetown University was founded.

It was a night for good food and laughter. She had hoped a romantic evening might provide a quiet setting to help resolve a few of their differences. But it was not to be. Tonight, George seemed even more radical, distracted and angry.

George Wilson was a good old southern boy from South Carolina who barely graduated in the top twenty percent of his class at the state university in Columbia. Nevertheless, with his family's pedigree and contributions his father made to his alma mater, GU Law School admitted his son with the thinnest of margins. George was now in his second year.

When they first met, Renee thought George was a bright, handsome young man from Georgetown Law on his way to becoming a successful lawyer. He was kind to her and considerate, a true Southern gentleman. Over time he had changed.

"George, are you okay? Have I done something wrong?" she asked.

George turned to see the men debating. "No, just drop it, okay?" he was quick to respond having just overheard the comment about a fellow law student from the man in the tweed jacket.

* * *

"I totally disagree. I don't think we can simply ignore what's going on with her. The University has got to step up," Stan declared to his boss and golfing buddy of many years.

"Stan, keep your voice down," Howard insisted. "Other people are trying to enjoy themselves."

Straightening his posture in defense of his embarrassment, Professor Howard Gerard's eyes searched the dimly lit room for any peers who may have taken offense at his tablemate's enthusiasm.

"Sorry. Bad enough one of our law students drug us into the fray, but since we're there we've got to support her," Stan whispered in a determined voice. "With the pounding rhetoric of the right-wing antagonists and the mood of the country right now on economic and social issues, intellectual honesty is at stake. That's pretty important for any university, don't you think?"

Adjunct Professor Stanley L. Parker, 37 years old and single, was a perfect match for the History Department of Georgetown University. Dressed as he was tonight – tweed jacket, blue oxford button-down and a blue and green striped bow tie – Stan looked the part of tenured professor. It was the 'single' part that concerned one of the female members of his Capitol staff from his full time job – the Architect of the Capitol. He was considered a bit of a playboy. Not a good thing if you live within the gossip-filled enclave of the beltway.

"Good evening, gentlemen. May I get you something to drink?"

"Howard, this is my treat. That way I can continue to rant on a bit longer. I'll have Gentleman Jack on the rocks, and, Howard, your usual … Johnny Walker Black neat?"

"Thanks," Howard nodded in agreement.

Washington was in more turmoil than usual during the 112th Congress. The Republican Party controlled both houses of Congress and were out to take down President Obama and his major accomplishment – the Affordable Care Act – any way they could. One way was to repeal provisions for contraceptive coverage. Georgetown University was caught square in the crosshairs of the debate. The Architect of the Capitol was too.

Stan was an accomplished designer but loved people rather than projects and the history of architecture even more. His credentials, family's wealth and political connections within the Democratic Party earned him a full-time position as the Architect of the Capitol in 2009. It was perfect for him. Not only was he able to learn more about Federal architecture and work with a great many dedicated people, but he also had the flexibility to continue with the faculty of Georgetown – now as a part-time professorial lecturer.

Yes, his job seemed perfect except for one thing – he hated getting beaten up by Congress during the budgeting process. Every year the same hurdle existed. He proposed the necessary budget to properly hold together the deteriorating buildings placed in his charge, but they apparently expected him to do it with duct tape. Each budget cycle, Congress tried to score political points and not raise the necessary funds to effectively run the government – October's proposed budget was no exception.

"Certainly our leadership, alums and donors will not be happy if we support Sandra Fluke. So why do it? This will pass. And like it or not, the Religious Freedom Restoration Act of 2012 will be law, count on it," Gerard said in the politically correct manner required of a Department Chair.

"Yes, it may pass, unless the Capitol dome falls down around their ears first."

"Oh yeah, I caught your testimony two weeks ago."

"I need a hundred million dollars to fix the problems and those cowards are still playing politics."

"Any movement yet?"

"No, of course not. They're still posturing. We'll probably never get a budget passed, but let's get back to the issue at hand. The health of half of the country's citizens is …"

Stan began to mount a campaign, when he drifted away from the heated conversation momentarily. Suddenly, his gaze met the eyes of one of his prior students across the room. Nodding, a smile crossed his face. She forced a smile in his direction and pushed away a tear.

"Stan … Stan? It doesn't seem like I have your attention anymore."

"Yes, I'm sorry, it's one of my students from a few years ago over there. She seems to be upset. Where were we?"

* * *

George Wilson was a devout Catholic and an arch conservative. He hated the demographic changes his country was going through. He grew intensely frustrated by the growing prominence and rise to power of women, African Americans and Latinos over the past several years. It was clear that he struggled to keep up with school and the changing world around him.

Renee was bright, liberal and agnostic. She had always been a shy girl, seeming to a casual observer that she was a little cold or aloof or at times somewhat meek. In truth, she was afraid of allowing herself to show her true feelings for fear of getting hurt as she had many years before. Her shyness made it difficult for her to make friends. Once secure in a relationship she had an easy-going personality unless she was provoked or had to take a stand for something she deeply cared about. She was far from meek.

Over the months, George's affection for her became obvious and she returned his affection. Their relationship grew. She became vulnerable.

Tonight, George's kindness toward her vanished. She absorbed his cruelty until she could do so no longer. *What's with George tonight? Wonder what's going on in his head* she thought, remembering the past few months of their relationship that seemed pleasant enough.

The South Carolina primary vote went well for his hero, Newt, but right after the Florida Primary he started getting weird and depressed thinking Romney might run the table, Renee thought. *It must be Super Tuesday coming up that's got him so upset.*

"George, what's wrong. Is it the election?" Renee questioned once again.

"I asked you to drop it …"

"I'm just concerned I may have …"

"You just can't let it rest, can you? You're not going to like it, but here it is. See those two guys over there?" he said gesturing with his head. "See the pretty one over there with the bow tie, facing you? He's been droning on and on about your friend, Sandra."

Renee soon found her thoughts about the looming Super Tuesday vote were wrong. That would have been simple. But George now revealed a part of his personality she had never seen before. He was no longer the bright star he once seemed, but was angry, mean spirited, and completely obsessed about her friend's recent testimony to Congress.

"I know she's a Protestant, but how could she possibly bring this shame on us? How could your friend testify before the committee on something as ridiculous as having American taxpayers pick up the tab for her week-end sex flings? How could she betray our Catholic values like she did? Christ!"

I should have known it would be about Sandra, something he knows absolutely nothing about. Why are these Neanderthals getting involved with women's health issues? Renee thought.

Instead of a romantic evening as she had hoped, Renee now sat shaking uncontrollably among the 50-plus guests surrounding her. She felt as though she had just been kicked in the stomach – physically sick, alone and betrayed. Had he changed or had she just not paid attention, until now?

"She even opened her testimony with, 'I attend a Jesuit law school that does not provide contraceptive coverage in its student health plan.' Well, duh, this is a Catholic school. She knew when she applied for admission, come on," George announced with the vitriol of a wounded combatant.

"But George …" Renee said, attempting to inject a thought.

He opened his leather-bound daily journal that was always by his side and turned to February 23rd for reference. He continued to bark, sarcastically mocking her testimony, "'Women who work for religiously affiliated employers suffer because they cannot get contraception.' Really? Of course they can, they just don't want to pay for it. Better their employers or the government should! And the whole idea of it being for health-related issues, what's that … maybe one person in a zillion? What bullshit. This whole line of thinking is just ridiculous!"

"Hey! Take a breath. What are you talking about? Am I going to get a word in here sometime?" Renee loudly whispered in total disbelief.

He continued his relentless attack, "I can't believe you would support such a radical thinker. It's just like the time you rallied in support of Harvard's president in her help-the-gays lawsuit to keep the military off the campus. That was another ridiculous stunt. She just wanted to pad her résumé."

Pounding on the table with the clinched fist of his right hand to make his point, Renee noticed him wearing a new piece of jewelry – a gold ring with a ruby stone and Maltese cross. "What's with the ring? Have you joined some sort of new religious cult? Is that why you're acting so bizarre?" she asked.

"No, you wouldn't understand!" he said. "And keep the knights out of it," George commanded.

"Knights? Ha! You ought to learn something about chivalry."

All of his testosterone-led ignorance is unbelievable. He's no more a knight than Monty Python's guy at the bridge. Why am I here with this idiot? He seems to be so much like the other religious fanatics trying to close abortion clinics or Governor Ultrasound's nonsense about vaginal probes. Things have really gotten out of hand. Do we really need government telling us how to provide for our own health care? Renee thought, fearing the worst was yet to come from Congress or from the courts.

Her attempts to quiet George, who by this time was causing a scene, were unsuccessful. "Enough!" Renee blurted out. *Enough, it's over,* she thought. *How could I have been so blind about him? I simply have to swallow my pride and get out of here!*

Renee pushed back the table in hopeless disgust. Their water glasses tipped in his direction. She abruptly stood and yelled, "George, you don't have any idea of what you're talking about … so just shut up!"

Now feeling more anger than hurt, she took a deep breath, gathered her purse and composure, and with a sense of righteous indignation calmly walked from a room full of strangers. Strangers who she would never see again, except for Professor Parker.

The wait-staff scrambled to handle the spilled water. The maître-de scurried to retrieve her winter coat and hail a cab. George sat alone to wind down his hatred – his soaked lap now chilling his uncontrollable passion.

Looking completely baffled by what had just happened, George reached for a napkin to dry himself. He offered an embarrassed shrug to his fellow guests, signaled for the check, and then began a notation in his journal.

Sunday, January 26. RE: Renee Gaston.

Dinner tonight was awful. Sandra's to blame. Must apologize to Renee.

* * *

"Howard, when is your research assistant's last day?" Stan asked.

"Next Thursday. Why? What do you have in mind?" Howard's response and furrowed brow suggested he already knew.

Smiling through his words Stan confessed, "I think I know the perfect candidate to take her place."

CHAPTER 3

SANTIAGO DE COMPOSTELA, SPAIN - NOVEMBER 2, 1934

The distant streetlight barely penetrated their murky living room windows. Even so, it provided enough light for the boys to see the silhouettes of two goons poking their father with sharpened bayonets.

"Stop! Stop hurting him!" the young voices of six-year-old Rafael and Miguel, age three, begged as they watched their father cower on the floor of their dingy second floor apartment.

"Please … please do not kill me!" pleaded their father, a frail man of fifty-one years whose failing health was the result of a lifetime of smoking. "Their mother is no longer alive. They only have me." As his terrified sons yelled with each recoil of their father's bloody torso, Ramon continued his relentless pleading to the butchers aligned with Mola's army. "Please. Please. I mean no harm to you or to the Church. I just want things better for my children. I want to live in peace."

Social activist Ramon Tuguía, himself a member of the Socialist Party, was a sympathizer to the growing movement of revolutionary Spain. King

Alfonzo XIII fled the country and later abdicated. It was a bloodless transfer of power. The military simply refused to support the king against the will of the people. A new constitution was written in 1931 and a provisional government established, but the King's abdication had little effect on the lives of the poor.

The land-owners still owned the land, the power structure of the ruling class remained intact and the powerful and conservative Catholic Church was still entrenched. All hope for change to the lives of the peasants and workers was dashed as three members of a right-wing political force were put in the cabinet of a coalition government of the new Republic.

There seemed to be only one choice remaining. Revolution erupted, led by a coalition of labor, Socialists, Communists, and Anarchists, as coal miners went on strike in northern Spain. In the province of Austurias, eight teachers, all Brothers of the De La Salle Catholic School, and their priest were brought to a mock trial and summarily executed by the revolutionaries. This act of insurrection set into motion what two years later became the Spanish Civil War.

"Get up, coward. We saw you share in the violence of the riotous forces two weeks ago. Do you deny you were there?"

"Yes, I deny it. I was here, I was not in Austurias. You can ask Father Ortega. I work as a custodian at the cathedral under his charge. Ask him. He will tell you I was here," Ramon said, holding his side as he began to stand.

"You were quick to mention Austurias. How do you know I was talking about Austurias?"

"That's the only violence I've heard of recently. Is there more?" Ramon asked somewhat sarcastically.

"Shut up. Your sarcasm will not help you," Sgt. Garcia said, striking Ramon in the mouth with the back of his opened hand. Ramon's head lurched back as the blood from his mouth flew across the room.

"We know where you work and what you do. We know about your traditions and your heresy. We know you clean the cathedral and about your measly little existence. We also know you stole something from the cathedral. So, tell me sinner, where is it?"

"Where is what?" Ramon asked.

Garcia knocked him to the ground and kicked him in the stomach, again. Miguel continued to cry. Rafael yelled once again for them to stop – this time beating on Garcia's back with his tiny, clenched fists. Rafael remembered what his father had told him only a few weeks before and tried to help him as best he could.

Garcia turned and slapped Rafael back against the wall. He then returned to his prey.

"You know damn well what I'm talking about. And, no, I don't believe you were here. We saw your ugly face in a picture of the crowd in Austurias. You were there with your comrades and yelled in defiance of the confederation and the new Republic. We followed you and your Jew friend back from Austurias. We have watched you since then. Do you think we are not informed? Do you think we are stupid? I'm going to ask you once again, you stupid, feeble little man. Where is it? I'll be damned if I'm going to let you rebel against the government and blaspheme the Church!"

Gasping for air, Ramon coughed, "I still don't know what you're talking about!"

"I'm talking about the thing you stole from the cathedral. I've been ordered to investigate the rumors you took a container of some kind from the crypt."

"I did not steal anything. What are you talking about?" Ramon exerted all of his strength to lie once more.

"Get up. José, tie him to the chair, and shut those kids up. They're getting to be a pain in the ass."

"No! Leave them alone!" Ramon cried out attempting to protect them from his adversaries.

"Shut up!" Garcia demanded striking Ramon with the back of his hand once again.

* * *

Ramon had confided in his young son three weeks before the miners' strike. "Rafael, I have something I must tell you. Please sit down and listen to me," Ramon said in a solemn tone gesturing to their thread-bare sofa.

"Yes, father, what is it?" Rafael asked in earnest.

"Spain is going through a very terrible time right now. People are divided into two groups who hate each other very much. One side, our side, are the people on the left, as we call them. Everyone on our side is poor. There are very few jobs for us. There is not enough money for us to buy what we need. There is not enough food to eat. The people on the other side …"

"The right, father?"

"Yes, the right," Ramon answered seeming somewhat amused by his son's alert reaction to his attempt to explain a difficult situation. "The people on the right have all they need. They are once again in control and continue to be very cruel to us."

"Rafael, remember we talked about elections before?"

"Yes, father."

"When you were three years old the people of Spain wrote a story about how we wanted to live. Your mother was so happy that you and our new child would have a better life than us. Her death was such tragic day for both you and me, but she delivered your brother into a world now filled with hope. She wanted nothing more from this life than to have her children grow and be safe from the hatred that surrounded us.

"We wrote some rules and started a group to carry out our rules. We called the group a Republic. During our first two years, we made a lot of changes. We removed the Catholic Church from power, allowed for people to be married outside of the Church, and started public education rather than having to be taught by the Jesuits. Our part of Spain was almost able to break away from the rest of Spain, as we wanted. Everyone was thought to be equal. Women were given the right to vote in elections. This was something your mother wanted very much.

"At that point it seemed things would be better for us, so we held our first election just last year," Ramon continued, "I was so sad your mother was not able to see her dream come true, but she would be happy her friends had the vote if she were alive, I know. Some of our people did not believe things would ever be better. They wanted no part of the Republic or to have property or bosses or the Church or even God."

"But we want God, don't we father?" Rafael asked, remembering the stories told to him by his father.

"Yes, of course we do. I said *some* people. But our beliefs are different from the Catholic Church. Just now when I said the people wrote a story, it's called a constitution and it gave people the right to think about God any way they chose and not just as the Catholics do. To us, Jesus was not a god as they would have you believe. He was a man who did wonderful things for both men and women when he was alive," Ramon stressed to his young son.

"Yes, I know father. You have told me about the wonderful things before," Rafael smiled.

"Rafael, please pay attention to what I'm about to tell you. A few months ago, when I repaired the floor of the cathedral crypt, I found a story written in an old, strange language. It was put deep within the crypt and hidden out of sight under some floor stones that had become loose. It had been there for a very long time. I knew no one remembered it being there and thought it might be valuable. I brought it home.

"My good friend Ezra Hitzig was able to make out a few words. It is in a language like his, but not exactly. The words he made out proved to me it was something of great importance. When all of the current conflicts calm down, I will have it translated. For now it remains safe from the leaders of the Church. They would destroy it if it says what I think it does. I have given it to my brother Juan for safekeeping. Other than me, your uncle is the only other person in the world who knows where it is hidden."

"I don't understand," Rafael said with a concerned voice and worried look.

"I know you don't, not now, but someday you will. Trust me. No mention must ever be made of it. You must keep this secret for me.

"When you get older, remember what I tell you now. If I am not able to get the story from your uncle myself, you get it. Also, I want you to remember a man named Gil-Robles. He and his confederation are the ones to blame for our troubles."

"Confederation, father?" Rafael questioned.

"Yes, Rafael. La Confederación Española de Derechas Autónomas, just remember the first letters in its name – CEDA. Gil-Robles and his followers, and the Catholic Church all want to remain in power. They formed the group they call CEDA. And even though the Church is involved, these rich and powerful people continue to look after themselves and do not care about us or the Republic.

"When we held our first election, they were able to get a lot of people to vote for them, even some of the women we helped get the right to vote. They got control of the Republic and everything shifted again to the people on the right. The leaders in Germany and Italy are also doing much the same thing. I fear more and more of our people are losing hope and ready to fight for their lives."

"What will that mean, father?"

"I do not know what will happen, but if any harm should come to me I want you and Miguel to live with my brother. I talked to him just last week. He agreed to help you if necessary. I also talked to my boss at the cathedral, Father Ortega. If something should happen, find him and give him this note. He agreed to take you and Miguel to Juan's home. It will be in the kitchen, here in the cupboard," Ramon said hiding the note.

"When you are older get what Juan and I have hidden. Make it known to the world if it has importance as I believe. And remember what I have said. Keep this a secret for now."

"I will, father," promised the confused and scared six-year-old

"Your uncle is a good man; he will help you. He secretly supports the left, but as a farmer his income requires him to look like he supports the government's farm program. Juan will keep you and Miguel safe."

* * *

Garcia threw a bucket of cold rainwater from the balcony on Ramon's face. He regained consciousness.

"Wake up. Enough of this shit. One more time, what did you steal? Where is it?"

Ramone remained mute and turned away his face. "Untie him … stand up," Garcia ordered, gesturing to José to lift and support his beaten prisoner. "Let's go."

As the men headed for the stairs, Rafael ran to the balcony and peered over its rusted wrought iron railing. "Stay inside Miguel," he said to his younger brother.

He watched Garcia tie his father's hands when they reached the ground. José pushed him to walk faster. His brown eyes filled with tears as his father's oppressors lead him out of sight. José pushed him once again. Ramon stumbled and fell. José picked him up and pressed his bayonet into his back marching him to a vacant lot a few blocks away. Ramon was made to stand in front of its perimeter wall and was asked once again about the object he reportedly stole. He remained silent. Suddenly, the pop of an army-issued Llama pistol echoed to the distant balcony where Rafael waited in terror. Ramon, shot in the head, fell to the ground – lifeless.

"One of these days you left-wing bastards are going to learn not to mess with us," Garcia announced, leaving Ramon crumpled up, like a mound of dirty laundry, for others to see what awaited their resistance.

Other Spaniards, like Ramon's sons, now sobbing and gasping for air from the distant balcony, were left to an uncertain future as the anticipated revolution began.

CHAPTER 4

WASHINGTON, DC - FEBRUARY 27, 2012

Renee tossed and turned in bed for hours. *Mon Dieu! It's one-thirty in the morning,* she thought as she rolled over to see the amber glow on the nightstand. *This is ridiculous. I've got to get some sleep. It's not a big deal. I'll just go in there and apologize to him for acting like a shrew. I don't care what he thinks. Dr. Parker won't care ... he barely knows me. I'm making too big a deal of this. I've got to get some sleep.*

In truth she held a great fondness for Dr. Parker and was embarrassed he may think less of her. She weighed the options over and over in her mind and began thinking about Stan rather than what she might tell him.

His class was really something ... so is he, Renee thought as she imagined him to be more than her professor. *I love his innocence ... his wit ... his boyish charm ... his whole persona.*

"America's Freemason-rebels-turned-constitutional-fathers embedded Masonic secrets into the planning and architecture of their new capital city as a means to protect and influence the public," he wrote in his doctoral thesis at Harvard Graduate School of Design. "The government's success was assured through its symbolic architecture. Symbolism that was embedded in the buildings with sculpture and detailing relating to the Greek goddess of justice, innocence, and purity."

He defended these observations in his thesis and to his class in the elective she had taken with such energy there could be no doubt America would be blessed by the heavens, or so the founders thought.

He has such passion for his work, she thought as she drifted off to sleep. … *I wonder if he could be as passionate about me? He seems so ...*

* * *

Renee woke to another cold winter's morning whose grey skies seemed to disappear by her continued fantasy about Stan. Her thoughts then turned to the twenty-five degree temperature outside, then to the warm bed in her apartment, and then the grey skies reappeared. *What's the use? I should just stay right here all day today.*

She spied some wool socks discarded on the floor from the day before. She put them on and meandered to the bathroom, knowing that she could not stay in bed. As she stood at the sink and brushed her teeth, she saw the image of a woman she didn't know. *This is ridiculous,* she thought. *I simply have to see him face to face and apologize.*

Renee was strikingly beautiful at age twenty-eight. With shiny jet black hair, emerald eyes, pale alabaster skin and high, flushed cheek bones, her thin frame stood 5' 9" tall and tipped the scales at just under 130 pounds. She could easily have had a career as a model, but Renee wanted none of that. Ever since she was a little girl growing up in the Languedoc region in the town of Albi, France, she shied away from exploiting her natural beauty. But this morning she did not shy away. Her continuing fantasy led her to choose her most tempting outfit she had and stop by Stan's office at the Intercultural Center before going to her morning class.

He was not there. His office schedule was attached at the entrance to his office cubicle provided to Adjunct Professors. It indicated that after his 8:00 a.m. class, 'The Influence of Monumental Architecture on Society', he would return to the office at 11:00 and be available to students until noon.

She penned a brief note explaining she had come by and would return at 11:45. It concluded, "Last night's outburst at the restaurant was not at all like me. I am terribly embarrassed by the whole thing. I would appreciate having a few moments of your time to explain what happened and clear the air."

Sheepishly she looked around the cluster of cubicles in all directions, so as to not be discovered. She entered. With an affirming sense she had committed herself to the right course of action, she folded the note and left it on his desk, next to the photograph of Stan and his golfing buddies – Howard, Josh, and Andy – cheering on McIlroy at last year's US Open in Bethesda.

* * *

Stan returned to his office on time and read her note. At exactly 11:40, he hurriedly dismissed an undergrad to ensure his appointment with Renee would not result in further embarrassment for her. He picked up her note once again next to the photo of his long-established foursome and reread it and smiled. He remembered McIlroy's come from behind one stroke win at the Congressional. *Anything is possible,* he mused.

Renee said goodbye to a friend as the elevator door closed behind her. The sound of her voice echoed in the distance and captured his attention. He stuck her note safely in his coat pocket. Her appearance and light fragrance of French perfume caused his palms to sweat and his heart to race. This was uncharacteristic for a man who was normally in control and comfortable in the presence of beautiful women. Uncharacteristic, but not unwelcomed this time.

"Please, have a seat," Stan said with a welcoming gesture so as to not have to shake her hand and blow his cover.

Seated, Renee began, "Professor Parker, last night …"

"You know on second thought, why don't we go to the small conference room where we might have a bit more privacy?" Stan asked, not sure where this conversation would lead, but having a pretty good idea of where he wanted to take it.

"Down the hall and to the right," he advised.

Seated once again Renee began, "Professor Parker…"

"Renee, please call me Stan," he interrupted. "I only teach one class now and you've already taken it."

"Thanks, I will."

She took a deep breath and swallowed hard as she now had to find the strength to start again. "Stan, last night was absurd on so many levels. My boyfriend of the past few months, George, turned out to be a copy of a horrific person from my youth; a real bastard to me. George's railing against a women's health and reproductive … well … rights … all started because he overheard a comment you made about my friend, Sandra. George was combative, degrading and, well, I just couldn't take it any longer. I had to get out of there. I'm so sorry …"

"No, no, please don't be," Stan interrupted. "I like assertive women. Renee, don't be embarrassed. This will pass. More importantly, how are you feeling about the loss of your boyfriend, if you don't mind me asking?"

"Fine. Really fine. I totally misjudged him. It's over and I feel relieved. I'm so glad I discovered who he was this early in our relationship," Renee admitted as she pondered *wonder why he's asking?*

"Well, good for you," he said. "You know, at embarrassing times I try to put them out of my head as quickly as I can and just move on. I know that's easy for me to say, but let it go. It's not a big deal. I guess what George heard was me telling Howard the university needed to support Sandra's position. Then, seeing you, it hit me. Howard's research assistant, Sara, is leaving next Thursday and I think you would be perfect for the job Want to chat about it over lunch? Hungry?"

Renee's anxiety vanished when she saw the charming and encouraging man of her imagination right in front of her. "Yes, I would. And thank you for supporting Sandra by the way," she said.

"You're welcome." He continued as they stood, "I dare say after you jumped up to leave and dumped the ice water in his lap, our old buddy George left the dining room with a shrunken ego as well as other parts."

A good laugh broke the growing sexual tension of the moment as they walked back to his cubicle. Photos of places he had enjoyed in Europe and a piece of abstract sculpture also made her realize they had so much in common – so much they could share. *He likes assertive does he? I'll show him assertive.*

* * *

Lighthearted conversation quickly consumed the five-minute walk from the Epicurean Center back toward the Intercultural Center. It was a conversation neither Renee nor Stan wanted to end.

The opportunity to work for Dr. Gerard sounds interesting, she thought, *but more importantly it will give me more time to spend with Stan. He and Howard are the best of friends. Stan said he's always in and out of Howard's office. This could work out well.*

George waited in the vestibule of the ICC to catch Renee before her next class. Stan and Renee passed without noticing him, focused on an exploratory conversation of growing intimacy. Through the prisms of the darkened glass and his darkening mind, he looked out on the pavement of Red Square. He watched them continue their leisurely stroll toward Copley Lawn and followed them until they came to Healy Hall and the open space of the Healy Lawn. George seemed confused and shaken by her apparent dismissal of their relationship in favor of the man before her now. He had to fix things.

The name Gaston was not unfamiliar to Georgetown. While living in France, Renee was able to trace her family roots back to her 9th great uncle, Jean Gaston, a French Huguenot. Family lore described Jean rejecting his Catholic siblings to narrowly escape the country's religious war of 1628 as Cardinal Richelieu and Louis XIII lay siege to the port city of La Rochelle.

Jean's great-great grandson was a second generation American. William Gaston was born to immigrant parents – an Irish, Presbyterian father, Dr. Alexander Gaston, whose revolutionary politics resulted in his early death as an ardent Whig, and an English, Catholic mother, a Margaret Sharpe. They settled in North Carolina. After a band of Tories killed her husband, Margaret saw to her son's proper Catholic education and enrolled young William in a fledgling preparatory school in 1789. William, Renee's 5th Great Uncle, entered Georgetown as its first student at the tender age of thirteen.

Throughout his life, this respected graduate, jurist and congressman attained such prominence that Gaston Hall – a performance auditorium seating 740 people located in the upper floors of Healey Hall – was dedicated to his memory. Six generations of Gaston graduates later, Renee added her name to the Gaston legacy. She now stood on Healy Lawn with the man of her dreams beneath the edifice dedicated to her family's luminary.

Renee was a brilliant student, graduating Summa Cum Laude in 2007 with a BA degree emphasizing Ancient Egyptian and Medieval European History. She was currently enrolled in the second semester of study toward obtaining a Master of Arts in Global, International and Comparative History. Known as the MAGIC program – a tongue-in-cheek acronym Georgetown unabashedly used – it was one of its most prestigious fields of study.

She had rejected the teachings of her maternally-imposed Roman Catholicism since becoming an adult, in favor of this more rational approach to MAGIC. Nevertheless, she valued the education she had received at the Jesuit institution and decided to stay at Georgetown to continue her studies. All she wanted to do now was work in investigative journalism on the global stage. MAGIC gave her training; Dr. Gerard would give her a first opportunity.

George had cautiously followed their meandering stroll from a safe distance. He watched as their flirtatious manner began to infuriate him, but he kept his composure and distance. As the couple parted, George saw Renee smile and nod her head up and down, not knowing she had just agreed to meet Stan at his Capitol office for drinks after work this evening.

George quietly followed Renee toward the ICC. Stan headed in the opposite direction, skirting the South Gatehouse to his parked car. Once Stan was out of ear shot George called out, "Hey, Renee, wait up."

His voice stopped her dead in her tracks. Turning, she saw the image of someone she had once cared about toss a cigarette on the ground and run toward her. "What do you want?" she scoffed. "Just leave me alone. I don't want to see you again!"

"Three things," George was quick to admit. "First, I want to apologize for the way I acted last night. I was rude. I apologize for the embarrassment I must have caused you. I don't know what came over me, let alone why I took it out on you. I hope you can forgive me and we can remain friends at least.

"Second, I want you to know a little about the Sovereign Military Order of Malta, or the Knights of Malta as we are commonly called. We're not a cult like you said, but a Catholic organization that is dedicated to caring for the poor, the sick, the elderly, and all those who suffer. We're especially involved in helping victims of armed conflicts and natural disasters. I'm proud of the work we do and don't think it should be minimized.

"And third, I'm not sure if I'll ever be convinced Sandra has a legitimate position, I just don't get it, but I'd be willing to listen if you would be willing to explain it to me some time," George said with the endearing smile that attracted him to her in the first place.

Despite his many flaws, George was captivating when he smiled; hardly anyone could resist him. "You're right. I apologize about the knight remark."

"And?" George pressed.

"What? Friends? Well, we'll see," Renee said hesitantly. "But for now, just stop bothering me. Let's give it some time."

"Sure thing," George agreed as he watched her turn and walk away.

* * *

George sat in the afternoon sun on Healy Lawn avoiding the cold shadow cast by Gaston Hall and lit another Marlboro. He scribbled his thoughts in the journal that had been with him since his junior year in college.

Monday, February 27th. RE: Renee Gaston.

I am convinced that Sandra is wrong. Drugs for birth control should not be provided by the state. It's just another form of abortion and is not in keeping with God's will. After all, He commanded us to "Be fruitful and multiply and replenish the earth and subdue it." Eve was created to be of service to Adam. God intended her to be submissive, to bring man pleasure. A woman is not intended to be equal.

God took one of Adam's ribs to make his companion. And like the other animals he named, Adam named her saying, "... she shall be called woman because she is taken out of man."

When will women ever learn the truth revealed by God and stop all of this equal rights nonsense?

George packed away his journal and headed back to the Law Center, convinced Renee was within his grasp, Sandra would be contained, the Religious Freedom Restoration Act would soon become a law and, once again, all would be right with the world.

CHAPTER 5

WASHINGTON, DC - LATER THAT DAY

The renamed Gerald Ford Office Building was quickly and inexpensively constructed in 1939 to house a growing Federal workforce under the FDR administration. It was a nondescript and unimpressive building, not one that should be home to the Architect of the Capitol. Stan passed the guard's station at the building entry.

"A good afternoon to you, Dr. Parker."

"Well, we'll see about that when I get to my office, won't we?"

"Yes sir," the guard said with a chuckle.

The building was buzzing with activity as the Congressional Budget Office prepared to release its assessment of the President's 2013 budget based on his remarks in the State of the Union Address.

"… In 2008, the house of cards collapsed. We learned that mortgages had been sold to people who couldn't afford or understand them. Banks had made huge bets and bonuses with other people's money. Regulators had looked the other way or didn't have the authority to stop the bad behavior. It was wrong. It was irresponsible. And it plunged our economy into a crisis that put millions out of work, saddled us with more debt, and left innocent, hardworking Americans holding the bag. In the six months before I took office, we lost nearly 4 million jobs. And we lost another 4 million before our policies were in full effect.

"Those are the facts. But so are these: In the last 22 months, businesses have created more than 3 million jobs. Last year, they created the most jobs since 2005. American manufacturers are hiring again, creating jobs for the first time since the late 1990s. Together, we've agreed to cut the deficit by more than two trillion dollars. And we've put in place new rules to hold Wall Street accountable, so a crisis like this never happens again."

Stan smiled and waved to a few friendly CBO staffers who scrambled to put together the first of many assessments to come. He knew that much of his proposed budget was on the chopping block but would fight hard to keep it in place.

Nancy Thompson, the Chief of Operations for the Architect of the Capitol, and Sheila Rosenberg, the Chief Executive Officer for Capitol Visitor Services stood chatting and laughing. They both had the look of guilty adolescents as Stan, rather than their parents, entered the room.

"Well, there's a couple of Federal employees if I ever saw one. Bonnie, what's going on?" Stan asked his administrative assistant.

"Stan, we have just had a couple of incidents." Sheila interrupted.

"Sheila, you got this?" Nancy asked. "I need to get back to work."

"Yeah, Nancy, go ahead."

"Okay, Sheila let's take it to my office," Stan said.

Sheila sat down and continued, "We had our usual eleven o'clock clash between reps from Planned Parenthood and the anti-abortion protestors in front of the Visitor Center. But the news today is really about the marble replica of the Statue of Freedom at the entrance to the Exhibition Hall. She came under attack by an extremely drunk, albeit amorous, visitor about thirty minutes ago."

"Yeah, I know. I heard a little about it on the radio on the way over."

She continued, "The President's Press Secretary is briefing on it right now."

* * *

Josh Morgan, the President's Press Secretary and third member of Stan's golfing foursome, completed his briefing and began soliciting questions. "Yes, Jim."

"I think we're all familiar with the Statue of Freedom on the Capitol dome and the Roman Goddess, Libertas, but what about the chicken feathers comment? What was that all about?"

"Well … wait a minute, ah, yes … here, my notes say … and you're going to find this interesting … Thomas Crawford's statue was very close to what War Secretary Jefferson Davis wanted … yes, that Jefferson Davis …" Josh said as he looked up to his audience for understanding. "One small detail, however, made him totally lose it. Davis apparently went ballistic when the sculptor's design for the Statue of Freedom included a liberty cap as she was normally depicted – hence the word liberty. Crawford's crowning symbol for our nation's capital was the Roman symbol of emancipated slaves. That just didn't work for Davis. Crawford reluctantly accommodated him. He replaced the liberty cap with an American eagle and a crest of feathers. This gave her crown the appearance of a Roman helmet which yielded the chicken feathers crack from today Okay, then. Who's next? Yes, Nancy."

"Any further news on protesters?"

"No, not really; seems they all dispersed without incident. Anything further? … No, okay then, I'll remind you there's a Pentagon briefing on Afghanistan today at 3:00 p.m. Anything else? … No. Okay. Well, have a nice afternoon."

* * *

"My old buddy Josh Wonder how's he's doing? We haven't played golf in about three weeks. I need to give him a call and get back together real soon," Stan said as he drifted away from his conversation with Sheila.

"Well … okay, you do that … but for now, apparently our assailant was ranting something about Congress not being able to get anything done because they were all a bunch of pagans working beneath a cowardly bronze statue with chicken feathers, rather …"

"Sounds about right for a Monday …"

"Rather than," she repeated, "and I'm quoting him now, '… our warrior Lord and Savior Jesus Christ.' "

Amused with the thought that members of Congress had any sort of religious principles at all, pagan or otherwise, Stan said, "You know, Sheila, I may be the only person in DC who understands what the Freemasons attempted to tell us. '… working under the influence of a cowardly goddess with chicken feathers …' now that's funny. Are we done, Sheila?"

"No … actually … just before going into the Exhibition Hall some high school kids from a DC American History class were studying Freedom's face and listening to their teacher explain why she was wearing an eagle on the top of her head, when our perp came out of the hall, approached Liberty from behind, jumped the barrier, began climbing her, and yelling, 'Bend over bitch, I'm gonna do you right now!' "

"Anyone hurt?" Stan said with a concerned voice feeling a little out of sync with the humor Sheila attempted.

"What?"

"Was anyone hurt?"

"Oh. No. No, not at all. Even Ms. Freedom is okay, but after the encounter, she did ask for a cigarette."

Stan, amused by her comments, let them pass. "Well, check in with the teacher, anyway, to make sure there's no fallout from the kids' parents. I've got to say this is pretty gutsy stuff on his part, considering she's like three times taller than an Amazon and her heart is made of stone," Stan said finally catching up to Sheila's intent.

She continued, "Of course, once he found his mark and started to unzip his pants, our perp fell to the ground, then tried to stand up to make another go at her, but then fell down again before he was able to climb back on. That's when the Capitol Police subdued and arrested him. No real harm done, but rumor has it Freedom is filing a sexual harassment claim. Other than that, it's been a pretty quiet morning. How about you?"

"My morning was … well … interesting, very interesting," Stan smiled.

Three years ago, Sheila Rosenberg and Stan were lovers. When the construction of the Capitol Visitor Center neared completion, she was a Vice President of Creative Ventures, Inc., the largest marketing and lobbying firm on K Street. At Stan's urging, she applied for the newly created position of CEO. She was eminently qualified to handle the job. She was hired, and Stan had to end their relationship. They were both aware it would have to end, but she always felt guilty about her career aspirations and having to sacrifice their relationship. Since then, Sheila thought she had to fix him up – constantly.

"Hey, speaking of the statue's sexual encounter – I have a name for you … Sally Fredericks," Sheila said as she stood. "She's a friend of mine who works at the EPA so I suspect you two will have a few things in common. She's looking forward to getting out of the bar scene and being able to have a conversation with someone who doesn't apologize by saying 'I should have *went* to buy some condoms,' as well as not forgetting them in the first place. Anyway, she wants improvements on both counts – to find a responsible, intelligent man and ditch the losers she been dating … and for some odd reason I thought of you."

"Not interested, but its great you are always on the prowl for me. You know, once upon a time I could do this sort of thing myself. Thanks for the help, but you really do need to get out of the Yente business," Stan said sarcastically.

Passing Sheila on the way out, Bonnie entered his office, "Here are your messages from this morning. Say, Stan, do you find her attractive too?"

"Who?"

"Ms. Freedom."

"Oh …get out. No … wait … speaking of attractive, I'm expecting a guest named Renee Gaston around 5:30 this evening. Will you please tell the guards she should arrive around then? Please show her back to my office when she gets here. Okay?"

She nodded.

"Thanks."

LATER THAT EVENING

The Capital Beltway and connecting interstate highways normally look like parking lots during the three to eight evening rush hours. As a result, the feeder road traffic has no place to go and backs up for miles. Renee knew this all too well. This evening was no exception.

She preferred taking the Metro and leaving her car at home. This required planning. The DC rapid transit system is precise.

I need to be at the bus stop in just fifteen minutes to catch the shuttle to DuPont Circle, Renee suddenly realized, knowing she had to allow thirty minutes for the two and a half mile trip. She gathered up her things and raced back in the direction of Epicurean Center to a crowded bus stop of twelve students waiting to board.

She arrived at DuPont Circle now breathing normally and right on time – exactly 5:00 p.m. A giant white letter 'M' marked the location of the escalator's descent to the dimly lit barrel-vaulted refuge and the Red Line.

The quiet sacred space for secular lives greeted her arrival. She pondered her surroundings and the evening ahead as she waited for the train to Metro Center. Fellow passengers scurried to and fro in the maze of underground tunnels. Their lifeless faces revealed what Renee feared could be her future after graduation.

There was hardly any noise. An occasional train rumbled through. High heels clicked off the pavement. These were the only sounds that echoed off the cavernous concrete paneled tubes. No talking. No laughing. No real joy as the next wave emerged from an open door and darted to their connecting train.

At the Metro Center Station, she took the Blue Line to the south. *Do we have any real purpose in our lives or are we just on a constant pilgrimage from one mindless activity to the next in search of the almighty dollar?* she wondered.

The army continued to march, briefcase in hand, newspaper tucked under one arm, passing one another in eerie silence. *There's got to be more to life than this.* Renee continued to ponder her fate. She hoped what awaited her at the end of this journey might take her in a different direction.

She left the congestion of her fellow passengers and ascended to the Federal Center SW Station. She surfaced to a crisp winter's evening from a portal about one-half of a mile southwest of the Capitol, and right in front of the Ford Office Building.

She shed her coat upon entering the building's warmth and presented her driver's license to the building's security guard. He greeted her, "Welcome, Ms. Gaston. I've been expecting you." She was stunned, but appreciative.

"Really? Okay … well … thanks. Could you direct me to the ladies' room please?" He inspected her purse and gave her permission to enter the screening device. He gestured in the direction she was to follow.

"Have a good evening."

Stopping briefly to check her appearance, comb her hair and adjust her skirt and sweater, she arrived right on time for her rendezvous with Stan. A gentle soul, whom Stan had retained in her job from the prior administration, greeted her as she entered.

"Good evening. Ms. Gaston, is it?" Bonnie asked. Renee nodded yes. Bonnie continued, "We've been expecting you. This way please."

Unlike all of the professors on campus and most of his fellow executives, Stan's office was not in disarray. He was meticulous and so was his office. His desk was in perfect order. His blinds were raised to the exact same height and tilt. His high-backed leather chair was a family heirloom – it certainly wasn't issued by the government. The books and art throughout his office indicated he was an affluent, cultured man with a keen interest in the sculpture and stained glass adorning the gothic cathedrals of the twelfth and thirteenth centuries.

"Welcome, Renee. This time we might have a little more privacy. I'm so happy you decided to come. Except for having to deal with the guy who tried to rape the Statue of Freedom this morning, I've thought about this evening for most of the day."

Renee blushed in response, "Yes, me too. I heard about the incident. Hey, what was Davis thinking about when we commissioned a statue of a Roman goddess anyway?"

Stan was excited to answer her question in detail and get the evening started. After a few minutes of idle conversation about Jefferson Davis and the Libertas commissioning, he coaxed, "Let's go. If you think that was strange, I have something else to show you. It will blow your socks off. Well, uh, you know what I mean."

Stan and Renee left the warmth of Ford, retrieved his car from the assigned lot and headed toward the main entrance to the Capitol. His permit allowed him to park along the southern perimeter road where they left his car and walked toward the entry.

"Aren't you cold?" Renee asked with motherly concern, as the evening had turned much colder in the short time she was in Stan's office.

"Yes, a little, but this morning was so nice I left my top coat at home." Stan chuckled, "So, what's with the face? Okay, okay… I'll be fine. We'll be inside soon. You really don't want to channel my mother, do you?"

Renee's smile said it all as she thought, *well maybe; she may be just the person whom I want to channel.*

They stopped for a moment on the Capitol steps. "Renee, I want you to turn around and look down the Mall at the Washington Monument. Now look to the right," Stan said guiding her head toward the Whitehouse, "and now turn to your right and look back at me."

She turned and smiled at Stan.

"That's the Spring Triangle."

With the Capitol as his backdrop he continued, "Greek mythology says the virgin goddess of justice, innocence, and purity fled wickedness, abandoned earth, and ascended to the heavens. She became the constellation Virgo. The three brightest stars surrounding Virgo – Spica, Regulus and Arcturus – established the positions of America's greatest landmarks. L'Enfant's plan for the entire city of Washington was based on the Spring Triangle and the goddess of justice. Think about that for a moment.

"On the Mall, Spica is represented by the Washington Monument and Regulus is the Capitol. Now follow the cars down the hypotenuse of Pennsylvania Avenue," he gestured, "Arcturus is the White House. Let's go inside. It's getting cold."

Stan presented his identification badge to the security guard; his photograph, name, and title were clearly visible. Quickly admitted to the building's ground floor, they made their way through the crypt to the stairs beyond.

The voices and footsteps of a growing crowd, clamoring to leave work, echoed a sense of chaos from the radiating stone floors and hardened walls surrounding them. The pair emerged from the stairs into the Great Rotunda to see statues of past presidents standing on sentry duty as they guarded the eight giant murals of American history.

"Look above you," Stan instructed. "See that?"

Renee looked 180 feet above her to the ceiling of the dome and what appeared to be a painting from the Vatican and said so.

"That's right," Stan agreed. "The artist was born and trained in Rome and painted at the Vatican before emigrating to America. The painting above us is titled the 'Apotheosis of Washington'. It literally means the raising of Washington to the rank of a god. That's George Washington in the middle rising to the heavens in glory."

"That's strange. Our war-hero-President was thought of as a god?" Renee asked.

"Perhaps, but probably not. What may seem even stranger are the six groups of figures around the dome's perimeter. These represent Washington's advisors on War, Science, Marine, Commerce, Mechanics and Agriculture. War is depicted as our friend from today, Freedom, who was based on the goddess Libertas. All the others have a god or goddess to secure his endeavors. Marine and Agriculture needed extra help and got a pair. All together there are three gods and four goddesses or five if you count Libertas. It's perfect.

"So what do you think, Renee?" he continued. "Is this simply a neo-classic gesture to a past Roman Republic or is it an attempt to keep America strong by paying tribute to these ancient gods and goddesses?"

"Got me," Renee shrugged. "How about you – symbol or tribute?"

"I think it's a little of both, you know, better to be safe than sorry. They were politicians after all. But I really think it's more about the vision Jefferson and architect Latrobe had for the capitol building and what the Freemasons brought to the table. What may be the real story is this," Stan continued. "Ancient civilizations saw value in worshipping both the male and female. This was often in the form of a powerful, warlike sky god and a goddess representing Mother Earth and bringing forth new life, what is often called 'the sacred feminine.' Somewhere along the line our society lost sight of this. Why? How did this happen? I don't know, but it seems our founding fathers, Freemasons all, did not."

Renee was fascinated by Stan's explanation of L'Enfant's plan for the city and by his thesis that the country's founding fathers once honored both the male and female. Her thoughts went to Sandra's inquisition during the Congressional hearing. *How times have changed since the Age of Enlightenment!*

They drove to begin an evening they had both anticipated all day as the snow began to cover the Capitol grounds. "Stan, I've been thinking about working with Dr. Gerard. Do you think I have a chance of getting the job?"

"Yes! It's a done deal if you want it. In fact, say the word, and I'll make it my personal mission next week."

A few minutes later, they dropped Stan's Prius with the valet of the historic Jefferson Hotel. A young lady greeted their arrival at the dimly lit Quill Lounge. She escorted them to a quiet corner in the far end of the room. A gentleman in his mid-fifties quietly played on the baby grand piano centered under a chandelier in the middle. It provided a pleasant background to mask an intimate conversation. Renee's thoughts went to her surroundings. *The elegance of the Quill is perfect for tonight. Good choice, Stan! Your stock just keeps going up and up.*

A waitress approached their table.

"Just one moment, please," Renee said while studying the wine menu. "I think I'll have a glass of your Gerard Bertrand Coteaux du Languedoc."

"And I'll have a Gentleman Jack on the rocks. Thank you."

Stan returned his attention to Renee. "So, you know your wines do you?" Stan asked fancying himself a bit of a wine connoisseur.

"No, not really. This wine comes from the Languedoc region near my parents' home in France. It's a household favorite. I haven't had it for a while. It's pretty good … I'll give you a taste … think you'll like it."

"I'm sure I will," Stan said, staring into her eyes, "I'm sure I will."

"So, what is Dr. Gerard's research about anyway?"

"As I understand it, he wants a better understanding of the Shell Pilgrimage to the Cathedral of St. James in Santiago de Compostela, Spain. He's interested in not only the history of the pilgrimage, but also what motivates the modern-day pilgrims. Why do they walk for such distances? What is the payoff for them?"

"Where is Santiago de … what's it called, again?"

"Compostela. In the Galicia Region of Spain, just north of Portugal. When we discussed it briefly, Gerard told me it was considered one of the most important pilgrimages back in the day, third only after Jerusalem and Rome. According to legend, this cathedral is the home of two saints, both with the name St. James. The one – probably the more familiar – is the Apostle James, James the Great. His tomb was supposedly discovered and enshrined there in the early ninth century. By the mid 800's orthodox Catholics began their pilgrimage from what is today Western Europe to pay homage to him.

"Then about 1200 what was thought to be the cranium of James the Less – the brother of Jesus and Bishop of the Church of Jerusalem – was brought to Santiago de Compostela and enshrined in the crypt beneath the cathedral.

"Non-orthodox pilgrims journeyed for him rather than James the Great. Since he was associated with Gnosticism, these pilgrimages were made in secret under the guise of James the Great. So it would seem that pilgrims journeyed for two different streams of Christianity – one orthodox and one heretical, one with the Pope's blessing and one in secret – to the same cathedral at the same time. How cool is that?"

Renee smiled and said with a bit of sarcasm, "Well … cooler than being burned at the stake, I suppose."

Renee was captivated by the history of the Gnostics and the Cathar heresy surrounding her home town. It permeated the stories of her youth. She often thought, *why did Christians turn against each other in the thirteenth century? Why were so many of my distant ancestors slain in a twenty-year crusade that made absolutely no sense?* Answers were made clearer to her during her undergraduate studies, but no more acceptable.

"Anyway, that's my understanding of what Gerard wants. Sara couldn't commit to spending a few weeks abroad this summer, so Howard needs to find someone new." Stan continued, "But enough of the Middle Ages. Let's fast forward to tonight and talk about you."

"Well for openers, I can really relate to the Gnostic Christians. Remember I grew up in the Languedoc region of France in the city of Albi?"

CHAPTER 6

A CORUÑA, SPAIN - NOVEMBER 3, 1934

Ezra Hitzig fled his hometown in August 1933. Earlier that year Hitler built the first of many German concentration camps. This one was twenty miles from Ezra's hometown of Munich – Dachau. Munich was abuzz with rumors that it was built to house political prisoners consisting primarily of rebellious Socialists and Communists who challenged the Chancellor's authority. That was short lived. Dachau's population quickly grew to include artists, intellectuals, those with physical and mental challenges, homosexuals, and anyone whom Hitler considered unfit for his new Germany. Chief among this population were tens of thousands of Jewish prisoners who lost their lives through forced labor, medical experiments, disease or extermination.

Ezra was a single young man of eighteen when he left Germany. He was Jewish. From his early teens, he had seen his friends and classmates, boys and girls alike, join the ranks of the Hitler Youth and the League of German Maidens and become indoctrinated in Aryan racial superiority and Nazi ideology that viewed Jewish people as less than human.

He had watched the movement grow tenfold to a membership of two and a half million young Germans between fourteen to eighteen years of age. His classmates, once his friends, now disparaged him.

Ezra and his parents had to leave their home and get away from this growing hatred. They escaped to France; he continued as far west as he could.

The hatred followed him to the town of Santiago de Compostela in northern Spain where Jewish people had not been welcomed since the Spanish Inquisition and were later expelled by the Ottoman Turks.

When he arrived, the Galicia region of northern Spain was a cauldron of civil unrest between the right-wing Nationalists and the left-wing faction of the Spanish Republic, between the Catholic Church and those who were not Catholic, between the haves and have-nots. It was in this environment that Ezra met brothers Ramon and Juan Tuguía.

Juan indirectly supported the Spanish Socialist Workers' Party in the early days of the Republic's coalition and his brother's early efforts to bring about change. But living in a rural area near the small coastal town of A Coruña, Juan felt as though he was isolated from politics.

His brother Ramon was older, a widower with two children who worked wherever he could find employment, but Juan was free to take advantage of Spain's scientific investments. As a farmer he embraced the changing times as Galicia, and other food producing regions of Spain, began to move from a peasant-based economy of land workers on large, failing tracks of land to one of small-scale family-owned farms. The government offered Juan and others a choice of crops. He chose to grow a new hybrid maize to feed both people and livestock on surrounding farms. He had to remain indifferent toward politics as the Republic shifted to the right and civil disobedience broke into war. He did so for three years before his life changed.

From his fields thirty-six miles north of the cathedral where his brother worked, Juan could see a distant cloud of dust moving in his direction. The dust encircled a borrowed black BMW with red side panels. It stopped alongside a weather-beaten plow and a decaying wooden ox cart resting in front of Juan's humble home. A man wearing a clerical collar stepped out from behind the wheel. Two boys clung to their possessions as they jumped from the backseat and bolted from the passenger door.

"Uncle Juan," the six-year-old sobbed, "our father was killed."

"How? How did it happen?"

"Two men broke into our apartment and started yelling and poking him with their guns," Rafael said, gasping for air. "Father would not give them what they asked for. He told me if something happened to him, we should live with you."

"I know," Juan said as his sweat and now salty tears stung his eyes. "I know."

Father Ortega introduced himself and handed Juan the note left by Ramon for Rafael and Miguel.

"Thank you, Father," Juan said. "And thank you for bringing the boys to me today. I will take good care of them."

Father Ortega gave an affirming nod, bowed his head in silent prayer, crossed himself and opened his eyes with, "Amen." Placing his hand on Juan's shoulder, Ortega looked into his sad eyes and said, "Your brother was a good man. He did a lot for me and the cathedral. I will truly miss him. He was taken to the morgue in town. They are holding him until I return to arrange for his burial at Cementerio Municipal de Boisaca, near the cathedral. Juan, these are dangerous times in Galicia. May God be with you, my son, and may your life and the lives of the boys be blessed and safe."

He had nothing more and departed as quickly as he had come.

The boys' small arms carried a few clothes and scant other possessions inside. Two windows and a single wooden door punctured the randomly cut and placed stones that formed the perimeter walls of their adopted home. Unwanted vines plugged a roof of broken clay tiles and prevented most of the rain from entering the 85-year-old make-shift dwelling. It was large enough for one person, but housing three would be not be easy. They did not know what would become of their lives without a father or mother. They only knew that their uncle had given his word to their father.

Attached to the dwelling was a modest barn of similar construction. A rickety barn door, pieced together with scrap lumber from a nearby mill, secured a bicycle, a mule for plowing and an ox for harvesting and trips to the market. It also secured a 2,000-year-old scroll, wrapped in sheep's hide, and placed in a clay jar beneath its dirt floor.

CHAPTER 7

WASHINGTON, DC - MAY 29, 2012

Renee was good at her job. During the week following her quarrel with George, Stan had worked his magic on Howard. He had persuaded Gerard to give her an interview to help with his research. Her personal knowledge of the Cathars and the Knights Templar was not only a plus during her interview, it would also lead Gerard to sort out the Templars' goal to unite Christianity, Judaism and Eastern religions

Stan realized he had a problem after her selection. He confided to Howard that he had a date with her a week prior to her interview. "Not only that, but I'm attracted to her. I'm not sure where this will lead, but if it gets serious, I will have to terminate my position with the university. At least until after she graduates."

Howard tried to talk him down and ask, "She's not an undergraduate. She's not in the class you are teaching now, right?"

"No, she took my class as an undergraduate, about five years ago."

"I don't see the problem then. The administration won't care if you are romantically involved with a twenty-eight-year-old grad student."

"I don't care if they care. I care and … by the way … so do you! The university policy does not allow me to have a romantic relationship with a grad student in the same department. End of story," Stan said.

"There are exceptions. Maybe we could find an exception."

A month later Stan turned in his letter of resignation to be effective at the end of the spring semester.

* * *

The spring semester had come and gone. It was the end of May and finally time to go on assignment for Gerard as agreed. Renee hated to leave. She adored Stan. They had been together for the past three months and discovered they had so much in common.

George on the other hand had become a constant source of friction and fear. She thought about the wonderful evening with Stan at the Quill. When he drove her back to her apartment he kissed her good night and watched her climb the stairs. She placed a key in the lock of the front door and waved, neither one of them seeing George who waited in the shadows. Stan waved back and headed home.

"Where ya been?" George snarled as flicked his cigarette in her direction.

"Oh, God … you scared me! What are you doing here? Where I was is none of your business. Leave! Now!"

"Okay, I will. It's just … you know … when I called your cellphone and then your landline and you didn't answer either, I got worried and came over," George said with his endearing smile.

"No, I got your call - I ignored it. I was busy. Now go. You being here like this creeps me out. I'm going to call the police if you don't leave right now!"

"Okay. Okay. I'm leaving. I'm leaving."

Her pounding heart muted the loud clicking sound of the door lock. She entered the vestibule and raced up the oak stairs of the renovated Georgetown mansion.

Nervously fumbling for her apartment key, she entered her third floor flat and turned the deadbolt to its locked position. She fell back against the door, closed her eyes and breathed a sigh of relief, thinking George had been scared off by the thought of the police.

The thought of George's stalking became even more unnerving.

I wonder if I dare trust him. He's changed so much. He waited for me. He hid where he couldn't be seen. I've got to put an end to this or protect myself in some way. Maybe I should buy a gun to keep in my purse ... she thought as she drifted off to a restless night.

* * *

"Are you okay?" Stan asked the next morning when she called.

"Yes, I'm fine. I worried about it a lot last night. Thought about buying a gun, but I finally decided George is just a little obsessed; I don't think he's dangerous."

"I wouldn't be too sure. Do you want me look into it?"

"That depends. What are you going to do?"

"Contact Andy and see what he suggests."

"Well, okay … but be careful."

Satisfied that she was not in danger, Stan hung up the phone and called his best friend Andy Miller on his private line.

"Good morning. Federal Bureau of Investigation, Special Agent Andrew Miller. May I help you?"

"Hey, Andy, I need to see you right away."

"Sure … where … when?"

"Meet me outside your building in thirty minutes. I'd rather not discuss this over the phone. Okay?"

Stan walked the twenty-five minutes rather than fighting traffic.

"What's up, buddy?"

"I need you go over to the Law Center and pay a visit to a second year."

"What are you talking about?"

"No threats, nothing like that. Just explain to this creep an arrest warrant for stalking Renee wouldn't look too good on a law student's résumé, followed by a calm, stern conversation between colleagues, if you catch my drift. Now, here's what happened."

Stan spent the next half hour catching Andy up on his new relationship and Renee's fear of George. What else could Andy say other than, "I'll try to do the best I can to help you, of course," knowing that he would have to stay within the bounds of the law.

Back in the day, Stan and Andy became close friends. Andy attended Boston University in Criminal Justice and Stan, Harvard University in

Urban Design. An unlikely pair, they had two things in common, vices actually – the Red Sox and golf. Stan lost so much money handicapping the major league teams with their made-up rules and betting on golf at ten dollars a point he came close to paying for Andy's tuition. Then the baseball season ended, and Stan's golf got a lot better, so Andy had to get a real job.

* * *

George never approached Renee directly during the next several months, but she sensed his presence lurking about all the time.

When she did see him, he stared at her and wrote something in his journal. When he was not in sight, she felt his eyes staring at the back of her head. She turned and he was nowhere to be seen. She heard his voice in a group conversation; he wasn't among the participants. She smelled the scent of his cologne when entering an elevator, but again, nothing. It was eerie. She knew he was there … somewhere.

Do I still have feelings for him? Is this the reason he's still in my head, she thought. *No, not even close. He's got to be following me. He's around somewhere. Either that or I'm really losing it.*

CHAPTER 8

PARIS, FRANCE – JUNE 1, 2012

Gerard asked Renee to take the Shell Pilgrimage from her hometown in Albi to Santiago de Compostela.

During the Middle Ages, the pilgrim believed his journey would result in him spending less time in purgatory. Gerard knew this. He also understood many of the pilgrims today were on the journey for personal reasons, not religious. He wanted to know why. He asked her to interview the pilgrims and synthesize their comments.

Gerard quickly learned Renee was not particularly religious and liked that from a clinical standpoint. He reasoned her spiritual growth could be measured and asked her to chronicle this as well.

Two weeks earlier, she called to tell her parents when she would arrive and that she planned to take a pilgrimage to a Spanish cathedral after a brief visit. Renee's flight arrived in Paris at 9:30 a.m. Her connecting train would leave the Charles de Gaulle station in a little over one hour. She had to gather her suitcases and clear customs. Time was tight.

She was tired by the trip from DC, but was able to catch a few hours of sleep on the train as it rambled through Bordeaux to Toulouse, near her hometown. Six and a half hours later, her parents waited for her arrival at the Toulouse-Matabiau Station.

From a distance Jacques Gaston's muscular frame outlined a much younger man. Closer, the greying temples of his coal black hair suited a father who kept himself in great shape at age fifty-five.

Normally a gentleman but easily angered, he kept his temper in check at home and was the father of every little girl's dreams. He made time for her, playing on the floor when she was little, listening to her concerns about boys as an adolescent, and helping her with math and science in high school.

The relationship with her mother, Marie Gaston, was never as strong as it was with her father. Renee loved her mother dearly, but Marie constantly pushed Renee toward a religious life and to compete for the opportunity she never had.

As a young girl Marie pursued a *baccalauréat général*. She was bright and talented, but with the early death of her father she was unable to complete her studies. Staying at home to care for a mother in marginal health became Marie's life after seventeen, a year short of graduation. She accepted her fate as God's will, assumed the financial and household responsibilities to care for her mother and younger siblings and looked inward to the Church for further understanding. Her Catholicism, her ability in the kitchen, and her obsession with Renee's education became the only things in her life as an adult. Now, only her kitchen skills and Catholic teachings remained.

Mama took so much pride in my accomplishments. When I was accepted to Georgetown she was overjoyed. I had to go to a Jesuit university, I really had no choice. Doing anything else it would have broken her heart, Renee thought.

"Bonsoir! How have you been? It's so good to see you. It's been such a long time." Renee said excitedly as she embraced them both.

Five years before Jacques and Marie had travelled to America to see their little girl graduate, the sights of the U.S. capital city and later the 'Big Apple' – New York City. It had been two years since her last visit to France, but this visit was different – she was returning home on her way to becoming an international investigative reporter.

Just prior to their visit to America, Renee landed a job as a French translator at the United Nations. A planned stop to tour the U.N. building and have her parents meet her new boss, Debra Herzog, was high on Renee's list of must-dos. And, of course, the highlight of her parents' trip was visiting their country's gift to the United States that boldly stood in the middle of New York Harbor.

Renee often thought about the enormous gesture of goodwill France made to commemorate the lasting friendship between the two peoples. She was inspired by the words, "… Give me your tired, your poor, your huddled masses yearning to breathe free …" like so many others. But she did not understand the opening words of the sonnet, "Not like the brazen giant of Greek fame …" nor its title "The New Colossus." Stan made it clear to her one afternoon before the celebratory dinner when she was hired.

She smiled remembering the afternoon of her interview with Dr Gerard three months ago. She closed his office door behind her and entered the reception office. She greeted Stan with a thumbs-up knowing she would start her new job during the following week. He blew her a kiss as he knocked and entered Gerard's office.

"Hey Howard. What do you think of the boss supporting Sandra the way he did? Pretty gutsy of the old man," he said tossing an article from the March 2nd *Washington Post* on Gerard's desk. Its headline read, "Georgetown president defends Sandra Fluke, blasts Limbaugh."

"Did you get the email?" Stan continued. "It said, 'She was respectful, sincere, and spoke with conviction. She provided a model of civil discourse. And yet, some of those who disagreed with her position – including Rush Limbaugh and commentators throughout the blogosphere and in various other media channels – responded with behavior that can only be described as misogynistic, vitriolic, and a misrepresentation of the position of our student.' "

"Yep, pretty strong stuff. Let's see what the alums do now," Gerard said.

"Howard, let me borrow your book on the Freemasons for a bit," Stan said, pointing to one of Gerard's prized possessions. "I want to read Renee a passage. What's with the face? Don't worry. I'll bring it right back."

Returning to Renee, Stan thumbed through the pages and began, "To celebrate Rhodes' victory over an invading Cyprus army, the Colossus of Rhodes was built to honor the Greek sun god Helios. It stood in defiance at the entrance to the Greek harbor repelling would-be attackers. As a counterpoint, Ms. Liberty was built to honor the star-maiden and Greek goddess of justice, innocence and purity welcoming everyone to America's shores. Renee, remember the Spring Triangle and L'Enfant plan for DC we talked about?" he asked rhetorically then continued. "Seems like the same idea was captured in Ms. Liberty.

"The US and France agreed the French would design and construct the actual statue and America would design and construct the pedestal. It was said the French sculptor, Monsieur Bartholdi, himself a Freemason, 'Caught a vision of a magnificent goddess holding aloft a torch in one hand and welcoming all visitors to the land of freedom and opportunity.' "

Stan advanced the pages of the book.

"Ah, here you go. 'About a hundred Freemasons attended the consecration ceremony of the cornerstone for the Statue of Liberty on Bedloe's Island.' " Stan continued, "The words of the Deputy Grand Master are recorded to say, 'Massive as this statue is, its physical proportions sink into comparative obscurity when contrasted with the nobility of its concept. Liberty Enlightening the World! How lofty the thought! To be free, is the first, the noblest aspiration of the human breast. And it is now an admitted truth that only in proportion as men become possessed of Liberty do they become civilized, enlightened, and useful.' "

Renee found these words strikingly contradictory to George's degrading attack on women and the unenlightened public servants in today's Congress and state legislatures. She just hoped one day these men might become possessed of Liberty ... civilized, enlightened and useful.

* * *

Renee settled into the back seat. A deep breath and long sigh followed her thoughts about Stan. The roar of her father's engine snapped her back into the moment and the trip ahead. Albi was another hour away.

Her father headed east to their hometown, a small medieval town of about 50,000 Albigensians. Albi was known for three things: the birthplace and museum of Toulouse-Lautrec, the Albigensian Crusade of the thirteenth century, and the large pink skinned garlics used to make the most delicious sea bass anywhere in Southern France.

Renee's mind began to wander as they drove through the countryside of southern France. The familiar open landscape reminded her of the days of her youth and the many trips between Albi and Toulouse with her parents to go shopping in a large city.

Jacques slowed the car as they drove into town and past her 350-year-old alma mater. Smiling once again, she thought fondly of her many friends at her high school, Le Lycée Lapérouse, and the hours they wasted in the Jesuit school's courtyard giggling about boys, knowing that the rippling waters of the central fountain masked the sounds of their secret conversations and laughter.

To her left was the old bridge, Pont Vieux. Spans of red brick arched between massive stone piers provided a visual base to the ruddy historic buildings that seemed to float above. It had endured the history of Albi for over 1,000 years and had been vividly etched in Renee's memory for the past twelve. Heading north to the new bridge, Pont Neuf, they crossed the Tarn River and finally reached the small two-bedroom home of her youth.

She tossed her suitcase and daypack on the bed and reacquainted herself with the Spartan room. She washed her travel-weary face and moistened her eyes. She now felt somewhat refreshed as Marie called her to dinner.

The dimly lit hallway formed a gallery of photos of family and friends. Among the many photos was a black and white one of Marie's investiture into the Dames of Malta. Pictured among twelve inductees Marie's cloak bore a Maltese cross. The old photo hung there in remembrance of an event that occurred long before Renee's birth. It was an image Renee had long forgotten. It went unnoticed as she entered the dining room.

Renee was famished. The aroma of garlic and basil from the soup, now warming on the stove, filled the air.

In her youth, Renee hardly ate anything. Marie constantly complained to anyone who would listen, "My little girl is just skin and bones. She will not eat. Doesn't she like my cooking?" The long trip, the late hour and Renee no longer being a child changed that. Renee wasted no time in coming to the table.

Marie Gaston's skills as a cook were well known in the community. This was especially true of Renee's friends who frequently invited themselves for dinner. "Mama, would it be alright if I invited Noelle tomorrow night?"

"Certainly, dear. You know she's always welcome. Speaking of Noelle, she's working with Father Dubois now," Marie said with a sense of pride knowing she had influenced Noelle Martine to rejoin the Church. "She started her job right after she completed her studies at the Université de Toulouse-Le Mirail. You know her parents were both killed in a plane crash from Rio three years ago, right? What a shame. As mayor her father was such a wonderful public servant for Albi. But I digress. With that and not having someone special in her life, Noelle is actually thinking about becoming a nun and joining the convent in Albi."

"You're kidding, right? I had no idea."

Marie presented Renee with a Provençal vegetable soup, soupe au pistou, followed by sole meunière, Renee's favorite, and a scoop of meringue floating on vanilla custard for dessert. It was fabulous, made even more so by her announcement.

"Mama … Papa," Renee began while sipping on a second glass of wine, "I have some good news to tell you. Three months ago, I met the most wonderful man. Actually, he was my professor years before that, but you know what I mean. For me it was love at first sight; I think for him as well. I can't wait for you to meet him, I'm sure you'll feel the same way." Renee explained, almost giddy with delight, Stan's background, education, personality, passions, position with the government, and the kindness shown to her. "Stan asked me to marry him next June, right after graduation. Even though it's only been a short while, it seems we've known each other all of our lives. I accepted. We'll plan the wedding so you can make it to both on a single trip."

"That's wonderful," Jacques boasted, choking back the tears as he imagined walking his little girl down the aisle.

"In fact, it's because of Stan I'm even here, now. As I told you, in a few days I'm going to become a pilgrim and join the Shell Pilgrimage to the shrine of St. James in Santiago de Compostela in western Spain."

"Renee, I've been concerned about this since you called. Will it be safe, dear? I mean … to go by yourself," Marie asked.

"Yes, of course it will be," Renee answered. "What do think will happen with all of the pilgrims around?"

"I don't know, but nevertheless I would feel better if you had someone to accompany you. Why don't you ask Noelle? Maybe she'd like to go on the pilgrimage herself or simply spend some more time with you."

"That's a good idea. I'll check with her," Renee said, turning her attention to her father. "Papa, after getting the assignment I read up on the Shell Pilgrimage to honor St. James the Great."

"Ah, the Shell Pilgrimage. There are lots of legends why it's called that," Jacques said. "One is about James being washed up on shore covered in scallops. Another describes the various routes converging on

Compostela looking like the ribs of a scallop shell."

"Yes, I learned about those, but when I was a child, you often spoke of Le Chemin de St-Jacques while telling your stories of the Cathars. Will you remind me about what you said?"

"That was one of the four paths taken by pilgrims from France toward the Cathedral of St. James," Jacques began. "Le Chemin de St-Jacques is southeast of us. It originated in the town of Arles and was the path taken by those influenced by Mary Magdalene and the Gnostic traditions of our region. It collected pilgrims through the Languedoc, attracting them from Montpellier, Albi and Toulouse. It continued through the Gascogne region to Pau, finally joining the main path in Spain.

"The Shell Pilgrimage to Compostela was taken by many of the Albigensians to honor James the Righteous, not James the Great. It was the first stop on their Path of Initiation. I think you'll find their path, El Camiño de las Estrellas and the Path of Initiation more to your liking."

"I don't understand," Renee was quick to admit. "I told Stan about our Gnostic heritage, and he mentioned the two Jameses, but I don't know anything about El Camiño de las Estrellas."

Jacques looked toward Marie for some sense of approval for what he was about to say. "Renee, we need to start at the beginning. The Gospel of John tells us in the last chapter that Jesus asked Simon Peter three times if Peter loved him. Three times his answer was 'Yes, Lord, you know that I love you.' With the first, Jesus said to him, 'feed my lambs', with the second he said, 'tend my sheep', and the third he said, 'feed my sheep'. He then warned Peter that when he grew older another would take him where he did not want to go. But he then commanded Peter to, 'follow me' implying that he should not follow the other. Peter then asked about the disciple whom Jesus loved the most standing with them, 'But, Lord what about this man?' Jesus responded, 'If I will that he remain till I come, what is that to you? You follow me.' "

Jacques continued, "And so began the struggle between Pauline Christianity and the Church of Jerusalem. Paul brought Peter over to his side and propped him up as the leader of a new faith story. Peter then rallied the other disciples to spread Paul's message of salvation through Jesus and the forgiveness of sin. They focused on the gentile world that grew into orthodox Christianity through a hierarchical system of priests, bishops and so on.

"Countering this, the disciple whom Jesus loved the most, Lazarus, and his sisters Mary and Martha stayed with James the Righteous and the Church of Jerusalem. They believed the human tragedy was not sin. Rather it was ignorance and sought to enlighten those who were spiritually dead or dying. They held to Judaic law and rejected the hierarchy forming in the orthodox Church as there was no reason to have another person intercede in what they believed was a personal relationship with God.

"This struggle lasted for about two hundred years until the some of the early bishops prevailed in that part of the world. The Gnostics were deemed heretical and were cast out. One hundred years later, Constantine convened a meeting of the two hundred or so bishops of the early Christian communities. They negotiated a common creed in the early fourth century. The Bishop of Rome later consolidated power as the Vicar of Christ, which assured apostolic succession. And that was that.

"Meanwhile, a later Pope deemed the Cathars here in southern France were heretical in Gnostic tradition and purged them with an orthodox crusade. Inquire about El Camiño de las Estrellas – the pathway of stars – when you get to Compostela. I think you will be glad you did."

* * *

Word spread quickly of Renee's return home and her work for Professor Gerard. Marie had seen to that. Like her parents and other generations before, many of her school friends remained in Albi after graduation, including Sebastian Philippe and Noelle Martine.

Twelve years before this return to Albi, Renee was the envy of all of her friends. Sebastian was tall, muscular and handsome. She forgave his imperfect grades in favor of watching his long blonde hair blow in the wind as he dribbled the football down the field.

Noelle Martine was Renee's best friend all through her years in Le Lycée. She was an outspoken and assertive young girl who seemed to take charge of any situation. She was also kind and had been a comfort to Renee during some very difficult months. Renee was excited about the chance to spend some time with her and catch up on old times and tell her about Stan. *I bet I can talk her into going with me on the pilgrimage,* Renee thought. *It would be wonderful to have a friend go with me on the journey.*

She also knew an encounter with Sebastian was inevitable. Renee began to dread even the thought of seeing him again. Sebastian was in his final year at Le Lycée Lapérouse and two years older than Renee when he had taken her virginity at sixteen.

It was only a five minute walk from their school to Pont Vieux where Sebastian had offered her a glass of wine in celebration of his upcoming graduation. After her second glass, she began to feel aroused. A feeling of sexual desire came over her to such a degree Renee could not stop the feelings. Nor did she want to. Nudging her along, Sebastian suggested they return to school and cycle to a spot to where they could be alone.

"Sure, that seems like a good idea," she said not knowing he had laced her wine with a tablet of ground ecstasy. "I would love to."

Two months later Renee came to the stark reality his drug induced rape had produced a child growing within her. The thought of carrying the child to term was painful, but the thought of having an abortion was even more gruesome. She knew safe medical care for those who chose to abort a fetus was available, but emotionally she couldn't bring herself to do it.

She could not confide in her mother. Marie's Catholic indoctrination would not allow her to understand this had not been an illicit affair. Her mother would not discuss the idea of having an abortion and even insist Renee keep the child, rather than allowing her to put the child up for adoption. Nor could she tell her father, whose temper would most likely result in his arrest. At her age, she could not easily provide for the child herself, she knew that, but it seemed she had no other choice.

She vowed she would not be a burden to her parents and knew that the road ahead would be terribly difficult, made even more so by the lack of responsibility shown by Sebastian. Raging that she had many such liaisons, he convinced himself he was not the baby's father. This was something she had to do by herself, somehow … someway.

One month later, the pregnancy resolved itself in the form of a miscarriage. The practical part of the dilemma was over, but the emotional side of her loss lingered. Renee remembered being despondent, feeling guilty, feeling angry for weeks on end, all the while resenting – even hating – Sebastian for what he had done to her. *Thank God Noelle was there to support me,* she thought. *I can never really repay her resolve, discretion and friendship.*

Despising him for these past twelve years, Sebastian had seemed to be a curse in Renee's life – a life that was otherwise quite wonderful – that is except for George who seemed to be cut from the same piece of cloth.

A chance meeting now provided her with an opportunity to let go of this hatred. Off in the distance she saw him with another man. Laughing, they seemed to be enjoying each other's company. Renee saw his youthful frame had grown into a mature god-like body of thirty, but Renee's contempt for him was unwavering and their meeting expectedly strained.

He saw her from a distance. He had heard the rumors of her work with the Dean of the History Department at Georgetown and became obsessed about seeing her once again wanting to be with her. He spoke to his companion who turned and walked away. Sebastian approached her alone to congratulate her and speak in private. He reached out to her revealing a ring emblazoned with a golden Maltese cross mounted on a ruby stone.

She was curt and dismissive toward his advances and wanted him to simply disappear from her sight. He was contrite.

"I asked my friend Paul to wait behind just now so I could have a private moment with you." He began to explain, "Renee, when you lost the baby that summer I was really happy. But I soon realized I was a fool. I turned my back on the best thing I had going for me."

"Yeah, you did. If it weren't for Noelle, I don't know what would have happened to me. Sebastian, this was the worst time in my life, and it was your fault. Do you understand that? Do we have to do this?"

"Yes, I do. Please hear me out. I want you to understand what happened after you left for America."

"Go ahead," she sighed, "but make it quick."

"I know it was terrible. Your hatred for me was obvious, as it should have been. But I could not stop thinking about you. I still do. During your last two years of high school, I never crossed the line. Not once. But I saw you as often as I could from a distance. When you left Albi, I felt alone and depressed. I lost my job and what little savings I had dried up quickly. I fell in with a bad crowd which led me to get involved with a powerful crime family in Corsica who was working in Southern France."

"Yeah, I heard all of the stories from Papa. You can imagine how much he enjoyed telling me how right he was about you."

"It's like that is it? Jacques never like me much. Did you tell him about us, back then?"

"Certainly not. Never. He likely would have killed you as not. He just didn't like you hanging around me and then years later you joined a gang and got arrested. He felt vindicated."

"You know what, back in the States you've got your fancy school and your sophisticated friends. I'm sure all of you think gangs are a waste of a person's life. But don't. They welcomed me when I had no friends or money or place to go. They gave me a sense of pride and my life a purpose. I was one of *them*."

"What happened? I heard you went to prison."

"I screwed up. I became arrogant and careless. After three years, I was arrested for breaking and entering into a home in Toulouse and spent the next two years in a detention center. When I was twenty-four, I was released and returned to the Church. I confessed my sins to Father Dubois and asked for his and God's forgiveness."

Looking at the ground, he pleaded, "Renee, I am so sorry for the pain I caused you. Father Dubois has absolved me of my sins from my prior life. God has forgiven me. I hope you will one day find it in your heart to forgive me as well and we could be friends once more."

Renee could not help herself and quickly stifled a laugh.

"What? Did I say something funny?"

"No, you didn't. I'm sorry for that. It's just you remind me of a law student back home named George Wilson. You two are just alike. Even the rings you wear," Renee said while shaking her head.

"Your friend, George Wilson is it, he is a member of the Order as well as Paul and me?"

"Apparently. I really don't know too much about it."

"The ring is a symbol we wear for our Church. Our select band is known as the Sovereign Military Order of Malta."

"Yeah, I know that much. Never mind. George told me about the Order's purpose and many accomplishments," Renee said, not being able to reconcile the duo's horrific personalities and the knights' public image. She knew nothing of Paul's background but was quick to judge him by the company he kept.

"Sebastian, we can never be friends. Not now, not ever," Renee said sternly. "I appreciate your apology, but we're done. Get over it."

Renee turned and walked away, hoping to never see him again. She did a month later.

CHAPTER 9

ALBI, FRANCE - JUNE 5, 2012

The day came when Renee and Noelle were ready to leave Albi. They would leave behind Renee's parents, Father Dubois and – thank God – Sebastian. They texted a few remaining friends that in nine days and 750 miles they would be at the Cathedral of St. James, and they were off.

Gerard had agreed to let Renee skip the starting point of the longer pilgrimage and drive for the first 680 miles. If they were to receive a certificate, Renee knew they must join the other pilgrims at the small Spanish town of Sarria for the last five days.

Their route paralleled the Pyrenees to the south traveling west across the Gascogne region of France and resembled Le Chemin de St-Jacques. Driving at a leisurely pace over a four-day period, they reserved the afternoons to reflect on what they had seen and what it must have been like for the pilgrims in the darkest period of history. Along the way, they studied the histories of the towns they visited.

The French town of Pau was their first stop, visiting the Château de

Pau, a medieval castle begun in 1307 by Gaston III and birthplace of King Henry IV. Born a Catholic and raised a Huguenot, Renee noted King Henry accepted Catholicism once again as a means to end the religious wars of France.

The afternoons also served as a time to renew their once close relationship. The first afternoon Renee asked about her friend's future.

"Noelle, before we left, Mama told me you were thinking about becoming a nun," Renee said.

"Yeah … well … I don't know. There's a Benedictine Order nearby and a Carmelite Order in Albi. But. I just don't know."

"Why the indecision?"

"That may take some time …"

"That's okay. We have a few days ahead of us."

"Well, for one thing why aren't women allowed to be priests? And then there's the whole neo-Gnostic influence over our region. Why do we even need priests and the hierarchy of the Church to intercede in our relationship with God?" Noelle began.

"Yes, knowing you years ago I was really surprised when Mama told me you were working for Fr. Dubois."

"I know, but he's a good sounding board and gives me a lot of latitude For example, last April the Vatican came down pretty hard on a group of nuns in America," Noelle continued. "Apparently, they signed a statement supporting health care for women. I was pretty upset that these men, men of God no less, entered into the fray, but nevertheless there they were. Fr. Dubois tried to walk me through their logic and listen to my arguments. It helped somewhat, but didn't dissuade me."

"And so, if you do not agree with these positions, why do you want to be a nun?" Renee asked.

"I think these are difficult times for the Church … a Church that is declining and out of sync with the people it serves … a Church that reacts in centuries to societal changes when the rest of the world reacts on Twitter. So, I'm torn. Of course I don't want to see the Church undermined, but I don't think that is what these nuns were doing. They were making a political statement, not a religious one. They seemed to be focused on real life issues that will go wanting if not supported by your Congress. They are not trying to destroy Church doctrine. As far as the male-only priesthood, that's one thing that will never change."

"Why? What do you mean? Doesn't this have to change if the Church is to remain relevant?"

"Yes, of course it does but I'm sad to say I don't think it ever will. The bible reflects the patriarchal society over the years it was written but continues to be thought of as the direct word of God. Too many people take it literally as if it's current today. Read it critically, Renee. I think you will discover that it suggests Eve was the root of evil, allows women to be considered as property, does not allow a wife to divorce her husband, treats menstruating women as unclean, and is virtually silent on the Apostle to the Apostles, Mary Magdalene. I don't think the Church will ever allow women to become priests until the Church accepts this truth. So, I'm not very optimistic," Noelle concluded.

"You know, I think I'm a little more optimistic about the Church than you," Renee advised, not knowing what the next two weeks would unveil.

Renee also remained convinced the history revealed in their pilgrimage was part of her heritage. The next day they continued south to Navarre, Spain, visited the Palace of the Kings and found Gaston IV, Count of Foix. Their next stop brought them to the town of Astorga. Once an abandoned village and buffer between the invading Moors of the eighth century and the Christian strongholds from Austurias westward, Astorga was a town rich in Celtic history with no Gastons in sight.

The final 115 miles of the trip carried them through the Spanish countryside to a medieval town of nearly 14,000 people – Sarria. They turned in the rental car, helped one another adjust their daypacks and prepared themselves to begin the journey to learn about themselves and others on the following day.

* * *

Sarria was a small yet welcoming town. Residents had seen many pilgrims come and go over the years. This morning was no exception.

The aroma of hot coffee, freshly baked bread and aged sheep's milk cheese of the Basque region greeted their arrival from the hostel next door. It gave them the nourishment they needed to begin their journey on foot.

The vine covered opening next to their table filtered the morning sunlight as Renee and Noelle sat in silence thinking about the day in front of them. They stared down the path that lay ahead. Small stone buildings. Alternating gravel and flagstone streets. Ivy covered walls interspersed with glorious patches of yellow and red flowering vines defined the town.

Beyond the edge of Sarria, the rolling hills of grassy terrain provided a backdrop for the pilgrims on their way.

They were surprised to see the great number of pilgrims who joined them from this starting point. Others had been walking for the past twenty-seven days. From the French side of the Pyrenees, 480 miles away, pilgrims collected their passports, which soon would be filled with the stamps from the villages they visited, and their scallop shell, the symbol of St. James and started walking.

Some pilgrims walked in solitude with only their thoughts about the meaning of life and the yellow-arrowed-shell-markers to guide their journeys. Others shared stories, friendship, laughter and spiritual bonds of human struggle. Some walked for religious reasons, some for physical. Some booked accommodations in advance, enjoyed Spanish wines and food along the way, while others stayed in the *refugios* with Spartan, sometimes unsanitary, conditions. Some were well groomed, others disheveled.

Nevertheless, they were all on the path to discover why they were on the path.

At first Renee had the feeling she was not welcomed as a true pilgrim by those who had started in France. "What are you thinking Renee? You look sad. This is a joyful thing we are about to do, no?" Noelle asked.

"I know. It's just the others look exhausted but are so happy. They've been together for such a long time. I don't know if they even want us here."

"Of course they do. Just give it a little time," Noelle urged. "You may even meet some new friends on the pilgrimage or in Compostela. You never know."

Noelle is right, of course, Renee thought.

After their first fourteen mile day of exhaustion from Sarria to Potomarin, they both experienced the camaraderie of these new friends and the joy in their purpose. *I'm really glad Mama suggested I take someone along. It's so great having Noelle here with me every step of the way.*

Renee awoke the next morning knowing the day before her would be like yesterday, and the days to come would be harder still. They would need to walk about sixteen miles to make it halfway to Azúra and the pre-booked hotel room for the night in Palas sixty-one miles more – up and down the hills and valleys, on alternating uneven dirt and paved roads – and embrace her resulting thirst, sore muscles, exhaustion and elements of an ever changing summer sky.

Their morning coffee and the news from the day's edition of *Libération* set the tone for the day ahead. "Hey, Noelle, it says here a group of Catholic nuns announced yesterday they are planning a bus trip beginning in Iowa and ending in Virginia with stops in seven other states. They're calling their journey 'Nuns on the Bus.' They're planning to stop by schools and healthcare and homeless facilities run by nuns in order to bring attention to their work and protest the Congressional Budget that cuts out these services."

"Well, good for them," Noelle said. "Renee, I have to tell you, your question on why I stay with the Church got to me. It's been on my mind ever since."

"I'm sorry, I didn't mean to offend. It just seems to me you're not very closely aligned philosophically with the Church. That's why I asked," Renee said.

"Oh, no, you didn't offend me. It was actually good for me to think it through," Noelle admitted. "I still am not sure about becoming a nun, but it's just there's so much that must be done to aid the poor, the sick, the homeless, the hungry, and the disadvantaged that Church politics are of little interest to me. Isn't that what the nuns on the bus are really about?"

Leaving Potomarin, Renee overheard the pilgrims discussing the last leg of their pilgrimage to Compostela, a twenty-four mile journey from Azúra. The ones who had been on the pilgrimage since the border had built up the stamina to accept the last leg willingly; in fact, at the end some were so eager to finish they almost jogged the last few miles. Renee and Noelle planned to walk from Azúra to Pedrouzo, a distance of twelve miles and from there another twelve miles would find them in Compostela. Renee began to doubt if that was the best plan after listening to the others. Certainly they could not make it in one day as some decided.

"You know, Noelle, by the time we get to Compostela all my body will want to do is crash, when my mind will want to go to see the town and the cathedral," Renee said. "I overheard several of the others discuss walking twenty-one miles and stopping three miles short at the Mount of Joy. From there it is possible to see the holy city of Compostela off in the distance. If we take three days rather than two it might be better. What do you think?"

"Well, if we walk what … about two and a half miles per hour for the next two days … we could spend some time in the villages along the way and save our energy for the third day to arrive in Compostela. It will take us six days rather than five, but so what? I could stay in Compostela one night rather than two and still be back in Albi in time for Sunday mass. So, okay," Noelle confirmed.

Several hours into their journey Renee thought about her studies and road beneath her where the footsteps and spirits of so many had come before. *Was the period of the Dark Ages truly that or had the Church deliberately obscured learning as a means of control? Matter always existed to the Egyptians; to them it was not logical for God to create something from nothing,* she thought.

"Noelle, do you remember our physics classes at Lapérouse?"

"My God, why did you have to remind me? I almost flunked out of school because of that class," Noelle readily admitted.

"I know. I didn't much like it either. But do you recall Einstein's theory that all matter is made of energy and can be transformed back to energy. Everything is alive. Even those rocks over there have particles moving within them," Renee said. "This suggests God did not create the heavens and the earth as Genesis says but is the source of all energy."

"Yeah, but the problem is the ancients were self-conscious and anxious. They did not think of themselves as holy beings who emanated from God. They thought and wrote that we are here and God is over there," Noelle said pointing to the clouds off in the distance. "We are separate. This alienation seemed so real, so powerful they created the story of Adam and Eve to explain their anxiety. God was good and we were not. We were degenerate if not evil and had to be forgiven by God."

"Noelle, that doesn't sound very Catholic to me. The separation thing you talk about took on a life of its own during the Middle Ages, especially in Albi. I don't know about you, Noelle, but the nuns and you just might drag the boys kicking and screaming into the twenty-first century yet. But you'd better be careful. The Vatican is on a tear these days. They might condemn you for having serious theological problems as well."

"I know, but thankfully Father Dubois does not."

They awoke from their last night's stay at one of the many hostels built to accommodate the pilgrims overjoyed to complete their journey. They walked the last three miles to Compostela on the last morning of their now ten-day pilgrimage physically exhausted, but spiritually rejuvenated.

After seventy miles and six days of thirst, sore muscles, and exhaustion they finally arrived at the Romanesque Cathedral of St James. The sheer size of the place was overwhelming, but more than that they immediately felt the impact of a spiritual presence, a feeling Renee needed to capture and document for Gerard.

The next afternoon, Noelle headed for the airport for her pre-booked flight back to Toulouse. Renee was saddened by her dear friend's departure and left alone to figure out what she had learned from the past ten days.

Remembering her many challenges along the way, she recalled one pilgrim saying to her, "The real journey is not the pilgrimage to the cathedral, the real journey is what you do with your life after what you've learned."

Little did she realize after three more days in Compostela a new journey would be made known to her – a journey that would change her life forever.

CHAPTER 10

WASHINGTON, DC - JULY 4, 2012

Renee's mind left Noelle, the Shell Pilgrimage, and the Cathedral of St. James and returned to the holiday before her. *I have to find a way to tell Stan what happened to me. And I have to tell him today. This can't wait,* she thought. She climbed down from the kitchen counter and walked across the room to embrace her fiancé.

"Here you go," Stan said, handing Renee a perfectly prepared omelet, bacon and strawberries. Why don't we go outside?"

A cool morning breeze blew across the Potomac and welcomed the couple to the terrace. As they ate, Stan's curiosity began to get the better of him. "What did you mean earlier by saying 'the past four weeks have been life changing', Renee?"

"Stan, this is going to take some time," Renee said.

"That's fine; we have all day."

Renee began by telling Stan about her father's story of El Camiño de las Estrellas, her friend, Noelle, and the many pilgrims she met along the way.

"Our route was lined with churches and monasteries. There was certainly no doubt that Noelle and I approached a holy city. Our narrowing, meandering roadway suddenly opened onto the huge central plaza of the city. I sat for hours in the plaza watching the pilgrims enter the cathedral. Their joyful spirit seemed to push them more and more to accomplish their shared goal.

"The first time I entered, I was struck by the magnitude of the cathedral," she continued with a growing excitement. "It's massive. It's one of the largest Romanesque cathedrals in all of Europe. Inside, its length is that of a football field and its height was as tall as a … well, a five-story office building. It's incredible. I guess you know this. You should have been there, you would have enjoyed it."

"It was weird, though. In spite of its grand scale, when you sit quietly and reflect on the past and the thousands of pilgrims who have visited the cathedral, it somehow feels intimate. There was a spiritual presence about the place. It could not be denied.

"In complete silence the pilgrims would enter, make their way to a pew, genuflect, kneel and begin to pray. At that point their faces seemed solemn, reflecting their reverence for their immediate surroundings. Following a period of silence and prayer, they would walk to one of the side aisles, cross a wide transept, and hesitate as they approached the altar. Their faces showed a childlike wonder and awe. Above the altar was an enormous canopy, a baldachin, I think it's called, with a statue of Saint James. It was in this moment each face appeared to change, exhilarated by a sense of joy and accomplishment. The pilgrims then walked in silence behind the altar and kissed the statue. They then went behind the altar to the … uh …"

"Ambulatory?" Stan suggested.

"… yes, to the ambulatory surrounding it. Every pilgrim would pause for a while at each of the five chapels to study the paintings, sculpture and relics collected throughout the centuries. The most interesting was the silver bust of James the Righteous. It is said to contain his skull. Afterward, they would descend to the crypt below the main altar. There, the substructure of the old cathedral could easily be seen. It was once dedicated to James the Righteous but now contains the remains of James the Great. This was their final destination, to honor these relics."

"So, were they both there?" Stan asked.

"Yes, in a manner of speaking, just like you said. Funny thing though, at the bust of James the Righteous the signage referred to him by his other name, James the Less, and cited him as the brother of James the Great rather than the brother of Jesus. I found this a bit odd. I guess it was to continue the Catholic implication that the Virgin Mary only had the one child by Immaculate Conception even though the Gospels of Matthew and Mark both say he had four brothers and at least two sisters.

"After Noelle left, I stayed in town for a few days more talking to other pilgrims and locals about their attraction to the Cathedral. I asked over and over about El Camiño de las Estrellas and the Path of Initiation without much success. Finally, just two weeks ago, on my fourth and last day in Compostela, a local man approached my table. He was an elderly Spaniard with slicked back grey hair and dark weathered skin. He extended his hand to me, as if he were an official welcoming me to his city and said, 'Excuse me, before your friends left, I overheard you asking about the pathway of the stars. My name is Rafael Tuguía. I was born here and have lived here all of my adult life watching the pilgrims come and go. Some return to their homes while others continue on horseback on El Camiño de las Estrellas to begin their Path of Initiation. I have some knowledge of this. May I be of assistance?'

"My father's brief explanation came to mind as I hurriedly said, 'Yes, you can. Do you know about it? Tell me anything … tell me everything.' As he sat, I noticed he wore a golden triangular shaped pendant. Mounted on the triangle was a golden cross with roses. It was hard to miss displayed against his brown, hairless chest and framed by his unbuttoned shirt. Seeing it like that made me admit, 'That's a beautiful pendant. I've never seen anything quite like it before.'

"'Thank you,' Rafael said. 'I am Rosicrucian.' "

CHAPTER 11

INTERLUDE – PRESENT DAY

History reveals that many ancient cultures used obelisks or pillars to express their connection to their god. For example, the Egyptians had a pillar in Upper Egypt and one in Lower Egypt joined by the sky goddess Nut, the mother of Osiris and Isis.

Egyptian customs and beliefs influenced biblical traditions. Joseph – Jacob's son, Isaac's grandson, and Abraham's great-grandson – was a dreamer. According to *Genesis* he was Jacob's favorite son and dreamt God had called him to greatness. He was sold into slavery by his jealous brothers. This led him to be imprisoned by a false accusation. Whether Joseph actually existed, or with his purported two sons and ten brothers personified the twelve tribes of Israel (formerly named Jacob) bearing their names, is not known.

Assuming Joseph was an actual person, again *Genesis* tells us that once his dreams proved themselves, this imprisoned son of Israel found favor with an unnamed Egyptian pharaoh. He then rose to become the second in command and saved his family from famine by bringing them to Egypt.

This story is cited as an antecedent to another biblical figure named Joseph (Spong, 2007, p 32).[3] In *Matthew 2:13-23* we find an angel appearing to this Joseph, who also had a father named Jacob, in a dream. The angel told him to flee to Egypt to protect and save another holy family – Mary and the infant Jesus – from King Herod this time, rather than famine. Coincidence? Perhaps, but doubtful. Reference? Probably, as any Jewish person in the eighth decade would have understood this reference to their patriarch.

The pharaoh discussed above was Akhenaten, according to Robert Feather, (Feather, 2005, p 87)[4] Akhenaten (reign: 1353-1336 BCE) was the tenth pharaoh of Egypt's Eighteenth Dynasty. He was perhaps the most controversial pharaoh in Egyptian history because of his break with Egypt's orthodox religion – a pantheon of some 2,000 deities. He and his queen, Nefertiti, formed a new religion, Atenism, and worshipped only the sun's disc, the Aten. After Akhenaten's death, Egypt returned to its polytheistic belief system. Their primary deities included the divine trinity Osiris, Isis and Horus as well as the god of evil and chaos, Seth.

"Now there arose a new king over Egypt who did not know Joseph." (Exodus 1:8). This is likely the beginning of the Nineteenth Dynasty of Egypt also known as the Ramessid Dynasty. Whether Joseph influenced Akhenaten or Akhenaten influenced Joseph or whether Joseph was only a literary figure is unknown and of little consequence; what is consequential follows.

When the Israelites fled Egypt – approximately one hundred years after Akhenaten's reign and most likely during the reign of Rameses the Great – they carried with them not only the "bones of Joseph" *(Exodus 13:19)*, but also a Canaan inherited or Egyptian inspired concept of monotheism, a belief in the powers of healing and regeneration derived from the Mother Goddess Isis, the concept of Egyptian pillars to connect to their god and the values of Maat, i.e., truth/morality and law/justice as personified by the Egyptian goddess of a similar name, Ma'at.

When Yahweh "… gave Moses the Ten Commandments he had clearly been reading from the Egyptian Book of the Dead … which includes the familiar words: I have done no falsehoods … I have not robbed … I have not killed men … I have not committed perjury … I have not (sexually) misconducted myself … I have done no wrong … I have seen no evil … I have not reviled God … I am not wealthy except with my own property .. I have not blasphemed God in my city … " (Pickett, 2003, p 162).[5]

The Israelites personified these pillars with the values of Maat to give their lives stability. Judaism reflects this in Moses and Aaron, David and Nathan, Josiah and Jeramiah, etc. – the king (law/justice) and the high priest (truth/morality). Bronze pillars representing this idea, named Boaz and Jachin, are said to have defined the entry to Solomon's Temple.

Around 200 BCE the Greeks controlled and defiled the Temple of Jerusalem. This sacrilege caused many of the extremely devout priestly class, i.e., the "Sons of Zadok" named by Solomon, to break away from the two dominant Hebrew sects – the Pharisees and the Sadducees. The Essenes, as they were later called, settled in Egypt for a brief while. Aspects of Egyptian culture combined with their traditional Judaic beliefs, customs and practices to shape a new, fledgling theology.

The Dead Sea Scrolls tell us "they stumbled around like blind men for twenty years." When they returned to Judah, led by the 'Teacher of Righteousness', the celibate Essenes settled in the wilderness of Qumran caves, approximately twenty miles from Jerusalem. Located near the northwest tip of the Dead Sea, it was in these caves that thousands of scroll fragments, multiple copies of Genesis, Leviticus, Deuteronomy, Isaiah and Psalms as well as other scrolls – the Temple Scroll, the Thanksgiving Scroll, the Damascus Document, Community Rule (Manual of Discipline), and the War of Sons of Light Against the Sons of Darkness – were found between 1947 and 1954. From the evidence in the latter document it appears the Essenes embraced the dualistic concepts of good versus evil in what may have been one of the earliest forms of Gnosticism.

Those who held the same beliefs but chose to marry, formed a separate but connected branch of the Essenes. The Nazarenes (meaning 'keepers' or 'preservers' of the ancient scriptures) married and settled at Mt. Carmel (Galilee), near the modern city of Nazareth. Recall that St. Paul refers to Jesus as "Jesus the Nazarene."

Borrowing from mainstream Judaism, their pillars were called: Mishpat, the Pillar of Justice, and Tsedec, the Pillar of Righteousness. Jesus Christ (Christos, Greek for 'anointed', the Messiah or the 'anointed one to be king') and John the Baptizer represented these two pillars. When John's mission and life were quickly extinguished, Jesus' brother, James, who was called 'James the Less' – to distinguish him from James the Great (aka James the Apostle and James, Son of Zebedee) – became the Pillar of Righteousness and was called James the Righteous (aka James the Just).

James became the first bishop of the Church of Jerusalem and singly shouldered the responsibility for the community of the Torah after Jesus' death. The Nazarenes continued the worship *of* God in strict Judaic sense under the Torah. By contrast St. Paul took his new religion, based on the worship of Jesus Christ *as* God, to the gentiles.

The pair fought over taking Nazarene thought outside of the Torah to the uncircumcised. A struggle between Pauline Christianity and Christianity rooted in Gnosticism then emerged. The Gnostics sought knowledge (gnosis) in all that they did. To them the problem humans faced was not sin, it was ignorance. They held that Jesus did not save people from their sins by way of the cross, rather he sought to teach spiritual fulfillment through enlightenment. They claimed they did not need the priesthood to intercede on their behalf, but could connect with God directly.

Fourteen bishops of Jewish origin followed James to serve the Church of Jerusalem. After suppressing the second Jewish uprising in 135 CE, the Roman Empire appointed Marcus as the first gentile bishop as the persecution of the Jewish people continued. Over the next one hundred years Pauline Christianity consolidated power, became Christian orthodoxy, and deemed Gnosticism to be heretical.

It is often asserted that after Jesus' crucifixion Mary Magdalene, their child and others including her sister, Martha, and brother, Lazarus, escaped from Jerusalem by boat and landed on the shores of Southern France. This is legend, but it is interesting to note that a new form of Gnosticism emerged in the form of Catharism from the Languedoc Region of Southern France.

This theology embraced the dualism of good versus evil having deities to represent either side. They rejected the hierarchy of the Church and what the adherents perceived as the abuses and corruption of the priesthood. This form of Christianity was once again deemed heretical by orthodox Christianity. In response Pope Innocent III (Papacy: 1198-1216 CE), who by that time had claimed supremacy over all European kings and initiated two crusades against Muslims – one in Iberia and the Fourth Crusade in the Holy Land – initiated a twenty year crusade against the Cathars known as the Albigensian Crusade.

French noblemen with orders from King Philip II killed well over 200,000 Gnostic Christians and even some of their own under the Pope's direction and in his name. For example, prior to the initial massacre at Béziers, where 20,000 men, women and children were killed, it is commonly held that Abbot Amalric, representing the papacy, was asked how they were to distinguish Cathars from Catholics. He responded, "Kill them all! God will know his own." This does not meet historical scrutiny, but captures the spirit of the Crusade. This genocide all but eliminated Catharism; survivors went underground. It also brought the Languedoc under the French crown.

So passionate were they in their thirst for knowledge that "... had it not been for the persecution of the Cathars, the culture of the Languedoc would have spawned a Renaissance nearly two centuries before that in Italy." (Wallace-Murphy, Tim and Hopkins, Marilyn, 1999, p 123). [6]

* * *

Our story resumes in Santiago de Compostela, Spain two weeks before Renee's July 4th holiday in Washington D.C. She is eager to learn about El Camiño de las Estrellas from a man who will teach her the true meaning of her fellow pilgrim's statement. "The real journey is not the pilgrimage to the cathedral, the real journey is what you do with your life after what you've learned."

CHAPTER 12

SANTIAGO DE COMPOSTELA, SPAIN - JUNE 19, 2012

"I have learned so much as a Rosicrucian. It means everything to me. I will tell you all I know about El Camiño de las Estrellas, but first tell me what brings you to Compostela?" Rafael probed, hoping Renee would reveal more about her character and integrity.

"Rafael … may I call you Rafael?" Renee asked watching him nod in agreement. "Rafael, my name is Renee … Renee Gaston. I grew up in Albi, France, not too far from here."

Renee began a superficial answer to his question – describing her assignment, Dr. Gerard, Stan and the building itself. It was a start.

"It's a pleasure to meet you, Renee. Yes, the cathedral is certainly a magnificent building, but why did you seek St. James?"

"As I was saying, I started on assignment to interview the pilgrims, but somewhere along the way this changed. Of course, I completed my assignment as promised, but that seemed secondary to my experience."

"Good, this is what I would like to understand."

"My companion, Noelle Martine, and I had time to discuss a great many things about life, politics, the future of the Church, and the way women are often mistreated. Through all of the soul searching and discussion, we got caught up in the joy of our shared experience with the other pilgrims. And then upon entering the cathedral I was overwhelmed by not only its grandeur, but also in awe of what we accomplished together. It was truly humbling," she continued, revealing a person whom Rafael now believed he could trust.

Better, he thought.

"I understand what you are saying. I've spoken with many who begin the journey as a lark and end the journey surprised by what they experienced and accomplished with fellow pilgrims. I am glad you were able to find purpose in your journey. Like your Dr. Gerard, I too like to know the reason people make this pilgrimage; that's why I asked. I hope my manner did not offend."

"Not at all," Renee was quick to acknowledge.

"Before, you asked about El Camiño de las Estrellas."

"Yes, I did. I asked many fellow pilgrims along the way and here as well since I arrived. But no one seems to know anything. My father suggested I might find this path, the "Path of Initiation" as he called it, even more interesting. My mother on the other hand, derides him every time he mentions this. She's a devout Catholic and still thinks Gnosticism is heretical. It's about the only source of friction between them, but it's ever present."

"I agree with your father. What is his name?"

"Jacques … Jacques Gaston … my mother is Marie."

"I think you would enjoy taking the Path of Initiation as well. The Cathedral of St. James is so much more than a building or a destination. It's a beginning. You will visit many such places of learning and spiritual awakening throughout France. I congratulate you. Finding humility is key to beginning your spiritual journey."

Rafael studied the intensity by which she hung on his every word and decided to go forward.

"Since you are from Albi, I assume that you are familiar with the tragic end to what Rome called the Cathar Heresy. Thousands of French Christians of Gnostic tradition lost their lives to French noblemen and the Roman Catholic Church during the Albigensian Crusade."

"Yes, of course I do. It's like a cloud that still hangs over our town and in my house. Why?"

"This so-called Cathar Heresy was the reason the Path of Initiation was devised and kept secret from the Catholic Church. The novice would begin and end his journey at two sculpted, Solomonic columns – pillars actually, as they were called. These pillars were thought to be joined by the glorious constellation of the Milky Way above France, giving rise to the name El Camiño de las Estrellas. The first pillar was in northern Portugal. There the initiate would go through a period of purification before returning to Compostela to begin his journey.

"From Compostela," Rafael continued, "the novice would advance east and north through France to five sacred sites that were once the locations of Druidic oracles, then Roman Temples, before becoming Christian cathedrals. At each site, the initiate studied and mastered academic subjects and gained spiritual enlightenment in progressive stages."

"This sounds familiar. It's like the ancient Egyptian pilgrimages along the Nile I studied about," Renee offered. "At the journey's end the pilgrim had achieved full illumination and union with the divine. He then had the right and the ability to read the ancient mystical books of Egyptian wisdom. You called it a 'Solomonic pillar', what do you mean?"

"Exactly. There are many parallels between the Egyptian pilgrimage and the Path of Initiation. Solomonic is a term whose derivation comes from the columns thought to have been erected at the Temple of Solomon. It's a twisting shape pillar."

"Okay, thanks. Please go on."

"After he completed the sixth degree the more advanced candidate would be invited to conclude his journey at the second Solomonic pillar in Scotland, the Apprentice Pillar of Rosslyn Chapel. There he would learn about human self-consciousness and the spiritual relationship of life and death, much like your Egyptian 'union with the divine.'

"Egypt had such a huge influence on Judaism. Aspects of Egyptian culture combined with traditional Judaic beliefs, customs and practices to create a new theology that was embraced by the Essenes and the Nazarenes. This evolved into Christianity."

"Rafael, how can you be so sure about all of this? Our traditional understanding of Christianity is rooted in Judaism and does not include a path through Egypt and has lasted two thousand years."

"You have heard accounts in the Dead Sea Scrolls, I trust."

"Yes, of course," Renee confirmed.

"These scrolls obscure a person's identity by using names such as the Wicked Priest or the Teacher of Righteousness and the like," Rafael said.

"I am aware. But as far as I know, none of this has been sorted out. Unless you are telling me something new," Renee said.

"I am. The Nazarenes committed themselves to honor women in the tradition of the sacred feminine and attempted to move away from a Judaic paternal society. Remember, one of the things St. Paul said about Jesus the Nazarene, 'In Jesus there is neither male nor female.'

"I will give you some commonly known examples to perhaps ease your mind. Brother John preached confession, baptism, redemption, and the promise of life after death found in the worship of Osiris and Isis. The Jewish people held no such beliefs. The Essenes also changed the Sabbath from Saturday to Sunday to honor the sun. They faced the rising sun to the east when they prayed. They used a solar calendar rather than the Jewish lunar one, and the list goes on and on. Much of this is revealed on the Path of Initiation."

"Wow, my head is spinning. I don't know what to think," Renee concluded. "I wish I had time to take the Path and slowly absorb all of this, but I'm returning to the States in two weeks. In the meantime, I need to return to Albi and work on my report for Dr. Gerard. Someday, perhaps."

"Pity. Maybe I could drive you as far as Toulouse so you could visit the Church of Notre Dame la Delbade. It was the next step of enlightenment. I've been there many times. Father Berger and I have become good friends. I am sure he would be most welcoming."

"No, I'm sorry, but I have a flight this evening," Renee confessed.

"But with two weeks remaining you must make time to visit the fourth site along the path, Chartres Cathedral. It's one of the most beautiful Gothic cathedrals in all of Europe. If you do, I think you will return one day to Compostela and take the entire pilgrimage."

"I could do that. If Chartres is the fourth, what is the third?"

"At Compostela the pilgrim learned humility and opened himself to a higher spirit. At Delbade he went deep into himself and learned to trust his own feelings. At the third site, Orléans Cathedral, he became a warrior and was knighted after he demonstrated the resolve and bravery to defend good and fight evil. The pilgrim, now a knight, progressed to the fourth site at Chartres. There he raised his spirit to an even higher level and resolved never to retreat from what was required of him. Chartres was at the heart –

the joining of the body's strength and mind's spirit. As you will learn, it became one of the most important Cathedral Schools in France."

"Rafael, before I go today, the thing you said earlier about 'the sacred feminine'," Renee said. "Does Mary Magdalene fit into the puzzle somehow?"

"Yes, but this should wait. You will learn more about her at Chartres. I will contact my brother, Miguel, who lives there. He's well versed on matters relating to the cathedral and to the Magdalene. I'll let him know you are coming and of your interest."

"Yes, please do," she said thinking about the time she had available. "I can meet him on Monday, a week from now, before I leave the country."

"Wonderful. I think you will enjoy what he has to say about Mary as well as the messages hidden deep in the art and architecture of Chartres." Looking at his cellphone's calendar Rafael confirmed, "That's Monday, July 2nd, right?"

Renee nodded in agreement.

"Perfect! On most weekdays during the summer months the chairs are removed from the nave. While you're there you likely will be able to walk the labyrinth. When you arrive contact Miguel on his cellphone at this number," he said handing her a slip of paper. "He speaks English as well. I will let him know you will call."

* * *

"Hello, Miguel. This is Rafael. I think our angel has fallen from the sky as you had hoped. Her name is Renee Gaston. She'll be there on July 2nd. You should give her a portion of the translation."

CHAPTER 13

TOULOUSE, FRANCE – TWO MONTHS EARLIER

David Hitzig was a quiet and thoughtful man of forty-three. For thirteen of those years, he taught Hebrew and Ancient Israeli Studies at Université de Toulouse-Le Mirail without incident. But things were changing in France and throughout the world.

For the past two months France seemed to be a cauldron of hate and anti-Semitism as white supremacists grew their ranks.

Earlier in the year, anti-Jewish thugs shouted down Arnaud Montebourg, a leading figure in France's Socialist opposition party "Juden, Juden, Juden … France is for the French," they claimed. "Jean-Marie Le Pen has given us the midnight permission to hunt the Jews in Paris."

Mr. Le Pen said he condemned the incident, but critics argued he was unwilling to challenge extremist elements within the National Front party. That was in Paris. David felt safe in Toulouse at the University of Le Mirail. But today his world was shaken.

Today, Wednesday, April 25th, Eva Sandler lit a candle at the memorial service in Jerusalem after her husband, a rabbi, and two sons were gunned down at a Toulouse café in March by Mohammed Merah.

Today, a delegation of Israeli students from Ben-Gurion University was midway through a tour of French universities when they visited Le Mirail campus, near where the Toulouse gunman grew up. They handed out leaflets and chatted with students on behalf of "What Is RAEL." Without provocation, protesters arrived and shouted anti-Israeli slogans saying Israel commits genocide, Israel is a criminal state, and they should be exterminated.

Today, Father Dominique Berger quietly knocked on David Hitzig's office door. Standing with Dominique was an elderly Spaniard with slicked back grey hair and dark weathered skin. He wore a golden triangular shaped pendant with a cross and roses.

"David, please allow me to present Rafael Tuguía."

"Father Dominique, Mr. Tuguia please be seated," Professor Hitzig said, swinging around his desk chair and gesturing to the two lounge chairs that filled his small office.

"No, I'm going to leave you two now, and go back to the church," Dominique said. "Rafael, are you okay?"

A slight smile crossed Rafael's tense face as he held up a hand to wave his friend away. Turning, he said to David, "Thank you for taking Dominique's call and agreeing to see me. A few months ago, I asked Dominique if he would attend a lecture you gave on the three early strains of Christianity and introduce himself."

David acknowledged Rafael's opening remarks with a slight nod and bewildered look. He said, "Yes, I remember. We shared lunch several days later. I'm sorry, but I do not recall him mentioning you at the time. It surprises me to hear this now. We have become fairly close friends since."

"David, Dominique did not mean to deceive you. He was doing me a favor. Please let me explain. I have known Dominique for years, ever since he came to Notre Dame la Delbade. I have grown to trust him. We are close friends and have a great deal of respect for one another. I asked if he would meet you and judge if you could be trusted. I think you will see why in a moment. Please do not allow my need to be careful diminish your friendship or his sincerity. He has written how much he has enjoyed your conversations and friendship over the months and has full confidence in your integrity."

"When Dominique called yesterday, he said something about you and my grandfather," David said in a suspicious tone. "I did not understand."

Dispensing with any sort of cordial small talk, Rafael continued, "Yes, I will come right to the point. David, even though you are not aware of this I have known you and your family for your entire life. When we were very young, my brother and I lived with my father in Northern Spain in the town of Santiago de Compostela. In fact, I still do. I just left there yesterday to meet with you. You may have heard of the town and much of what I will share with you."

"Of course, the destination of the Shell Pilgrimage," affirmed David.

Taking a deep breath Rafael continued, "When Hitler became chancellor of Germany, he targeted the Jewish people as a serious biological threat to the purity of the Aryan people. I know you know this, but because of this your grandfather, Ezra, fled his home and travelled as far west as he could, and settled in Compostela. He and my father, Ramon, and my uncle, Juan, became close friends. They had very much in common. They all were subjected to persecution from the right-wing Nationalists, much like France has experienced here during the past few months.

"In 1934 my father was murdered by two thugs who supported Gil-Robles and the right wing group CEDA. My brother and I grew up in A Coruña with our uncle to care for us. My uncle and your grandfather remained friends over the years. I also had the pleasure of getting to know him as well on our trips to visit my father's grave. Several months before our civil war started, when I was eight, he married a lovely, local girl by the name of Elisa Diaz before she changed her name to Hitzig."

"Yes, of course," David confirmed, "I'm so sorry to hear of your father's death, especially in that manner. You must have been devastated."

"Yes, I was, but much of the pain was eased by your father. When I was thirteen, your father, Jacob, was born. As he grew, he treated me like an older brother. I enjoyed his company very much."

"Thank you. It's nice to hear he meant so much to you during this time."

"Yes he did, but times were tough for all of us. Two years before he was born the Republic was toppled, hundreds of thousands of Spaniards died and Franco became dictator. In the early years things were extremely difficult, especially for the men who originally supported the left leaning policies of the Republic. It was worse for women.

"Things eased up a bit a few years later. People migrated to the cities and gained employment. If you were a member of the Nationalist

Movement, male, white and Catholic things were a lot better. Ezra, Juan and I were only two of those things."

"And my grandmother, Elisa, only one" David injected with some understanding of the time being described.

"Of course. Seven years later, in 1948, David Ben-Gurion proclaimed to the world that Israel was a new state. This joyous moment was simply overwhelming for your grandfather. He spoke of nothing else for the next five years. Then in 1953, when Jacob turned twelve, the Israeli Minister of Education initiated the Israel Prize to be awarded annually for achievement in the humanities, Jewish studies, the arts, and so forth. This act helped shape another degree of Jewish pride and that was that. Ezra decided his son must have his bar mitzvah in Jerusalem, so off the three went, never to return."

"I remember hearing stories about his early years in Israel," David smiled, "but I never knew very much about his time in Spain."

"I was sad to see him leave, but I knew it was for the best. We corresponded often. He sent me these pictures from his marriage to your mother, Sharon. She was so beautiful and Jacob was so happy," Rafael said reaching in pockets for the proof. "And then you were born. Jacob was so very proud. When you learned to walk, then talk, your early years in school, all through your adolescence, and of course your bar mitzvah, all I heard about was David … David … David."

"Okay, this is getting embarrassing, now."

"I was in my early 60s when he wrote to me of your time at the Hebrew University of Jerusalem and your studies of history, Judaism, English and Semitic languages and your further research into early Christianity and Gnosticism. Jacob was so proud of you then, maybe even more than when you first started to walk. How far you have come!"

David set back his chair with a puzzled look on face thinking. *I wonder where all of this is going.*

"You'll forgive an old man's ramblings, but I wanted to remind you of these times. Times when you seemed like a son to me even though we had not met. Because, David, I have something to tell you. I must confide in you. Something not even Jacob knows."

David sat at attention and asked, "Well, what is it?"

"I will tell you but first you must swear to me that you will not tell anyone about what I'm going to reveal to you in this document."

TWO DAYS LATER

Is that it? Rafael asked.

"Yes, it is. Quite a story you have there. You say your father found it in the crypt?" he asked as Rafael acknowledged his question with a nod.

"It was written in ancient Hebrew," David continued. "I added the punctuation and broke it into paragraphs that seemed to make sense."

Rafael thanked him, handed him the €5,000 agreed upon for translating the photocopy of the scroll and confirmed his promise to pay David an additional €10,000 for his silence until he was ready to share his father's discovery.

"Here is my friend's name and phone number and the name of his company. They can provide carbon dating services on your scroll. Tell him I sent you," David said passing him a slip of paper.

"I will keep quiet, but if it turns out to be real and originated in Jerusalem, as I suspect, you know it should be turned over to the Israel Antiquities Authority and housed at the Israeli Museum with the Dead Sea Scro..."

David's voice faded to a dull buzzing sound as Rafael began reading the translation to himself.

Peace be with you from peace, my son.
To you, whom the Master loved most deeply.
Peace be with you from peace, Brother Lazarus,
Love from love,
Grace from grace,
Life from holy life. Amen.

The end of days are near ...

"Rafael," David interrupted. "You are reading the literal translation of the scroll. This helped me prepare a more modern one. One that would be more understandable to a prospective owner. You will have all three for presentation and negotiation – the original, the literal translation, and the updated version."

Rafael took the second document and started again.

Blessings to you, Dear Lazarus,

The end of days will soon be here for us. Before I die I will use this time to record the truth as I know it to be for you and those whom you may encounter.

When our people asked the Savior, who would lead us after his death, he told Brother Thomas to go to me, James the Righteous, the Son of God.

Since the time of Moses and Aaron our people have been led by the King and High Priest. As written in the Torah, King Solomon selected the sons of Zadok to be the High Priest for all time. Seven hundred fifty years later Menelaus expelled Jason, and stole the office for himself. Two hundred years ago our ancestors fled to Egypt when this wicked priest profaned and plundered the Temple. Twenty years later the boy who was our rightful High Priest, grew to be a man. We found the strength to return to Jerusalem through this man, the Teacher of Righteousness, but he was denied once more. The Temple was desecrated with statues of Greek gods, but Judas Maccabee and his brothers soon bought the light back to the Temple. Even so, we could not abide the new practices and broke away from those who tolerated them. We returned to the faith of our ancestors and will remain here in the wilderness to prepare for the Kingdom of God.

Herod Antipas now sits on the throne as a puppet of Emperor Caligula. Theophilus, son of Annas, was appointed by Rome and is now High Priest. This is the very same person, who with his father and four brothers, plotted to kill you after you were raised and reborn with the spirit of John the Baptizer within you.

We are now without a legitimate King or High Priest – ones of our own choosing.

It was left to my brother, Jesus, the Savior, the Son of Man and me, the Bar-aba, the Son of God to fulfill these roles within our community. Pilate, the governor, knew he did not have to kill both of us to tear apart our stability. He offered the people a choice.

Joseph of Arimathea has been able to protect you, and your sisters, Mary and Martha, until now. But he is a hunted man because he dared to claim the body of the Savior and seal him in a tomb lest he be cast into a mass grave and forgotten. Tensions in Jerusalem grow worse and I fear for...

Moments later he neared the end of the translation. The growing intensity of David's voice refocused Rafael's attention once more on his surroundings.

"Rafael … Rafael are you still with me?"

"Yes, sorry, I was … you know, lost in this. My brother and I were able to sort out bits and pieces, but never knew the depth of what we had."

"As I was saying, if this was actually written 2,000 years ago, it will need to be returned to the Israel Antiquities Authority. I will remain silent unless you do not do this."

"Yes … yes, of course."

"There's one other thing. Two days ago when I told you Dominique and I met for lunch I forgot to mention he brought a young lady with him by the name of Noelle Martine. Dominique met her when visiting a friend in Albi, a Father Pierre Dubois. Noelle held a lengthy conversation in Spanish with another visitor while Dominique waited in the outer office for Pierre to arrive. Later, Dominique complimented her on her command of English and Spanish. Noelle thanked him and was quick to tell him of her time at Le Mirail, knowing he was from Toulouse. Apparently, she also told him she was one of my students nine years ago.

"When you asked Dominic to contact me, I guess he felt more comfortable having a mutual friend who spoke French as her native language but could also speak Spanish and English to act as a translator if needed. He invited her to join us for lunch. I really didn't think much about it until I started my work on the scroll. It jogged my memory of her. As a student from Albi, she seemed quite interested in Gnosticism and was quite inquisitive. It was actually good to see her again. She's turned into a beautiful young woman with a serious nature rather than the silly girl who was so infatuated with another one of my students and fellow countryman, Yossi Wolff."

"I think you may want to contact Noelle. She gave me her cellphone number … here it is. Please keep in touch. And don't worry, I have a vested interest in ancient Hebrew culture. I will not mention your scroll.

CHARTRES – TWO DAYS LATER

Miguel waited in his car at the train station near Chartres. The harsh yellow streetlight revealed the aged face of an eighty-one-year-old man. It was a tired, deeply lined face racked by years of fear and worry. His older brother's train arrived from Toulouse on time.

Miguel exited the driver's side of the car to greet Rafael. "Is that the translation?" he asked.

"Yes," Rafael said, handing the briefcase to his brother.

"You drive," Miguel directed in a hoarse voice.

Rafael headed west and followed the road signs in the direction of Chartres. "The good news is David is fully on board," Rafael said. "He wants to help us get the scroll released and back in the hands of the Israeli government. He has become the friend we once had in his father."

Miguel turned on the ceiling light and began reading.

It had been forty-seven years since François Mitterrand consolidated the Workers, Communists, Socialist parties and other liberal thinkers to nearly defeat Charles de Gaulle. The following year Miguel sought a new life in France away from Franco's fascist regime as did thousands of Spaniards from the Basque countryside.

Times had been better for Miguel in France. He helped Mitterrand get elected sixteen years later, celebrated the victory with his brother's visit and fell in love with his adopted city, Chartres. It was an easy place to live, and an easy place to get around. Buildings that were hundreds of years old, cobblestone roads, lush parks and public walkways along the Eure River blended to create a welcoming and joyful place to be. He chatted with customers in his flower shop, gave directions to tourists, and embraced a culture that allowed him to close at one-thirty and have a late lunch with friends.

In this environment Miguel was able to focus his time and energy on what was important to him, Chartres' cultural and spiritual center - the thirteenth-century Cathedral of the Black Madonna, Notre-Dame de Chartres. But his life was changing again.

Miguel finished reading the translation and sighed deeply. "Rafael, I have something to tell you," Miguel said closing the translation and his eyes. "Last week I was diagnosed with stage four lung cancer. It is not operable. They are not sure, but believe I have less than four months to live."

Rafael slowed the car and pulled to the side of the road. "Oh my God," he said. "Are they sure?"

"Yes, I'm afraid so. I went to the doctor after I coughed up some blood. They're sure. Rafael, we have to make sure the scroll is made public immediately, before I die. It is no longer possible to wait. It is urgent we do it now."

"I understand," Rafael said returning the car to the road and his thoughts to the scroll. "I understand."

"Miguel, after my meeting with David I contacted a young lady from Albi by the name of Noelle Martine, as he suggested. She was a student of his years ago. He thought she may be able to help us. I arranged for an appointment with her and the priest of her parish on Wednesday. I'll get back to you after we meet and tell you what she said. You and I will need to quickly develop a plan to do this thing. Is the scroll safe?"

"Yes. I made sure on Friday, knowing you would ask," Miguel said. "Will Noelle be able to raise the money we need?"

"No, I don't think so. She works as a parish administrator in Albi. But she may be able to help us find someone who could help raise the money."

The outline of a massive building with flying buttresses and asymmetrical spires came into view as the hour-long car ride was ending.

"Then it would seem we need to have an angel fall from the sky," Miguel said.

CHAPTER 14

ALBI, FRANCE – THREE DAYS LATER

Noelle Martine escorted their guest into the walnut-paneled pastoral retreat. "Father, please allow me to introduce Rafael Tuguía," she said to Pierre Dubois.

Rafael surveyed the room as he entered. Hundreds of books lined the shelves of the study creating the correct impression that Dubois was a well read and educated man. Among the books, Rafael saw a photograph of Dubois with Cardinal Joseph Ratzinger now known as Pope Benedict XVI.

His picture served as a painful reminder of the horrific time when the Archbishop of Munich, the man who had ordained Ratzinger fifty-four years before, agreed with Hitler's remarks: "… these sub-humans, incited by the Jews, created havoc in Spain like beasts." It was a cowardly derision of Rafael's father and the poorest members of a Spanish society engaged in civil war. It was not easily forgotten by Rafael or his brother

A tall, thin, grey-haired man wearing a black suit and a clerical collar rose from behind his desk. Rafael's eyes left those of his host. They stared at a black and white picture on his desk of a much younger priest. He stood among four other men, all smiles, arms draped around each other's shoulders and holding a black flag emblazoned with a white Maltese cross with St. Peter's Basilica in the background.

Dubois extended his hand. "Welcome, Rafael. I am Pierre Dubois."

Rafael's eyes returned to his host. He was slow to grasp Dubois' hand as the Archbishop's voice echoed in his mind. "Thank you, Father."

"Those are friends of mine in the Order of Malta from the late '70s. The flag is actually red," he said with a nod and smile in response to Rafael's questioning face. "Noelle has told me a great deal about you. Please, have a seat. Noelle, please join us."

"Thank you, Father." Rafael began as he sat down, "Noelle, my request of Fr. Berger to arrange a meeting with David Hitzig put him in an awkward position. He was comforted to have you join them. Thank you for attending the luncheon and for inviting me here today. And thank you, Father."

Noelle smiled and nodded, "Of course."

"Dominique Berger and I have been friends for a long time," Dubois said. "It was my pleasure to allow Noelle to take some time off to help you. What can I do for you now?"

"Father, when I spoke to Noelle last Friday I told her David said many wonderful things about her language skills and about her time at Le Mirail. He indicated that she was a student of his as well as a student of the Gnostic influences surrounding Albi."

Noelle smiled, yielding to her mentor for comment. "Yes, we discuss this frequently."

"David recently helped me with a private matter and told me with Noelle's personal interest in antiquity she may be interested in helping me as well."

"For the record," Noelle interrupted, "After we spoke, I called David to see how I could best help you. David seemed guarded and chose his words carefully. He said he could not speculate on what you might want. He did tell me about your families' relationship, how your father died and what his father meant to you, but that was it. He said that if I wanted to find out more I would have to ask you. I shared this with Father Dubois."

"Yes … yes she did. Rafael, I'm terribly sorry you lost your father in that horrific manner. It was an awful time during the war."

"David did say that if you needed a contact in Israel, he thought his father may be able to help. He gave me his current address and phone number," she said handing him a slip of paper for Jacob and Sharon Hitzig.

"Oh my," Rafael said, choking back his tears. "Thank you, I lost contact and have not spoken with Jacob in several years. I was going to ask David but wanted to wait for the right moment."

"Rafael, again what is it you wish us to do?" Dubois pressed.

"I'm not sure at the moment. Father, I just wanted to meet Noelle and you today and ask your permission to contact Noelle in the future."

"Of course you may…" Dubois began.

"I'm not sure how I can help," Noelle interrupted, "but please let me know if I can. I did have one other thought after we spoke. A good friend of mine from America, Renee Gaston, will be visiting her parents here in Albi in a few weeks. As kids we discussed a lot of things about her father's Gnostic heritage. If this is of interest to you, she may be willing to help you as well. If you want I will ask her and let you know what she says."

Rafael nodded in agreement. Dubois could not let the moment pass without offering yet another opportunity to their guest.

"Rafael, when Noelle told me about the death of your father I contacted one of my past associates in Rome. He said the Order is generally familiar with a Ramon Tuguía and his politics before the war. He said your father may have been connected to the coal miners' strike in Austurias that resulted in his death during that horrific time."

"Father, he was a custodian. How could he possibly know of him?"

"But he was a custodian in the Cathedral of St. James. There are rumors that linger about his time in the cathedral. I do not know anything beyond this, but I thought you should know. Should things not work out with your plans for Israel, Rafael, my friend may be able to help," Dubois said, pointing to the picture on his desk.

"If his speculation is accurate, I'm sure the Order would compensate you handsomely for whatever you received from your father. If you want to discuss it, I will make arrangements."

"Thank you, Father. I will keep this in mind."

Noelle's eyes met Rafael's as she turned away from Dubois in disbelief. *Did he use the information I gave him to go behind my back? Did he just offer to buy something that Rafael inherited from his father?* Noelle thought. She grimaced at what she just heard from her mentor and wondered if he could now be trusted. *David said something about a secret that Rafael held, but he would not tell me anything more. I dare not tell Father Dubois about this, now.*

Noelle stood to counter what he had suggested. Dubois stood as well.

"Thank you for your visit. God be with you, Rafael," Dubois said to preempt her further comments.

Noelle forced a smile and escorted Rafael to the outer office where Sebastian waited. "Sebastian, you are here again?"

"Noelle, Renee's mother told me that she will be here in a couple of weeks? Did you hear about this?"

"Yes, but you do know Renee is engaged to be married, right? Marie has said such wonderful things about her fiancé."

"Yes, I know. Just a little wishful thinking, I suppose."

"I suppose," Noelle mimicked.

Actually very little thinking at all, Noelle imagined. *Just give it a rest. You do not begin to measure up to her fiancé. Dubois is not going to help you with her mother and drive a wedge between a parishioner and her husband – a man who despises you. You have got to get over this obsession of yours.*

"Rafael, please allow me to introduce Sebastian Phillipe. Sebastian this is Rafael Tuguía."

Sebastian extended his hand to Rafael revealing a ring emblazoned with a Maltese cross. It resembled the one on Dubois's desk.

"Thank you for visiting today, Rafael. I will be in touch," Noelle said.

Sebastian quietly knocked and entered his priest's office.

"Just a moment, Rafael," she said as he opened the outer door. "I did not want to say this in front of Father Dubois or Sebastian, but David hinted that you may be looking for help with releasing something to the public. From my days at Le Mirail he knew that my father was once mayor of Albi. He trusts me, but even so was cautious about what he said. He only asked if any of my father's friends may be politically connected on a national level. I could not think of any who were and with my father's death three years ago I told him I have lost touch with most of them. But I have an idea. Meet me at the palace gardens next to the Lautrec Museum at 5:30 this evening."

"Yes, of course. I will be there."

"Goodbye for now." *After Pierre went behind my back I will definitely find a way to help you now,* she thought.

* * *

Text Message
Noelle Martine

Sun, May 3, 13:47

Rafael, thanks for contacting me & your visit. I spoke to David again. My friend, Renee, is expected in about four weeks. I'll be in touch with you soon. Peace, Noelle.

Mon, May 16, 20:55

Her mother expects Renee on June 1st. More later.

Mon, May 29, 9:24

I convinced her mother I should join her on El Camino. See you in Compostela.

Tue, Jun 5, 7:37

Leaving Albi now. Arriving there on June 14, late. Renee is tall and thin, black hair, green eyes. Watch for our arrival. Peace, Noelle.

I will. Thank you. It will be good to see you again, Noelle. RT

Mon, Jun 11, 20:55

Changed: Jun 15 mid-morning.

Got it

Fri, Jun 15, 10:25

Perfect! I saw you arrive and enter the cathedral. RT

Sat, Jun 16, 15:18

On the plane to Toulouse. I will check in with David and discuss Jacques' protest in Paris then back to Albi. Peace, Noelle.

Renee's talking to some friends. I'll pick my moment. More Later. RT

Fri, Jun 29, 14:18

David and I are going to pay a visit to her father on the 3rd. We have the photos of Paris. Thanks. RT

CHAPTER 15

CHARTRES, FRANCE – JULY 2, 2012

Renee arrived two hours before her meeting with Miguel at Chartres Cathedral. She studied the library of knowledge revealed, not in words, but in the sculpture and stained glass. The ending of the high-pitched Gregorian chant of the choir's rehearsal still echoed off the stone surfaces surrounding her. Closing her eyes, she smelled the fragrance of scented candles as the congregants offered their flames for reasons known only to them.

This is truly the most sacred space I have ever been in ... even more than St. James. She wandered through the nave, studied the light filtering through the various tapestries of stained glass, and tried to ignore the renovation.

Renee's quiet reflection was shattered when she overheard a tour guide's amplified voice, "Please avoid the scaffolding around the building's perimeter as you move through the cathedral. We are now in the fifth year of its restoration. Even so, I think you can imagine if the northern spire was laid on its side its height would be the exact length of the nave plus the choir while the shorter south spire comes exactly to the radius point of the semicircular east end."

She observed the crowd surrounding him and thought, *some of his audience appear to be a little disinterested ... as if all they want is to simply check Chartres off their itinerary. And others seem to be permanently attached to their cameras. Neither allows the Cathedral to work its magic.*

"The rose window up there," he said as he pointed in its direction in the west end, "is so positioned that if the western façade were to be turned down flat against the floor it would overlay the exact position of the same size labyrinth, over there."

Casting her eyes in the direction of the portion of the floor he pointed out, she thought, *the more devout choose to take advantage of today and walk the 365 stones of the labyrinth.* She observed their quiet mediation *Their spiritual journey is not unlike mine during the last few days of the pilgrimage.*

Her attention returned to the reason she was there when a man's hoarse voice whispered, "Renee? … Renee Gaston?"

"Yes. Are you Miguel?" she asked of the man who wore a golden cross pendant covered with roses.

"Rafael described how beautiful you are, Renee. When I saw you standing there, I thought you must be the person he so inadequately described. Thank you for your call. I am a little early; I hope you don't mind."

She saw the man's resemblance to Rafael and felt a little more comfortable by his approach. "Thank you," Renee blushed. "No, it's fine. I got here early myself to study the cathedral. Clearly not enough time."

"No, not enough time. Some have studied this cathedral for years and years and keep coming back to learn more. I am sure you will return one day as well. Are you enjoying your time here?"

"I just arrived late yesterday afternoon, but yes. So far so good," she said remembering her first, distant glimpse of the cathedral seeming to grow out of the rooftops of the surrounding homes. "I love being here. The cathedral is an amazing building! But your brother talked about its importance as one of the cathedral schools as well. Can you tell me about this?"

"Yes, but before I do I need to tell you a little about how the cathedral came to be. Early in the twelfth century some of the wealthiest and most influential families in Europe sponsored a band of nine knights to go to Jerusalem. In fact, some of their descendants are alive today and still control a great deal of European wealth.

"The nine knights were charged to search for any ancient text hidden deep within the Temple Mount in Jerusalem. After they returned to France, the Abbot of Clairvaux and his wealthy benefactor created a school for training stonemasons in the ancient art of sacred geometry. The Knights Templar, as they later became known, received the Pope's endorsement in 1129. Ten years later they were granted special authority and raised vast sums of money."

"Was the cathedral based on what they found?" Renee asked.

"Perhaps. No one really knows for sure," Miguel said. "But the ancient art of sacred geometry was lost to the world until the nine returned from Jerusalem. Coincidence? Maybe, but from this beginning the Templars accepted the Abbot's charge to build the Kingdom of God. Come over here Renee, I want to show you something.

"See that window?" he continued his presentation pointing to the window on the south wall high above them. "You can see the men pulling the carts or even carrying the stones for its construction. The cathedral's construction involved the entire community of Chartres and pilgrims from other regions of France as well. Everyone joined in the labor of love no matter what their station in medieval life. Lords, Ladies, architects – or Masters of the Compass as they were known then – stone masons, artisans, servants, and peasants. Everyone was engaged, but no one took credit. It was all for the glory of God. Money came from all over Europe for its construction, much of it from the Knights Templar. As it neared completion, Chartres became one of the most important centers of learning for the pilgrims on the quest for enlightenment."

"Were the Templars responsible for the cathedral's construction?" Renee asked.

"Some disagree with me, but I believed they were. This is especially evident when one considers the West façade and the hidden symbolism that is present. Only the Templars could have communicated this religious unity with such elegance. This façade was begun in the middle of the eleventh century. So, the timing is right. Much later a fire erupted in the roof's structure and nearly destroyed the entire cathedral. A great deal of the nave had to be rebuilt.

"Before the fire," Miguel continued, "Chartres was one of the premier locations for teaching. Remember we are talking about a period during the Middle Ages when the vast majority of people could not read or write. The images surrounding us were the only way the Church could tell the biblical story to the masses. It is all here from Adam and Eve to the Savior to the Saints who came after. The energy of this city attracted many scholars of the day to teach subjects in math, alchemy, language and the like – even Jewish philosophers came to learn and teach."

"What happened to the school after the fire?" Renee asked.

"It continued for a while during the reconstruction, but by the early thirteenth century the school at Notre Dame de Paris was on the rise. Chartres Cathedral then became an important destination for secretive, pilgrimages."

Renee's mind drifted to the Middle Ages, as she imagined the pilgrims who, like her, had seen the asymmetrical spires, the massive buttressed stone walls and giant openings of multi-colored glass for the first time.

"There is such a sense of joy in my father's voice when he speaks of the pilgrimages to Chartres during the late twelfth century; a time before the Albigensian Crusade killed so many of our people."

"Yes, but the pilgrimages continued well after that time. They were made possible by the Templars' use of the Tarot."

"The Tarot?" Renee questioned. "The cards of fortune tellers?"

"The cards back then actually had two layers of meaning. One suggested they were used to predict one's future making them safe to carry. The other, the true meaning, told the story that the novice, or Fool, can achieve salvation through his own actions, independent of the Church. One card, the Hierophant, or teacher, shows a regal figure between two pillars wearing a bishop's mitre. But it is not the Pope. It is Jesus' brother, James the Righteous, the bishop of the Church of Jerusalem. And the card that was most offensive to the Church was Jesus' High Priestess, Mary Magdalene. She also sits between the two pillars of Judaism. So yes, the Templars are often credited with building Chartres Cathedral and a number of the Gothic cathedrals bearing the name Notre Dame."

"Our Lady," Renee confirmed.

"Yes, Our Lady, but perhaps not the mother of Jesus."

"So, who then? What are you saying?" Renee asked with a sense of wonder and excitement.

"Just look at the difference between the statue on this pillar," Miguel said while pointing, “and the other artistic expressions of the Madonna and child surrounding you. I think you can tell me.”

“The Magdalene?” Renee suggested with astonishment.

“Yes, Mary the Magdalene. Mary the Magnificent … Mary the Great. The cathedrals built during the time of the Templars and bearing the name Notre Dame are thought to glorify the Virgin Mary, but here, as well as in other churches all over France, there are black Madonnas present. This replica replaced the original after it was destroyed. Surely it and other Black Madonnas are tributes to Jesus’ queen of the South, Mary Magdalene. Not only is she believed to have come from Ethiopia and had dark skin like Solomon’s Queen of Sheba, but also in a Gnostic tradition the Magdalene is thought to be divine wisdom – the goddess Sophia, herself.”

“But I’ve also heard it argued the Madonna and child were derived from the Egyptian goddess Isis holding her child Horus.”

“Yes, that is true, Renee. The stories are all intertwined.”

Miguel coughed several times, cleared his throat and took a deep replenishing breath to prepare himself for what he was about to say.

“I want to show you something. These photos are yours to take. This is a photograph of an ancient scroll, a letter if you will, written by James the Righteous. Rafael and I have the original hidden for safekeeping. These photos are portions of the original scroll. It is written in ancient Hebrew. These are translations. My father discovered the scroll seventy-eight years ago. My brother and I have held its secrets since we were very young. But we are now old men so we have agreed we must bring the scroll to the world quickly before it is too late. Start reading here,” Miguel said.

Blessings to you, Dear Lazarus,

The end of days will soon be here for us. Before I die I will use this time to record the truth as I know it to be for you and those whom you may encounter.

When our people asked the Savior, who would lead us after his death, he told Brother Thomas to go to me, James the Righteous, the Son of God.

“Now here,” Miguel said pointing once more.

With the death of the Savior we know the war will soon be upon us. The final battle between the Sons of Darkness and the Sons of Light.

Renee responded with a mixed sense of curiosity and fear, asking, "Before what is too late? Why are you telling me this? I came to you wondering about the cathedral school. I don't want to know about this."

"Please continue reading here. I think it will soon be made clear," Miguel said pointing to another part of the translation.

Remember the stories of our ancestors as you leave Caesarea for open waters. From the time of King David, Judah remained strong for four hundred years. We were blessed as we worshipped Yahweh and Yahweh's wife, our Mother Goddess, Asherah. It was after this time King Josiah removed her from the places that King Solomon built for her, saying Yahweh commanded him to do so. Our people chose to follow Josiah and denied Asherah.

Yahweh abandoned Judah and Josiah was killed in battle. We were later overwhelmed as Babylonia defeated the Assyrians and Nebuchadnezzar turned his armies on Judah. We were forced into captivity. Jerusalem, the Temple and the monarchy were lost.

"Are you saying…is this suggesting the reason Nebuchadnezzar crushed Judah and the reason the Jewish people suffered at the hands of the Babylonians was because they turned away from their goddess Asherah? And they believed this?" Renee asked.

"Yes. But please do not be so quick to judge their beliefs," Miguel said. "Please continue here."

Jesus sought to restore the ancient ways and return to the importance of love and wisdom derived from the goddess. In so doing, he chose your sister, Mary, to fulfill our ancient mysteries. It was the Magdalene whom the Savior chose to be his High Priestess – to determine when he should die, anoint him in preparation, attend his burial, and bring him out of the underworld to bestow the blessing of regeneration.

"I don't understand. What is this saying?" Renee asked.

"There is an ancient Egyptian rite known as *hieros gamos* – or sacred marriage." Miguel said. "It was based on the mystical union of Osiris and Isis and later carried into Canaan with the worship of Yahweh and Asherah. In the ritual, the High Priestess played the part of the Mother Goddess and symbolized fertility and reproduction. She anointed the pharaoh in preparation for his symbolic death. At that point, the pharaoh or king was considered the son of god and became one with the father in a cosmic heaven. Three days later, thanks to magical intervention of the goddess, she brought him out of the underworld, and he arose to make the land fertile once more."

"But his was not a symbolic act. He was actually crucified by the Romans, right? Again, why are you telling me this?"

"I will tell you in a moment, but before I do it is important for you to know the history of our scroll. King Philip IV was highly in debt to the Templars and fearful of their potential dominance of Europe. In 1307, he had thousands of French knights arrested. But when the King's men were sent to confiscate their treasure, most of the Templars' vast wealth and documents had vanished. My father found a scroll buried in a waterproof tube-like pouch of a sheep's hide, in the crypt of St. James Cathedral. We assume it must have found its way to Spain through the Knights of Calatrava."

"And? Again, why are you telling me this?"

"Rafael told me about you and your fiancé. He believes you to be honest and circumspect and thinks you are the perfect person to reveal the truth to the world about the goddess Asherah and our High Priestess, Mary Magdalene. Think about how the world may have been different if the Mother Goddess had prevailed over the god of power, or at least had been an equal partner since the time of the ancients.

"Renee, we have waited for a long, long time for the right person to be revealed to us. All we ask is for you to keep this secret until the time is right for its revelation; that and fifty million dollars."

"You're selling the scroll … to me?" Renee's voice began to increase in both volume and pitch.

"Sssshhhhh! Keep your voice down. Well, not so much me personally … or for that matter we are not selling the scroll at all."

"What the hell are you talking about then?" Renee asked. "Even if I wanted to help you, where could I get that kind of money?"

"Renee, I am an old man. I have been diagnosed with lung cancer and

only have months to live. We must act, now. We think with all of your resources, you and your fiancé will be able to figure it out. May I have your telephone number? I will contact you in one week for your decision. Renee, we are depending on you."

"Yes, I guess so, here it is," she said as she scribbled her cellphone number on a piece of paper. "I'm not sure why I'm giving it to you. I really do not want to be part of this thing."

"I think you do, Renee. Rafael told me about your concern for the way women are treated throughout the world. This thing right here, this rejection of Asherah and rejection of the Magdalene is the reason so much of the world has been in crisis. I think you know this and want it to change."

Renee nodded in agreement.

"But what can I possibly do? I am just a student. I don't have the resources to …"

"I will call you in a week," Miguel interrupted.

* * *

"Hello, Rafael. This is Miguel. It is done."

CHAPTER 16

WASHINGTON, DC - JULY 4, 2012

"I don't quite know what to say," Stan confessed as Renee finished. "It's … well, you know … uh … unbelievable. Not only the story itself, but also the fact you were singled out to be the messenger. How does it make you feel? Do you want to be?"

"Yes, I think so, but now what do I do? If what he told me is true, it will turn the world upside down. I'm not sure I want to be responsible for that. But if it's true, then it has to be made public."

"Get dressed and I'll call Howard to see if we can come over today. With Miguel's failing health it seems we now only have a few weeks to make this happen."

"Stan, I don't think that's such a good idea," she said. "That was my first thought as well, but do you think a Catholic institution, even one with the intellectual integrity of Georgetown, is going to want to take the lead on something like this? I don't think so."

"No, you're probably right. I still have some contacts at Harvard. Maybe its Divinity School would be interested. Or better yet, it seems to me the scroll eventually needs to wind up under the protection of the Israeli government. I met Ambassador Ben-Artzi when he was a visiting prof at Georgetown a few years ago. Maybe he could help get us in touch with the right people."

"Perhaps. Both are worth exploring at some point, Stan, and I'm sure we'll think of others. But the thing is, right now, I don't yet understand why the Tuguía brothers picked me to broker this deal for them. Something's weird about the whole thing."

"They were probably just grasping at straws. Two old men stumbling around and found a likely possibility. With you asking questions about El Camiño de las Estrellas they just got lucky."

"Yeah, probably. But it just seems strange; like I was somehow set up. But enough of that.

"Renee, you've been thinking about this a lot longer than me. How do you want to proceed?"

"As a first step it might be wise to contact my old boss at the United Nations, Debra Herzog. I don't remember if I ever mentioned her, but she is an Israeli, reads and speaks Hebrew fluently and actually served as a translator in both Hebrew and French at the UN. Miguel told me the language in these photos is not Aramaic, but ancient Hebrew. The photos seem to be large enough to read, so I think Debra may be able make it out and come close to verifying Miguel's translation. I think we should give it a try anyway. I want to make sure he's not a con-artist before we go too far. Then we'll have to verify the dating of the scroll somehow."

"Good idea. Remember my golfing buddy, Andy Miller, with the FBI who helped us out with George?"

"Well, I actually never really met him. It's like you were embarrassed to introduce me or something."

"Come on. You're kidding … right? It's really just the opposite. Andy can be quite full of himself sometimes. Anyway, I thought I might touch base with him. We may need his help. Okay with you?"

"Fine. I know you trust him, but for now keep it vague."

"Okay. So for tomorrow and Friday, why don't I tie down a few things at work, you report back to Gerard on your trip and we'll contact Debra Friday night after work to see if we can drive up this weekend," Stan was quick to organize. "Meanwhile let's get dressed and enjoy the holiday."

"Or not get dressed, and enjoy the holiday," Renee said. "Maybe we'll just get lucky," she said with a smile. "I mean maybe someone will just give us the fifty million."

"Yeah … right. That's going to happen."

THE NEXT DAY

"Good morning, Dr. Parker. Did you have a nice holiday?"

"Yes, thanks. It was a bit strange, however. How about you?" Stan asked as he passed the guard's station at the entry to the Ford Office Building, one of the few buildings in his charge that was not in desperate need of repair.

"Yep, the family and I did our annual picnic gig on the Mall again. Great fireworks last night, but, man, was it hot!"

"We stayed away, but we had a great night watching from afar. See you later," Stan said entering the elevator.

"Good morning, Bonnie. Any messages?" Stan asked upon arriving at his office.

"Just three. Andy returned your call from Tuesday afternoon and Nancy wants to talk with you when you have a few moments."

"Good, thanks. I need to talk to both of them. And the third?"

"We received a fax from someone posing as Queen Elizabeth in celebration of July 4th saying since the US banks continue to wreak havoc on the global economy and since our inept government can't control them she must revoke our independence and retake control of the colonies."

"Yeah, must be from one of my students adding to the other messages floating around. I've got to say, it's better than King George's reaction. At least she's not sending in the redcoats."

"By the way, Stan, she added a post script, 'PS Daily tea time will now begin promptly at 4:00 p.m. with bone china cups and saucers. The use of mugs is strictly prohibited.' I prefer Earl Grey. What would you like?"

"Bonnie, you know I enjoy sparring with you, but not today. You win. I have a lot on my mind. How about a two-day truce?"

Stan made his way down the hall to his office, adjusted the blinds and immediately picked up the phone and returned Andy's call.

"Hi, Andy. I originally called about golf for this weekend, but something else has come up. I have to go out of town. Do you have time for lunch next week? … Right, I'll call you when I get back. We can hook up at Old Ebbitt. … Okay, sounds good. Talk to you later."

Stan then turned his attention to his Chief Operating Officer. "Hey, Nancy, I'm here. Back for another day of fun and games brought to us by our esteemed elected officials. The message from Bonnie said you wanted to talk to me about the Capitol dome. Why don't you gather up Larry and come on over?"

Larry Simmons, an accounting major with a MBA from the Kellogg School at Northwestern, served as a political operative in Illinois during President Obama's run for the US Senate in 2004. He now served as CFO to the Architect of the Capitol.

"Good morning, everyone," Stan began. "Have a seat. So, Nancy, tell me, any problems from yesterday?"

"No, not really. It was pretty calm considering all of the people who were here. The National Symphony did a terrific job, as usual. Besides the normal traffic jam and mess to clean up, which the Park Service put into high gear this morning, the July 4th concert and fireworks went off without a hitch."

"Good for them. You wanted to talk to me regarding the Capitol dome?"

"Yes. We're still hearing from the American Institute of Architects and the other professional groups who wrote to the Congressional leadership in support of our proposal on the Capitol dome. They're wondering what else they can do."

"Larry, any movement on the hill yet?" Stan asked, already knowing the answer.

"No, they're still doing their political speak and not solving any problems. This whole thing makes me weary. How are we expected to do our jobs like responsible adults, when we have to take direction from the kids?" Larry asked.

"Listen, tell the AIA and anyone else you speak with to keep pushing on the Chair of the Sub-Committee. He's got to bring this home. Also, be in touch with Senate leadership. They're in support as well. In fact, most of the Senate Appropriations Committee members seem to be on board. It's the House that's in disarray, as usual. Tell the AIA to push their membership to contact the Chair and anyone who sits on Appropriations of the House. I'll be in touch with them next week."

"So tell me guys, how does funding for Covert Ops work?"

"What do you mean, Stan?" Larry asked.

"I need to find some money somewhere, before the Capitol dome and society collapse. The CIA budget might be a good place to start. Think they might have a few shekels to spare?"

"I still don't …"

"Never mind … just kidding. Thanks. Now go do your thing … whatever that might be."

LATER THE SAME DAY

Sebastian arrived early Thursday afternoon at the office of the Registrar of the Georgetown Law Center.

"Pardonnez-moi, where may I find a Monsieur George Wilson?"

Sebastian's long blond hair and muscular frame quickly grabbed the attention of one of the female clerks. His arrogant manner and pretentious sounding French accent, however, was too much for the West Virginian clerk to deal with. *I think I'll pass*, she thought.

She greeted him at the counter. "I'm sorry. What did you ask?"

"I'm trying to locate one of your students named George Wilson. He was my fraternity brother a few years ago," he said pointing to the Maltese cross of his ring. "I've lost touch with him over the years. I heard he was attending Georgetown Law School."

"May I have your name and ID please?" she asked without hesitation.

He presented her with his passport, bearing the title Passeport, Union Européenne, République française. "Please permit me to introduce myself. My name is Sebastian Philippe," he said.

"Excuse me while I photocopy your information," she said

She returned to the counter moments later and returned Sebastian's passport.

"The Law School is closed for the summer session so I'm not sure what we will have," she said as she pulled up George's information on her computer.

"Looks like George lost a few pounds over the years," he lied to continue the ruse. "Good for him."

She turned the screen away from him.

"Thank you. Anything you have would be helpful. I have not seen him in such a long time. I thought I would check on him while I'm in town."

"You're in luck. It says here he is enrolled for the summer and taking a graduate level National Security Law course on the main campus."

She looked up the course location. Her screen read:

National Security Law
Associated Term: Summer 2012
Registration Dates: Feb 6-10, 2012
Levels: Graduate/LL.M.

Main Campus
Seminar Schedule Type
3.000 credits

Type	Time	Days	Where	Date Range
Seminar	5-8 pm	W * * Th 7/5	Intercultural Center 212	6/17-8/10

"Normally the class convenes on Wednesday evenings, but with the holiday it was rescheduled for this evening from 5:00 until 8:00 p.m. at the Intercultural Center."

"Great. How about an email address in case I miss him?"

"I'm sorry, I'm not permitted to do that. Would you like directions?" she asked.

"Yes, thank you. This is my first trip to your nation's capital city. Maybe a fellow student will know how to contact him."

She handed him a map, circled the ICC's location and highlighted the streets from the Law Center to main campus.

"You can either head south on I-375 or north to Massachusetts and jog around here to you get on K Street then west. Since you're new to town staying off the interstate system would probably be best. You can park here on Canal Road and walk for about 15 minutes to the ICC, here. It's not hard to find. Five story, modern brick building."

"Another question, please. Where may I find the History Department?"

"You're kidding, right?" she said.

Sebastian shook his head and mouthed the word, "No."

"It's in the same building – the Intercultural Center," she said thumping the circle on the map.

Sebastian left the office and took the wheel of a rented convertible. To a man who was used to the 50,000 person medieval town of Albi, the numbers of cars and street patterns of Washington were most confusing.

"Merde," Sebastian said loudly to himself in anger. *I should have turned right on 1st St! I've got to find Renee this afternoon and return after class to find George. At least, they are in the same building so I won't get lost when I find it now.*

Exasperated by the traffic, horns and jeers, Sebastian seemed overwhelmed by the campus and distance he had to walk to the ICC from the remote lot offered to him. A half a mile later he entered the lobby of the ICC and found a listing of thirty-four departments, programs and centers of excellence. A third of the way down the list he read, 'History Department, Dr. Howard Gerard, Dean, Room 407.'

He entered the elevator and pushed the button for the 4th floor. No one spoke or made eye contact. He arrived without being noticed. From a distance he saw Renee through a sidelight of Gerard's office door.

"Mission accomplished," he whispered to himself.

Gerard's door swung open. A student rushed out on his way to class. "Excuse me," Sebastian said grabbing his arm. "I need to come back to see someone later. What time do the offices close this evening?"

"Most people leave around 4:00 p.m. You know the traffic in DC after five is terrible."

"Thank you. That will work."

Sebastian left the ICC and walked five minutes south. He entered the office of the campus police. The Georgetown men's soccer schedule was posted on the wall behind the undergraduate and summertime clerk.

He greeted Sebastian's arrival. "May I help you?"

"Yes, please. My name is Sebastian Gaston. I came to find out the location of one of your lots," he lied to the clerk to dodge the question. He pointed to the poster with the nod of his head. "Looks like Virginia is first on your list next month."

"Yeah, we didn't play them last year. I think it is part of the conference realignment. Rumors are flying around campus. Seems the Catholic schools that don't have American football programs are going to leave the Big East. We Hoyas have a good goalie and a couple of good forwards. Virginia split the season last year, so I think we have a pretty good chance against the Cavaliers."

"Do you play?" Sebastian asked and found that the student in front of him was a Junior and starting midfielder for the team.

"I used to play as well," Sebastian said describing his many victories at Le Lycée Lapérouse.

A bond quickly grew between the two athletes as they shared stories of past glories, each trying to outdo the other. After thirty-five minutes of football banter, Sebastian gave him Renee's name and produced a picture of her from his wallet. It read, "To my big brother Sebastian, love Renee." It was enough proof to score a goal on the Hoyas. The midfielder matched her name and picture to his computer image and broke with security protocol to reveal the campus location of Renee's parked car, a late model dark blue Volkswagen Jetta … Lapérouse 1 – Georgetown 0.

"Good luck this season," Sebastian said. "You'll likely need it.

Sebastian now knew she was assigned a spot in the Leavey Garage. He returned to the ICC and studied the campus map he had been given earlier in the day. The faculty, staff, and students began streaming out of the vestibule doors at the four o'clock hour as promised. Ten minutes later he saw Renee.

Sebastian jogged the half-mile to his parked car and raced to the side of the Leavey Garage where vehicles exited. He waited patiently in the shadows of the health center for her dark blue Jetta to emerge.

Renee left the ICC and meandered in the direction of the Leavey Student Center. She made her way past the students, the shops and the student amenities and took the elevator down to level P-2.

The listening device he planted in her daypack just two days prior was in range and working perfectly. He heard the sound of her tires squeal and the music of her radio. Her cellphone rang. "Hello. … In about two hours," she said in response to a question Sebastian could not hear, "see you then. Love you."

Sebastian remained in the shadows being careful not to be seen. He saw her exit the garage. She turned right. He followed her to her Georgetown apartment.

One and one-half hours later, the girl from Sebastian's youth, now a refreshed and beautifully made-over woman, came through the front door of the subdivided mansion. She hurried to her parked car unaware that she was being watched. Her daypack was constantly with her. The photos and papers weighed heavy on her mind. The listening device Sebastian planted in Paris went undetected.

Sebastian followed at a safe distance to the heart of Old Town North, in Alexandria. He parked in front of Oronoco Bay Park.

He had a clear line of sight, made even sharper by the binoculars purchased for this purpose. He watched Renee enter the apartment, set her daypack carefully on the kitchen counter, and embrace Stan as if they had been apart for months.

Sebastian's mind began to wander as he listened in on their intimate conversation and remembered the days of his youth in Albi. He remembered her as a teenager. Her youthful innocence. Her adoration of him. The time he had enjoyed her lustful passion. "Enough of that," he mumbled to himself. *I now know where I can find her when I need to – at work, at her apartment and here. Renee has been warned,* he thought.

"Stan, it's 6:30. I think it's time we made the call," she said.

Sebastian listened in as Renee called a stranger to him, but a person he would soon get to know very well.

"Hello, Debra. This is Renee Gaston. … Yes, it's been almost a year. I need to see you this weekend about something extremely important. Will you be in the city? … May I drive up to see you for lunch tomorrow? … Good, I'll meet you at our favorite grill in the Flatiron District at noon."

"Here we go," Sebastian said to himself listening to the balance of their conversation about a secret Renee needed to share. "And so it begins," he said now leaving to return to the ICC.

* * *

"George? George Wilson?" Sebastian called out as the National Security Law seminar adjourned for the evening.

"Yes, who are you?" George said backing away.

"I'm sorry I startled you. My name is Sebastian Philippe," he said. With his palm facing down and his ring clearly visible Sebastian extended his hand in George's direction to greet his new friend.

"You don't know me, but we have a mutual friend in a woman named Renee Gaston and the bonds of brotherhood in the Order. She's from my hometown in France and is in grave danger. I've come to America to try to protect her. But I cannot stay here for long. I must return home soon."

"What do you mean grave danger? From whom? How?"

"All in good time. I'd like to discuss a proposition with you. Will you join me for a drink?"

CHAPTER 17

NEW YORK CITY - JULY 7, 2012

Debra Herzog was seated at the bar when they arrived. She took the last swallow of a grapefruit mojito when she saw Renee and a man she did not recognize enter the grill. She stood and waved rapidly to attract their attention, gave the bartender a generous tip, and returned her wallet to a small clutch bag. She was glad, but puzzled, to see her prior co-worker and now distant friend. Renee had not given her much information about the meeting, only that she had an important document written in ancient Hebrew and needed her help.

Debra was a petite woman who appeared to be in her late twenties, but was actually thirty-five. With long, curly red hair, light skin with fading freckles, she normally wore tailor-made business suits to work at the UN. But today was different. Weekdays were a time for decorum. Weekends were a time for her to let loose. Dressed in her Christian Louboutin stilettos, improving her height by three inches, skin-tight jeans, and a form-fitting sleeveless sweater, she knew today she could make even the most casual observer pay close attention.

Renee returned the wave and dashed across the room to greet her old friend and colleague. They hugged and had exchanged pleasantries from a time fondly remembered when Stan caught up to them.

"Debra, I'd like to introduce my first big surprise, my fiancé, Stan Parker," Renee boasted. "Stan, this is my good friend Debra Herzog."

"What a pleasure it is to finally meet you, Debra," Stan said. "I've heard so much about you that I feel like I know you already."

"Thank you, Stan. I'm sorry to say I can't say the same." Debra said looking somewhat embarrassed. "Renee, why didn't you tell me before now you were engaged to such a handsome man? Tell me all about him."

"Ladies, please, let's do this another day … when I'm not here," Stan urged seeking a way out of the embarrassment that would surely ensue.

* * *

The listening device worked perfectly. Sebastian had listened intently to their conversation the night before. Renee had not revealed much detail about their plans to meet Debra. Sebastian had no other choice but to return to his vantage point at Oronoco Bay Park and track their every move from Alexandria to the Flatiron District of New York City.

Once there, he double parked and watched as they parked at a neighborhood lot and entered the restaurant. The listening device still worked perfectly.

"Ladies, please, let's do this another day …" Sebastian mocked as he waited for a break in traffic.

He continued south on 5th Avenue past the grill in search of a parking spot. He returned on foot where he could hear their conversation. A few laughs later the threesome returned to the entry and the maître-d's station.

"If you don't mind, we'd like to be seated upstairs and away from the other guests. It looks a little less crowded up there in back," Stan advised. The maître-d' directed a hostess to seat them as requested, where Renee could discretely spill the beans.

"Good afternoon, ladies and gentleman, may I offer you something to drink," the waiter greeted them upon arrival.

"Nothing for me, thanks. I just had one of your famous mojitos and it was terrific. You guys might want to try it," Debra coaxed.

"No, thanks. We're not big citrus fans," Stan confessed. "Renee, how about a Bloody Mary?"

Renee nodded in agreement as Debra asked, "So what's your next big surprise?

"Okay, well, here's the thing … you are only the second person who will know what I'm about to tell you; Stan was the first," Renee cautioned. "Unless … Stan did you say anything specific to Andy?"

"No, nothing at all, actually. I arranged to meet him next week for lunch to see how this weekend panned out first."

"Good. So, Debra, as I was going to say, I hope I can count on you to keep confidential what I'm about to tell you. It can't be made public until we have thoroughly checked its authenticity and are ready to release the information."

"Knowing you, Renee, you would not ask unless you had a good reason, so yeah, sure, mum's the word."

Renee signaled the waiter for service. "Okay, why don't we order something to eat first and then I'll tell you something you're not going to believe."

"May I help you?" the waiter asked, as their drinks arrived.

"I'll have the blue corn crab cakes," Debra was quick to respond.

"Poached salmon salad for me," Renee said.

"Well … she tells me you're noted for your burgers," Stan said, nodding in the direction of Renee. "Make mine medium."

Renee waited patiently until the waiter was out of sight and said again, "Debra you must keep this confidential."

"Okay, okay, what is it?"

Renee braced herself for what she was about to say.

"Last month I traveled to Spain and then France and met two elderly gentlemen who were brothers."

Renee relayed the story as told to Stan three days before. When she introduced Chartres Cathedral and Miguel, the meals arrived as if on cue. She continued the monologue through lunch to the point of discussing the reason for their meeting.

"And then Miguel said, 'These are photos of an ancient scroll. My father discovered it in the Cathedral of St. James 78 years ago. My brother and I have held its secrets since …' "

Debra interrupted the conversation, lowering her head and her voice to a quiet whisper, "Wait a minute, Renee, are you telling me they have an ancient scroll in their possession?"

"That's exactly what I'm telling you, Renee confirmed. "Let's get the dishes cleared and I'll show you the photos I brought back."

"I think I *will* have that second drink now," Debra said.

"Waiter," Stan called out. "Please have someone take away the dishes and bring us two more Bloody Marys and a …"

"Make mind a Blood Mary also, with a double shot of vodka," Debra added.

"Okay, three then," Renee added. "So here are the documents Miguel gave me, Debra."

Renee eagerly produced the documents from her daypack. "These are photos of the scroll, and these are portions of the scroll and their translations – one is literal and the other easier to understand. Are you able to read the text? Can you verify the translation?"

"Well, let's see," Debra said with some doubt.

Debra read the translations and studied the Hebrew lettering for nearly 10 minutes. She gazed up at Renee and Stan in disbelief and said, "From what I can make out in the photo, it parallels the translation pretty closely. I think I might be able to say more conclusively if I studied it for a while."

"Great, that's what I hoped you'd say," Renee said, retrieving the photos from Debra. Returning them to her daypack, Renee's fingers brushed an unfamiliar object in the side pocket. She pulled out a small plastic box about the size of a quarter and laid it on the table. Sliding back the top cover of the black plastic case, marked *'Made in China,'* she discovered the electronic components of a wireless transmitter. She brought her fingers to her lips, signaling for her tablemates to remain quiet as she pointed to the object.

"Well, Debra, it's been great catching up with you. Think about all of this and I'll get back in touch with you next week to arrange a time for us to get back together," Renee said as she scribbled on a piece of paper. "I think someone is listening in on our conversation. Can we leave here and go to your office?"

Sliding the paper to Debra and Stan, Renee continued her deception, "Stan, it's getting late; we need to be thinking about heading home."

Stan called for the waiter as he watched Debra write a hurried response and continued the conversation with Renee about the trip home. Debra wrote: "Instead, come with me to my apartment. If we get separated, meet me there in 30 minutes. It's in the Upper East Side. Take the 6 Train on the Lexington Avenue Line. Get off at the 96th St. Station. Address: 175 E. 96th, The Monterey, 28th floor."

Stan and Renee nodded in agreement. He paid the check, and the threesome left the building. They waited momentarily under the entry canopy to make sure whoever was listening could see them leave.

"Why don't we walk you to your train station? Where is it?" Stan asked.

"I take the L Train to Greenwich," Debra lied. "It runs along 14th Street down there. I can pick it up at Union Square, just a block over there."

Sebastian heard every word of their conversation. He saw them depart. They walked along 15th toward the middle of Union Square and headed right to the station at 14th and Union Square. Sebastian followed at a safe distance. Hearing Renee and Debra talk about their days at the U.N. and Stan and Renee discuss their plans to return to DC, Sebastian was convinced the day was now coming to an end. He held his distance and waited close by.

They reached the domed portal serving three lines and eight trains. As they descended the stairs, Sebastian watched from the shadows of the park's urban forest and listened as the three said their goodbyes. Then silence. Taking comfort that his hastily conceived pursuit and reconnaissance had succeeded, Sebastian waited for the pair to emerge in a few minutes. They did not.

Instantly he knew he'd been duped and now must reclaim lost ground. His athletic prowess kicked in as he darted past the resting tourists, who claimed the shade of the park; past the parents, who watched their children chase pigeons from their pecking waddles into flight; past the lovers, who strolled arm-in-arm along the park's pathways, until he reached the domed portal to the subway.

Without concern for safety, his or anyone else's, he leapt down the portal's stairs touching down on every third step. He pushed aside both map-holding-subway-novices and veterans of the underground tubes, jumped over the turnstiles and rushed toward the L Train platform.

The threesome was not to be seen on either side. *Damn it! ... Not Greenwich ... then where?* Sebastian questioned himself in between taking deep gasps for air to relieve his aching lungs. He studied the subway diagram on the wall. *North. They must be heading north.*

Sebastian's passion to follow them reignited as he gathered the needed oxygen to chase the signs to the Lexington Avenue Line. He raced onto the platform, again pushing people aside to achieve his goal.

Fellow passengers pushed back. Sebastian absorbed the verbal and physical attacks without regret. He had to get on board their train.

Renee was the first to spy the commotion caused by his relentless pursuit. "Stan, quick, give me your phone," she commanded.

Sebastian watched the train's doors close. He was exposed. He was vulnerable. *What will I do now?* he thought. *Renee knows I am following her. I have failed in my mission. I must ask God's forgiveness.*

Renee's and Sebastian's eyes met from a distance of only five feet away. Her face contorted in anger.

She took multiple pictures of her adversary's dripping face gasping for air as the train began to move. Her horrified voice penetrated his ear, "How could you? Why are you doing this, Sebastian? Go to hell!"

He watched her arm swing toward the ground as the crushing sound of her heel destroyed the transmitter against the car's floor. It was the last thing he saw and heard as the 6 Train pulled away from Union Square.

* * *

Stan stared off into the distance, attempting to steady his nerves. His eyes combed the East River and west end of Long Island, scanned the caravan of cars traveling across the Triborough Bridge, traced the northeast edge of Harlem and fell upon the Islamic Cultural Center of New York directly below.

He watched the Muslims enter their place of learning and worship, inhaled deeply then slowly released the air against the 28th floor window of Debra's apartment. "Fantastic view from way up here," Stan said. "The cultural center down there enjoys a pretty good reputation from what I hear."

Debra's hands were still trembling. She tried to steady them as she gestured for Stan to sit down.

"Yes, it does," she said clearing and moistening her throat. "In fact, right now, and every Saturday afternoon, they have a class going on, an outreach program to discuss Islamic customs and traditions. Terrible what's happening. Several of the U.N. Ambassadors from Islamic countries are on their Board of Trustees. Many of whom I …"

"Okay, stop it people! What are you doing? What are we going to do about the scroll?" Renee demanded.

"… know well." Debra concluded.

"You guys are acting like this whole spy thing never happened," Renee said. She had not yet chosen to be involved. Miguel trusted her. Sebastian betrayed her. "I really don't like the fact I found that thing. How much did Sebastian hear anyway? Right now, I'm somewhere between furious and I don't know what! Afraid, I suppose."

"Renee, who is Sebastian? You've never mentioned him before," Stan asked cautiously, not sure he really wanted to know.

"Sure I have," she said.

"No, you really haven't."

Renee mentally reviewed their many lengthy conversations over the past four months. "Stan, do you remember in late February when I came to your office to apologize for the horrific evening with George at the restaurant? I said something like, 'George was like the bastard of my youth'. Well, Sebastian is, in fact, the bastard of my youth. He deserted me then and he's apparently trying to harm me now. I don't know what's going on, but he followed me in France to Chartres. I didn't tell you about it because … well … I didn't know if I would get involved in all of this and I didn't want to worry you. I just thought it was Sebastian being Sebastian and he was back in France and … you know … out of sight, out of mind."

"Didn't want to worry me? I can't believe you didn't tell me. Now, I really think we need to get Andy involved," Stan said unapologetically.

"You're probably right." Renee reluctantly agreed. "There's one other thing I did not tell you. When I was at the airport in Paris, Sebastian followed me there as well and told me I should forget this whole thing. He warned me my involvement could be dangerous and if I didn't believe him, I should call my father."

"Did you?"

"Did I what? Believe him?"

"Did you call your father? Come on Renee, this doesn't have to be tedious."

"Yes, I was getting to that. Papa told me two men approached him a few hours before I got to the airport," Renee rambled on. "Apparently, some associate of Sebastian must have watched our house from the time I left for Chartres and called Sebastian when the men showed up. It could have been his friend Paul. I don't know.

"Who's Paul," Stan asked.

"I don't know. I never saw him before my trip. A recent friend from

Albi, I suppose. Papa told me the two men handed him some photos when he was a young man before I was born. It seems he got caught up with an Armenian group who protested the genocide of their people by the Turks. Fortunately, his grandmother was not among the ones who were tortured or executed, but she was deported from Istanbul in 1915, along with other Armenians. Papa was campaigning for President Mitterrand in Paris during the '81 election when it happened. It was all very innocent. He was gone before it turned into an attack on the Consulate, but the militant Armenians killed a guard and wounded the Turkish Consul. They took fifty-six hostages as well. The two men implied that the photos could be a real problem for Papa if they were released.

"The men also reminded him of his Gnostic heritage from both Armenia and Albi, told him about the scroll, my involvement and what was at stake. He wasn't sure what they meant, but he was frightened, and Papa doesn't get frightened very easily. He said they were more informative than threatening, but he was so afraid of what might happen to me that he told Mama everything. I think he's ready to kill Sebastian the next time he sees him. I'm worried he just might … his temper, you know. So, Stan, do I want to get involved? No, not really … well, maybe. But I don't think I have a choice. And as you said, we only have a few weeks … three days less now … to make this thing happen! Debra, I'm sorry I drug you into this mess," Renee continued. "I didn't think it would be dangerous this early."

"Well for now, he doesn't know where I live or where I work, so there's no real harm done," Debra offered. "Going forward, we have to be careful."

"Going forward? ... *We?*" questioned Renee.

"Yes, we. I'm in if you're in with me. Let's see those photos of the scroll again. You shut down the conversation so quickly I didn't have time to study them," Debra said.

Renee handed her the photos and began to pace the floor in fear of what she may find. Debra reviewed the photos for what felt like hours, jotting down clues as she tried to unscramble the ancient script.

Renee periodically stopped her to anxiously ask what she had discovered only to be rebuffed by Debra's hand gesturing for quiet. Stan calmed his nerves by staring into the darkening sky, wondering about Sebastian and silently counting the headlights crossing the bridge as the rain began to fall.

Debra scribbled down a few words she recognized and guessed at others. At long last she began to paraphrase the words on the photo.

"As we read in the translation James the Righteous was the scroll's author. He says here the final battle is upon them. Joseph is a hunted man and could no longer protect Lazarus and his sisters so they must leave the place where they were hiding. It describes Asherah being abandoned and them being forced into captivity. Next it says that Jesus sought to restore their ancient ways and chose Mary to be his High Priestess.

"The words in the photo seem to track very closely to the translation. As far as the other portions, and I'll be guessing at some of this but as I can make out, this next part describes their time in captivity. Years later they rebuilt the Temple, but a priest turned against them and they fled to Egypt. And then he talks about Saul killing Stephen, not trusting Saul, now called Paul, and Paul threating their existence. Next, he says the Savior loved the Magdalene and she loved him. And here James concludes with Mary being chosen to lead but Simon Peter challenged her authority. He then charges Lazarus to continue Jesus' teachings and protect his sister."

"Debra, do you think the translation is accurate?" Stan asked.

"Yes, I do. Mine is a lot of guess work, of course, but I think it is generally correct. I want both of you to get this. If the scroll is to be trusted, what's being said is the most prolific Christian writer and evangelist, the person who basically started the Christian movement, Paul, this icon, distorted the true will of Jesus for his own purposes.

"We are way over our heads here," Debra continued. "We've got to get some help. I think I can get the attention of the Israeli Ambassador to the UN, Ambassador Chazan. We've become friends since his arrival. He'll know who to contact. But before I get him involved, we have to somehow confirm the scroll is authentic. I really don't want to pull strings with the Ambassador only to find out the whole thing is a hoax."

Renee took back control, "Stan mentioned he had befriended Ambassador Ben-Artzi when he lectured at Georgetown. Maybe he could help as well. I expect a call from Miguel sometime during the middle of next week. I'll let him know he'll need to arrange to have the scroll dated and authenticated in some manner and the three of us will meet him in Chartres next weekend, agreed?"

"No." Stan said firmly. "I don't want the two of you in any danger. Just tell him I'll be there next Saturday. I'll get in touch with Andy when we get back. Debra, may Renee stay with you over next weekend?"

CHAPTER 18

WASHINGTON, DC - JULY 8, 2012

"Yeah, George, this is what I'm telling you. I overheard their conversation yesterday in New York. They do have a copy, photographs really, of an ancient scroll. We must do something to prevent it from becoming public. We also have to make sure Renee is not harmed. Meet me at St. Matthew's for 11:30 Mass," Sebastian insisted, then turned off his cellphone.

Silently Sebastian stood before the mirror of his hotel room and prepared for his morning penance. His mood was reflected in the glass – hopeless, desperate. Kneeling, he offered himself to God.

"Hail Mary, full of grace. The Lord is with thee. Blessed art thou amongst women, and blessed is the fruit of thy womb, Jesus. Holy Mary, Mother of God, pray for us sinners, now and at the hour of our death. Amen.

"Heavenly Father, I seek your favor and forgiveness. Please forgive my stupidity. I have let you down in the task given to me. I have made myself known to them. But I will not fail you in the end. I will uphold the teachings of St. Paul and the Church. I will not permit these infidels to desecrate his name or yours or that of your Son. Please forgive me. Be with me now and in my future efforts to glorify your name, I beg you. I am given now to St. Paul when he said, 'In my flesh I complete what is lacking in Christ's afflictions, for the sake of his body, that is the Church.' "

Sebastian stood once again and removed his clothes to inflict the punishment against his flesh that he knew he must endure to atone for his sins.

"I will not fail again," he promised. "Thanks be to God."

* * *

"Stan, calm down," Andy said returning his empty glass to the bar. "I've never seen you like this, even the time with George."

"After we dodged him the jerk even went back to my car and left this note on the windshield. 'Don't think you've gotten away with anything. I know where you live and where you work and what you are up to. We'll be watching. You will make a mistake and it will be over.' What's with this crap? Man, this guy is really pissing me off. Can't we get a restraining order?"

"Hang on. You said something about a picture."

"Here you go ... here's the bastard," Stan said handing Andy his phone. "Renee snapped several pictures of his sweaty face just before the train left."

"Okay, just calm down. Take a deep breath. We'll figure it out. Why don't we go over to a table, order some lunch and then get back to it?"

"Fine … okay," Stan agreed. "Andy, I appreciate your meeting me downtown today and giving up your Sunday."

"No problem. This place works for me any time. And your timing was perfect. The Nationals aren't playing today. Teams are gearing up for the All Star Game on Tuesday. Did you hear – we're sending five players this year?"

Stan did not respond. He had more on his mind than the Nationals. Recognizing Andy, the waiter was quick to arrive at their silent table. He took Stan's order and turned to Andy. "Would you like the grilled fillet with Béarnaise sauce today, Mr. Miller?" he asked.

"Yes, of course, medium rare. And as long as he's buying, I'll have another Dewar's and soda. Thanks, Frank".

I have to stop doing this at some point, Andy thought. *I was still a slim 165 pounds when I joined the Washington Field Office. Now look at me two years later. Fifteen pounds heavier. Even my time in the agency gym doesn't seem to be working.*

"Hey Frank," Andy yelled. "Let's skip the Béarnaise today, okay?" Then quietly to Stan he asked, "Is he working alone?"

"Could be, but Renee seems to think George is somehow involved. She keeps saying that he seems to be ever present, but invisible. This whole thing is starting to wear thin. She noticed Sebastian and George wearing similar rings … belonging to a religious order of some sort. I don't know. Just her intuition, I suppose, but I would not be surprised if she was right."

"Stan, why don't you have Renee file for a protective order, not a restraining order, against Sebastian first thing tomorrow morning at the Superior Court? Stalking is one of those things the courts take pretty seriously. The note will certainly provide sufficient evidence she is being stalked. Judge Black and I go back a ways. And now that I'm heading up the Criminal Division in DC, he and I have even more contact. I'll see if I can't get the protective order expedited. And I'll keep an eye out for George. Meanwhile, stay away from Sebastian. Don't do anything stupid."

"I know. I won't get near him, even though I'd like to take a two by four to the bastard's skull!"

"What's this all about anyway?" Andy asked.

Stan spent the next twenty minutes describing as much as he could remember and concluded with, "All of this needs to be kept under lock and key. We can't let it go public. Not yet."

"I understand. So tell me, what's your next step?"

"I'm going to Chartres to see if I can't get more information. Renee was so shaken by what she heard, the details are a little fuzzy. She's at the condo right now making arrangements. I'm leaving Friday and returning Sunday."

"Want some company? Sounds like you could use someone with my background … in an unofficial capacity, of course. Besides, I like French wine and cooking."

"Thanks. I'd appreciate your help on this. This is way over my head. I'll give Renee a call and tell her to book two tickets. Listen, Debra's flying down on Wednesday for some meeting having to do with the U.N. Human Rights Council. Why don't you join us for dinner?" Stan asked.

"Is she married or dating someone?"

"No, single. I don't know if she's dating anyone special, but I think not."

"Sounds good. I'd like to meet her."

"You two might just hit it off. With the way she jumped in to help Renee, she seems like a glutton for punishment, so I'm guessing she just might like you. I'll check with Renee about dinner plans and give you a call."

* * *

The brick and sandstone edifice was home to the Cardinal and the Archdiocese of Washington, DC. George entered the center portal of the Italian Renaissance styled cathedral feeling the weight of both bronze doors closing behind him and what he was about to hear. Above him, St. Matthew greeted his arrival, as he had on the past six Sundays. *Ground zero and home for the nation's fight for religious freedom,* George thought, as he entered.

The magnificence of the barrel-vaulted, coffered ceiling could not be ignored. It captured the worshiper's eyes and spirit as it soared high above the nave where about 200 out of the nearly1,000 seats were occupied. Sebastian knelt in prayer toward the back. George joined him.

The Cathedral of St Matthew the Apostle seemed an unlikely spot for a clandestine meeting of potential criminals, but nevertheless there they were kneeling in prayer to a savior they hoped to save. "Amen," Sebastian concluded, crossed himself and returned to his pew. George followed suit.

Sebastian leaned in toward George and whispered, "It was just as I thought and told you last week. They do have access to an ancient scroll. It may prove devastating for the Church, if authentic. George, you need to be my eyes and ears over here."

"How you propose I do that?"

"I planted four bugs in both her apartment and Stan's condo on Friday. Here are the receivers," Sebastian said, handing him a small suitcase. "There's one for Stan's apartment; one for Renee's. Each contain four receivers. The transmitters should broadcast clearly for about three hundred yards."

"Got it."

"Follow Renee. Try to make sure no harm comes to her, but she's in this thing now and I'm afraid she does not know what can happen. Let me know what she and Stan are up to. I have to return to France tomorrow and contact the Colonel. Believe me, I won't forget our deal."

As the organ called those assembled to worship, they both stood from guarded positions in the rear of the church and said their goodbyes. Sebastian exited through the center portal. George moved closer to the front to continue the mass. The morning's bright light filtered through the lantern high above the altar illuminating the pages of George's daily journal:

Sunday, July 8th. RE: Sebastian Philippe.

Reports of an ancient scroll confirmed. May be devastating for the Church. Sebastian returning to France. Gave me his cellphone number today. Not sure who he has involved or what he's planning but he needs help. Promised to keep him informed.

CHAPTER 19

WASHINGTON, DC - JULY 11, 2012

Sebastian's involvement in Renee's earlier and current life occupied only a few moments of early dinner conversation. They set it aside in favor of letting Debra and Andy get to know each other a little better. A second bottle of wine arrived. Then dinner. Plans for Stan and Andy traveling to France were finalized, wedding plans for Renee and Stan were discussed, and Debra reinforced her resolve to help Renee. A moonlit stroll from King Street to Stan's apartment continued what was becoming a budding relationship between Andy and Debra.

"Nice place, Stan," Debra said upon entering his condo. "And thanks again for dinner. It was great."

"I agree," Andy said. "My steak was perfect."

"My pleasure. Glad you both could join us here tonight. It is good to get back to a little sanity after spending last Saturday chasing round the streets of New York," Stan said.

"Andy, I was able to get the protective order yesterday. Thanks for your help. Sebastian has turned into a madman. I'm really scared about what he may be up to," Renee confessed.

"And don't forget about George," Stan added.

"I've got this. Both of you should try to relax a bit."

"Yeah, maybe we should take a little break from Sebastian and George for a while and talk about something else," Stan said. "It's probably too hot for the terrace, so why don't we just enjoy the evening inside. I have some wine I've been saving for a special occasion. Renee, why don't you put on some music? I'll be right back."

Stan withdrew to the area of the great room that was the kitchen. Only a high granite topped bar formed a barrier to separate Stan from his guests. It was an austere space. Everything needed for the gourmet cook was available, but neatly organized and put away behind cabinet doors. The stainless-steel refrigerator and freezer columns complemented the wine preservation column, Stan's pride and joy.

When he became of age, his parents made sure he was well versed in the principal grape varietals and the areas of the world where they were cultivated. He took this seriously and completed several courses toward becoming a sommelier.

He also took the selection of his wine preservation column seriously. It maintained his 146-bottle collection at the perfect temperature and humidity with a tinted glass front to protect the wine from ultraviolet rays.

Stan inspected and wiped four thin-stemmed crystal wine glasses and opened a bottle of 2008 Henschke, Mt. Edelstone Shiraz. Passing out the glasses and beginning a pour, he said, "I think you'll enjoy the taste of plum and blackberries from this vintner. It is a little peppery, which I really like. … So, what do you taste?"

"A little sage, perhaps?" Debra asked.

"And chocolate?" Renee added.

"Very good," Stan said, praising them both.

"Andy, you look a little puzzled," he said.

Andy swirled his wine, put his nose deep into the glass and said, "What I particularly enjoy is the resounding bouquet of rose petals with a hint of lavender." Then lifting the stem toward the ceiling and chugging the balance he asked, "May I have another pour, s'il vous plait?"

"Oh, shut up," Stan said, passing him the bottle. "Hey Andy, did you catch the ball game yesterday? It was some game. Can you believe the American League was shut out? La Russa did great. With that win under his belt, he's managed to chalk up an All Star win in both leagues."

"We just got lucky," Debra said.

"Lucky?" Andy took the bait.

"The National League may have won, but it was the Yankees who won the day. New York rules!"

"You seem to be a bit confused, Debra. You said, '*we* just got lucky.' You do know that Yankees are in the American League and the National League won eight to zip, right?" Andy asked.

"Silly boy, of course I do," Debra was quick to respond. "But please take a note. Giant's Melky Cabrera hit a two run homer in the 4th and was voted as the game's MVP. Thing is … he's an ex-Yankee. I'm a Mets fan. New York rules!"

"Uh-oh, strike one?" Andy asked.

"Yes, but not a complete miss. I set you up. I'll call it a foul ball." Debra said. "Just hang in there. Keep yourself open to the pitch, your arms up and eyes on the ball. You'll do fine."

Stan laughed and looked at his friend as if to say, "Why don't we drop it."

"How was your meeting today, Debra?" Stan asked wanting to change the subject. "Let's see … you met with an Israeli committee, right? What was that about?"

"Well, for starters, you should all know the American Israel Public Affairs Committee is the largest pro-Israeli lobby in America, and they're good at what they do. They keep the US powers-that-be pretty close to what's going on in Israel. AIPAC's latest concern is the U.N. will soon take a position on the legality of Israeli settlements on Jerusalem's West Bank. The U.N. plans to investigate the rights of the Palestinian people in the occupied Palestinian territory, as they framed it. A friend asked if I would meet with a few of their members since I know the region well and work at the U.N."

"Given the never-ending conflict over there, it seems reasonable for the U.N. to take a position on this, don't you think?" Stan asked.

"Maybe, but Israeli officials say Israel will not cooperate with the current mission and condemned the U.N. Human Rights Council's treatment of Israel."

"Why do you think they reacted so quickly and negatively?" Stan asked.

"It's just never ending. With the war, the Human Rights Council investigated alleged war crimes in Gaza. Their final report accused both

Israel and Palestine of war crimes. Later the panel members amended the report in favor of Palestine. As a result, Israel doesn't have much confidence in the Council or in the U.N."

"Yeah, I remember. But that was a long, long time ago. What's AIPAC concerned about now?" Andy asked.

"Several months ago, a report issued by a retired Israeli judge found the settlements occupying the West Bank were *not illegal*. The US State Department immediately rejected it and continues to put pressure on Israel not to implement his recommendations."

"So what did a high ranking U.N. official tell them? Legal or not so legal?" Andy asked with what seemed to be a slight edge to his voice.

"Hmmmm. So it's like that, is it?" Debra quipped, "I have no idea what a high ranking U.N. official would have told them, but I told them what I thought."

"Oops, strike two?"

"Yep, that was a complete swing and a miss … I didn't set you up this time … you didn't foul that one," Debra laughed. "I thought you may be different. Oh, well – zero and two, but who's counting?"

"Well, that was stupid," Andy acknowledged.

Debra smiled, "You still have one strike left, don't blow it."

"Speaking of people acting stupid, I haven't seen George around lately. Have you, Renee?" Andy asked. "He may not be linked to Sebastian, but he's not very bright and could get in the way."

"Not for a week or so. Maybe he's decided to leave me alone."

"Maybe. But keep your eyes open. Debra, what did you tell AIPAC?" Andy tried again, filling her glass with a little more wine and mouthing the words, "I'm sorry."

"I gave them my views on why I thought Israel's position on the West Bank was wrong. I reminded them that Jordan gave up any claim to the area in 1988. Israel annexed East Jerusalem and the area along the border, but the areas now considered the West Bank were never annexed. I know this from personal experience."

"Personal experience? How so?" Andy asked.

"I really don't want to get into all of that right now. So I'll just say this. My parents hoped the West Bank would be annexed, but it never was. As a result, my mother felt it was dangerous living there and insisted we leave."

"So if the West Bank was never annexed and Jordan gave up any claim shouldn't the Israeli settlements be considered legal? Shouldn't both sides be permitted to settle there?" Stan asked.

"You would think so, but it's tricky. The West Bank still remains under Israeli military control and has since the Six-Day War. In fact, most of the world, including the U.N. by the way, refers to the West Bank as 'Occupied Palestinian Territory.' Israel insists, however, that the Palestinians were never a sovereign nation and only territories captured from a sovereign nation, like Israel did with the Golan Heights, can be considered occupied territory. But a lot of people argue the military is only there to protect Jerusalem from foreign invasion. So there you have the stalemate that's existed for forty-five years."

"But don't the Israelis have a reasonable point? By keeping troops in the area, doesn't this protect the Israelis who live there?" Stan asked.

"Of course they do, Stan, but the stalemate needs a resolution. The other big problem is East Jerusalem. It is recognized as part of the West Bank, but Israel insists it is part of Israel's capital city and can't be separated."

"You said, 'a lot of people,' but what do *you* think? What did you tell the AIPAC people?" Andy continued to press.

"I told them by signing the Oslo Accords, Israel agreed to remove its troops and work toward resolution of statehood for Palestine in the region. They never did. And for good reason since radical Palestinians continue to blow things up. So, reluctantly I told them I thought the Israeli settlements were not legal."

"Good for you," Andy concluded. "With your personal involvement it must have been tough for you to have come to that decision."

"It was," Debra said.

"Well, people ... I have an early morning. I took a vacation day to see some of the sights here before heading back to New York and I want to crowd in as much as possible. Stan, would you mind calling me a cab?" Debra asked. "I need to go to the Willard InterContinental Hotel on Pennsylvania."

"Hold on, Stan, don't call. I'd be happy to drive you."

"Thanks. I appreciate that.

"Renee, is everything squared away for Friday's trip?" Andy asked.

"You bet. To recap, you'll arrive Friday evening. Meeting's set for July 14th at 10:00 a.m. with Miguel at the cathedral. Stan can fill you in on all the details. I booked you a room with twin beds at l'Hôtellerie Saint Jean for two nights. It's cool. It was built on the site of an old monastery. I figured the vibes would keep the two of you away from any French women. Stan already has one back in the States. Besides, it's really close to the cathedral," Renee said.

"Debra, I'll fly up Friday evening and call you when I land. I'll take the train to your place."

"Hey, Andy, take good care of my man here, please," Renee said as she clung to his arm.

"Thanks again for a great evening, Stan. Take care, Renee," Debra said as they left the comfort of Stan's air-conditioned condo and joined the humidity of a still summer night in DC.

* * *

The bugs Sebastian had planted on Friday worked perfectly. From his vantage point near Oronoco Bay Park, George noted their conversation.

Wednesday, July 11th. RE: Stan Parker, Andy Miller, Renee Gaston and Debra <u>*????*</u>

Conversation among Stan, Renee, someone named Debra and Stan's FBI stooge, Andy. Informed Sebastian. Parker and Miller staying at l'Hôtellerie Saint Jean for two nights, July 13th and 14th. Meeting arranged at the cathedral on July 14th at 10:00 a.m. Renee going to stay with Debra in NY Friday. Informed Sebastian.*

** You bet your ass I'm going to get in your way. We'll just see how stupid you can be, Mr. FBI agent. I'm in control now!*

MOMENTS LATER

"Thanks for the lift, Andy. I thought you'd probably be driving a late model, government-issued sedan, not this machine. I'm pretty impressed. I'll take back one of your strikes, but remember you still have one against you. Want to come in for a nightcap?" Debra asked with a smile.

"Don't mind if do. We kind of got off to a rocky start back there … so, I appreciate the invite. The government-issue is for my job, not personal use. This one gives me a lot of pleasure. Glad you like it."

Andy powered down the beast and handed the key fob of his new Audi Spyder R8 to the valet in front of the Willard. A smile crossed his valet's lips. "Please be careful," Andy warned as he flashed his FBI badge. "It's not paid for." The valet's smile vanished.

Debra's high heels echoed off the marble floors and hard surfaced walls of the Willard. It was like walking back through history – two story marble columns supported a structure sheathed in a deeply coffered ceiling, pendant light fixtures represented a time when ambiance was more important than efficiency, Persian rugs helped to mute the echoing noise, brocade laden wingback chairs defined the corners of the individual spaces contributing to the lobby as a whole – to the time of Abraham Lincoln. In fact, the entire feeling of this historic landmark captured a sense of decades gone by – charming and sophisticated, albeit a bit outdated.

Turning to Debra, Andy said, "I can't believe in all of these years this is the first time I've been to this place. Maybe I should have told the parking attendant to wreck the car rather than being careful. From the looks of the Willard I may have been able to collect more than the car's worth."

The aroma of the finest collection of cordials and liqueurs in Washington beckoned them toward the Round Robin Bar and Lounge – home to beltway and international power brokers. Their waiter arrived after a few moments with a menu. Debra glanced at the offerings.

"I'll have Dewar's times two with soda and the lady will …"

"I think I'll have a Monumental Mojito. Thanks."

"You know, Renee really appreciates you getting involved with this albatross she's been handed," Andy said.

"Yes, I know. She's been a good friend for a long time … always so positive and energetic. I hate to see her stressed out like she is. Glad she was able to find someone she loves so much."

"Yeah, they make a great pair," Andy quickly confirmed. "I've known Stan for a long time as well and I've got to tell you that guy is completely off the market. He's pretty smitten." Looking around at the elegance of the lounge, he asked, "Do you always travel like this?"

"No, not really. I haven't been to DC in quite a while … wanted to take in some sights downtown while I'm here and well … I guess I just wanted to splurge a little on myself. Everyone deserves to do that every once in a while. Don't you think?"

Andy smiled, nodded in agreement and gave his credit card to the waiter.

"Cheers," he said clicking their glasses together. "Debra, earlier tonight you said, 'I thought you may be different.' What did you mean?"

"You really want to do this now?"

"Yes, I do. It kind of hit me between the eyes. I have no idea if you meant it, why you said it, or even what you meant."

Debra began, "You said, 'So what did a *high ranking* U.N. official tell them?' Why do you guys think sarcasm is a good idea? I was enjoying the evening until that point. Why do men have to be on the attack? With their sarcastic wit it seems like all they want is a one night stand, then they're on to their next conquest. They're never interested in anything serious, not even a serious conversation. Just a quick-bam-thank-you-ma'am kind of guy."

"Wow! That's pretty direct. But you're wrong, I'm not that guy."

"So what's your story then?" she asked bluntly.

"My story? I'm sorry … what did you ask?"

"You know, what makes you tick … what do you do for fun?"

"Let's see, I like baseball and golf, an occasional well-prepared steak, scotch whisky, playing poker with my buddies at the club, Tom Clancy, a good cigar every now and again … all the guy stuff."

"Really, I never would have guessed that," Debra said. "No … wait … I'm sorry. Let's back up. I can't very well pick on you if I'm going to be guilty of doing the same thing. Can I?"

"No … no … not so much," Andy said. "Debra, are you sure you're interested in finding a serious relationship or do you just use the push back thing as a means of defense?"

"A means of defense? Now who's talking in riddles? What do you mean?"

"Well, some people would think my sarcasm, as you say, is just a little innocent flirtatious banter and not characteristic of a 'quick-bam-thank-you-ma'am kind of guy.' So, when you resist flirtation, do you do it as a means of defense?"

"Andy, I don't want to scare you off here or anything, but yes, I'm looking for a relationship. In case you haven't noticed, I'm not getting any younger. And I don't have time to waste with a little banter. So yeah, I am a little up front about it. Just now, you said 'some people would think'. You pushed back on me earlier with a similar comment, so … what is it that *you* think?"

"I think you just stand at home plate with your bat on your shoulder and hope you'll get on base, rather than swinging the damn bat."

"No, I don't. I swing the bat … at a good pitch."

"Well then, are you saying I'm not a good enough pitch for you? How do you know I'm not the kind of guy you're looking for?"

"Well, I don't ... really. Are you?"

"I could be."

"Maybe we should find out. Maybe I should start over and swing the bat," she said with raised eyebrows. "Since I took back one of your strikes, you still have two strikes available. Don't blow it, again. Aw, what the heck, let's start a new inning. Want to get in the game?

Andy was taken aback. He was cautiously silent. He nodded yes. He was no longer in control of the situation as he had been trained. He was unsure of what to do next. They exchange phone numbers,

"Why don't you take tomorrow afternoon off and spend it with me? The Capital Fringe Festival is in full swing. It'll be fun."

"What's the Capital Fringe Festival?"

"It's an annual festival for the performing arts in DC. It's cool. It's uncensored. All the material is created and produced by the artists themselves. Andy, first you've never been to the Willard and now you don't know about the Capital Fringe ... are you sure you really live in DC?"

"Sure you don't want to see a ball game? Wait ... we can't ... the All Star break. Damn."

CHAPTER 20

WASHINGTON, DC - JULY 12, 2012

"Excuse me, Stan," Bonnie said knocking on his office door. "There's a young lady here to see you without an appointment … a Debra Herzog. Should I send her away?"

"No … no. I'll see her. Please show her in."

"Stan, she's cute. Does Renee know about her?" Bonnie asked.

"Of course, she … oh, just get out!

"Stan, Ms. Herzog," Bonnie said upon returning.

"Well, this is a pleasant surprise," Stan said gesturing for her to be seated. "Would you like a cup of coffee or something?"

"No. Thank you, I just finished breakfast."

"Thank you, Bonnie. That will be all. Now go back to the solitaire game on your computer," Stan said laughing and gesturing for her to go away. "When you said last night you were going to do some sight-seeing today, it didn't occur to me you would start at the Ford Office Building. Pretty grim, huh? So what brings you here?"

"It's about Andy," Debra confessed.

"Oh?"

"Yes. It's all a bit confusing for me right now. But before we do this, let me tell you again how much fun I had at dinner and the conversation afterward. I'm glad Renee has you in her corner, especially right now."

"Thanks. She's still pretty tense about this scroll business."

"I know. Just give her some time to process this. It's weighing pretty heavy on her right now," Debra advised. "Stan, last night, at your place, Andy started getting under my skin a little with his snarky comments."

"Yeah, I could tell. He can be a bit over the top sometimes. Pretty competitive guy."

"Yeah, that's one word for it," Debra added. "But when he dropped me off at the hotel, his whole demeanor seemed to change. It was like he was trying to impress you back at the condo or something."

"I hardly think he was trying to impress me of all people. He just likes to show off a bit, regardless of who's around. I think you were the real target."

"Well, anyway, when he dropped me off I asked him in for a drink. Our conversation got personal, pretty quickly. I think I pushed his buttons back at your place. He said some things that caught me off guard and made me wonder if I was seeing him through the lens of my prior relationships, and not who he really is. He said I act defensive and didn't swing at the pitch."

"I don't under …"

"Oh, never mind," Debra interrupted. "I'll get to the point. Stan, is Andy a good man?"

"A good man? Of course he's a good man. Why? What are you asking?"

"I think I'm falling … oh, I don't know … he's just interesting and I don't want to go down that path if it turns out he's just another schmuck."

"Have you talked to Renee about this?" Stan asked.

"No. Like me, she barely knows him."

"Well, that's true."

"So what then? What do you think?"

"Do I think Andy is a good guy?" Stan asked himself. "Yes, I do. He confronted George when I asked and volunteered to come to France with me, didn't he? Two things he didn't have to do."

"Yes, of course. But that was in support for one of his buddies. I mean is he a good man? Can he be gentle and kind? What's his track record with women?"

"I plead the fifth on that one. You're going to have to find out for yourself. Just let me say this. You two just come at the world very differently. For example, Andy grew up in New York City in a poor household. Andy and his brother ran with a pretty rough crowd. His father let them get away with a lot, but his mother kept them in line.

"At the time the city's housing authority maintained a separate police force and neighborhood cops became the norm. His buddies got involved with a local gang, but his mother got them to turn away from them and encouraged Andy and his brother to befriend their neighborhood cop, instead.

"This cop was great. Andy said she was like a member of the family. Not just theirs, she took lots of kids under her wing. It was because of her that Andy decided to go into law enforcement in the first place. From this childhood he went to Penn State. After a year there, he transferred to Boston University and graduated in criminal law. From there he went on to earn his law degree at Georgetown and is now a public servant.

"You, on the other hand were born in …?"

"Israel," Debra filled in.

"Grew up in …?"

"France."

"Graduated from …?"

"The Paris-Sorbonne University."

"And studied …?"

"Arts, humanities and languages."

"Majoring in …?"

"The most beautiful language in the world and French literature with a minor in drama … also took some acting classes with Pratique Théatrale."

"Exactly. This is what I'm talking about," Stan said confidently. "Now don't get me wrong, I think yours was a wonderful education and fits you perfectly. It gave you an opportunity to be thoughtful, reflective, and creative – qualities that are still with you today."

"Thank you," Debra said somewhat embarrassed.

"Now Andy, rather than choosing to earn a lot of money as an attorney, chose public service. He's always been competitive as a student and as an athlete. You saw some of this last night. He has been conditioned by his job. He needs to be in control. He needs to dominate the situation. His life may be at risk if he doesn't."

"Of course, I get that," Debra confessed. "But at the end of the day, will he be able to leave all of that at the office and have any sort of intimate relationship? Can he relax or must he always be in control?"

"Let me try to answer you by saying this. Andy joined the bureau in July 2001, shortly after graduating from law school. Two months later the nine-eleven attacks happened, and the World Trade Center buildings collapsed. Even though it had only been on the job for two months and it happened in a different city, he has always felt he was somehow partially responsible for the 3,000 deaths. It was on his watch. How could he and his colleagues could have let it happen? It gnaws at him. Now here's the kicker … his parents were visiting the first tower when the plane hit. They were among those who were killed."

"Oh my God. I had no idea. Thanks for telling me. Andy never mentioned anything about them."

"Okay, but here's the answer to your question. He was angry at first to be sure, but this tough guy … this guy who always needs to be in control, is a different person when it comes to his parents. Years later when he speaks of them, he speaks with a sense of reverence. Even though they didn't have much money, he has such fond memories of his childhood and of them. He still speaks of them with such love and tenderness. So, yes, once you've broken through the shell, I think he can be intimate. And I think you have a good start … just continue to play hardball."

"I want to build a relationship and this is what you're telling me … 'just continue to play hardball?' "

"Yes, but just until he figures out you're someone who will be his equal … his partner, not someone he can easily control. It won't take much time. You'll see. And speaking of time, even though we're running out of it, I'll try to give Renee enough time to process all of this. I know it's difficult for her; she's pretty stressed. I think that was good advice."

"Certainly better advice than 'just continue to play hardball.' "

* * *

A familiar sound rang in Debra's purse. Andy's name appeared on the screen of her cellphone.

"Hey, Andy, where are you?"

"Just leaving the office now. Had to get a few things squared away before our trip to France tomorrow."

"Great. Guess what? I'm at the Fringe and just bought a pair of tickets for the 7:15 p.m. show. It's called *A Night In – Or the Night My Wife Left.* It's about a dude with multiple personalities whose wife is divorcing him because she says she doesn't know him anymore. She just leaves him a note and splits before he gets home."

"I don't know. Sounds kind of depressing."

"Well, maybe, but they say parts are funny. I'm thinking there might be some pointers here we could take away or at least it would be interesting to talk through. It's billed as, 'Rude, crude, but brutally honest. It explores that first night of being alone and the questions we hate to ask ourselves when we realize maybe our ex-partner was right.' Sound okay? I could take them back."

"No, let's try it, but if gets too weird, I'm out of there."

"Don't worry ... it's all done with puppets that reflect character's persona. Like his pothead friend is made from a bong. You'll be fine. Meet me in front of the National Archives Building at 1:30. We'll go from there. Lots to do."

"Puppets?"

CHAPTER 21

CHARTRES, FRANCE - JULY 14, 2012

Sebastian followed Stan and Andy from l'Hôtellerie Saint Jean until they sat down to have a cup of coffee and fresh croissant. It was an hour before their meeting with Miguel.

An elderly gentleman waited in front of the cathedral for their arrival. They approached him at 10:00 a.m. "Mr. Parker?" he asked.

"Yes, but call me Stan. And you must be Miguel Tuguía. Allow me to present my friend, Special Agent Andy Miller."

The formality and strained greeting was lost on no one, especially Sebastian, who had now caught up with the pair. He watched the meeting unfold from the patio of a small café. He remained out of sight. He had no need to hear them. Their early departure allowed Sebastian enough time to find and enter their austere, monastery-like-cell, plant a listening device, and take the three minute walk to the cathedral by the appointed time.

Stan and Andy entered the center portal and were immediately in awe of its magnificence. "It's beautiful," Stan remarked looking toward the Rose Window. "I've studied the cathedral extensively, but this is the first time I've actually been here."

"Even with all the scaffolding, she is beautiful, no?" Miguel asked. Our Lady of Chartres reveals many of the world's religions under her crossed copper roof. You can even see the influence of Eastern religions in the organization of the western façade. Let's take a walk back outside for a moment and I'll show you."

Sebastian was noticeably shocked when saw them exit the center portal. "I wonder if it's over?" he whispered to himself, hiding behind that day's copy of *Le Figaro*.

As they passed, Sebastian left the safety of the patio and rounded the corner of the medieval stone building that encroached on the cathedral's plaza. He watched as they walked to its center and stopped.

"The west façade is organized into three distinct elements – the central portion flanked by the two asymmetrical towers," Miguel began. "In the center at the top Jesus stands like the crown chakra with an infinite number of lotus petals of Hindu tradition. Now move down the façade, the two angles represent the two lotus petals of the brow chakra and surround Mary and the infant. Below, the sixteen figures in the Kings Gallery represent the sixteen lotus petals of the throat chakra. In the middle, the rose window with its openings in groups of twelve suggest the twelve lotus petals of the heart chakra. This organization continues all the way down to the simple unadorned doors of the root chakra. The Templars took such care for unity," Miguel said in child-like adoration of his lady.

"Miguel, you do know why we are here, right?" Stan asked bluntly.

"Yes, of course I do. It seems serendipitous you should be here this day, La Fête Nationale, to visit the cathedral. When the Third Estate broke from the nobility and Catholic Church and stormed the Bastille in Paris, the cathedral was also briefly attacked. There was some fear she would be lost. But the riots around her stopped. She was not hurt of course, but with the scroll's revelation to the world I fear she still may be, or God willing she might be rededicated to *our* Lady. Let's go back inside, shall we?"

Sebastian put down his newspaper and sighed with relief as they reentered the building.

Stan focused his mind, not really caring to understand Miguel's veiled remark. He began, "Renee brought back the most fantastic story from her time with you – one that is extremely hard to believe. We're really struggling to get our heads around it."

"I assume she also told Andy. Are there others who know?"

"Yes, Renee confided in an old friend of hers named Debra. She's with the United Nations and may be able to help us. And one other person knows – or maybe from him there may be others who know by now. A man named Sebastian Philippe from Albi whom Renee knew as a young girl. He followed her here and saw you talking with her. He tracked us down in New York and eavesdropped on our conversation with Debra. From what Renee told me, he's a devout Catholic and apparently a member of the Sovereign Military Order of Malta."

"I know a number of people who are members of the Order. It sprang from the Knights Hospitaller founded during the crusades to care for their wounded fellow knights. They carry on their tradition of care. They are not normally people who get caught up in such things," Miguel said.

"Maybe not. I don't know if there's a connection between the Order and his involvement with you, but he has a fanatical interest in what's going on. He even left a note on my windshield to make the point on the day we ditched him. 'Don't think you've gotten away with anything. I know where you live and where you work and what you are up to. We'll be watching. You will make a mistake and it will be over.' " Stan recited the words etched on his brain. "We're not sure, but Renee thinks Sebastian is working with another member of the Order of Malta, an American named George Wilson."

"And so it begins," Miguel said sadly.

"And so what begins?" Andy asked.

"The fear. The fight. The bloodshed. The struggle continues. I had so hoped it could be contained until after …"

"Until after? After what?" Stan impatiently demanded.

Miguel continued, "… until after we are no longer in possession of the scroll or alive." He cleared his throat. "Gentlemen, my brother Rafael and I have been in conversation with an ancient religious sect of Mandaeans. Their ancestors fled Jerusalem right after the fall of the Second Temple and settled in an area in southern Iraq near the confluence of the Tigris and Euphrates rivers. They are among the last surviving Gnostics from antiquity.

"When the US invaded Iraq in 2003, these people were driven from their homes. We read they wanted to leave Iraq, but the British refused to grant them asylum and the Bush administration simply discounted their plight as a consequence of war. Over the past nine years, refugees have left one by one, some going to the US, but the US has done very little to relieve their suffering as a group of people."

"So what do you think? Do you think I'm in the position to drive the US government to its knees on their behalf?" Stan demanded once more.

"No, of course not, just hear me out. Prior to the war, the Iraqi people considered the Mandaean people just one of the many religious minorities inhabiting their country. They were middleclass artisans. They were left alone. During the war Islamic extremists constantly harassed them. Women who refused to veil themselves were repeatedly attacked and beaten by the extremists. As a result, most Mandaeans from Iraq scattered to different parts of the world, and those who remained faced extinction. A small portion of them escaped to Iran. There, they do not have a problem with violence, but they are prohibited access to employment, education, and a lot of other things because of laws that screen people for devotion to the tenets of Islam."

"What does this have to do with Renee ... with us?" Andy asked.

"A few months ago, we contacted several of the Mandaean priests. We told them about the scroll. Its content lends credence to their Gnostic beliefs and ours. We also told them we had it well hidden, but wanted to make it public, within the next few weeks now. They obviously want the scroll to be made public as well because it forms the basis of their faith and validates their existence. However, they told us about their current plight and asked if the US might be willing to pay for wartime reparations as a means to obtain the scroll.

"They asked if we would intercede on their behalf," Miguel continued. "They suggested fifty million US dollars would be a reasonable amount, considering the US virtually annihilated their 2,000-year-old culture. They intend to use the money to bring their brothers and sisters, now scattered throughout the world, back to rebuild their lives in Iraq since the war has subsided. They are a quiet, religious people and did not wish to prosecute this claim themselves. We agreed to help them encourage the US to provide the money and in turn we would release the scroll to you as a gift."

"Well, that's not going to happen," Stan exclaimed. "The US may go around the world blowing stuff up, but it is simply not in the position to buy a religious artifact or to give preferential help to any religious group. That's not what we do. If it became public that the US Treasury helped finance a religious institution in Iraq ... well ... it just isn't going to happen."

"What then? This scroll is extremely valuable. We asked them to allow us to pursue the matter on their behalf not only because we share most of their beliefs, but also to honor the memory of our father. Rafael and I are near the end of our lives. We do not want anything for ourselves. We could simply release it to the world, but we would not be believed. We are just two old men. We are not credible.

"Our mother goddess, Asherah, sent an angel of mercy to us. It is because of Her gift of Renee, and now you, we have the possibility of righting a terrible wrong and helping the Mandaeans survive. But we must hurry."

"Yes, I know," Stan said. "Renee told me of your diagnosis. If we do get involved, we will try to get this done as quickly as we can."

"Thank you," Miguel said acknowledging Stan's sincerity.

"And speaking of credible," Stan said as his due diligence kicked in, "were you able to have the scroll authenticated and dated?"

"Yes. I told Renee we would furnish you with a report. Here is a copy for you to take back. As you've noted, we're being watched so we all must be careful with the report. Any further contact with the man who dated the scroll will arouse suspicion. We must now turn over the scroll to someone who is strong enough and credible enough to protect it and present it to the world."

"Miguel, there may be another way," Stan said. "I've been thinking a better solution might be to involve Israel. Any problem with getting Israel involved?"

Miguel shook his head while saying, "Not at all. Rafael and I both agree this needs to happen in the end."

"You know if Israel gets involved, maybe one or more of its enemies – Syria or Iran or the Palestinians in Gaza or the West Bank or factions in Egypt, whomever – might get involved," Andy warned. "This whole thing could escalate pretty quickly and blow up in our faces. And yet, Stan and I agree. I too think Israel is your best shot. If the scroll is authentic it needs to be made public and housed with the Dead Sea Scrolls."

Turning to Miguel, Stan suggested, "You know fifty million dollars is a lot of money – too much to hide even in the US budget. If we can convince Israel to pay the Mandaeans a substantial amount of money, say twenty-five million, will you release the scroll to them?"

"I think they may accept such an offer. Assuming they would, then yes."

"You realize the only way this could work is by contract. The payment would only take place after the scroll is in Israel's possession and once again carbon dated, authenticated and translated to confirm your thesis."

"Yes, of course."

Sebastian watched as they departed – Stan and Andy walking back to their hotel, Miguel returning to his white Citroën sedan.

* * *

"Hey, Renee. … Yeah, I know … it's a little after noon here. Sorry for the early hour, but I wanted to get to you before Debra left for Temple. … She didn't. Oh, well maybe Monday would have worked after all. Sorry, I guess this could have waited. Listen, Miguel's good with Israel as a surrogate and a contract to purchase. The Tuguías are representing an ancient religious sect of Mandaeans now living in Iran. They want to return to Iraq, since the war is over. Tell you all about it when I get back. If Israel can fund this thing to the tune of twenty-five million, I think we have ourselves a ballgame. Andy's concerned that Israel's enemies may get involved if Israel pursues this. See what Debra can find out from the Ambassador. Meanwhile, tell her not to mention anything to anyone else, especially those board members across the street. I should be back around 6:30 tomorrow evening. Okay, see you then. … Yeah, me too. Bye."

"Israel. Mandaeans. Israel's enemies. Iran." Sebastian repeated to himself. "Gotcha."

CHAPTER 22

WASHINGTON, DC - JULY 16, 2012

After an early morning class and a long day at the office, Stan's exhausting weekend trip to Chartres finally caught up with him. Irish stew and a pint of Guinness seemed about right for the evening meal; cooking was clearly not in the cards. "Comfort food ... yes, that's what I need tonight," Stan said to Renee as they approached his condo. "Want to stop by O'shea's first?"

"Okay, but let's do takeout," Renee reluctantly agreed remembering her splitting headache from the massive amounts of green beer she had consumed on St. Patrick's Day. She called ahead.

Stan double parked on King Street allowing Renee a few moments to dash in and pick up a quart of stew. They arrived at Stan's condo at 7:15 to be greeted by Skype's irritating call to action. Debra's red hair and freckled face appeared on the screen when they answered the call.

"Hey, Debra. Any news?" Stan asked. Renee joined him at the computer.

"Hi. Yes. I spoke to the Ambassador today. I was pretty vague, but I told him I needed to contact someone within the Israel Antiquities Authority and asked if he had any suggestions. He said he didn't have any direct contacts but told me he would write me a letter of introduction. I also told him I needed to get some documents to the Israel Antiquities Authority without inspection, but didn't tell him about the scroll per sé. He agreed to allow me to courier them. I asked him if he could expedite the letter and the pouch because I planned to go to Israel this week, as soon as I could set something up. It will be good to get this thing behind us as well as to see my family while I'm there. I am so looking forward to the trip. Can you tell me more about Andy's thoughts on Israel's enemies?"

"Yes, of course. Andy seems to think Israel's adversaries might get involved if it becomes public knowledge that Israel intends to purchase the scroll," Stan said.

"That goes to my earlier point," Debra recalled. "I can't get the Ambassador involved more than I have without definitive information. Right now, the only thing we have is Miguel's word and a copy of a report that the scroll is the real deal."

"Andy also told me there have been rumors floating around the Department. It seems the CIA is concerned about an Iran-Vatican alliance against the US and Israel," Stan said.

"Why would the Vatican want to get in bed with them?" Debra asked.

"Well, it's not so much the Vatican wants to, as much as Iran is looking for a defensive ally. The Pope has been pretty quiet on all of this so far, but according to Andy, Iran's thinking goes something like this – if they continue to enrich uranium and the US escalates its stance toward military action, it would be to Iran's benefit if the Pope interceded on its behalf. He could sway public opinion in Iran's direction and buy some time. He also said, 'I'm not sure who the Pope considers to be the criminals, but he did express a pretty strong objection to the US-led invasion of Iraq. It seems the Vatican may think the US-Iran thing is more of the same.' "

"So do you think Iran has enough time to get the Vatican on their side?" Renee asked.

"Andy seems to think Iran already has. He said they've been working at it a long time with their embassy at the Vatican. He told me that before the State of Israel was established, the Vatican opposed Zionist policies. Pope Pius XII in fact called for Jerusalem to be in the international domain to keep the holy places away from either Arab or Israeli sovereignty.

Because of this, Israel has only had diplomatic relations with the Vatican for eighteen years, but Iran's been there for the past fifty-four. And it appears that Iran looks for opportunities to win the Pope's favor from time to time. Remember back in 2007, in April, when Iran released the 15 British sailors it held? Iran's President called his action 'an Easter gift' to the British people. His decision came the day after Pope Benedict XVI sent a private letter asking for their release. Coincidence? I don't think so.

"Debra," continued Stan, "I spoke with Ambassador Ben-Artzi today as well. I told him much the same as you told Ambassador Chazan. Ben Artzi did not know anyone at the Israel Antiquities Authority personally, but thought if we contacted the Security Services Branch, the director would most likely be willing to see us.

"I also spoke to Andy first thing this morning and again this afternoon, assuming you would want him to go. I asked him if you were able to get a meeting, whether he would be willing to accompany you to Israel. I knew you were anxious, so I told him it might even be this week. He not only agreed, he insisted on going. He's expecting his in-country firearm credentials from the Israeli Ministry of Public Safety to be shipped to him by Wednesday mid-morning. He had to pull some strings, but he got it done. You seemed to have made quite an impression. Both Renee and I think it would be best as well. I know I felt a lot safer with him in Chartres."

"Sure, that makes sense," Debra said. "I could use the help and a little security would be good too. If I call Security Services in the morning at 6:30 a.m. NY time, it would be what …1:30 p.m. Israeli time, right? I'll give the director a call in the morning and see what I can arrange. Talk to you soon. Bye," Debra concluded.

"I really don't think Debra should go there by herself," Renee said. "I'm glad Andy agreed to go. It makes me feel a lot better."

Picking up the copy of the *Washington Post* from the coffee table, Stan said, "Hey, the Associated Press is reporting Israel was Hillary's last stop on her whirlwind twelve day trip through Asia and Europe. It says, 'Shimon Peres voiced support for the Obama administration's pressure on Iran to halt its nuclear activities.' Hope the pressure is not too much. I'd hate to see the Pope get involved. Maybe we can enlist Hillary to go back to Israel and do our bidding?"

* * *

George lowered the windows and turned off the engine of his parent-furnished, red BMW convertible.

"Yeah, you probably should get Hillary involved if you think you can pull this thing off," George said to himself while writing:

Monday, July 16th. RE: Stan Parker, Renee Gaston and Debra Herzog

Followed Renee to Stan's condo. Conversation among Stan, Renee and Debra via Skype. Debra plans to go to Israel and meet with the Israel Antiquities Authority regarding the scroll. Iranians interested in helping the Papacy. Andy will accompany her. Obtained a license for firearms. Debra's last name is 'Herzog'. Found it on an org chart of U.N. personnel; head of translation services. Informed Sebastian.

George threw his cigarette butt to the curb and settled in for the night in front of Oronoco Bay Park. "I'm tired of listening to you two. You keep on talking. I'm going to sleep. Damn, it's hot."

* * *

"Stan, remember part of Miguel's translation … the part about Jesus wanting to restore the importance of love and wisdom represented by the goddess … and choosing Mary to fulfill the ancient mysteries?" Renee asked.

"Yes, of course I do. Why do you ask?"

"I truly believe that were it not for the paternalism of the ancient Hebrews, women would not have the legitimacy problems we do today."

"That's probably true. But don't be too hard on them," Stan replied. "You can find male dominance in most religions even in Hinduism. Women are first protected by their fathers, then by their husbands, and finally by their sons – a woman it seems was never fit for independence."

"Yes, but our culture has grown out of Judaic-Christian beliefs, so that's where I have to focus."

"Okay, so tell me, Renee, what's on your mind?" Stan asked.

"I've been thinking about this a lot with the revelation of the scroll. It was Mary who broke the barriers of their sexist society. But the early orthodox Christians couldn't deal with it. She was maligned as a prostitute in the second century and Pope Gregory's homily instilled this in the sixth.

This label stuck until the late twentieth century.

"Stan, isn't it time we recognize that the Church ignored Jesus' support of Mary, elevated Peter to power, organized itself in a patriarchal manner, created a hierarchy of male domination, and suppressed alternative thought as heresies in order to control the destiny of this new religion? Isn't this the reason we have a legacy of the inferiority of women?

"That's why I'm in this thing," Renee continued.

"I know," he said.

"It was through the reenactment of the sacred marriage with the Mother Goddess that the king was actually acknowledged and allowed to rule though another growing season. Without her, he was nothing."

"That sounds about right." Stan quipped.

"That's why it's so important to make the scroll public. We've got to find a way to help, Stan."

"We will," Stan reassured her. "We will."

* * *

The beeping of Skype woke the pair up from a sound sleep – George woke as well, as he listened in from his parked car. "Good morning, Debra, at least I think it could be," Stan said, yawning through a glazed stare at the computer screen.

"I apologize for the early call, but I just got off the phone with Amir Katz. He's the Director of the Security Service Branch of the Israel Antiquities Authority or the IAA as I have now learned to call it. I told him about the scroll and the general situation and made it clear I needed to see him right away. We set an appointment at the IAA on Friday morning at 9:00 a.m. He insisted we conclude our business to allow him to be home before sundown. It will be Rosh Chodesh Av on Thursday evening and a day of rest for women on Friday, so he must prepare the Shabbat dinner for Friday evening. I made arrangements to fly Lufthansa to Tel Aviv leaving JFK tomorrow at 3:30 p.m. and connect through Frankfort. It will get me to Tel Aviv at 12:30 p.m. on Thursday. I'll spend the weekend with the family then head back Monday. I should be back in DC in the evening around 6:00 p.m. I'll brief you when I get back. A few seats are still available. I'll call Andy and fill him in on the details. Send copies overnight of everything you have on the scroll to my apartment for delivery tomorrow morning. Do you still have the address?"

"Yes. This is moving fast," Stan said. "You don't waste any time."

"Hey guys, this is all my doing. Don't you think I should go with you?" Renee asked.

"No, not now. I really don't see the need at this point," Debra said. "Let me gauge their interest and I'll keep you posted."

"Well, okay, but again I'm feeling some guilt at putting you in this spot."

"Don't do that to yourself. I'll be fine. Andy will help. Talk to you soon. Bye for now."

* * *

Tuesday, July 17. RE: Stan Parker, Renee Gaston and Debra Herzog Early morning Skype.

Debra and Andy will arrive in Tel Aviv, Thursday afternoon at 12:30 p.m. aboard Lufthansa flight from Frankfort. Meeting with Amir Katz, the Director of Security Service Branch of the Israel Antiques Authority set for Friday 9:00 a.m. July 20, 2012. Visiting her family over the weekend. Will return to DC on Monday evening. Sent general description of Andy and other info to Sebastian.

CHAPTER 23

ROME, ITALY - JULY 17, 2012

License plate SMOM 40 identified the polished black Mercedes that chauffeured Sebastian to his destination – Via Dei Condotti 68 and the headquarters of the Sovereign Military Order of Malta.

Sebastian was excited to be in Rome. His work had won him the recognition of the highest-ranking members of the Order and in particular a complimentary message from the Grand Master delivered through his aide Colonel Bonito Sordi. He was on a path that would most likely place him among the elite Knights and Dames of Honour and Devotion if he were successful in his mission.

A flag of four equally sized red rectangles fluttered ten yards above the street and marked the portal where cars approached the inner sanctum. A band of shuttered windows wrapped the interior perimeter of the second floor and opened to a bright blue sky. Below, a giant Maltese cross defined the limits of the cul-de-sac.

A white Maltese cross, displayed against a crimson background, branded the pale orange, stucco façade and directed his path. He stepped out of the car and entered the Italian Renaissance headquarters.

"Good afternoon. My name is Sebastian Philippe," he said with a smile, upon entering the headquarters and official residence of Brother Frederick Schmidt. "I'm here to see Colonel Sordi."

"Colonel Sordi is with Fra' Schmidt at the moment. He's expecting you. My name is Erma Müller. Please come with me," she smiled and said with a flirtatious look.

As she stood, she tugged at the hem of a sweater-dress that clung to the curves of her body. She was young and beautiful and seemed bright, at least to Sebastian.

She had been Schmidt's assistant for seven years and moved to Rome when he was elected Grand Master of the Order in 2010. She guided Sebastian down a regal passageway and up the grand staircase to Schmidt's office.

"Say, Frau Erma Müller – or would you prefer Fräulein – I noticed you are not wearing a wedding ring. How about showing me some of your favorite night spots this evening?

Erma's rosy cheeks grew even redder as the handsome man asked her for a date. "Nein. As much as I may like to," she said. "Fra' Schmidt is a quite proper older gentleman and has a strict policy about me not dating brothers in the Order."

"Brothers? What makes you think I'm a member of the Order?" Sebastian asked.

"This time look at your own hand. I may not wear a ring, but yours … well, it's a big clue," Erma said. "Fra' Schmidt, Sebastian Philippe is here for Colonel Sordi."

"Yes, thank you. Please show him in," Schmidt directed.

"Ah, there you are my boy. Please come in," Schmidt said rising and extending his hand in welcome. "Benito here has just been telling me about your membership in the Order and reminding me of your recent work."

A six-foot-two-inch, heavy set, burly man stood and extended his hand as well. "Hello, I am Bonito Sordi. How was your flight? Please have a seat."

"It was fine, Colonel, thanks. And thank you Fra' Schmidt for your note and chauffeur. I am not accustomed to being greeted in such a manner."

Sebastian's eyes roamed the brocade wallpaper decorating the well-appointed office of the Grand Master. He studied the photographs that surrounded him. Images of aid being given to babies in hospitals, the elderly and disabled, earthquake victims and war-ravaged soldiers were but a few of the photos that called to account the services provided by the Order. At the end of his reconnaissance his eyes fell upon Fra' Schmidt's leather topped desk and what appeared to be a military award of some type.

"Sir, what is this medallion? I've never seen anything like this before," he asked as he studied a silver Maltese cross adorned by a center swastika, a pair of swords, and four eagles with four more swastikas.

"It was awarded to my grandfather in 1939. It's called a Spanish Cross. My grandfather and other volunteers from the Luftwaffe were members of a German unit known as the Condor Legion. I know we were on the wrong side of history during that time, but he is my grandfather after all and was a damn good pilot," Schmidt replied. "They fought with Franco and the Nationalists during the Spanish Civil War."

"Well, isn't that a coincidence? He must have been in Galicia about the same time as …"

"Excuse me, sir," interrupted Colonel Sordi. "Sebastian, let's take a walk. Frederick, you don't want to get involved with this. I'll see you later."

Colonel Sordi was a no-nonsense Italian. His twenty-seven years of military service as an intelligence officer left him hard, direct and without feeling. "Follow me," he ordered.

They walked through the porte-cochere and the portal and onto Via Dei Condotti in silence. Heading in the direction of the Spanish Steps, Sebastian asked, "Where are we going?"

"Away from this place," Sordi barked.

"Have I done something to offend you?" Sebastian asked.

Sordi stopped walking. "Listen, Phillipe, I want you to understand this fully. Before he moved to Albi, your priest, Father Dubois, was with me in Rome. He joined the Order in 1970, before he became a priest. We met five years later and have been friends ever since."

"What does he have to do with you … with us, now?"

"If you'd wait a damn minute, I'll tell you. Two months ago, Dubois contacted me about a man he was going to meet that afternoon," Sordi said. "His assistant, Noelle Martine, had arranged the meeting between him and a man named Rafael Tuguía from Santiago de Compostela. Martine told him that Tuguía's father worked as a custodian in the Cathedral of St. James and was killed just prior to the war.

"Dubois called me to prepare for Tuguía's visit. He knew Fra' Schmidt's grandfather was involved in the war in northern Spain and thought there may be rumors about the custodian's murder. He thought I might have heard something. I had. I'd heard a lot actually, but did not share any of the details with him. I just told him the Order was suspicious of Ramon Tuguía and investigating his time in the cathedral. I also told him the Order would be interested to know if he had received something from his father, as Fra' Schmidt suspects, and if it belonged to the cathedral we may be interested in purchasing it.

"Dubois also told me you were a devout Catholic and a member of his parish and the Order," Sordi continued. "Apparently, you followed his meeting with Tuguía and became curious about the Spaniard. He told you what little he knew and later called me to say you may be interested in helping me investigate the matter. The Spanish Cross you saw in Fra' Schmidt's office just now …"

"Yes, sir."

"Well, the old-man's grandfather earned it for bombing runs during the war. He and some of his fellow pilots were Catholic and kept the stories of European pilgrimages in their flight plans. They made sure the runs never got near the cathedral. Rumors persisted from some of the locals that an anti-Catholic custodian named Ramon Tuguía stole something valuable from the cathedral and had been killed. Since he was a young boy Fra' Schmidt listened intently to all of grandfather's stories including the one about the custodian at the cathedral. The name Tuguía has been held in contempt and under scrutiny by the Order since Fra' Schmidt has been among the leadership. Until now we had hoped that Ramon's sons would simply die and their secret would die with them."

"That would have been helpful to know at the time of my conversation with Renee at the airport," mused Sebastian. "Hoping to scare her into submission, I made up a tale to warn her to stay out of it, not knowing what I was really talking about."

"I'm not sure that was such a good idea," explained Sordi. It probably put her on guard. But had I had your limited knowledge, I may have done the same thing. The Sunday after your friend, Renee, went to Compostela … what's her name again?"

"Renee Gaston," Sebastian answered.

"Yes, Gaston. The Sunday after she made the pilgrimage to Compostela, her mother was so proud of her she couldn't contain herself.

She told everyone in church including Father Dubois about her daughter taking El Camiño de Santiago de Compostela. She relayed Renee's story about meeting an elderly Spaniard, Rafael Tuguía, who had seen many pilgrims come and go."

"Her father then spoke up and said Renee had taken his advice and was going next to visit Rafael's brother, Miguel, in Chartres to learn a little about El Camiño de las Estrellas," Sordi continued. "Dubois called me again and told me of their ramblings. That's when it all fell in place and I called you to get your butt to Chartres and follow her to Washington."

"Yes sir, when I got your call, I had no idea what you were talking about or what I could find out. It just seemed like a wild goose chase going to Chartres let alone to Washington. But you were right."

"Who else is involved with her now? Tell me what's going on."

"Renee of course you know about. There is Renee's father, Jacques Gaston; Stan Parker, her fiancé; Renee's friend and ex-boss Debra Herzog, an Israeli immigrant to the US who now works for the UN; Andy Miller, Stan's friend who's an FBI agent …"

"The FBI, huh? That's not good," Sordi interrupted.

"… Rafael and Miguel who are in possession of the scroll; some priests from the Mandaean faith in Iran and Amir Katz, the Director of the Security Service Branch of the Israel Antiques Authority," Sebastian continued. "That's all for now, as far as I know."

"Okay. You need to understand that Dubois is walking a fine line between two of his parishioners. When you returned from America and confessed to him about spying on her and what you discovered, Dubois violated his vows and brought the matter directly to my attention. He knew I would be interested in making sure the scroll never saw the light of day, not knowing you and I were already working together.

"This thing, and what we have to do in the future, is between you and me personally. Let's be clear. The Order is not involved. That's why I told you to meet me here today to make damn sure you understood this. I wanted to tell you this face to face. What we have to do does not and cannot involve Father Dubois, the Fra' Schmidt, or any of the members of the Order. Ever. Got it?"

Sebastian cast his eyes toward the ground. "Yes sir, of course," Sebastian said somewhat sheepishly, but with a slight smile knowing what they had to do would ultimately bring him success and praise from his fellow knights.

"What's with the smirk? I mean it! I will kill you if I have to."

"What *we* have to do?" repeated Sebastian, now afraid of what might be asked of him.

"Yes, *we*," Sordi said harshly. "You don't think you could actually pull this off by yourself. Do you?" Colonel Sordi's demeanor and gruff manner revealed a man who was not to be toyed with. He simply would not tolerate any imperfection.

"I'm not exactly by myself; you do know George is involved too, right? Oh, I forgot to mention him," Sebastian said.

"Who's George?"

"George Wilson. My friend in Washington. A trusted brother. My eyes and ears at the moment."

"That's it. The circle can't get any larger until I'm ready to add a couple of my old comrades. What's the current status?"

"Debra and Andy are flying to Tel Aviv tomorrow and have a meeting scheduled with Katz in Jerusalem on Friday morning. They're making arrangements to sell the scroll to Israel for twenty-five million dollars."

"Okay, here's what I want you to do," started Sordi. "Go to Tel Aviv and meet their plane. Stay out of sight, just follow them to Jerusalem and see if you can find out anything about the sale – when it will take place; where; how. Find out as much as you can. Do either of them know what you look like?"

"Yes sir, well, here's what happened. Renee discovered a bug I had planted in her daypack and then set me up. I followed them to a subway station in New York and then lost them. When I chased them down, Renee, Stan and Debra were already on the train. Renee took my picture, so I'm guessing they probably all can recognize me by now."

"Damn it!" exclaimed Sordi. "No more screw-ups! Understand? Just follow them and keep out of sight and keep me posted."

"Yes sir, I will. I was planning to go there already."

"When they head back to the States, let them go," continued Sordi. "Just let me know when they do. Have George continue his surveillance in DC. You stay in Jerusalem and see what you can find out about the exchange. And follow the money. A purchase in this amount will need to be appropriated by the Knesset. You'll have a sense of the timing if you follow the money."

"Right. There's a 5:10 p.m. flight I was going to take tomorrow, but I'll head to Tel Aviv this afternoon instead and get set up early. It will get me there a little after midnight Wednesday morning. I'll meet their plane Thursday morning. That'll give me an extra day in case there's a problem."

Handing Sebastian his card, Sordi said, "Here's my cellphone number. I'm going back to patch things up with Schmidt. Keep in touch and don't make any more mistakes!"

CHAPTER 24

NEW YORK CITY - JULY 18, 2012, 3:30 P.M. EDT

Andy's foul mood was lost on no one when he entered the upper cabin of the Airbus. He had already spent two and a half hours in transit from DC to meet Debra and was not looking forward to another fourteen. Their flight was announced. They boarded on time.

Andy met with the pilot, showed him his badge and firearms authorization letter from Israel, and explained he had an FBI-issued Glock in his personal belongings. The pilot was not happy and welcomed him on board with a curt, "Keep that damn thing in your bag and beneath the seat in front of you."

"The airline industry has done a real good job scaling back on convenience to optimize occupancy and profit," Andy complained to whoever was listening. Today was no exception. Nearly every one of the 555 seats was taken. "Whatever happened to the joy of flying?" he asked. "They sure hit the nail on the head by incorporating the word bus into this beast."

Debra and Andy's first date had ended with a passionate kiss. Debra had hoped seeing *A Night In* at Fringe Festival would be the catalyst to create a meaningful dialogue about relationships. It did.

"You okay? You seem preoccupied with something … things okay at work?" Debra asked, knowing she had to get out in front and redirect Andy's attention toward her and the trip ahead. "You know, you really do need to start looking on the positive side of life every once in a while. This could be a fun trip. You're with me. We're going to my hometown. We could have a good time if you'd just relax a little."

"What are you talking about? This is who I am, relaxed a little."

Securely buckled in, Debra, Andy and their fellow passengers were now armed with the flight attendant's presentation of what to do in case they tanked in the Atlantic Ocean.

"Really, so the seats act as a floatation device, do they?" he mocked. "I think we'd be better off to just bend over and kiss our asses goodbye," Andy said as he nervously watched what appeared to be smoke coming from the upper air supply registers. His eyes focused on the name tag of the nearest flight attendant.

"Hey, Inga. What's with the smoke?"

"It's not smoke, sir. It's just condensation from the humidity. Just relax sir. It will disappear soon."

"Yes. You're right. It does seem like you're relaxed quite a bit," Debra teased.

The comforts of their double-decked, wide body aircraft were short lived. They sat on the tarmac at JFK Airport for the next fifty-five minutes waiting for the deluge and lightning to pass.

Adults took the complimentary cocktails; teenagers ignored their parents and their surroundings and plugged themselves into the inner world of smart-phone technology; younger children squirmed in their seats, unable to move around the aisles; most of the infants and toddlers cried in discomfort. It promised to be an incredibly bad flight … as usual.

They adjusted their reading lights and air supply controls. A hush fell over the cabin when the engines began to whine. The captain's Germanic accent broke the quiet of the nervous crowd as the plane approached the active runway. "Good afternoon, ladies and gentlemen. I am Captain Eric Snyder. I apologize for today's delay. We are now currently number three for takeoff. When we reach our cruising altitude of 37,000 feet, we will turn down the cabin lights. This is for your comfort and to enhance the appearance of your flight attendants. So sit back and relax. And thank you for flying Lufthansa. We'll do all we can to make your flight as comfortable as possible."

"Why don't you start that comfort thing by shutting up the kid behind me?" Andy muttered.

"Try to relax. He'll be quiet in a few moments," Debra promised.

"Okay … Okay. Hey, Inga. You really going to let Captain Snyder talk about you that way?" he smiled and asked.

"Don't worry. I'll get even later," she responded.

The initial two hours was consumed by reading the inflight magazine, talking about the news, an occasional conversation about current events or briefly sharing personal anecdotes while probing for other areas of common interest.

"Guess what, Debra, at least here's a bit of good news!" he said, lifting his eyes from the sports page to boast to the traveling companion on his right. "The Nationals did it again last night. This gets us way out in front with the best win/loss record in the league and continues our first place standing in the National League East. Zimmermann pitched six innings allowing just four hits and no runs. They went on to give up a run in the seventh and two in the ninth, but my boys hung in to beat the Mets 4-3."

"And you think that's a good thing?" Debra questioned.

"Oh, yeah, I forgot. You're from the Big Apple, aren't you? No offense intended. Follow baseball much?" he asked.

"There's that guy again, but, hey, no offense taken. Let's just put it this way, R.A. Dickey is the starting pitcher for the Mets today. He's twelve and one. No one – and I mean no one – can hit his knuckleball. He's fantastic. I'm sure he'll give your precious Nationals a run for their money."

"Okay, Debra, now I'm really impressed. You're beautiful, brainy and know baseball. I just thought you got lucky with the All Star game at Stan's place last week."

"Funny. Did you play baseball in school?" Debra asked.

"Yeah, in high school … I got an all-state mention from New York where I grew up. Thing is, I could have been a starter in college and was recruited for some smaller schools, but I wanted to go to the Big Ten. I walked on at Penn State during my freshman year but rode the bench for most of the season. Then I decided to major in criminal justice before law school. Altoona was 45 minutes from the ball field in University Park and I didn't have a car, so both of these things weren't going to happen. I decided to transfer to the city that suited me better, Boston, and enrolled at BU."

"Is Boston where you met Stan?" Debra asked with a smile already knowing the answer to her question.

"Yep, he was going to Harvard at the same time I went to BU. Great times, but even so, high school baseball was a real exciting time in my life. I thought for a while I had a shot at the show, but it turned out to be just a fantasy. So I decided it was time to enter my life of crime and transferred. Fast forwarding from then 'til now, I lead a pretty boring life as an FBI agent. It's not as glamorous as it once seemed. Lots of paperwork, always at the gym – although not so much lately, got to get back there and drop these extra pounds. And, like I said, I like all the guy stuff for entertainment. Now, how 'bout you? Tell me about your job, and your connection to Israel."

"My job … my connection to Israel?" Debra repeated. "Do my ears deceive me or is a man really asking me about me? This might be a first."

"Doing your defense thing, again?"

"Touché. Well, let's see … my father is Israeli. His two brothers and sister and their families all live there. Six of my cousins are there – two in the West Bank and four in western Jerusalem. My father was born in Jerusalem just before Israel became a state in '48. He fought in the Six-Day War in '67. After the war ended and Israel took control of the West Bank, Golan Heights, the Sinai and Gaza, there was a huge influx of US Jewish people ascending to Israel. My mother was among those immigrants. She initially came to Israel just to visit a few college friends from NYU, but she met my father at a party, immediately fell in love and stayed. She constantly tells me how handsome he was in his uniform, and he was! They were married a few years later and made their home in a place Oslo II later called Area C of the West Bank near Bethlehem. I came along in 1977 and then we moved to France when I was ten years old."

"Why? Your relatives are still there, right? What happened to your parents?"

"My mother was never comfortable living there … too many conflicts; too many wars; too many Arabs. In late '87, before the Oslo Accords, a violent Palestinian uprising began in Gaza and the West Bank that protested the Israeli occupation and that was enough for her. So we left and moved to Paris where they stayed until '99, then they moved to New York, largely as a result of the growing anti-Semitism in France at the time. It seemed to follow us around the world."

"You say '*they* moved to New York.' Didn't you go with them?"

"No, when I was eighteen the second Oslo Accord was signed and it looked as though Israel and the Palestinian Authority had agreed to agree and there would finally be peace. So I returned to Israel to fulfil my military obligation as an Israeli citizen."

"Are your parents still in New York?"

"Yes and they love it. My mother returned home and my father fell in love with baseball. One year after I joined them in New York, the Mets played the Yankees for the World Series. My father never lets me forget this proud moment in his life – a new beginning for him and for the Mets. He taught me so much, and in the learning, I got addicted."

"Sounds like it. If he had as much influence on your love for baseball as it seems, I think I'd like to meet him."

"I think he would like to meet you as well. Say, Andy, Stan told Renee and me about your take on Iran's nuclear program and relationship with the papacy. How close are they to developing a nuclear bomb?"

"I'm sorry I can't tell you that. It's classified. All I can tell you is what you read in the papers."

"Speaking of classified, I need to classify all personal opinions I voiced about the politics of Israel when we get in country."

"Of course. No problem," Andy confirmed.

"Well, what are we doing other than the economic sanctions?"

"I can't tell you that either. But we're not sitting on our hands; that's for sure."

"You know Renee got pretty worked up about Sandra's testimony on the Affordable Care Act and her later encounters with George. What did you find out about him? Do you think he's dangerous? … I know … you can't tell me that either."

"No, I can actually, but there's not much to tell. He seems harmless enough. I gave him a pretty good scare right after his initial run-in with Renee. Seems to me this Sebastian guy is the one we really need to be concerned about. Stan sent me a picture of him you guys took from the train. Pretty intense day, I bet."

"You have no idea. I'm just looking forward to turning this whole matter over to the Israeli government and getting out of it."

Then came a before-dinner cocktail, dinner with two glasses of wine, a couple of after-dinner drinks, and two more hours of conversation, this time laced with flirtatious remarks and laughter.

Andy leaned into the aisle and watched her walk away from him toward the lavatories in the middle of the aircraft. She returned with a hint of freshly applied perfume. He stood behind her to let her in, close – ever so close – her fragrance working its magic. He gently held her arm as she sat. She lifted the barrier separating their seats. For the next two and one-half hours of their flight to Frankfort there was quiet. Eyes closed, Debra's head rested against Andy's shoulder; her hands touching his arm. He sat motionless with his eyes glued on the bag that contained his Glock. They were both settled in, at least for a while.

The flight attendant's amplified German accent startled them. "Achtung. Ladies and gentlemen, as we start our descent, please make sure your seat backs and tray tables are in their full upright and locked position. Make sure your seat belt is securely fastened and all carry-on luggage is stowed beneath the seat in front of you or in the overhead bins. Please turn off all electronic devices until we are safely parked at the gate. We'd like to thank you for flying with us today."

Twenty minutes later they were startled by a hard landing and the awareness of how little time they now had. They again heard the voice of their inflight comedienne who masqueraded as a flight attendant. "Ladies and gentlemen, please remain in your seats until Captain Smash 'n Dash brings the aircraft to a complete stop, oh about five feet or so from the gate. He'll then lurch forward once more and demolish the front end of the plane. But don't be alarmed, once the smoke and debris clear and the sirens go quiet, we'll open the door and you can jump to what's left of the jetway.

"No, hang on … that was for his flight attendant crack earlier. I should probably do that again. Ladies and gentlemen, welcome to Frankfurt, Germany where the local time is 6:25 a.m. and the temperature is already a warm 25 degrees Celsius. For your safety and comfort, we ask you to please remain seated with your seat belt fastened until the captain turns off the fasten seat belt sign. This will indicate we have parked at the gate and it is safe for you to move about. As you exit the plane, please make sure to gather all of your belongings and most importantly be sure to take your children. Anything left behind will be mine and as you may not know … I'm allergic to boys under the age of 19."

They arrived at the gate with only sixty-five minutes remaining to catch their connecting flight to Tel Aviv. Quick to stand, they bolted ahead of a few passengers, but it seemed the remaining passengers had conspired to delay their exit.

Winded, they arrived at their gate just in time to walk onto the jetway and their connecting Lufthansa flight. Andy spoke to the captain about his carry-on while Debra secured their seats for the four hour trip further east.

Thirty minutes out, Andy retrieved his jacket from the overhead bin and bag from under the seat. “I’m going to clean up a bit before we arrive,” he said as he left Debra for the lav. There he washed his face, threaded his holster through his belt to his right hip, and mentally prepared to go to work. Twenty-five minutes later he checked his watch to confirm the flight attendant’s arrival time – 12:45 p.m. Israeli Daylight Time, fifteen minutes late.

CHAPTER 25

TEL AVIV, ISRAEL - JULY 19, 2012

They were exhausted by the flight but exhilarated by what lay ahead. Not only was there the opportunity to present the privileged information to Amir Katz, but also the possibility of what seemed to be a budding romance.

Andy excused himself and headed for the privacy of the first men's room along Concourse C. He holstered his gun, steeled himself for the day ahead, and returned to her side. After fourteen hours and little sleep, her eyes were half closed when he returned. Instinctively, she reached for the familiar arm she had held on the plane. He moved her to his left side. He offered his left arm without her being aware of the change or why it was necessary. They followed the crowd toward Terminal 3 of Ben-Gurion Airport.

"I hate to be this guy, Debra, but when we leave the secure area, I have to have my arms free. I convinced my boss to send me here in an official capacity. He did and he expects me to do my job and keep you safe. Besides we'll have plenty of time when we get back to the States."

"Aren't you Agent Kill Joy."

"Well, that's Special Agent Kill Joy, but no I'm not that either."

Debra's international credentials allowed her to bypass the line that waited for processing. She presented her Israeli passport, U.N. Identification Badge and Israeli Identity Card for her diplomatic mission to the customs official.

He looked at her, then her picture, her once again and asked, "What brings you back to Israel? Business or pleasure? Or are you returning to stay."

Handing him her US passport for processing, she reached out her other hand for the documents to be returned. She explained her dual citizenship of both Israel and the United States.

"I will not be staying," Debra explained. "I'm here for both business and pleasure, but only for a short while. I have an appointment with Director Amir Katz of the Israeli Antiquities Authority tomorrow morning and then plan to visit my relatives over the weekend. I will return to the US on Monday."

"So tell me, Ms. Herzog, why is your name so familiar?"

"Maybe you're thinking of a distant relative of mine, Chaim Herzog. He served as the Israeli President in the '80's. Remember?"

"Yes, I probably am. Where did you perform your military service?"

"Golan Heights from 1995-1997. I left Israel in 1987 and lived in France with my parents until 1995, then moved back when I was 18 and joined the Women's Corp.

"Before leaving France I had the opportunity to meet the Israeli Ambassador. After my military service I returned to France to attend the University and kept in touch with the Ambassador as we both shared a passion for French literature. He later became the Israeli Ambassador to the United Nations and offered me a position on his staff after graduation. I was later appointed to my current position as Chief of Interpretation Services of the UN," Debra said matter-of-factly and handed him a second document. "This is a letter signed by Ambassador Chazan, Israel's current Ambassador to the UN. He appointed me to deliver these documents to Director Katz."

She lifted the brown leather briefcase marked with the logo of the United Nations and labeled "Israeli Diplomatic Pouch – This Bag Has Diplomatic Immunity from Search and Seizure."

He looked over the letter, studied the bag, and stamped her passport.

"Very well, proceed. Welcome back. Enjoy your stay in Israel."

Andy followed. "My name is Special Agent Andrew J. Miller with the Federal Bureau of Investigation of the United States of America," he said, handing the customs official his passport, visa, FBI credentials, badge and gun.

"I'm here on official business to protect the life of the young lady who just entered your country. My checked luggage also contains a FBI-issued Glock 23 handgun with six magazines of ammunition. The US Ambassador to Israel and your local authorities are aware that we will be in country for the days outlined by Ms. Herzog." Handing him the authorization letter that served as his license, Andy continued, "Your Ministry of Public Safety has authorized me to carry these weapons in country. It has been all prearranged. He will be able to verify this information."

The customs official signaled for an off-duty co-worker to come to his booth and take his place. He said, "Thank you. Please follow me."

He led them to a guarded waiting room. Concealed cameras and uniformed and plainclothes armed security guards were everywhere, in what is known as one of the world's most secure airports.

"I apologize, but I must retain you here for a few moments while I verify your information."

Moments later he returned with an armed guard at his side. "Ms. Herzog, it turns out it wasn't your distant relative, President Herzog. Please come with me. We have a few questions for you."

Andy stood and held on to Debra's arm. "Where are you taking her? Can't you ask your questions in here?" he asked.

"Ms. Herzog, please," the customs official said once again.

Andy stood in front of her. The guard pushed him back with his assault rifle.

"I'm a US Federal Agent. I don't think you want to be pointing that thing at me!" he growled.

"That may be, but your jurisdiction does not extend to Israel. Now back off."

Andy began to pace the floor. The brightly lit, sterile room contributed to his growing anxiety of not knowing what was now happening to Debra. Ten minutes later, the customs official and Debra returned. The guard took his post outside the door.

"Thank God!" Andy said, jumping from his seat. He grabbed her shoulders and drew her close. Surprised at his reaction, he backed off and asked, "Are you okay? What's happening?"

"A bit of a mix up really," Debra said with a trusting smile. "A routine check of my name uncovered someone the government suspects of being a traitor. It seems a Jewish man living in Gaza during the Israeli attack three and a half years ago also has the last name of Herzog. He's not related, but they wanted to make sure he was not one of the family members whom I planned to visit. Seems this Herzog guy sided with Hamas and protested against the Israeli invasion to end the rocket fire coming from Gaza. He was caught on camera and later identified by the military."

The customs official's eyes circled the room as he handed Andy's passport to him.

"I apologize for the manner of the inquiry, but it was necessary. All of your information seems to be in satisfactory order. I have your visa and have stamped your passport. Here are your credentials, badge and gun. Try not to use it while you're here."

The customs official left the room and they lingered for a moment. "Debra, before … I'm sorry about that. I was angry thinking about the way they handled things and about how they may be treating you. And I was so glad to see you when you returned, I guess I just lost …"

She placed her fingers gently on his lips interrupting his bungled apology. "No, don't be," she said returning the embrace and leaning in to surround his open mouth with hers."

"Glad you're okay," he whispered.

"Yeah, me too. Thanks for your concern."

* * *

Sebastian paced nervously around the arrival hall periodically looking at the arrival monitors and checking his watch, now reading 1:45.

"Their plane arrived an hour ago. Where could they be?" he muttered to himself. He then spotted them walking toward the luggage carrousel. He watched them gather their belongings and followed as they headed upstairs to the car rental desks.

"Good, Hertz," he said to himself.

He had been there the day before to rent his car and knew their procedures. While Andy signed the contract and got directions for their trip to Jerusalem, Sebastian headed downstairs and brought his car around to the exit of the Hertz parking lot.

Debra and Andy emerged from Terminal 3 fifteen minutes later, went straight to their appointed car, and headed east. Sebastian, cautiously out-of-sight, followed two cars behind. An hour later, they passed the graffiti-laden concrete walls that cordoned off the West Bank and finally reached their hotel near the Old City of Jerusalem and the Israeli Antiquities Authority.

ONE HOUR LATER

The city of Jerusalem was alive with tourists. Bus after bus passed the Mount of Olives heading to the common debarkation point for the best initial view of the eastern wall of the ancient city. Tourists stationed themselves at the balustrade, sidestepping the camels that existed for staged photo ops. Multiple languages competed for attention to share the stories of Judaic tradition relating to the life of Jesus – stories that were hardened like concrete into the minds of the locals who recited them. The heat and the dust went unnoticed by the tourists as they strained to hear their guide yell information about the city's ancient history in a language they could understand.

"Would you like some water, Debra?" Andy asked, taking a bottle from his daypack.

"Yes, and maybe some shade and a break from all these tourists."

A tour guide holding a red, triangular flag began his tale in English. Debra and Andy joined his group for the brief time he spoke. "Down below us and to the left is the house where his disciples shared the Last Supper with Jesus. Above us and to the right is the Basilica of Agony and the Garden of Gethsemane on the Mount of Olives where Jesus was betrayed. We will stop and visit them in a just a little while. Please look toward the wall, there on the left, is the Essene gate where Jesus entered the city of Jerusalem and was greeted by waving palm branches and Hosannas. Unfortunately, it is now sealed and not available for entry.

"Between us and to the right of the gate is the Jewish Cemetery. We have used this sacred site for burial for over 3,000 years. We believe when their resurrection finally does come, Elijah the Prophet will blow the shofar beckoning them to rise from their graves and follow the Messiah. Because of this, they are all buried with their feet facing the Temple Mount, over there," he said pointing in the direction of the golden dome, "where you also see the Dome of the Rock. We'll also visit those, later. We'll stay here for a few more minutes so you can take some pictures. …

"Okay, everyone back on the bus. Please stay together."

Debra and Andy wanted no part of a chaotic guided tour, but knew they had to stay awake for a few more hours to be in sync with Israel Daylight Time. They lingered at their vantage point for a while longer as the tourists shuffled to their buses. Quiet at last, Debra's eyes traced a path from the Essene Gate eastward to the Mount of Olives.

"I wonder what the terrain was like east of the mount 2,000 years ago?" she asked imagining what lay twenty miles beyond the olive trees. "I've been here many times, but never thought about Gethsemane being on a direct route between the Essene gate and the wilderness of Qumran where the Dead Sea Scrolls were found. Seems to give further credence to the theory that Jesus was an Essene."

A short taxi ride brought the pair back to the ancient crossroads and the Jaffe Gate of the western wall of the old fortress. They meandered through the crowded streets of the Christian Quarter. Priests in Greek Orthodox vestments greeted their arrival at the Church of the Holy Sepulcher. Believed to be the location of Calvary and the tomb of Jesus, the opulence of the many competing iconic symbols from the Eastern Orthodox, Roman Catholic and Armenian Orthodox traditions were captivating, but lost on them as they fought to stay awake.

They continued their trek on the cobbled streets of the Old City on their path toward the Jewish Quarter. A great energy engulfed them as a cacophony of multiple languages echoed off the stone walls. The black suits of Haredi men and the white headscarves of the Islamic men anchored the color spectrum of traditional dress. In between an occasional brightly colored abaya of a Muslim woman blended with the modernity of people of all ages and faiths, or no faith at all, to create a visual excitement found only in Jerusalem. The visual and audible intensity grew as crowds formed to bargain for the best deals at the shops now embedded along the Via Dolorosa - a path that is said to be the one Jesus walked, but it was not. His was about five yards below their feet.

Along their path Andy and Debra took time to relax a bit and have some refreshment. They looked across a vast plaza to a section of King Herod's retaining wall of the Temple Mount, known as the Western Wall. Israelis from Jerusalem and the Jewish diaspora continued to mourn the loss of the Temple. And, as they have for centuries, communicated with

God by placing hand-written notes between the ashlar cut stones

Andy took his iPad from his day pack and began reading the latest English edition of the *Ha'aretz.* "Says here a bus carrying Israeli youth exploded yesterday in a Bulgarian resort, killing at least six people and wounding thirty-two. The Prime Minister called it 'an Iranian terror attack' and promised a tough response. I don't think this is ever going to end. Oh, by the way, Yahoo's reporting the New York Mets won today nine to five. Hate to say you were right, but maybe. We've still got you by seven games don't forget."

The ten minute walk back to the hotel allowed them to get some dinner before turning in. A brief good-night kiss seemed like the requisite response for their fledgling relationship as they parted to go to their respective rooms.

"Good night, Debra. See you at 7:00 a.m.," he said.

Andy turned on the television to see the burnt skeleton of the bombed-out school bus in Bulgaria. He turned it off, not wanting to think about it. He closed his eyes and tried to sleep, but the images of the dead and wounded children kept flashing through his head.

He tossed and turned and could not sleep. *What the hell are we doing here? We need to get this thing resolved tomorrow and get out of here,* he thought. Finally giving up after thirty minutes he got up and got dressed.

"Who is it?" Debra asked in response to the knock on her door.

"Special Agent Kill Joy. I couldn't sleep. Thought you may want to go downstairs for a drink."

"I can't sleep either," she said peeking around the partially opened door while dressed in a form fitting satin and lace gown. Her curly red hair rested on the lace straps surrounding her neck and complimented its sea green color. Its plunging neck line accented her cleavage and captured his immediate attention. Her choice of color went unnoticed.

"Why don't you come in and we'll not sleep some more?" she asked. The long slit of the gown's left side not only allowed her to easily step to the side, it also revealed a beautifully sculpted piece of art that started at her hip ran all the way down to the floor.

"Should I go downstairs and buy some …?"

"And spoil the moment?" she teased. "No. Just relax. I don't need the insurance. I can afford to take care of myself."

She stepped back to a spot directly beneath an overhead light. His eyes began to wander and traced the sheer lace that outlined the gown's satin cups. The lace continued around her body to partially expose her waist and hips and joined the other side at the base of her spine. Crossover back straps barely held the gown in place and completely exposed her back to his delight.

"Wow! I didn't see that thing from behind until now," he said as she turned to walk to the outside wall of the room.

The city lights bleed through sheer drapes and silhouetted her petit, shapely body. She was everything he had imagined. She thought of Stan's advice and the mention of Andy's parents. *He still speaks of them with such love and tenderness. So, yes, once you've broken through the shell, I think he can be intimate.*

"So, Andy, the bat is off my shoulder and I'm ready to swing at a good pitch. Are you?" she asked to break through the shell.

He nodded. "Just a minute," he said removing the magazine and chambered round from his Glock and placing it on the night stand. He tossed his jacket in the direction of the room's single chair. It missed and landed on the floor. It was of no concern to either of them.

Her shiny red hair reflected the city lights and drew him closer. He stretched out his hand to caress her head and gently stroke the evening's reflection. She held the back of his hand and moved it first to her cheek, then to her lips and began nibbling his fingers.

He reached for the lace on her shoulder with his free hand and guided the strap down her arm. As her hand slid through the opening a satin cup fell to one side unmasking the statuesque charm of Venus di Milo in human flesh. She turned her back in his direction to offer her opposite shoulder. With his fingers still at her lips and elbow now draped over her bare breast, she raised his arm just enough to allow her sea-green-invitation to hit the floor. She kicked it the direction of his jacket.

She placed her hands on top of his, guided them to her breast and pressed herself into his lap. As she felt him growing against her, she spun her body toward his, ripped open his shirt and began kissing his hairless chest over and over as she raced toward his mouth. Their open lips met. Their tongues intertwined. A long, passionate kiss followed. Their breathing grew more intense as their bodies heated.

Stepping back from their embrace she revealed herself to him for the first time. His eyes widened, then crinkled as he smiled. He tore his shirt from his arms and threw it in the direction of the growing collection.

She smiled as the look of complete surrender and joy filled his face.

Slowly tracing the line of his collarbone and upper shoulder with her fingernails she circled behind him and continued to trace his shoulder blade. The soft skin of her pale arms wrapped his torso. He felt her breast press against his back. She loosened his belt. Then his pants. Then stripped his boxers to the floor. She grabbed his arm and pulled him in the direction of the bed.

They made love for nearly an hour. Slowly, tenderly at first, kissing, touching, and exploring the body of a new lover with anticipation and pleasure until their passion increased with a sense of reckless abandon. Moments later Andy collapsed on the pile of sweat-soaked sheets.

Exhausted by the day and her intensity, Andy lay motionless. After a few minutes the silence was broken. He began to laugh. "This homerun was way better than getting to second base! I wonder what my report will say about the protection game tonight."

"Let me read it before you send it in, will you? I may have to classify it."

"I think I'll go back to my room, take a shower and try to get some sleep. Bet I won't have any trouble now."

"You could do that, or you could stay here and shower with me," she smiled with a raised eyebrow.

They stood in front of Debra's mirrored bathroom wall waiting for the hot water to reach the oversized shower head. Smiles crossed their lips as they held each other's sleep deprived gaze in their sights. With one eye on Debra and the other on the mirror Andy said, "Yep, got to do something about these fifteen pounds."

"Nah, you're just fine. You know what, I think Stan was right about you."

"What? What did you say?"

"Never mind, I'll tell you later. Water's hot. Let's get in."

CHAPTER 26

TEL AVIV, ISRAEL - JULY 23, 2012, 8:00 A.M. IDT

"Colonel Sordi? This is Sebastian. … Yes sir, we're at Ben-Gurion now. … Pretty uneventful. I saw them enter the Israeli Antiquities Authority around 8:45 a.m. on the 20th, three days ago. I assume they met with Katz around 9:00 as planned. Must have given him whatever she was carrying in the briefcase, 'cause she didn't have it with her when she came out. They left the building around 10:30 and then went back after lunch for about an hour. I followed them to a house near Bethlehem. Looked like a family reunion of sorts. Fourteen people waited for their arrival; three generations. They hung around the house most of the weekend. I'm going to head back to the Authority after they have checked in. Hang on a minute. I'm about to go through a security check point so I can get on the airport property. … Okay, I'll call you back later."

The young Israeli sergeant cradled his standard issued Tar-21 assault rifle. He ordered Sebastian to stop, then cautiously approached the car.

"Name and passport, please."

“Sebastian Philippe. Yes, here it is.”

He studied Sebastian’s face and passport. Returning the passport he said, “Open your trunk please.” Signaling for his buddies to check the trunk, the sergeant stuck his head inside the car and checked for anything on the seats and floor.

Two other soldiers joined the sergeant. They placed what appeared to be oversized dental mirrors beneath the car and inspected its chassis looking for explosives. Satisfied, they moved to the trunk. After making sure it did not contain weapons or explosives or petroleum products, they closed the trunk door and slapped the car twice, indicating to the sergeant it was secure.

“Proceed,” he ordered.

Sebastian parked and jogged toward Terminal 3 at a fast clip. He slowed to a brisk walk, noticing the armed security guards stationed at the terminal entrances had readied their weapons.

“Good morning,” he said as he passed the guards.

“Halt! Passport please,” one of the guards ordered.

“Okay, here it is. I was just trying to catch someone before they departed.”

Checking him for weapons, the ranking guard said, “Well, slow it down. We stop and question anyone who runs through the airport. Go ahead.”

Inside the building, more uniformed and plainclothes security officers paced the facility and kept alert for would-be assailants.

Andy and Debra were at the ticketing agent’s counter three hours ahead of their flight as advised. Andy declared his firearms. They checked their luggage and headed toward their initial screening. A security agent checked his FBI credentials, questioned him about their stay in Israel, checked the outside of their carry-on luggage and asked about their travel plans for today. He then collected their luggage, personally checked Andy’s and ran Debra’s through the X-ray machine, followed by a pressure chamber to trigger any possible explosives. The agent was satisfied, and Debra and Andy avoided having to submit to a body search. Many others in line were not so lucky.

They picked up their carry-ons and headed in the direction of the Departure Level. They entered the Buy and Bye to purchase two cups of coffee and a breakfast roll to share. As the vendor opened the pastry cabinet to get the roll, Andy saw Sebastian’s familiar image in the reflection of the glass doors.

"Debra, don't turn around, but our boy Sebastian is lurking at the newsstand about fifteen yards behind you," he said. "I guess he's been following us. Whatever he has in mind, he won't attempt anything in here – too many guards. Let's just calmly head to the gate. Unless he has a ticket for the flight, it's over. Seems like Katz was right to get my phone number in addition to yours. We know mine is secure; yours, maybe not so much."

Debra texted Renee, "This is Debra. I'm using Andy's phone. Our flight leaves Tel Aviv at 11:17 a.m. We have one stop. We should arrive in DC around six in the evening your time. I'll call you when we land."

Thinking he had gone unnoticed, Sebastian watched the pair proceed to the security checkpoint where they were again questioned and their credentials re-inspected and their boarding passes now called into question. Once again, they cleared their carry-ons as before and passed through the metal detectors and out of sight. Sebastian did not follow.

"That's that then," Sebastian said to a passerby.

"Hello, George, this is Sebastian. … Yeah, I know it's two in the morning there. I assumed you were still studying. Listen, they're headed back to DC on time. Should be there about six in the evening your time. Stay after them. Talk to you later."

Once again, he reported in. "Colonel Sordi? … They're gone … Yes sir, no problems. I'm heading to the Authority now to see what I can find out. I call you when I do."

JERUSALEM - LATER THE SAME DAY

"Director Schulman," his assistant announced to the assembled crowd as she opened the door to the Director's conference room.

"Good morning, Eli," Katz said.

Nodding and shaking his subordinate's hand Schulman said, "Good morning, Amir. Everyone, sit … sit, please. Now what's this all about?"

Katz began, "First let me introduce you to Yossi Wolff, Even Nagar and Gil Hassan. Yossi is an archeologist with Dr. Horovitz and a scholar of ancient Hebrew writing. Even and Gil are both security guards with me in Securities Services. They all volunteered for the assignment when I put out the word on Friday."

"Thank you, and I guess you all know Dr. Yvonne Horovitz, Director of the Archeological Division, and David Cohen, Head of the Knesset Lobby," Schulman said.

"Let me start by saying I am not sure what I'm about to tell you is fact," Katz said. "At this point it is speculation, but we need to investigate it to be certain. On Friday, I met with a woman by the name of Debra Herzog. She works for U.N. Ambassador Chazan. Accompanying her was a man from the FBI by the name of Special Agent Andrew Miller."

"Did they come as an official envoy from the US?"

"No, it's a private matter. And, in fact, Herzog said her friend who got her involved, Renee Gaston, is most concerned that what I'm about to tell you not be made public until the story can be verified."

"Herzog explained that two elderly brothers – one from Santiago de Compostela, Spain, a Rafael Tuguía, and the other now living in Chartres, France, a Miguel Tuguía, approached Gaston during her travels to the two cities. The brothers apparently have an ancient scroll in their possession they say dates from the first century CE. They say their father found it in the crypt of the Cathedral of St. James in Santiago de Compostela in Spain and claim it was written by the brother of Jesus, James the Righteous."

"Did they offer any sort of proof?" Shulman asked.

"Yes, as a matter of fact they did. As of now it is unsubstantiated, but these are copies of photos of the scroll as well as portions in English. Yossi reviewed the documents over the weekend and as far as we can tell, the translations are accurate. He also translated the balance for me. That doesn't mean the scroll itself is not a forgery, of course."

"So, what's the issue?" Shulman said, growing somewhat impatient.

"If the scroll is authentic, it pretty much spells out an egregious deception of St. Paul. The scroll indicates the first-century Church of Jerusalem was headed by James the Righteous. It says the Essene brotherhood of Qumran followed the ancient scriptures being practiced much earlier in Egypt. This is also evident in the Dead Sea Scrolls where the authors speak about the Wicked Priest and the Teacher of Righteousness as you likely know. James' branch were from Mt Carmel and called themselves Nazarenes, meaning 'keepers of the ancient scriptures'.

"So, two things are at issue. First, apparently Paul usurped James' authority and thrust Peter into a position of prominence. And second, it seems he departed from the Nazarene teachings of Jesus and the Church of Jerusalem to preach a message aimed at growing his own faith among the gentiles. I say this because the scroll clearly documents that Mary Magdalene was to be next in line to lead after Jesus' death.

"This brings us to the Tuguía brothers and what they want. Modern day Mandaeans, who once mostly resided in Iraq, are as close to modern day Nazarenes as it gets. If fact, they call their priests by a similar name – Nasoreans. This sect of early Christians fled Jerusalem 70 CE when the Romans destroyed the Second Temple and murdered so many of our ancestors. They venerate John the Baptist as their most sacred prophet, not Jesus. At the time of the Iraqi invasion by the US and allied forces, the Mandaeans scattered to various places throughout the world. The largest group now reside in Iran. Since the war is now over, they want the ability and right to return home."

"Where have I heard that before?" Shulman asked callously.

Katz acknowledged Shulman's sarcasm with a slight smirk and said, "Sir, be that as it may, the Bush administration did very little to help these displaced people. Now, Rafael and Miguel are attempting to leverage the scroll to help their brothers in faith before they die and with them, the scroll.

"Here is where we come in. The Tuguía brothers are willing to give the scroll to Israel if we are willing to give the Mandaeans twenty-five million US dollars in return. I should point out they were originally asking fifty million, but have accepted the twenty-five in principle."

"I don't care what they're asking," Shulman said, "the scroll is Israeli property and by law we're entitled to have it. We'll negotiate the compensation later."

"Excuse me, sir, that's not exactly the way it works," interrupted Dr. Horovitz. "I'm sure you're aware the law actually says when an antiquity is found in Israel it shall become property of the State, provided compensation is given and other prescribed matters are in compliance. The simple truth is this scroll was apparently found in Spain. How it got there and whether it's even real are subject to further investigation. Assuming it is real, and assuming it says what it's supposed to, as explicitly as it seems, the twenty-five million would be a small price to pay for this discovery."

"At this point the Tuguía brothers are willing to trust the Authority to take control of the scroll for testing and verification if we provide them with a contract for purchase," Katz said. "At my request, Debra and Andrew confirmed this again after our morning meeting and returned later in the day to assure me this was the case. The terms of contract would basically state that after we are satisfied the scroll is authentic we would pay them twenty-five million US dollars for the right to own the property."

"I thought the money was supposed to go to the Mandaeans," Dr. Horovitz said.

"It is. That transaction will be between Rafael and Miguel and the Mandaeans, but I guess we could have some sort of provision for joint payment," Katz added.

"Here are the problems as I see them," Schulman said. "First, that's a lot of money. We have to get the Knesset involved, quickly but quietly. Thinking that something like this might be involved is the reason I invited you to this meeting, David. You need to start working on this. I'm not sure what we tie it to or how we explain it, but the money needs to be appropriated before we can authorize a contract for purchase."

"Let me suggest this. If I can informally get sixty plus members of the Knesset to commit to funding this purchase will that be satisfactory?" Cohen asked.

"I think so. Just be sure to get a solid majority from the Prime Minister's Party. We don't want this thing to be a referendum on his leadership," Schulman said. "The contract will need to have a caveat stating something to the effect that a significant number of our elected officials have informally agreed to funding, but the purchase is subject to the future approval by the Knesset. I think the Tuguías will understand that the funding for the purchase of the scroll could not be made public and debated at this time. Just get it done as quickly as possible."

"Okay, I will. Even so, I think I'll need at least a week to make all the arrangements and make it happen."

Schulman continued, "Good. Let's use next Monday as a target date to pull this together. The second problem, the contract must explicitly state we are not responsible for security or transportation of the scroll until it is within Israeli borders. The last thing we need is to be obligated for twenty-five million and the scroll is stolen or damaged before we can verify its authenticity."

"There's another major concern, sir – a political one," said Cohen. "If the scroll is real and says what we're assuming at the moment and if Israel presents this information to the world, I'm pretty sure we will lose US political support for confronting their dominant religion in this way."

"Good point, David. The Prime Minister is tied up today with plans for Mitt Romney's visit on the 29th, but when the dust settles, I'll touch base with him and let you know his take on it," Shulman agreed.

"I'd like to get back to your earlier concern about securing the scroll until it arrives at the Authority," Katz said while passing a photo around. "This man has been stalking Gaston and Herzog for about two weeks. His name is Sebastian Philippe. He's a French Catholic and apparently obsessed with the scroll. Herzog called me from Ben-Gurion this morning, just before they departed Tel Aviv, to inform me he was at the airport. I'm guessing he is still in Israel, so be on the look-out for him. If he followed Herzog to Israel, he must know the Authority is involved. Herzog and Gaston believe he will stop at nothing to ensure the scroll is not made public. He represents a real threat to them and us and must be neutralized."

"Is he acting alone?" Schulman asked.

"Andrew told me Gaston believes he's engaged an American named George Wilson to help him track their moves in the US although this has not been verified. The Knights of Malta seem to be their connection; they are both members. This may be just a coincidence or may be the reason Philippe sought him out. Other than these two, we do not know if anyone else is involved," Katz reported.

"The other thing that could be of real concern from a security point of view is Iran. Herzog mentioned the thing we know all too well. Iran has been attempting to curry favor with the Vatican. Once we get involved with this thing, Iran may also.

"My plan is to send Yossi, Even and Gil to meet with the Tuguías, present the contract and retrieve the scroll. I guess my question is this – with Philippe and the possibility of Iran's involvement, do you think we should get a few members of our military to escort them?"

"That's probably a good idea. Why don't you finalize the logistics of this thing and get back to me with your recommendations? I'll take it from there. Anything else?" Schulman asked as he studied the faces in the room.

"So, we're all in agreement then?" he said looking around the table.

Everyone nodded in agreement.

"Good. I'll prepare a letter notifying the Tuguías that the antiquity they possess is of national value to Israel and have our lawyers draw up the contract as discussed. Let's keep a tight lid on this. David, make sure the people you contact do as well."

"Eli, I'll follow up with Herzog and Miller and let them know what we decided," Katz said.

"Okay, please keep me informed."

WASHINGTON, DC - THE SAME DAY, 6:11 P.M. EDT

Debra's phone indicated multiple emails waiting for her attention. One was from Amir Katz. It read, "Debra, please have Andy check his phone messages. I left you a message." She asked to borrow Andy's phone. A voice mail message from country code 972 was among the others. She listened and became excited by its content. She returned his phone and picked up hers once again.

She pressed the screen for her favorite contacts. "Hey, Renee, we just landed. Andy got a call from Katz while in route. Really promising. … Yeah, okay, we'll be at Stan's place in about forty-five minutes. Andy knows the way.

* * *

George had staked out a position in the garage of National Airport waiting for Debra and Andy to appear. *So that's what Debra looks like,* George thought, *and there's the jerk, arm in arm with her. Wonder what that's all about? I bet he poked her while they were away. Can't wait to tell Renee her good friend slept with a member of the gestapo. Wonder if she hit up her Congressman for some birth control pills before she left?"* He followed them to Stan's condo, parked in front of Oronoco Bay and turned on the receivers.

"Hi guys," Debra said, almost giddy to be there. "Great trip. Lots to tell you, not the least of which is the news that Andy and I really enjoyed each other's company while we were away."

"Yeah, can you two do that later?" Andy suggested.

"I knew he poked her," George muttered. "Damn him!"

"The meeting went really well with Katz and ..."

"Excuse me, Debra," Andy interrupted and passed them a note: "Stan, I'm worried your condo may be bugged. Why don't we go onto the terrace?"

They opened the door to the terrace and heard the squeal of tires. Renee spotted a red BMW convertible race away from the curb and pass under a streetlamp. In the shadows and nearly one hundred yards away she could not clearly see the driver's face. "That looked like George's car," she said. "I haven't seen him in a while. I thought he had dropped the whole stalking thing with the threat of a protective order and what it might do to his career. Let's walk over to the park and take a look."

The smell of burnt rubber still hung in the air when they arrived. The filter end of two Marlboro cigarettes lay next to the tire marks on the pavement. "George's brand of cigarettes. That must have been him just now," she said.

"I'm guessing you're right," Andy began. "If so, that solves one mystery. Sebastian followed Debra and me to Israel. We saw him at the airport this morning, but we were careful not to let him know he had been spotted. I didn't know how he knew we were there, but there he was. Someone is monitoring our every move. It would seem that someone is George. We have to assume he's involved and treat this like the dangerous mission it very well could be. I'll have some guys from the office come by tomorrow and sweep the place for any bugs. Any place else they should check?"

"You probably should check Renee's apartment as well." Stan said. "I'm not too worried about my office or Renee's office. Plus, I don't want to arouse suspicion at work. After you check them out, we'll limit our conversation to those places plus your office, Andy. Debra, did Sebastian ever find out where you lived?"

"No, I don't think so, but by now he must know where I work."

"So, okay then, we'll limit our conversation to your apartment. We don't know if he has any U.N. connections. You'll need to check your luggage and clothes from your trip as well," Stan concluded.

"I want you to listen to this voice mail, individually; I don't want to put it on speaker." Andy said passing his phone to Renee.

"Hello, Debra, this is Amir Katz. I assume this phone is secure as Andrew indicated. Going forward, we need to treat all of our communications in a secure manner. Things went well with Director Schulman this morning. He assembled a team of the right people for discussion and everyone's on board in concept.

"Several things are at issue, however. First, there is concern about a potential Christian revolt if the scroll turns out to be a real thing. It may result in political fallout for Israel from the US. Schulman's going to work through this with the Prime Minister and will get his take on this.

"Second, the head of our lobbying team indicated he needs a week to coordinate all the parties here and secure enough promised votes for Katz to proceed. Meanwhile the Director is working up the contract, so we'll have it if we decide it's a go.

"And third, and this is my biggest concern at the moment, the scroll needs to get out of France, assuming that's where the Tuguía brothers are hiding it, and into our borders. We need control before we're committed to the deal.

"We're tentatively targeting August 9th as the day of the exchange so plan accordingly.

"I informed the boss about your call this morning. Before you spotted the stalker in Tel Aviv, I had planned to have two of my security guys accompany one of our archeologists, but now Shulman and I think it may be necessary to have more fire power around them. We're working on that … possibly the Israeli military or the French Police, but not sure at the moment.

"Please get back to me at the number I gave you this morning and let me know who will join us from your end, and specifically if Andrew can come – we'll need all the help we can get, I'm afraid. Also, please check in with Miguel and see if he will tell you generally where the scroll is hidden. I need to know this for security planning. This is not going to be easy. Good luck."

Stan's turn was next. After hearing the recording he said, "Think I'll give Miguel a call now. See what I can find out."

"So what do you think about being involved, Andy?" Renee asked.

"Probably a good idea. We need to hear what Katz comes up with and then I can fill in the holes or offer a suggestion or two. Since Stan and Renee live in DC, this would logically fall in my jurisdiction. Lots to do. First, I need to get in touch with our Ambassador to France to have the French government invite me to get involved, get the Director to treat the scroll's transfer as a potential terrorist threat, grant me authority to protect US citizens overseas, set up a case file and find a way to keep this classified. I'm on it."

Stan was able to make contact. "Yes, Miguel we need to let you know what's going on. Remember the number we gave you for Andy's phone? … No, stop, don't repeat it. Just go to a telephone you know is completely secure and dial it. Make sure you're in a secure place as well … maybe outside. Go now. I'll wait," Stan directed.

A few moments later Andy's phone rang. "Just a minute; I'll put him on."

"Miguel, this is Stan. We have a security breach on this side of the Atlantic. We're convinced it's a man named George Wilson. Tell your brother. You might have a breach there as well. In the future only call this number if you need to and I need a secure number where I can contact you. … Okay, when you get a new phone number call me back. And only call from a secure location. Now here is what's going on …" Stan discussed Katz's call while the other three listened to his side of the conversation.

"Don't forget to ask him where the scroll is hidden," Renee said.

Nodding, Stan asked, "Listen, Miguel, Katz is working up the logistics for the exchange now and needs to plan for security. Not sure at this point what steps will be taken, but he needs to know generally where the scroll is hidden so he can plan for everyone's protection. … Okay, then North Central France. He'll work out the specific details and let both of us know. The exchange is tentatively scheduled for August 9th if all goes as planned. Andy, Debra, Katz and his delegation will be at CDG airport on the 6th at 9:30 to brief you and your brother on the details face to face. I'll call you later."

"Hand me the phone, please," Debra said, "I need to call Katz."

"So what did he say?" Renee asked.

"He seemed really encouraged by the news and hopeful everything will work out for the Mandaeans. Also, he was grateful for Katz's focus on security and was forthcoming with the general location. He plans to get another cellphone right away and call us back tomorrow," Stan reported.

Debra left a voice mail for Katz. "Hello. This is Debra Herzog. Yes, we got your message. And yes, this is a secure line. Sorry for the late call, but we just spotted George Wilson spying on Stan's condo. This confirms what Andy told you on Friday. Also, the scroll is located in North Central France, probably near Paris, I suspect. Andy and I will return but I'm not sure who else at the moment. I'll let you know. As soon as you work up your security plan, please let us know. Andy could be of help. Thanks. Talk to you later."

"Let's go, Andy," Debra insisted. "I'm exhausted."

"Okay, one minute more. So, Stan, how about a game of golf on Saturday?" Andy asked. "I have something I need to talk with you about."

"Sure, sounds good."

"My club or yours?" Andy yawned.

"Why don't we go to mine?" Stan suggested. "I'm going to terminate my membership soon so I want to get as much play in as I can before I do."

Stan's family's wealth and political influence in Washington had provided him with an invitation and opportunity to join the prestigious

Burning Tree Golf and Country Club in Bethesda. Renee did not find favor with its male-only policy and occasionally told him so.

"Okay, so what's with the face, Renee?"

"You know how I feel about their exclusionary policy."

"I know. I know. And I did promise to resign after we get married, but for now the $75,000 initiation fee is just a little hard to walk away from. It's really a great club, and it may change in the future. … You know there are rumors Augusta may soon take the plunge. Smile, times are changing."

CHAPTER 27

BETHESDA, MARYLAND - JULY 28, 2012

"Good ball. You're probably out there about 230 yards and in the fairway for a change. Let's see. Straight shot … par 4 … 410 yards … no wind … beautiful Saturday morning … great. Only one problem; I really hate to tee off in front of everyone in the clubhouse," Andy said.

"I understand. You really do need to take some lessons. What are you now … a three handicap … give me a break!" Stan replied. "Hey nice drive! Looks like you're just shy of the 150-yard marker. So, you got lucky again, eh."

"Just like swinging a bat. No big deal. You know what they say, luck is simply when preparation meets … the other thing, can't remember. And as I said … I really do enjoy it when everyone is watchin'. Let's go."

"Hey, your guys swept the condo last Wednesday and found four bugs. They found four in Renee's apartment as well. Guess you were right about that," Stan said.

"Yeah, they told me. They checked them for fingerprints, but they were clean. I guess Sebastian and whoever's helping him know what they are doing after all. Maybe Sebastian planted them when he was in town and didn't care if you found them after he left."

"Well, maybe," Stan cautioned. "Renee is convinced George is involved, as you know. She is sure she saw his red convertible Monday night and the cigarette butts and tire marks all point in his direction. Someone's helping, but why would George risk his career with a felony? But who knows? She's likely right. She knows him pretty well and claims he's not very bright. It's like you said, we all just need to be a little more careful and keep our eyes open."

"Hey, Stan, did you catch the opening ceremony of the Olympics last night? I thought the stunt with the Queen's double parachuting into the stadium was priceless. She was such a good sport to let it unfold."

"London really did themselves proud," Stan agreed. "All of it was spectacular of course, but the thing I thought was most interesting was the pitch on Britain's National Health Service. Not only do they have universal health care, but they're so proud of it they presented it to the world as one of their major accomplishments … as a model really. Think we could ever provide universal coverage with Republican control of the House?"

"You're kidding right?" Andy quipped. "I wish we would have had it when I was growing up. My parents would have been so much better off. Yeah, not as grand as Beijing, but what the hell. What country could compete with the number of people and precision of the opening in Beijing? London's was smaller but simply a class act."

"The other thing I thought was amazing was the construction of the Aquatics Centre. About two weeks ago, in fact just before we went to Chartres, I caught a documentary about how the roof was constructed and raised in place. The gigantic structure was designed to rest on two points in the south wall and a third point on the north and span over 520 feet. The coolest part was once all of the steel trusses were lifted and fitted together, they had to raise the entire thing on hydraulic jacks about five feet to remove the temporary supports and then lower it into place. Lots of people holding their breath!"

"Speaking of Chartres, are you and Renee planning to go back? Debra pretty much volunteered me, so we're heading back on Tuesday for a few days in Paris before meeting Katz."

"Probably. Renee has it in her head she got everyone involved so she wants to see it through. We'll be alongside, I'm sure. I'll check in with her when we finish the game and have her coordinate arrangements with Debra. I have a few things to do before leaving so we'll be along a couple of days later. Hey, good par."

"Stan, I need to talk to you about something for a moment. I need some help."

"With your golf game?

"No, seriously, about a personal matter."

"Okay, hold on. … I got a bogey. Par five coming up. I need to nail the next hole. The last thing I need to do is buy you drinks when we're done. I know how much you drink. I can't afford it on my government salary."

"Look around you, man. You're telling me all of this is from your government salary? I don't think so," Andy asked.

"So what's up, my friend?"

"When Debra and I went to Israel, things got hot and heavy pretty fast."

"It sure seemed that way on Monday night. After you guys left, Renee was so excited she couldn't stop talking about what a cool couple you two were."

"That obvious, huh? It's just Debra is amazing. She's bright, good looking, self-confident, and determined. I just love the little things about her … her knowledge of baseball, for example, and her loyalty to the Mets. Now that was a strange conversation … right out of left field, so to speak. I never saw it coming. I've never felt like this before. I'm not sure where all of this is headed."

"Ah, frailty, thy name is woman … unless your name is Debra," Stan quipped. "With her confidence at least you know she can take care of herself. She wouldn't be looking to bump you off and marry your brother, like Hamlet's mother. You remember Gertie, right?"

"No seriously, I've been mulling over the idea that once all of this business with the scroll is over, I may ask for a transfer to the New York Field Office to see what might unfold between us."

"Why, I think that's great, man. What's the problem?"

"It's just this all seems pretty reckless for me. I don't do things like that. I don't even think things like that. I've got a good gig going on in DC. I'm getting some good assignments, know the turf and have built a good relationship with the Assistant Director … even to the extent he put me on special assignment to go to Israel in the first place. I'm not sure if Debra feels the same or if it's just my imagination. You and Renee seemed to hit it off right away. Hell, you even got engaged after two months. What was that like?"

"Yep, but we did put off the wedding for a year just to make sure. I don't know really how the stars aligned so fast, but they did. She seemed so vulnerable yet strong at the same time during her break-up with George. And her embarrassment and apology to me were priceless. I was attracted to her from the start. She is just so smart. Someone I can just sit with and have a conversation and neither of us has to say a word – if that makes any sense. We have so much in common, communication comes easily. And laughter … what a huge thing laughter is. That's most of it. Compatibility and laughter. They say opposites attract … well, don't believe it. I'll tell you one thing. From the little I've observed about Debra, you need to take the ambivalence out of your voice. Make a decision one way or another and go for it. She'll definitely like it if you take control. But let her think she is in control. Trust me."

"Out of the bunker in three with two putts. Par for me on number two. Say, Stan, will you mention this to Renee for me and see what she thinks? I'll start nosing around about a transfer and get a lay of the land. Hey, great putt."

"Thanks, I will. And that, my friend, is a bird. All tied up."

CHAPTER 28

WASHINGTON, DC - JULY 30, 2012

"Good afternoon, Bonnie," Stan said arriving at his office at half past three in the afternoon.

"Well, hello, Stan. Glad you could join us today. How was your morning?"

"Don't start with me. You know I have a class on Mondays and had some business to take care of after. Anything aggravating you today or do you just like to harass your boss?"

"No, nothing unusual. So why don't we just start over. Stan, how was your morning?"

"It was pretty good. Had lunch with Gerard. He couldn't seem to say enough good things about the report Renee prepared, her attitude, and the quality of her work. It was great to hear. Can't wait to share it with her tonight. He even said that because of her language proficiency and her research for him, she would be able to finish a semester early if she wanted to."

"Think she will?" Bonnie asked.

"I think so. She would not be able to attend graduation until May, but she's ready to be out of school. And that would also mean we could have a Christmas wedding. She'll be all over that."

"And your class? How was your class today?"

"Pretty good, but my students keep bugging me about the Capitol dome; like I'm not trying to do anything about it. Even they understand the importance and the iconic nature of what Congress is screwing with. This insanity is making me nuts. Anything the Senator needs? He's making another pitch to his colleagues today."

"No, I haven't heard anything."

"Well, would you please check with his staff and ask?"

"Sure … just a minute. Good afternoon, Architect of the Capitol. … Stan, you have a call on line two from Andy Miller. Something about a message from Katz." Bonnie said.

"Thanks. I'll take it in my office. … Hey Andy, what's up?"

* * *

At three in the morning, the fourth ring of Sebastian's cellphone penetrated his drunken mind and startled him into semi-consciousness. He had a splitting headache and a desire to kill whoever was at the other end of the call. As his world spun around him, he pushed his body to a seated position. He groped in the dark for the ear-splitting object on the nightstand and knocked his glass of water to the floor. Shards of glass now blocked the path to the bathroom. The unconsumed water was in his shoes. In desperation to stop the pounding in his head, he pressed the bridge of his nose with one hand and reached for the light switch with the other.

Next to him, Fra' Schmidt's naked assistant pulled the down-filled comforter over her head. "Sebastian," she said, "das telefon."

"Yeah … I … I … know, Erma." Sebastian managed to say in between hiccups

His phone displayed the name of his American partner, George Wilson. "What the 'ell … 'ell does … does he want?" he muttered to the non-responsive lump on the bed. "Yeah," Sebastian growled.

"George here. I was able to overhear Stan explain Katz's plans to Renee a little while ago."

"Do you haff any freak'n … idea of what the 'ell time it is?"

"Where are you?"

"Italy. Get … get on … on with it."

"Yeah, it's 9:00 p.m. here. I was going to wait for another four hours to call you, but I thought you would probably want to know this right away. Besides, I owe you one. You okay?"

"Yeah, I'm … I'm fine … just a little too … too much to drink."

"Here's what Katz said …"

"Good. Hold on a … a minute."

Sebastian brushed the spilled water on the nightstand onto the floor and set the phone down. He rubbed the heels of his hands into his eyeballs, attempting to clear his head. His water-soaked shoes came next so he could navigate around the glass. Carrying his phone and stumbling around the bed, he found the bathroom door, chugged a glass of water, and swallowed a deep breath to form a belch and stop his hiccups.

"You okay?" Erma murmured as her German accent, the down comforter, and her drowsy voice stole all clarity from her question.

"Yeah, I'm fine. Go back to sleep. Hey George, how did you hear them anyway? I thought the FBI would have swept for the bugs by now."

"They did. But after the agents left, I broke back in and planted another one – actually, three in the condo and another on the terrace this time. Just like you taught me. I didn't bother with Renee's apartment; she's never there anymore. I followed Stan home after work today and listened to him tell Renee about Katz's updates. He spilled his guts, 'cause the place had just been swept. But I'm in control, again. I even rented a new blue sedan so I wouldn't be so easy to spot," George reported.

He began describing what he had learned from his recent neophyte reconnaissance.

"Hold on. Give me a moment to get settled." Sebastian said sitting down at the hotel desk to scribble a few notes. "Okay, go ahead."

- Exchange confirmed to be August 9th, in the morning
- North Central France, probably near Paris
- Introductory meeting among Miguel, Rafael, Andy, Debra, Katz, and the Israeli delegation set: CDG Airport August 6th, 9:30 a.m.
- Israel's Prime Minister is on board for now
- Herzog and Miller arriving in Paris on Saturday, August 4th, staying at the Coachman on Rue Jean Rey
- Gaston and Parker will follow later. Unsure of date.

"Thanks. I'll move the info up the line after I get some sleep. Keep me posted on anything further. Check your watch next time!"

"Okay, I will. Take care of yourself. Hey, where in Italy are you?"

"Rome," Sebastian answered.

"Thought so. Say hello to Schmidt and the Colonel for me. Talk to you later."

* * *

George planned to graduate from Law School, then run for Congress from the 6th Congressional District of South Carolina. His hometown of Sumter and surrounding counties needed his brand of politics. His election would mean he would defeat the single Democratic Congressman from the state. The current congressman was just not in sync with the rest of SC's delegation. As a Tea Party advocate, George knew he would be. He'd made the rounds on Capitol Hill. He'd get the delegation's support and the Republican National Committee's support and he'd win, he was sure of it. He was now more confident than ever, since Sebastian promised to bring adequate funding from Rome and organize an army of knights to work on his behalf.

He no longer had to concern himself with nickels and dimes, or report the source of funding – the Citizens United case saw to that. What he needed was a sugar daddy and he had one in the Colonel. All the Colonel needed to do was funnel money through an American and then to George. No problem. As long as he kept doing a great job for him, Sebastian would make it happen. He promised. George continued his surveillance from his parked office to uphold his end of the bargain. That was the deal.

* * *

"So, what do you want to do about the trip?" Stan asked.

"I don't see we have a choice. We've got to go. I made arrangements to join Debra and Andy in Paris at the Coachman on Rue Jean Rey on Monday night, the 6th, after their meeting with Katz," Renee said. "We can have a couple of days together in Paris before the scroll is transferred."

"No, we really do have a choice. I've got a bad feeling about all of this. We don't know what Sebastian is up to or who may be with him. George, of course, but he's of little consequence."

As he listened George snarled to himself, "Little consequence, my ass! We'll see how inconsequential I've been on the 9th. Just keep deluding yourselves."

"Well, I have to go. You can stay here. I started this mess. Miguel trusted me. I've got to see it through."

"That's what I thought you'd say. And don't be so self-righteous. If you're going then of course I'm going."

"Stan, are you really worried about this? Katz seems to have everything handled."

"You bet I am. Let's see ... transporting a 2,000-year-old scroll that could turn the entire Christian world upside down from somewhere in France to the airport, what could possibly go wrong? Do you think the Church will allow it to happen? I don't think Katz is even remotely close to understanding the history of the Catholic Church. They'll stop at nothing to control this outcome. Count on it. Katz said the French government would not allow the Israeli military to escort them, but offered them four French policemen instead."

"Do you think the Iranians have gotten involved? Maybe they're doing the Church's bidding," Renee asked.

"I asked Andy about that at golf on Saturday. A week or so ago he had a friend in the CIA start nosing around to see what he could come up with. So far, nothing. Andy doesn't think they're in the loop – at least for now. There's something else Andy told me on Saturday."

"Oh yeah, what's that?"

"I know it's a strange time to mention this, but Andy has a thing for Debra."

"A thing? What's a thing?"

I knew it, George thought. *The jerk did poke her. Back to the Iranians again? Come-on. Jesus! It's just a few of us doing our thing for Christ and his Church.*

"You know a thing ... like you were saying Monday night. He's head over heels in love with her. He's so confused he can barely function. He's not sure what his next move will be, but he's checking out a possible transfer to the New York Field Office. He wanted me to ask you if you thought he was imagining all of this or if maybe Debra, you know, has a thing for him as well? So what do you think?"

"I'm pretty sure she does. She seems to have changed a bit since their trip, but I'll ask her when I call her in the morning."

"No, no, don't ask her! He was just interested in your opinion."

"Come on, Stan, give me some credit. I'm not going to just come right out and ask her. I'll be subtle. Nose around a bit. This is too exciting to leave it alone."

* * *

The streetlight provided some illumination for George as he scribbled

Friday, July 30th. RE: Stan Parker, Renee Gaston and Amir Katz

Able to bug Stan's condo again after he and Renee went to work on Thursday. Notified Sebastian this evening about the meeting at CDG Airport with the Israeli delegation on the 6th with Andy and Debra, the Tuguía brothers and the Israeli delegation. New relationship between Andy and Debra. May be a point of leverage if needed. Need to update Sebastian about the police escort and that Renee and Stan will join them on the 6th.

CHAPTER 29

ROME, ITALY - THIRTY-TWO YEARS EARLIER, 1980

Lieutenant Benito Sordi and Second Lieutenant Alberto Moritti transferred from a mechanized outfit in Milan to Rome and Military Intelligence when the Italian Army reorganized in 1975. They received training in clandestine operations. This preparation led them to join with other right-wing sympathizers from the Second World War referred to as the stay-behinds: code name, Operation Gladio.

Fourteen European countries were secretly engaged in this Cold War operation. Their goal was twofold – to provide intelligence gathering through the various European secret service organizations in coordination with the CIA and the British MI6, and to withstand a possible Soviet invasion until further military build-up could occur.

After their training in London, three young unemployed civilians – Guy Romano, a prior Italian security guard, Daryl Rousseau, a newly released pilot from the French Air Force, and Father Pierre Dubois, a freshly minted French priest – joined Sordi and Moritti in Rome. Fighting for a common purpose and watching each other's backs for the three grueling months of training resulted in the five becoming the closest of friends. The bond that initially existed among the five remained strong through the years, as with most men who rely on one another for their lives. But there was something more. They all were devout Catholics and members of the Knights of Malta. With that came an even stronger bond through God, the Church and their brotherhood.

The expected invasion never came. Operation Gladio slowly morphed into a right-wing organization used to overturn the growing influence of the Communist Party in Europe, especially in Italy. Four of the friends were right wing zealots and joined with others to fight Italy's changing politics. The fifth, Father Dubois, was equally dedicated to the movement, but lacked the stomach for what was now happening.

Bombings and gangland style shootings of their own countrymen seemed to be the new normal in a covert war waged to stop the Communist influence.

Things were improving as the alliance between the right wing Christian Democratic Party and the Italian Communist Party started to develop. Without warning, the hope splintered in 1978 when the Red Brigades murdered the right-wing leader. But the final act of violence came August 2, 1980.

* * *

"In the name of the Father, and of the Son, and of the Holy Spirit. Bless me Father for I have sinned." Crossing himself, Benito Sordi began his confession to Father Dubois. "It has been two months since my last confession. Father, last Sunday a time-bomb exploded in the waiting room of Bologna's Central Station. Being summer, the air-conditioned room was full of people. The explosion destroyed most of the building. Father, the roof of the waiting room collapsed, killing 85 people and wounding 200 more."

"I know of this, Benito," Dubois said. "What is this to you?"

"The very next day, the Communist press attributed the massacre to the neo-fascists. Later, the government said the right-wing terrorists prefer massacres because they promote panic and confusion. Rumors regarding the types of explosives used, Comp B and TNT, are pointing to the military.

"Father, I have been in a few skirmishes over time, but nothing of this magnitude. My difficulty is, I know who is responsible. My confession to God and you is that I lied when questioned. Three high ranking officers, my superiors in military intelligence, are now purposefully misdirecting the investigation away from their right-wing comrades and implicating others. I cannot now, nor can I ever, reveal the names of these men. Even so, I hold to the truth that the conservative right is on the side of God," Sordi rationalized. "Father, I am sorry for these and all the sins of my past life."

"Benito, for the sin of lying, your penance shall be to pray at the third station of the cross asking forgiveness from our Lord and Savior. Reflect on the story of Jesus falling to the ground because of the heavy cross burdened with the weight of your sins and those of others. You can relieve His burden by always telling the truth. I will offer absolution for the sin of lying, but your silence has contributed to the sins of the three you protect. For this sin and for your future sins of withholding what you now know, I cannot offer you absolution. Rather, you must find your own measure of penance on a scale worthy of eighty-five of God's children and seek absolution after reconciling these deaths."

"Yes, Father. My God, I am sorry for my sins with all my heart. In choosing to do wrong and failing to do good I have sinned against you whom I should love above all things. With your help I firmly intend to do penance, to sin no more, and to avoid whatever leads me to sin. Amen," Sordi offered.

"God the Father of mercies, through the death and resurrection of His Son has reconciled the world to himself and sent the Holy Spirit among us for the forgiveness of sins; through the ministry of the Church may God give you pardon and peace. I absolve you from your sin in the name of the Father, and of the Son, and of the Holy Spirit. Your sin of lying is truly forgiven, Go in Peace," Dubois concluded. "Thanks be to God."

The sanctity of the confessional now over, the two spoke candidly once more as friends.

"Benito, this latest attack … well, it is all I can endure. I'm sorry to leave you and the others now, but I must return to France and minister to those who are receptive to Jesus' teachings."

"I understand, Father. I will miss you. You have been a good friend. Thank you for hearing my confession today. Perhaps our paths will cross again one day."

ONE YEAR LATER

Seven weeks after President Reagan was shot by a deranged gunman in Washington, it happened once again to another world leader. This time it was the Pope. Gunned down in the Vatican City.

"Open his cell door," ordered First Captain Benito Sordi of the Italian Military and Secret Service Agency, commonly known as the SISMI.

The sergeant standing guard at the Rome prison complied with the order, revealing a small man of Turkish origin. A bruised cheek and split lip marked the face of a man held for the attempted assassination of Pope Jean Paul II.

"Stand up. You wanted to see us?" said Captain Alberto Moretti, Sordi's best friend and comrade.

"You clearly did not act alone. We are here again because we are told you are ready to confess and save yourself the misery of all of those unnecessary beatings. I'm going to ask you once again, who planned the assassination attempt? Who are your accomplices?" Sordi demanded.

It was late afternoon when John Paul did the thing he and his flock enjoyed the most – connecting with each other. Standing in his open, specially designed, white Jeep, he reached to touch the children being raised by their parents to receive his blessing. He waved and bent over the side to touch as many hands and heads as his slow-moving vehicle would allow. Suddenly, four gunshots rang out from the crowd.

The Pope stood immobile for a second or two, then fell to the seat of his jeep and into the arms of his private secretary. The crowd was chaotic … crying … screaming … running toward the Pope in anguish. Why would anyone shoot His Holiness? Almost immediately, Daryl Rousseau and Guy Romano and six other uniformed police officers of the Central Security Office surrounded him. He was hit, but would soon recover.

Rousseau and his detail detained a 23-year-old man and recovered a nine caliber pistol from the pavement. The gunman said he acted alone.

"So you no longer claim to have acted alone?" Sordi asked.

"No, I had an accomplice with me. We were to be paid by a Bulgarian to do this thing."

"Why?" Moretti asked.

After a long period of silence, the accused said, "I join with my Communists brothers in the Popular Front for the Liberation of Palestine and oppose the two-state solution as proposed. Israel must be totally destroyed. They have no right to exist, especially in Jerusalem. The Pope weighs into political matters in Moscow and Israel, and places and things where he has no business. Bulgaria is our ally in this fight to control our destiny. They sent me to Syria and paid for my training there and with that came the expectation to follow through with this assignment."

"What is the name of this Bulgarian?"

The Turk remained quiet, and finally said, "I do not know. Our plan was to escape and meet at the Bulgarian Embassy here in Rome after the shooting. There I was to receive the money."

"Anything else?"

"No."

"I will pass along your latest claim. There will be others who will follow me in due course. I suggest you and your attorney settle on a single story before your trial."

Sordi reported the latest information to Inspector General Luca Favero, head of the Central Security Office of Vatican City.

"That's a lie!" said Favero, the Pope's bodyguard and the man responsible for bringing the Pope's assailant to justice.

"Why? What do you mean?" Moretti asked.

"He indicated two days ago he was a member of the Popular Front, but they have denied any ties to him. He's not a Communist."

"Why did he claim to be in the Popular Front? What did he hope to gain?"

"Disinformation … to throw us off of the track. Another story indicates that he's a member of the neo-fascist Grey Wolves from Turkey. More disinformation. The real story that is beginning to surface involves Boris Volkov and the KGB."

"Are you hearing Volkov was directly responsible for the attempted assassination?" Moretti asked.

"No," Favero abruptly said. "All of this is conjecture at this point, but we're hearing the KGB instructed the Bulgarian Secret Service to carry out the mission because of the Pope's support of Poland's Solidarity movement. About a year before his imprisonment in Turkey, our shooter had apparently made several trips to Bulgaria in a drug smuggling operation to Western Europe."

"He was in prison in Turkey?" Sordi followed up.

"Yeah, but not for the drugs. He was found guilty of murdering a journalist in 1979 and sentenced to life in prison," Favero said. "After serving only six months, he escaped and returned to Bulgaria. Apparently, he was going to be paid a substantial amount of money for the assassination. He has no ideological interest in what he did. He is just a scum sucking mercenary."

"Have things settled down with the announcement of the Pope's improved condition?" Sordi asked.

"A little, but this whole ordeal has shaken the department pretty hard. One of our officers has already resigned for his inability to keep the Pope safe. It's a major blow for us. Not only was he an excellent pilot for the Pontiff during John Paul's trips abroad, he also serves in a protection detail when the Pope is at the Vatican. In fact, you know the guy."

"Who?" Sordi asked.

"Daryl Rousseau turned in his badge and gun and said he had to get away from Rome and the memory of his failure. I understand he plans to return to Paris."

"And Guy Romano? Remember I recommended him at the same time."

"No. He's still with us."

"That must be a terrible loss. Daryl is a good friend of both Captain Moretti and me. We all go back a long ways. I'll see if I can catch up to him before he leaves the city. Thanks for telling me. I'll let you know if he says anything else."

In the outer chamber Sordi turned to his friend and said, "Alberto, Inspector General Favero still seems to be in the dark. Don't forget the Grey Wolves grew out of the stay-behinds from Turkey associated with Operation Gladio. If our prisoner is connected to the Grey Wolves, Favero must never tie this thing directly to them. Favero needs to continue to protect the Pope at all costs and not join our world of politics. All roads must lead back to Moscow and away from our comrades on the right."

CHAPTER 30

ROME, ITALY - JULY 31, 2012

Thirty-two years after the massacre in the Bologna railway station, retired Colonel Benito Sordi started planning his penance. Sebastian brought him the opportunity for his road to salvation.

The final trial and 1995 sentencing of his superiors had relieved Sordi of the burden of having to identify those responsible for "… the most criminal enterprise that has ever taken place in Italy," according to the Italian President. Constantly maintaining their innocence, those convicted and sentenced to life in prison were neo-fascists leaders – a former general and deputy director of Italy's military intelligence agency.

Now all that remained was for Sordi to do his penance. Capturing the Papal-condemning-scroll and embedding it safely within the Vatican Archives would be the sort of penance worthy of withholding information on eighty-five deaths.

His cellphone startled him from his dream of redemption and return to God's grace. "Hello, this is Colonel Sordi. … Yes, Sebastian. … Okay, meet me at headquarters about 10:30 this morning."

Sebastian arrived fifteen minutes early and entered the office of a woman he had left only a few hours before. He showed complete indifference toward her not wanting to blow her cover and risk his opportunity to gain further insight into the Knights.

"Colonel Sordi will be right down," Erma volunteered after ringing Fra' Schmidt.

"Thank you," Sebastian said coldly as he gave her a wink.

"Ah, there you are, my boy," Benito said. "Let's take a walk."

Benito led Sebastian out to the bustling streets of Rome. "So, tell me, boy, what have you found out?"

"George reported to me the exchange is confirmed to take place next week … on August 9th to be precise. The scroll is currently located in North Central France, probably near Paris. Katz is planning for additional security, but found he is unable to bring Israeli military into France. He was offered four police officers for security purposes. Finally, there's a preliminary meeting among the parties planned for 9:30 a.m., August 6th at Charles de Gaulle Airport."

"Good work. Thank you. Why don't you head back to France for now, but plan on being back to meet with me and my comrades on August 7th," Sordi directed.

Sebastian returned to Via Dei Condotti 68 to say his good-byes to Erma. Sordi walked in the opposite direction.

"Hello, Pierre. Yeah, this is Benito. Your call last month started me wondering if you have kept up with Daryl Rousseau over the years. … I thought maybe you had. I saw him a few years ago in Paris. He told me he had gone to work with the Police Nationale. I tried contacting him just now at the Central Directorate of Public Security, but he is no longer there. Do you know how to get in touch with him? … Oh, good, that's even better. … Never mind, thanks. Listen, one final thing … if something should ever happen to me, contact Cardinal Ricci. He'll know what to do. … No, not at all. I'm just saying 'if'. I'll talk to you later. Thanks again, Pierre."

* * *

"Bonjour, Service de Protection des Hautes Personnalités."

"Bonjour, je m'appelle Benito Sordi. Parlez-vous Anglais?"

"Certainly. How may I help you?"

"Do you have an officer by the name of Daryl Rousseau?"

"Yes. Capitaine Daryl Rousseau."

"Would you connect me, please?"

"Bonjour, Capitaine Rousseau."

"Hello, Daryl. This is me, Benito Sordi."

"Benito. Well, this is a surprise. It's been what … three years?"

"I know. Keeps going by faster and faster. When did you transfer?"

"About two years ago."

"What do you do now?"

"We're responsible for protecting French and foreign dignitaries traveling in France. Why?"

"I thought so. Before contacting Pierre, I thought you were with Public Security. Your transfer will make all of this so much easier. Here's what I need you to do. Find yourself a secure phone, one where you can speak freely, and call me back on my cellphone," he said giving him his phone number.

After a few minutes Daryl had called back. "Okay, I'm outside on my cell. Make all of what easier? What can I help you with, Benito?"

"Daryl, what I'm about to tell you can go no further. Do you remember the day John Paul was shot?"

"Of course I do. It was the worst day of my life. It was the reason I resigned from the corps."

"I know. I want you to remember how you felt that day. You said you would never forgive yourself until you were able to truly glorify God and seek his forgiveness. That's how I felt after the Bologna massacre."

"Yes, I'm sure. I heard the story of Bologna. What does that have to do with Jean Paul? With me?"

"Have you?"

"Have I what?"

"Have you forgiven yourself yet?

"No. The whole thing still depresses me every time I think about it. The Pope may have been killed … on my watch. What's this all about, Benito?"

"I just may have the opportunity you've been waiting for. I can take an Air France flight to Paris this afternoon getting me there at 4:45. I'll land at Terminal 2 B. Can you meet me at the airport's Novotel check-in desk at six?"

"Can't you tell me more, now?

"No. I'd rather tell you this in person."

"Well … okay then. See you there at six. Au revoir."

* * *

"Bonjour, my friend," Sordi said as he returned to the check-in desk to greet his old friend. "Let's go to my suite where we can have some privacy. I have arranged for room service."

"So when's the last time you've seen Guy and Alberto?"

"It's probably been two years ago. Why? Benito, what's going on?"

"Hang on. We're almost there."

Opening the door to his suite, Sordi presented a fairly modest, almost austere, suite of three rooms, but a secure environment for their clandestine business plans. Dinner was waiting on a rolling table.

"I'm planning to get the gang back together soon," Sordi began. "The only exception is I'm leaving Dubois completely out of it as well as Fra' Schmidt and the Order."

"Out of what?"

"I'm getting to that. How are things going for you in your job?"

"Okay … well … to tell you the truth … not so good. My boss, Général Dupont, is constantly up my ass about something or another and I'm facing retirement soon with little savings and just a small pension. How about you?"

"I'm doing okay. Living on my army retirement and doing a few things for Fra' Schmidt ever so often. You look good … looks like you're still in good shape. Listen, I need to think I can trust you with what I'm about to tell you. Even if you decide not to join us, you can never make this public. Can I trust you?"

"I suppose so, unless you've decided to shoot the Pope or burn down the Basilica."

"No, far from it, but it may prove to be just as dangerous. About a month ago I learned that a 2,000 year old scroll was on the market. A pair of brothers, Rafael and Miguel Tuguía, currently have the scroll. They plan to sell it to the Israeli Antiquities Authority next week and transport it back to Israel."

"There was some mention of a few Israeli dignitaries coming to France on the 9th during our briefing yesterday. Dupont put out an email this afternoon asking for four volunteers. It's going to be a strange mission from what I hear. So, what about the scroll?" Rousseau asked.

"That's why we're here. The scroll was written by James the Righteous in the 5th decade. Dubois is trying to secure a document from Rafael for us by peaceful means, but I had to lie to him to make sure he was not in the loop."

"Lie to him about what?"

"Hold on. I'm getting there. He doesn't know the document is a 2,000-year-old scroll or what it says. I told him it was a document that we were interested in, but not to worry. Dubois is done and I'm letting him off the hook. Noelle Martine, Dubois' assistant, befriended one of the scroll's owners, a Rafael Tuguía. She informed Dubois that Tuguía is committed to handing the document over to the Israeli authorities. She does not know what he has either, but seems like she wants to help him according to Dubois. There's some debate about the scroll's authenticity, but I'm absolutely certain it is real, or I wouldn't be asking you this."

"Asking me what? That is great news about the scroll, right? The more we learn about the history of the Church, the better it is, right?"

"Not this time, Daryl. This time … unlike the Dead Sea Scrolls or the Nagamati Gospels … this time it will completely destroy the Church. I am told the scroll was translated to say Jesus chose Mary Magdalene and her brother, Lazarus, to lead the Church of Jerusalem after his death, not Peter. Everything the Gospels and Paul's writings say is potentially called into question – including his selection of Peter to head our Church. This means the entire line of Popes who succeeded Peter will be discredited and our beloved Church with it. Christianity as we know it could be undone. Imagine the catastrophic events that could ensue!"

"Hold on. Do you have any doubt about what you're saying? Is there any chance the scroll is a fake?" Rousseau asked in earnest.

"None. The Order has kept a close watch on the Tuguía brothers for a long time. Schmidt's grandfather fought with Franco against the liberal rebellion. He discovered that their father had stolen something from the cathedral. This information was passed down through the Order not knowing what it was, just wanting it back for the Church. Schmidt still doesn't know, nor am I going to tell him, but I recently found out the thing stolen was the scroll. But I'll ask you, even if there is a slight chance of it being a fake, do you want to take the chance it's not?"

"So what do you plan to do, Benito?"

"Steal it, by force if necessary, and turn it over to the Vatican. Guy and Alberto are on board with me. And there's another fellow involved, actually two, a Frenchman named Sebastian Philippe and an American, George Wilson. Both are members of the Order. George has been Sebastian's eyes and ears, tracking the Americans who were first approached by the Tuguía brothers. Wilson will remain in the States, but there are four of us ready to do the right thing for God and the Church. Will you be the fifth? Are you with us?" Sordi asked, anticipating a positive response. … "Well, are you with us or not?" Sordi pushed.

"Just … just … a minute! This is a lot to process. I'm on the other side of the law … remember?"

"But this is God's law, not man's."

"Yes, I know, but still … give me a minute!"

"I've also been in touch with Cardinal Ricci in Rome. Remember, he was our priest when we first arrived in Rome after England … he gave Pierre his first job. He's now a Cardinal, and the Cardinal Vicar to boot reporting directly to the Pope. Can you believe it? Anyway, I let him in on what was at stake and what we're planning … almost. I promised him our plan does not involve hurting anyone. He was shocked of course by the news, but thankful for our initiative. He is confident if we're successful in our mission he could round up the equivalent of what they are asking for the scroll, twenty-five million US dollars. That's a million for George and nearly five million for each of us just to sweeten the deal. So what about it … are you in?" Sordi pressed once more.

"Okay … sure. Let's do this thing. We're all still bachelors, right? No ties to family … nothing to lose right? Everything to gain!"

"You do understand that, in spite of what I told Ricci, there may be some bloodshed, right?"

"Yeah, I know."

"Now here's what I need you to do. Tomorrow morning you need to volunteer for the assignment, first thing. I'm departing Paris this evening on the nine-ten flight. I should be back in Rome around 11:30. Give me a call and let me know how it's shaping up. You need to be our mole going forward."

"Maybe volunteering will even win me a few points with the boss."

"Well, maybe … but not if you're found out … so be careful. Why don't we go downstairs and have drink and toast to our new fight … just like the old days in Gladio?"

CHAPTER 31

PARIS, FRANCE - AUGUST 9, 2012

Renee returned to France to fulfill a promise she had made to two strangers three weeks before. The past two days had been a wonderful time for the two couples to enjoy the celebration of food, wine and life in the city of lights. For them the normal tourist attractions took a backseat to simply strolling through the lively, flower-filled outdoor markets or stopping at the tempting bakeries and tiny shops. Anything to distract their minds.

The early morning hour closed in on her as Renee's thoughts grew dark. Stan and Andy had departed for Orléans to meet with the security detail on the day agreed upon. Debra was in a nearby room. It seemed like miles away. Restless and unable to sleep, Renee now lay in an empty bed alone and afraid.

A loud knock startled her fully awake.

"One minute," Renee said slipping on her robe.

A tall, thin, grey-haired man wearing a black suit and a clerical collar greeted her at the door.

"Father Dubois, why are you here?"

"Bishops' conference on priest recruitment," he said handing her a sealed envelope. "A note from a friend. I hope you know what you are doing." He turned and walked away without another word.

Tuesday, August 7th

My Dearest Renee,

Marie is so very proud of you. When you were due to arrive she told everyone about your life at Georgetown and impending marriage to the Architect of the Capitol. She is so excited and happy for you.

When Sebastian heard that you were returning to Albi in June, he became obsessed with you. He was deranged and would not let it go. He even told Fr. Dubois to plan for a fall wedding. At the same time Rafael asked if I knew anyone who had the stature to introduce his revelation to the world. I immediately thought of you. It was as if Asherah reached down from heaven and guided you to me to Rafael. Renee, you should know that I only tried to help you. Please forgive me for not telling you, but I could not. Sebastian found out that I was helping Rafael and threatened to harm your parents if I warned you. I knew he was still in love with you and would not hurt you.

Whatever Rafael's plans may be, Renee, I know that you are the right person to bring Asherah and Mary to the world's attention.

Be careful. God be with you. As ever, Noelle

ORLÉANS – LATER THAT MORNING

Miguel joined Stan as he nervously paced the ambulatory of the Cathedral of St. Croix. "Good morning, Stan," Miguel began, "where are the ladies?"

"Andy and I thought it best to leave them back in Paris for the day," Stan responded.

"To tell you the truth I'm not sure why I'm even here. As a boy I got to be pretty good at shooting skeet, but that's about it. If we have some clay pigeons thrown at us today, I can be helpful, but beyond that I'm not sure what I can contribute. Andy wanted me to come along, so here I am."

"I had hoped to see Renee once more, but it's probably best she's not involved today. Please thank her and give her my best when you see her again," Miguel said. "I do pray nothing will happen to us while en route."

"You and me both."

Off in the distance, Stan could hear Andy and the police talk about being ready for the danger that may lie ahead. Stan's breaths grew shallow and more frequent. His mind began to wander, imagining the most horrific things that could result from today's action, even his death. Pacing the floor once again, Miguel heard him mutter, "What the hell am I doing here?"

Miguel sensed the need to bring Stan back into the moment and took the conversation in another direction. "Stan, I assume that Renee told you about the Path of Initiation and the reason she came to Chartres."

"Yes of course."

"Chartres was the fourth stop along the path. Compostela was the first, Toulouse was the second and Orléans was the third before going to Chartres," Miguel said. "Here, at the Cathedral of St. Croix, once a candidate gained sufficient strength and moral conviction to represent good against evil, he was considered a warrior and knighted."

"Miguel, are you trying to tell me something?"

"Oh, no, never," Miguel said with a smile. "I would not presume to do such a thing."

"Well, okay," Stan said, now taking deeper breaths to calm his nerves."

"I just think this cathedral is a wonderful place to launch the revelation of Asherah and Mary Magdalene, that's all. If you take something else from it, so much the better," Miguel challenged.

"Well, I missed the first two stops so I doubt I will become a warrior with this morning's visit."

"Fair enough. Return one day and take the entire Path of Initiation. Maybe you will then."

Miguel decided to change the subject.

"Isn't this statue of John the Baptist exquisite?" Miguel asked kissing the hand holding the scallop shell. "It's the shell that is so telling. It links John directly to Santiago de Compostela and James the Righteous. It symbolizes the beliefs and love for Mary and John that the Templars held."

"Did the Templars build St. Croix?" Stan asked, now thinking about the architecture of the place rather than the danger that may come from it.

"Oh my, yes, but it has gone through fires and numerous renovations since then." Miguel continued, "You know, I think it is strange that only two people are named in the New Testament as having officiated at major rites in Jesus' life – John who baptized him at the beginning of his ministry and Mary Magdalene who anointed him at the end, and yet both of these people have been marginalized in the Gospels. Don't you find that strange?"

"To tell you the truth, I have never really thought about it."

"It is as if they were only included because what they did was too important to have been left out altogether. I think there's a simple reason for this – not only does a baptizer and an anointer bestow authority upon another, they have the authority to do so. The Templars tried to tell us this in all they created."

The arrival of the three Israelis meant everyone was now present and accounted for and the mission could proceed.

It had been only three days since Monday when Amir Katz flew to Paris to execute the contract with the Tuguía brothers, attend the briefing and approve the mission of the security team from the Police Nationale. Général Dupont presented him with two options for the flight returning to Tel Aviv. In the first, he proposed to contact the French Air Force and request landing authority at the Orléans-Bricy Air Base, about twelve miles from their staging area at St. Croix. The second was to be met by two customs officials and immediately cleared at the closest international airport, Paris-Orly, just south of Paris about seventy-five miles away from Orléans. Even though a shorter distance, the plan involving the Air Force seemed to be a far greater risk for leaks to occur. Katz opted for Paris-Orly.

They gathered to stage their convoy at the Cathedral of St. Croix as Miguel had suggested.

Capitaine Daryl Rousseau had successfully wormed his way on to the team Dupont assembled. As the ranking officer, Rousseau was in charge of the detail whose members he had met only days before.

He began, "In the lead will be Guardiens de La Paix Dominique Richard and Jean Durand. Following them I want Even Nagar, Yossi Wolff and Gil Hansen in the second car; after them Stan Parker and Andy Miller in the third; followed by Miguel and Rafael Tuguía in the fourth. Sous-Brigadier Leon Roux and I will bring up the rear. After the scroll is transferred to Wolff, the Tuguías will drop out and return to Chartres, while we go to the airport. You were all briefed on Monday by Général Dupont and there's been no change since then. Use channel 11 for all communications today. Any questions?" Seeing none he said, "Okay it's 9:00 a.m., let's roll."

The morning was overcast and cool. It began to drizzle. It was a welcome relief from the summer heat as the four uniformed police officers and seven civilians approached their now-radio-equipped vehicles. As directed, the caravan took shape – a blue and white Renault police vehicle pulled out in front, followed by two black Mercedes rentals, Even Naggar driving the first, Stan Parker driving the second, followed by a late model white Citroën sedan, and finally the two Yamaha motorcycles of the Police Nationale.

En route, Durand found it necessary to turn on his overhead lights and touch the siren every few seconds to clear a path, as the caravan snaked its way west along the French streets.

The famed statue of the maid of Orléans, Jeanne d'Arc inside the roundabout greeted their arrival. Her statue presented a woman of unusual courage and moral leadership mounted for victorious battle. It memorialized a time when God had instructed her to support the Dauphin and retake France from English control. Ironically, this armor-clad Catholic woman now seemed to guard the bank containing the esoteric contents about the two goddesses that the newly minted warriors of St. Croix had come to claim.

The caravan entered Rue d'Illers and stopped alongside the bank. The drizzle turned into a light rain. Roux and Rousseau parked their motorcycles across the one-way street to block further entry and directed oncoming traffic to continue around the circle. Wolff, Hansen, and the Tuguías entered. Richard and Durand guarded the door; the balance stood with their vehicles on heightened alert – their eyes in constant motion. Ten minutes later, Wolff reappeared carrying a specially designed leather case.

Rousseau commanded once again, "Okay, let's roll."

Leaving the caravan, the Tuguías headed toward highway E-5 and Chartres. The balance continued west along Rue d'Illers until reaching the perimeter highway to the west and then north to Rue de Paris and farming country. On Monday afternoon Dupont briefed the security team that he thought staying off E-5 on their way to Paris-Orly Airport would be best. Everyone, including Katz, agreed. Later that evening Rousseau briefed Sordi.

Twenty-five minutes after leaving the bank, Rousseau tuned to channel 19. "Colonel we just entered Chevilly. We're a little more than one mile from the overpass. Get ready. I'm on the cycle on the east side, near the shoulder."

He returned to channel 11. Sordi and Moritti were ready and waiting near the top of the northwest side of the embankment. Sebastian, a new recruit for the Gladio comrades, positioned himself on the overpass above the Rue de Paris. Romano drove their stolen, five-year-old Hummer into position. It was large enough to carry the four men and an arsenal of weapons in the rear. The front end faced in; the rear compartment was easily accessible

"Okay boys, get ready." Sordi shouted. "Ski masks … gloves. They'll be here in less than two minutes. Rousseau is on a cycle on the east side near the shoulder of the road. Don't hit him!"

The planned ambush was to take place in the open farmlands between the town of Chevilly and the northern village to the north – La Croix Briquet, Chevilly. The A-19 overpass above the Rue de Paris provided Sordi and his team the perfect opportunity to hide and take advantage of the high ground above the caravan. The plan of attack was directed toward the lead car in an attempt to halt the vehicles. A radio-controlled improvised explosive device was planted in the early morning for that purpose. The rain was not planned, but was a welcome addition to the chaos that ensued.

The lead car traveled beneath the overpass and entered the graffiti-scarred concrete holding back its embankments. Just as it emerged, Sebastian detonated the IED with his cellphone.

The thunderous explosion hurled the Renault fifteen feet into the air, flipping it over and landing it on the roof. The shock wave brought Nagar's Mercedes to a screeching halt and thrust it back in the direction of Stan's matching car.

The fireball billowed through the air. Shrapnel cut through the embankment and the northern end of the enclosed structure but did not hit any of the men. Black smoke rising from the scene drew the attention of curious residents of the sixty person village of La Croix Brique, one-half mile north, and town Chevilly, one and one-half miles south.

The impact crushed the Renault's roof. Windows shattered and littered the road. Instantaneously the flipped vehicle formed a barricade, blocking the caravan's further movement north. Nagar and Stan slammed on their brakes. Wheels locked. Tires squealed and smoked. The two Mercedes slid across the wet pavement and into each other.

The two bloody policemen hung motionless from their secured seatbelts inside what was left of their flipped vehicle.

Romano raced the Hummer backwards onto the Rue de Paris to block the south bound lane and plug the potential escape route. Moritti and Sordi took cover on the passenger's side of the vehicle and made a full-frontal-assault on the immobile caravan.

Rousseau covered the rear, shooting in the direction of the attackers. With planned deception, his bullets ricocheted off the concrete wall behind them, rather than into the bodies of his comrades.

Andy took cover on the passenger's side of their car. He sprayed bullets from the police-provided-carbine in the direction of Sordi and Moretti, giving Stan just enough time to escape.

From the southwest embankment, Sebastian unloaded half of the magazine from his semi-automatic rifle in the direction of Sous-Brigadier Roux, killing him on the spot. He then ran down the embankment taking aim at Stan and laughing at his attempt to flee. He missed him once, but the next bullet grazed Stan's arm.

"That's for taking Renee away from me, you son of a bitch!" he yelled.

With only a superficial wound and another burst from Andy's carbine, Stan ran to the passenger's side for Andy's protection. Andy tossed him his Glock. Stan unloaded the magazine in the direction of Sebastian. He fired wildly missing his target.

Now blocking the south bound lane, Romano slid to the passenger's side of the Hummer to make his escape. Bullets struck his vehicle. He waited to get out. Andy took aim. His bullets crashed through the rear window on the driver's side and into Romano's back, thrusting him into the dashboard. Wounded, but still alive, Romano's blood splashed against the passenger's side window.

Nagar and Hansen climbed out the passenger side of their vehicle leaving Wolff to cradle the scroll on the floor in the back. About a dozen red streaks from Moretti's weapon zipped by their heads, one finding Nagar's arm. A required change of magazines allowed Hansen a few seconds to explode a bullet into Moretti's head.

Andy took aim at Sordi as he aimed at Hansen. Andy fired, hitting Sordi in the forehead. Suddenly there was silence.

The silence broke as Sebastian sprinted to the Hummer spraying bullets in the direction of the two Mercedes now riddled with bullet holes. Hansen swung and fired in the direction of Sebastian, but missed. Then silence once more, except for the squeal of tires coming from the Hummer. The south bound lane was now clear. Andy's training kicked in as he took note of Sebastian's license plate speeding away with Romano still bleeding.

In minutes it was over. Roux, Moretti, Sordi lay dead on the blood soaked pavement, Richard and Durand appeared dead in the crushed Renault.

Two of Rousseau's best friends from his days with Gladio were now dead. He was left with a decision. He thought about Sordi's warning to be careful and about his choices. Either he could complete the mission, perhaps be successful and collect the money, or he could join in a fake pursuit and come out clean. He chose the latter. He muttered to himself, "Sebastian is dedicated to the mission; he'll keep after the scroll. If I help him escape, he has no reason to turn me in."

Rousseau tuned into channel 19 to call the Hummer. "Sebastian, the two Americans are coming after you. It will look like I am too, but I'm not. A road through the town of Artenay is up ahead. Take it through town. Don't bypass it. Trust me. We can deal with the scroll later. Don't forget the Tuguías are on their way back to Chartres. How's Romano?"

"He's hanging on. I'll be in touch," Sebastian responded.

Stan blotted his bloody arm with his sleeve and retook the wheel of his car. He jammed the gear shift into reverse. After a minute of wheel spinning and jockeying the car back and forth, he broke free of Nagar's vehicle and raced backward.

Turning back to channel 11, Rousseau said, "Let's go. I'll take the lead."

"Okay, I'll notify the police and get them to the crime scene." Andy said.

With Rousseau's police light flashing and siren blaring, the three were now about two minutes behind the Hummer. The Israelis stayed behind. Their mission was to protect the scroll, not apprehend their assailants. Hansen called his boss,

"Hello, Amir. We've come under attack," Hansen said. "Five are dead - three policemen and two of the attackers. Nagar was shot in the arm, but he's okay. Wolff and I are fine. Stan was shot in the arm as well, but he's driving so I guess he's okay. Andy's fine. One of the police officers and the two Americans are in pursuit of the other two attackers."

"What about Rafael and Miguel?" Katz asked.

"They left the caravan as planned and were not with us when we were attacked."

"Good. We exchanged phone numbers last Monday. I'll give them a call and make sure they're okay. What about the scroll?" Katz asked.

"We have it," Hansen reported. "We're still about an hour away from the airport. I'm going to bypass Artenay and jump on E-5. I think it will be safer out in the open rather than going through all of these small towns."

"Okay, be careful," Katz said. "Let it go if you have to. Just get back home safely."

* * *

Andy switched the radio to the emergency frequency, channel 9. "Aide. Aide. Parlez-vous Anglais?" His panicked voice drew a quick response.

"Oui, monsieur. Certainly. How can I help you?"

"My name is Andrew Miller. I'm with the United States FBI. We were just ambushed. Several are dead."

"Try to calm yourself, monsieur. Where are you?"

Andy swallowed hard. "We're on the Rue de Paris just south of Artenay heading north in pursuit of a black, late model Hummer, license plate … wait a minute …" Andy said, reaching for his note. "French, license plate AB-4274-AC. A few minutes ago, our caravan was ambushed beneath the overpass for A-19 north of Chevilly. I think five are dead, but someone may still be alive. We're with Capitaine Daryl Rousseau of the Police Nationale. Send help, now!"

As instructed, Sebastian left the Rue de Paris and drove straight ahead. Farm country soon bled into the rural town of Artenay. The 1,800 person village was a community of trusting friends and families, rarely locking their doors when leaving their homes. These Frenchmen had no police force or the need for one, until today.

The thunderous explosion, rising black smoke and the screaming police siren demanded that volunteers from La Croix Brique and Chevilly create a barricade to stop oncoming traffic from both directions. In response, a few stunned residents grabbed scraps of lumber, sawhorses, flares, colorful flags, whatever they could find, and ran to strategic locations in a desperate attempt to halt the infrequent vehicles traveling along the Rue de Paris. Stan's rearview mirror filled with images of the scrambling volunteers as the pair of Americans gained speed toward the French town of Artenay. Now only two hundred yards behind the Hummer, the invading chase flew past the aluminum sheathed warehouses, manufacturing facilities and a concrete batching plant of Artenay's industrial region in the town's south. The newer housing districts coming next also offered little traffic to impede their chase.

As they approached the older part of town, refurbished and dilapidated, one and two story grey buildings crowded the narrowing streets. Their pace stayed constant but seemed to increase as the Hummer's size dominated its surroundings. Sebastian's driving became erratic. Romano's life hung in the balance as his bullet-ridden body was tossed about. Rousseau's flashing light and siren kept the pedestrians on the sidewalk and stilled the cars traveling on the village street.

From behind it looked as though Sebastian would drive straight ahead, but then he took an immediate hard left giving Rousseau the opportunity to slow his speed, slide through the turn and lay down his motorcycle. Rousseau prepared himself for the slide out. Leaning hard to the left, he slid across the pavement while throwing gravel and the cycle into the path of the fast-approaching Mercedes in pursuit. His cycle flipped over and over and crashed into a parked vehicle, sparing a young mother and her child just ten yards beyond. Stan instinctively reacted, jerking the car to the right over the curb and crashing into a grand spruce tree that anchored the triangular shaped flowered island separating the intersecting streets.

Their heads thrust forward upon impact plunging their faces into the deployed airbags. Recoiling, their heads jerked back against the headrest. Andy stretched out his battered left arm reaching once more for the microphone, barely able to move. "We crashed. Need help … Artenay," he pleaded before dropping the microphone and passing out.

Sebastian's rearview mirror filled with the scene of the Mercedes' right front fender buried into the tree. Three pedestrians ran toward the wreckage. Stan struggled to get out. His face now bloodied from broken glass, he pushed the start button cutting the engine, unbuckled his seatbelt, grabbed his gun resting on the seat, and slid his back toward the open door.

Sebastian's eyes left the mirror and refocused on the signage ahead, letting the scene vanish from his mirror and his mind. He slowed his Hummer to twenty miles per hour, not wanting to attract further attention, and headed west in the direction of Chartres.

Stan stood and felt weak and disoriented. One of the pedestrians ran to his aide. "Allongez-vous. Allongez-vous," he said, gesturing for him to lie down in the grass.

Pulling away Stan yelled, "My friend. I must go to my friend."

"Non, allongez-vous!"

The other two hurried to Andy, still unconscious and trapped. They punctured the air bag to give him some relief. His left leg was clearly broken. They feared injuring him even more if they tried to forcibly remove him from the wreckage. With no smell of gasoline present and the engine shut off, they decided to simply move his seat back as far as possible, raise his legs to the extent possible and recline the seat back until medical help arrived. His skin grew cool and clammy, his pulse seemed weak and rapid, but there were no signs of impaired breathing. Covering his body with their jackets to keep him warm, one yelled to his aide, "Il peut être en état de choc."

"What are they saying?" Stan whispered.

"Pardonnez-moi," the pedestrian said to him. "They say to me, he may be … how you say … shocking."

Suddenly Sebastian saw a sign pointing to a supermarket on the left. "Hey, Guy … Guy … damn-it, Romano … open your eyes."

Stan grew more anxious with the news Andy was in shock. He tried to stand up but felt nauseated and fell back. "Non, allongez-vous!" he said again. Stan gave up and waited for help to arrive.

As Sebastian suspected, the supermarket's parking lot was filled with at least two dozen cars and vans waiting for their owners to return. Three were parked on the sidewalk adjacent to the store, unlocked. The passenger's wheels rested on the sidewalk while the driver's wheels remained on the pavement, beckoning him to look inside. He scanned the interior cabs and steering columns for the least difficult to steal. He spied the key fob of a dark blue, late model VW Touareg resting in the console.

"Come on, let's go," he said while helping Romano to his feet and into their new SUV. Sebastian made a U-turn and headed back to the Rue de Chartres. The roundabout's sign indicated the road to Paris was at the first exit, Chartres was second, and E-5 was three-quarters of the way around.

"Perfect," Sebastian said to Romano, now drifting in and out of consciousness from the loss of blood. "We know where we're going, but the police won't." Taking the second exit onto the safety of the road to Chartres, Sebastian said, "Okay, old men, where in hell are you?

CHAPTER 32

ARTENAY, FRANCE

The closest police station was in Saran, a community near the northern suburbs of Orléans and about six miles from the crime scene. Four police officers responded to the call, passing travelers and improvised barricades. They arrived at the ambush site moments later. Officer Laurent remained with the carnage; headquarters dispatched his partner on to Artenay in response to a second message. The other two left the scene to erect official barricades and reroute traffic to E-5 between Chevily and Artenay.

Laurent surveyed the bloody battlefield and found two dead civilians and what appeared to be two dead police officers lying among hundreds of spent shells. Guardien de La Paix Jean Durand had unbuckled his seatbelt shortly after the explosion and lay on the crushed ceiling of the overturned Renault. He was now unconscious and barely breathing, but still alive. His partner's body still hung over a pool of his own blood.

Officer Anton Bertrand arrived in Artenay and quickly surveyed the scene. He saw a police officer getting to his feet, two people tending to the man in the car and another bent over a man on the ground. He went to Stan first. “Are you okay?” Bertrand asked.

“Yeah, I’ll be fine. Just a little dizzy. Go check on my friend, will you?”

“He looks like he’s in good hands. Why don’t I stay here with you? What’s your name?”

Reaching in his pocket, he presented his passport. “Stan Parker. My friend over there is Special Agent Andrew Miller with the US Federal Bureau of Investigation.”

“Why don’t you let me take your gun for now? What happened here?” Bertrand asked securing his weapon.

“My friend and I and Capitaine Rosseau over there attempted to apprehend one of the assailants after the attack. We were in a high speed pursuit of his vehicle when Rousseau lost control of his motorcycle. I reacted and crashed. Listen, can we do this later? I’m feeling a little nauseous.”

Bertrand jotted down their names. “Sure. This can wait. An ambulance will be along shortly. I can find you at the hospital if necessary. Give me your phone number and I’ll call you later. Help will be along soon. Try to rest.”

* * *

Le Service d'Aide Médicale Urgente d’Orléans dispatched two Mobil Intensive Care Units. They arrived at the ambush scene five minutes later. Officer Laurent directed the first vehicle on to the crash scene at Artenay and the physician from the second to Jean Durand in the Renault. He determined Durand was still alive and yelled to the balance of his team to secure his patient. In response his nurse and EMT gently placed Durant on a folding stretcher and carried his seemingly lifeless body to the MICU. The doctor made a quick examination of the other four bodies and pronounced them dead at the scene. Tossing Laurent some blankets, the team raced to the hospital in northern Orléans in an attempt to save Durant’s life. Laurent covered the bodies and waited for the cornier to arrive.

The second MICU arrived at Artenay only moments after Officer Bertrand had arrived. The medical team went to work immediately. Rousseau had abrasions on the left side of his torso and left leg – he had to wait. Nurse Andrée Fournier went to Stan's aid; Dr. Martin and her assigned EMT, Jean, focused on Andy.

The hood and the right quarter panel of the Mercedes were crushed, but inside the cab was left intact. Andy was still unconscious and had a badly bruised right cheek and blood coming from a lacerated forehead. Dr. Martin positioned a cervical collar to temporarily immobilize his neck then raced to the driver's side. Jean lowered Andy's torso around the collapsed airbags and into the arms of the waiting physician. She slid him from the car, strapped him to a spine board, and with Jean's help carried him to the MICU. Jean administered intravenous fluids and oxygen. She left to check on Officer Rousseau.

Dr. Martin determined Rousseau's injuries were superficial. She directed Bertrand to help him to the MICU and have her technician clean and bandage his abrasions. He would be released at the site. Meanwhile she turned his attention to Stan.

Nurse Fournier reported Stan was slightly disoriented, but his temperature and pulse appeared normal. Dr. Martin checked his pupils and breathing and asked if he could stand. Stan was able to walk. Martin held his arm as she escorted him to the MICU. Fournier cleaned and bandaged his face and gunshot wound.

Stan retrieved Andy's credentials and authorization for firearms from his jacket pocket and presented them to the officer. He indicated where the weapons could be found. Bertrand secured them and the ammunition from the back seat of the wrecked Mercedes. He cleared the ammunition, locked the safeties, and placed them along with Stan's Glock in his vehicle.

Their two new patients and the medical team headed west toward the roundabout and entrance to E-5 en route to the hospital. Stan's guilt felt a lot worse than his injuries. His lifelong friend still remained unconscious.

"Where are they taking them?" Rousseau asked.

"Le Centre Hospitalier Régional d'Orléans," Bertrand said. "Why don't you come with me back to Saran and answer a few questions, Capitaine Rousseau?" Bertrand asked. "You can call in your report from there. We'll send for your cycle to be picked up."

"Okay … thanks." Rousseau said, then informed Bertrand of the events that unfolded earlier as they headed south on the Rue d' Orléans.

* * *

Three officers were at the crime scene when Rousseau and Bertrand returned. Barriers were in place permitting only a single lane of travel and only a few vehicles at a time. Behind the barriers, the location of the dead bodies had been marked in anticipation of a later investigation. The corpses now lay covered waiting for the coroner to remove them.

"I called in the status here a few moments ago," Laurent reported.

"Take the weapons in the back of my car to the hospital in Orléans, will you please? I called ahead. Their security detail will secure them for Agent Miller. This man and I are going back to the station."

"Sure, no problem," Laurent said. "Headquarters is sending two inspectors over in a few minutes. Looks like a war zone here. Maybe the casings or bomb fragments might give them something to go on. There're two of them still at large, right?"

"That's correct," Rousseau confirmed.

"There's only four corpses. What happened to the fifth?" Bertrand asked.

"The fifth, an Officer Jean Durand I believe his name was, was found alive, barely alive mind you, but he was still breathing," Laurent said. They attempted to stabilize him and transported him to Orléans." Rousseau, visibly shaken by the news, was later relieved by Laurent's concluding comment. "He died while en route to the hospital."

"Sacrebleu, my entire team … dead!"

A radio message interrupted Rousseau's act. "Go ahead," Bertrand said.

"Dr. Martin reported she spotted an abandoned, black Hummer on a side street in Artenay before reaching E-5."

"We need to get back," Bertrand said. Why don't you two go check it out and see if there's any sign of his escape to Paris-Orly".

* * *

Sebastian's cellphone beeped to indicate he just received a text message. "They're en route to the hospital – Le CHR d' Orléans."

Five minutes later and about a mile in front of him, Sebastian caught sight of the Citroën he had seen once before in Chartres.

He pushed the gas pedal to the floor and caught up to the Tuguías. "We caught 'em Guy," Sebastian said. Romano was not responsive. "Guy … Guy … are you okay?" Sebastian pressed his finger into Romano's neck.

No pulse. "Damn it!" he screamed.

Miguel was driving. Sebastian lunged past him then swerved to his right forcing the Citroën off the road. Leaving his dead comrade to be discovered and tied to the massacre, Sebastian raced to the car and pointed his handgun at Miguel's head. He jumped in the back seat and ordered, "Let's go."

"Where?" Miguel quivered in a hoarse voice.

"Orléans. Use the back roads. Don't get anywhere near Artenay."

Moments later Miguel's cellphone rang. "It's from Stan."

Now holding his gun on Rafael's head, Sebastian said, "Answer it and put him on speaker. Don't do anything stupid or so help me your brother's dead."

"Hello, this is Miguel. ... Just a minute, Stan; Rafael asked me to put you on speaker. ... Okay, we're back."

"As I started to say... the caravan came under attack about thirty minutes after you left. Two of the assailants and I hear three of the police escorts are dead. The Israelis have the scroll. Andy and I were injured in a crash. He's in pretty bad shape. We're on the way to a hospital in the center of Orléans by ambulance right now. I'm calling to check on you. Are you okay?"

"Yes, we're fine. Does Renee know?"

"I just got off the phone with her," Stan said. "She and Debra are on their way to the hospital right now. I'll call you later. Bye."

"Where in Orléans?" Miguel asked Sebastian.

"Town center, just north of the Loire River. For now, head toward Saran in Orléans-nord. I'll tell you later," Sebastian said.

Ten minutes later Tuguía's cellphone rang again. "It's Katz," Miguel reported.

"Don't answer it," Sebastian ordered. "Let me have the phone."

"You know of him?" Miguel asked.

"Do you actually think we would engage in this and not know everyone involved?"

Sebastian waited. A moment later a beep and a message indicated Miguel had a voice mail. "Hello, Miguel, this is Amir Katz. The caravan came under attack. I'm calling to make sure you're okay. Call me back."

Continuing to hold his gun to Rafael's head, Sebastian returned the phone to Miguel. "Call him back. Here's what you tell him ..."

CHAPTER 33

NEAR PARIS, FRANCE

"Hello, Yossi. This is Amir Katz."

"Yes sir," Wolff said. "We're about 15 minutes from Paris-Orly Airport. No problems so far."

"Yeah, well I have a problem … a big one! After your earlier call, I spoke with Director Schulman and Dr. Horovitz and informed them about the attack and murders. A few moments ago, I received a call from Miguel Tuguía. Apparently, his brother, Rafael, has been kidnapped and is being held for ransom. He asked that we cancel our contract and return the scroll so his brother won't be murdered. He also told me Andy and Stan were seriously injured in their pursuit and are now en route to a hospital in Orléans. I called him back and told him Schulman, Horovitz and I were all in agreement we should honor his request and return the scroll to him. He asked that the scroll be taken to Orléans; Rafael's kidnapper will call me later with specific instructions. Yossi, for now, we're going to cancel the flight and do as he instructs. I will tell you where to take it when I know."

"Are you sure?" Yossi asked. "We are so close."

"Yes, I'm afraid so. How's Even doing?"

"He seems to be doing okay. He lost a little blood, but the bullet went clean through his arm and did not hit an artery. I'll get him to a hospital and get it cleaned up as soon as we're able."

"Okay. I regret this decision, but we really have no choice. Tell your team everyone here appreciates their effort, but we have to let it go."

"We'll turn around and head back on E-5," Wolff confirmed. "Let me know where to go when you find out."

"I will. We also believe if anyone else was a part of the plan they would have been involved in the attack. According to your earlier report, it looks like we're dealing with five criminals, or zealots, or martyrs, or whatever the hell they think they are. I doubt if any others are involved. Seems like their only motivation was getting the scroll. Once we return it, you should be safe. But stay alert."

"Amir, when this is all over, I need to take some time off and visit an old friend from Albi," Wolff said. "Tell Dr. Horovitz, will you? I'll be back to work when I figure it out."

"Figure what out?" Katz asked.

"Never mind. Just tell her I'll be back when I can, please."

* * *

"Hello, Papa. Stan and his friend, Andy, have been in an automobile accident. Stan's doing okay, but Andy is seriously injured. It's all my fault." Renee said, her voice beginning to crack as she thought about how Noelle had unknowingly betrayed her. "Debra and I are heading to the hospital in Orleans right now. It's the one in the center of Orléans. We'll be there in about an hour and a half. Papa, I could really use your help with all of this; are you able to meet us there? … Okay, good, I'll see you later this evening. Papa, thank you."

Debra and Renee arrived at the hospital a little a little before one. Their faces showed signs of stress and worry as they hurried past dozens of people streaming out of the hospital entrance on their way to lunch. Tearful and blood shot, Renee's eyes scanned the hospital directory and found directions to the ER. They entered the waiting room and approached the nurses' station.

"Hello, I'm Renee Gaston and I'm here about Stan Parker."

"And my name is Debra Herzog, here for Andy Miller."

"Just a minute, I'll call the doctor in charge."

A few moments later the attending physician greeted their arrival. "Good afternoon. My name is Dr. Beaudry. Which one of you is Renee?"

"This is Debra. I'm Renee. Why?"

"Mr. Parker asked me to meet you when you arrived and assure you he is okay. I examined him and found him lucid and his vital signs and EKG all satisfactory. I want to keep an eye on him over night, so I admitted him for observation. If he sleeps well and there's no problem during the evening, I will release him tomorrow morning during rounds."

"Oh, thank you, thank you so much," Renee said overcome with emotion.

"Debra, I'm afraid Mr. Miller's injuries are more extensive. When he arrived, he was unconscious, but his vital signs all improved under Dr. Martin's care during transport. He regained consciousness about an hour ago. He has a fractured tibia and fibula in his left leg, which we set immediately. His EKG indicated a slight abnormality, but there was no base line data available for comparison, so I'm uncertain as to the extent of injury or degree of trauma. He complains of a sharp pain radiating across his shoulder through his arm and down through the tips of his fingers. Occasionally he says he has a numbing or tingling feeling in his thumb and index finger. His neck was not broken, but I suspect he may have sustained a neck injury and suffers from a cervical radiculopathy or injury to the upper lumbar area of the neck, probably in the form of a herniated disk. If this diagnosis is correct, he will require surgery. This may just be a temporary condition or something more complicated. I've ordered an MRI to confirm my suspicions; we'll know more afterward. Right now, he's resting in Trauma # 2. I'll take you to see him."

"Thank you, Doctor."

Beaudry escorted the pair to Andy's bedside. "Before you go in there's one final thing. Mr. Miller asked me to release his weapons to you, Debra. He asked that you to lock them in your car's trunk for safe keeping. Our security team is holding them. I'll make arrangements for you to pick them up later."

Debra stood at the draped opening of the sterile environment. She watched him sleep for a few more moments before entering. She walked to his bed side, kissed her fingers and placed them gently on his bruised forehead. He woke and attempted a smile in her direction.

"I'm so sorry, Andy," Renee said from the foot of his bed. "If I had listened to Stan, you would not be here now."

"I'll be fine. Don't do that to yourself," he whispered. "You didn't force me; I made the decision to come. And besides, I will be okay. Stan seems to be doing fine, they tell me."

"He is. Dr. Beaudry said he probably will be released tomorrow morning," Renee confirmed.

A nurse pulled back the drawn curtain. She and an orderly entered. "Mr. Miller?" the nurse inquired. "What's your date of birth?"

"June 26, 1975."

"That is what it says here," she said checking her records. "Ready to go?"

As they began to wheel his bed from the room, Andy noticed the clock on the wall on the far side of the room read 1:20 and asked, "Did you and Renee have lunch yet?"

"No, we just got here as quickly as we could drive," Debra said.

"They're here to take me for an MRI," Andy said. "Why don't you go see Stan, grab a bite to eat and by then we may have a better idea of what's going on after the results come back. Okay?"

"Well … okay," Debra reluctantly said, leaning over to gently kiss his cheek. "We'll be back in an hour."

CHAPTER 34

SARAN, FRANCE

"Bonjour, Bureau de l'inspecteur Général Dupont."

"Bonjour, this is Capitaine Rousseau. May I please speak with Général Dupont."

"Rosseau, Dupont here. Good to hear from you. I just got a call from Amir Katz. He said you came under attack. What the hell is going on?"

"Yes, sir, I'm here with Officer Bertrand now. Five are dead; three of our own and two of the assailants," Capitaine Rousseau reported. "They were in position when we crossed under an overpass about 30 minutes from the bank. They blew up the lead car, killing Richard and Durand, then began shooting at the vehicles. Roux was killed by one of the snipers. I was able to take cover from the assault and engage in the fight.

"Two of the assailants escaped. The Americans and I chased them into the town of Artenay, then we lost control of our vehicles and crashed. The two escaped as a result. The Americans were in pretty bad shape from the crash and were taken to Le Centre Hospitalier Regional d' Orléans. The Israelis managed to escape with the scroll. Hopefully, they made it to the airport and out of the country."

"No, unfortunately Katz told me he had to turn them around," explained Dupont. "Apparently, Miguel Tuguía told him his brother, Rafael, was kidnapped. His kidnappers want the scroll in return for his safe release."

"Damn. Well, that's regrettable. I had hoped at least our mission would have been accomplished."

"Daryl, please know that your department thanks you, your country thanks you, and I thank you for your heroic efforts today," Dupont said. "It will not soon be forgotten. I plan to recommend you for Médaille d'honneur for your bravery today."

"Thank you, sir, I'm truly honored. The loss of our officers is, of course, beyond tragic. But know we did our best here today to protect the lives of our visitors; we were simply out gunned. Katz probably should have realized what he was dealing with and requested more security. I'll tie up loose ends here in Saran and make a full report when I get back to Paris. Thank you again, sir."

"Sounds like Général Dupont is pleased," Bertrand said continuing his inquiry of Rousseau. "So, tell me, Daryl … may I call you Daryl?"

"Yes, of course," Rousseau responded.

"At the scene of the ambush, the bad guys seemed to be pretty well prepared. You know … they apparently knew how many of you there were going to be … the route you took and so forth."

"Yes, I know," Rousseau interrupted. "I've been thinking a lot about that myself … trying to figure it out."

"And what have you determined?"

"What's been going through my mind is the number of people who had knowledge of our plan … several of the officials of the Israeli Antiquities Authority, the Knesset members, maybe some of whom were not so loyal to the Prime Minster, the Iranians were likely aware of the situation and may have wanted to stop the transfer and embarrass the Israeli government even if there was nothing more sinister involved, the Tuguías, of course …"

"Why would the Tuguías possibly want the secrecy to be compromised?" Bertrand interrupted.

"I've been trying to piece that together as well and the thought that struck me was this. They never were going to be in danger. The plan called for them to exit the caravan before it got started. Their real motivation might have been to get the scroll out there in the public's attention. The notion of the Mandaeans could have been simply a ruse to distract from their true goal. You know the press is going to have a field day with this when it becomes public."

Rousseau thought quickly about the recent revelation and said, "Now, with the news of the kidnapping this may just add fuel to the fire. Général Dupont told me Miguel, not the kidnapper, called Katz. If the kidnapping is also a hoax and they control the scroll when the news hits, they'll be seen as heroes."

"Anything else?"

"No, not really … you know it's still pretty confusing to me at the moment. And the loss of my team … and the impact on their families … it's all just beginning to sink in."

"Excuse me for interrupting," Officer Blanc said knocking on Bertrand's office door. "We found the Hummer abandoned next to the supermarket west of town. Pretty shot up and bloody, but no clear fingerprints on anything. It all was a mess. The DNA should give us something to go on, but for the driver, I guess he wore gloves the whole time. When we got to the scene, a middle-aged man, a resident of Artenay by the name of Denis Marchand was beside himself. He kept waving his arms and pacing the ground where his new VW Touareg once was … the Hummer was left blocking the street."

"Do we know how to get back to him when we sort all of this out?" Bertrand asked.

"Yes, I have all of his information and will get back to him later. Meanwhile, we impounded the Hummer. A tow truck has it and is now en route here together with the motorcycle."

"Anything further?"

"Yes, sir," Blanc said proudly. "As ordered, we left the scene and traveled in the direction of Paris for a few miles but returned when there was nothing obvious to pursue. We notified the authorities to be on the lookout for Marchand's Touareg and headed back to Artenay. Then we caught a break. When we approached the roundabout, the driver of a vehicle coming from Chartres saw us and began blowing his horn and flashing his lights to get our attention. He flagged us down and said he saw what appeared to be a dead body left in a VW Touareg about two hundred yards down the road toward Chartres. He was right. On the side of the road was Marchand's car with a dead man inside. I assume it to be another assailant. My partner is with him now waiting for forensics to arrive. I left him to pick up Officer Laurent and come back here to give you the latest info."

"Thank you," Bertrand said. Turning to Rousseau he said, "Okay, for now we'll check on any link among the three dead assailants. Our investigative team is at the ambush site documenting what they can. Apparently, there's another team on its way toward Chartres. I'll let you know what they find out."

"Thanks. I'll take the train back to Paris tomorrow, but for now can someone drop me off to get a rental car?"

"Of course. There are several spots along the road to the train station in Fleur-les-Aubrais. It will connect you to the Austerlitz station in Paris. Officer Blanc can take you. In the meantime, stay in touch."

"Thanks, I will."

ORLÉANS

Rousseau began to clean and dress his soon-to-be scabbed over skin when his cellphone rang. Sebastian Philippe's name flashed on the screen.

"Rousseau here," he answered.

"Daryl, where are you?"

"At a motel in Saran, north of Orléans. Where are you?"

"We're nearing the town of Ormes on our way to a hospital in Orléans. Are you okay? I need your help."

"Yeah, just a little banged up, but otherwise okay. Hang on a minute," he said checking the map app on his phone. "Here's what I need you to do. From Ormes, take Avenue du Général de Gaulle east. It will turn into the Rue d'Orléans. When you pass over D2701 you'll see Le Motel Orléans-Nord on the left. I'm in room 105 … direct entry from parking lot."

Sebastian knocked on his door fifteen minutes later. Rafael and Miguel were with him. "Get inside," he commanded.

"Ah, we meet again Capitaine Rousseau," Miguel said in disgusted rasp. "You being here explains a lot."

"What's going on?" Rousseau asked.

"One scroll for two maybe three hostages. Seems like a fair price," Sebastian answered.

"Three?" Rousseau asked not knowing what Sebastian had in mind.

"Yeah, I've got an errand to run. Give me your car keys. Here's the keys to the Citroën. I'll hang here for a few minutes while you tear up one of those sheets, tie them up and gag them. You need to baby-sit these two old men for a while."

"No! No, please! I will not be able to breathe," Miguel pleaded.

* * *

The pair walked from the hospital on their way to lunch. They did not see Sebastian until he grabbed Debra's arm from behind.

"You two come with me," he said.

Gesturing to Rousseau's rental car across the street, he placed his hand inside his jacket pocket and stuck his gun in Debra's spine. She flinched. Her body contorted as he jammed his gun harder into her back. Instinctively she spun around breaking free from his grip, threw her free arm into his jacketed hand, grabbed his shoulders and began wildly thrusting her knee upward toward his groin as she had been trained to do 17 years before.

Sebastian recoiled and winced in pain. He grabbed her leg on her third thrust, pushed her back, and aimed his gun at her head as she lay on the ground.

He opened the driver's door. "Get in," he ordered Renee.

"No!" Renee resisted. "Stan and Andy are hurt. I need to get back to the hospital."

"I told you to get into the damn car!" he said pulling at Renee's hair then pushing her on the shoulder, still pointing his gun at Debra.

"Okay … okay. I will. Just don't hurt her!" Renee pleaded.

"Get up," Sebastian commanded Debra. "I want you to go back in there and make it damn clear to the boys that I've got Renee, Rafael and Miguel and I don't intend to release them until the scroll is turned over to me. I have assurances that it will be."

"Who's got it?" Debra yelled back.

"I don't know. Ask Katz! When he gets it to me, I'll call your FBI clown to let him know where the hostages can be found. If not, the pretty lady and the two old men will be dead, if and when you find them. You have two days."

Sebastian handed Debra his cellphone. "Enter Miller's name and number. Tell him I'll call him when it's over."

"Andy's pretty banged up. Why don't you call Stan instead? I'll enter his number, too."

He grabbed his phone from her hand and ran to the passenger's side. He then turned his gun on Renee and got in the car. Let's go! Straight ahead for one mile … then north. I'll tell you when."

* * *

Ah, good, you're back," Stan said as Debra entered his room. "But why so early? … And why are you out of breath?"

"It's awful! Sebastian kidnapped Renee," she gasped.

"What do you mean she was kidnapped?" Stan asked as panic set in.

"Just now, Sebastian kidnapped Renee."

Stan took a deep breath to calm himself and said, "Tell me what happened."

"He was waiting for us. Somehow he knew we were here. We walked out of the hospital on our way to lunch and he came up from behind us and stuck a gun in my back …"

"Are you okay? Are you hurt?" Stan interrupted.

"Yeah … no … yeah, I'm okay. I was able to get in a couple of good kicks to his groin before he forced Renee into the driver's seat holding a gun on her all the while."

"You did what?"

Debra managed a slight smile in response.

"What were they driving?"

"A dark blue Peugeot sedan."

"Did you get a license plate number?"

"No. It all happened too fast … it was so confusing. He said he has Renee and Rafael and Miguel and he doesn't intend to release them until he has the scroll."

"What else did he tell you?"

"Once he has the scroll, he will call to tell you where they can be found. I asked him who has the scroll now. He didn't know … he said to ask Katz. Stan, if he doesn't get the scroll, he threatened to kill them all."

"Anything else?"

"He said we have two days."

"Okay, we'll figure it out. Take a few deep breaths and sit down for a while. Hand me my cellphone, before you do … thanks."

"Hello, Amir … Parker here."

* * *

"What are you doing, Sebastian. Are you crazy? Are you trying to get arrested and go to jail for the rest of your life? If you stop this insanity now, you could escape. What are you doing? Let it go. It's not worth it," Renee pleaded.

"Shut up! You wouldn't understand."

"Like, I wouldn't understand about your precious knights?"

"Yeah, something like that. Just keep driving and shut up."

"Or what? You'll kill me now instead of later?"

"I don't want to kill you now or later, Renee, but I will if I have to."

"Are you going to kill the Tuguías also?" she asked. "You and your knights are really brave men … threatening the lives of two men in their eighties and an unarmed woman. You just don't understand what you're doing. You can escape. Stop the car and let me out, now!"

"I don't expect you to understand. I don't care about my life. I won't be around very much longer anyway. But neither will the scroll, I'll see to that! Turn here … north.

* * *

"Yes, Stan," Katz said, "I've been expecting your call. I didn't want to disturb you or Andy until one of you was ready to talk."

"You know what's going on then?"

"Yes. Yossi contacted me right after the ambush and later Miguel called. Apparently, one of the escaped criminals kidnapped his brother. He is being held for ransom."

"It's worse than that," Stan said. "Sebastian is the kidnapper … the man who followed Debra and Andy to Jerusalem … he's still alive. Not only does he have Rafael, but he also kidnapped Miguel and Renee. He's holding the three of them all hostage somewhere … I don't know where. He demanded that the scroll be delivered to him, or he plans to kill them all."

"Yes, I know … at least I knew about Rafael," Katz said. "Miguel asked us to break the contract and return the scroll. We agreed. Yossi and his team are headed to Orléans right now. The kidnapper is Sebastian, right? Is that what you said? Then it will be Sebastian who contacts me to tell me where to make the drop."

"Yes. He told Debra that we just have two days. Can you deliver it by then?

"Yes, Yossi is ready to act as soon as Sebastian calls us. Stan, since you know who it is, are you going to get the police involved?"

"No. They had their chance to protect us once and blew it. I'm going to take care of it. I'm not trusting Renee to them. Call me the moment you know the location."

"Okay, I will. Are you sure about this? You know what you are doing?"

"Yes, I'm sure about this. Whether I know what I'm doing remains to be seen."

"Then, God be with you, my son. Good luck!"

Turning to Debra, Stan said, "Hand me my robe, please. We need to go downstairs and tell Andy what's going on."

* * *

"What do you mean?" Andy asked.

"Just that. Sebastian kidnapped Renee. He kidnapped Rafael and Miguel earlier. He demanded the scroll be turned over to him, and then he would release them all," Stan said.

"How is that supposed to happen? The scroll must have been flown out of the country by now. We'll never get it back."

"Not so fast. We're on it. Katz stopped them from leaving. I'm expecting a phone call from Katz telling me where and when Yossi's team will deliver the scroll," Stan said.

"Yeah, but look at me," Andy demanded. "I can't do the job. You've got to get the police involved."

"No. It's too late for that. I'll be with them every step of the way, Andy. I'll find Renee and take care of Sebastian once and for all," Stan tried to assure him as the tragic turn of events caused Andy's heart to race.

Pulling the curtain aside, the on-duty nurse frantically raced to his bedside. "Are you okay?" she said. "Our monitors indicated a sharp rise in your heart rate."

A minute later Dr. Beaudry followed her unaware of the current situation. "Mr. Miller," Dr. Beaudry began, "I have some good news for you."

"Excuse me, doctor, Mr. Miller's pulse jumped from 75 to 113 beats per minute almost instantaneously."

"What is it, doc? I need some good news, after what I just heard," Andy said to Beaudry.

"What did you say?" Beaudry asked the attending nurse.

"His pulse …"

Stan interrupted, "The woman who was with me earlier …"

"Stan, maybe later," Andy said.

"Okay … well, anyway she just left me. When I told him just now, Andy got upset that he could not stop her in his condition."

"I'm sorry to hear that, Mr. Parker. She picked a heck of a time. Mr. Miller, try to relax and calm yourself. We'll see if your pulse will return on its own. If not, I'll order you something to take the edge off. For now, close your eyes, take deep breaths, and try to relax."

"You may as well order it now. I don't think I'll feel less anxious on my own anytime soon."

"Hopefully what I'm about to tell you should make you feel a little better. The MRI results are negative. There does not appear to be a ruptured disk. It appears your neck was hyperextended, or in other words you suffered from an extreme case of whiplash. You will not need surgery after all, but your neck will be sore for a while, and your arm and hand will continue to tingle until the inflammation goes down. You're going to need some bed rest for a few days, and I want you to wear a cervical collar for at least the next two weeks. If the pain persists after the two weeks, continue with the collar until it subsides. When you get back to the States, and your pain lessens, I would also like you to schedule an appointment with a neurosurgeon and get another MRI to confirm my opinion. For now, we're going to keep you here for a few days and let you rest and start a rehabilitation routine. You should continue it after you leave. Any questions?"

"No, not really. Glad to hear the results," Andy said.

"I'm leaving to admit you now. Someone will be here to take you to your room. I'm sorry to hear about your loss, Mr. Parker … I'm sure everything will be fine, soon."

"Say, doctor, the second bed in my room is vacant. Any chance you could arrange for us to share 407?" Stan volunteered.

"I'll check on it. Meanwhile, Mr. Miller, get some rest. You will feel much better very soon."

"Thanks, doc. I'm not so sure about that, but I hope you're right."

Two anxious hours had passed since Dr. Beaudry left Andy's bedside. Debra assured him she had secured his weapons in her car. Andy noticed the clock now read 5:25 when his nurse returned with two young orderlies. "Mr. Miller, your pulse rate is now down a bit from the 113 it was, but it's still in the high 90s. Dr. Beaudry admitted you to Room 407. He asked to have a valium prescription filled and administered once you arrive and are comfortable. Do you need anything before leaving here?"

"No, I'm okay. Thanks."

Debra and Stan waited Andy's arrival.

"Anything new?" Andy asked.

"I left a message on Renee's cellphone telling her you didn't need surgery after all," Debra confessed. "I thought if she was able to hear the news, it might ease the burden a bit."

"Good, thanks. Hey wait a minute … Renee's cellphone!" Andy cried out.

"Yeah, it has a tracking device on it she enabled," Stan interrupted. "Maybe the battery will last long enough to be of some use."

The knock on the door of Room 407 startled them as a small-framed Frenchman entered the room. "Bonsoir, my name is Jacques Gaston. I am Renee's father."

"Bonsoir," Stan answered. "I'm Stan Parker."

"Stan, I'm so very glad to finally meet my future son-in-law. But I wish it could be under different circumstances."

Pointing to his friends, he said, "This is Debra Herzog …"

"Why, yes, Debra, it's been such a long time," Jacques said. "It's so good to see you once again."

"And Andy Miller."

"Yes, Andy. Renee spoke of you often while she was with us in June. She said you're with the FBI. That's got to be a dangerous job Better you should be an architect," he said gesturing to Stan.

"Well, I'm an architect and I'm a little beaten up at the moment so I'm not so sure about that," Stan said.

"Renee told me you and Andy were involved in the accident. You don't look so good, Andy. Are you okay?"

"A pair of broken bones, whiplash and a little shaken up … but I'll be okay. Just need some rest. Thanks."

"Is that all she told you?" Stan asked.

"Yes. But she did ask if I could meet her here. She sounded upset," Jacques said. "Do you know where I might find her?"

"Jacques, I think you should sit down for a moment. Renee did not mention anything about an ambush?"

Jacques sat. His knuckles grew white as he gripped the arms of the chair. "No. What are you talking about?"

"Andy and I came to France to assist two men transfer a document, a scroll actually, to the Israeli authorities – a Rafael and Miguel Tuguía," Stan began.

"Rafael and Miguel Tuguía? They're the people Renee met on her pilgrimage. In fact, Rafael came to visit me, if visit is the right word. Rather harsh and threatening. I knew this would have a tragic ending."

"En route to Paris, our caravan came under attack," Stan continued. "Five people were killed at the scene. Andy and I chased one of the assailants through the town of Artenay, but I lost control of the car and crashed into a tree. That's how we came to be here."

"Jacques," Stan said, then paused to swallow. "Renee was kidnapped earlier today. So, no, we don't know where she is at the moment."

"Kidnapped!" Jacques repeated in anger. "Mon Dieu, who would do such a thing? Was it one of the assailants?"

"Yes, and you're going to like this news even less," Stan cautiously said. "It was someone you know … Sebastian Philippe."

"Sebastian Philippe? … Once more I have to deal with Sebastian Philippe … that bastard," Jacques said in a rage. "I should have killed him years ago and we wouldn't be in this situation now."

"Hang on," Stan interrupted. "Let us catch you up. Plans have been finalized. We're confident he will contact us tomorrow and when he does, we're ready to bring him the scroll. Doing so will secure Renee's release. What did Sebastian do to you years ago?"

"Never mind. It was something involving Renee. She doesn't know that I know. Are the police involved, yet?" Jacques ask.

"No, I'm going to take care of it. Trust me. This scum is mine," Stan swore.

"Count me in," Jacques said.

"I don't think that's such a good idea," Andy said. "The violence is likely to continue. It's going to be dangerous for both of you."

"Regardless, I'm going," Stan repeated.

"Me too. You can either take me with you or not take me and I'll go alone, but I'm going. He kidnapped my little girl. I'm going to kill the bastard myself, with my bare hands, or die trying."

Stan knew any further discussion was out of the question. He also knew he could use the help. "Okay. Jacques, why don't you find a place for tonight? Do you have a cellphone?"

"Oui, Renee got me one for my birthday last year."

"Okay, what's the number? I'll call you when I hear something. If you don't hear from me tonight, meet me back here tomorrow morning at 10:00. Get some sleep. We're going to need it."

CHAPTER 35

SARAN, FRANCE - AUGUST 10, 2012

"Bonjour, Bureau de l'inspecteur Général Dupont."

"Bonjour, this is Guardien de La Paix Bertrand de Saran. Please let me speak to Général Dupont."

"Dupont here."

"Monsieur, this is Guardien de La Paix Anton Bertrand. I'm calling about yesterday's shootings near the town of Artenay. Three of your officers were killed at the scene, together with two of the assailants. Later, a third one was found dead."

"Yes, I'm aware. How can I help you?"

"Sir, through Interpol we were able to identify the first two dead assailants as Benito Sordi and Alberto Moretti. The third was identified as Guy Romano."

"Yes, thank you, I've been able to determine that much from here," Dupont said with a degree of arrogance that annoyed Bertrand to his core. "I look forward to receiving your complete report."

"Yes, sir," Bertrand said, "but the thing is when we crossed checked the names against the database, something interesting showed up."

"And what was that … Officer Bertrand?"

"Sir, all three were members of the Operation Gladio forces that trained in England in 1975."

"Yes, what of it, man?"

"Well, sir, for the last twenty-one hours I've been puzzled about the fact the assailants knew precisely where and when to attack the caravan. Doesn't that puzzle you as well, sir? The thing is there was a fourth man trained for Gladio in England in 1975 that was involved with yesterday's massacre."

"You've captured the fourth killer?"

"Not exactly, sir."

"Well, what then … spit it out, man."

"Sir, Capitaine Rousseau's name appears on the roster as well."

"What? Are you accusing Capitaine Rousseau of being involved in this gruesome act? I find that very hard to believe. We have the finest officers in public service."

"We're not yet ready to accuse him, sir. I just want to give you this heads up and request your silence and your cooperation as we continue our investigation."

"Well, be careful. Capitaine Rousseau is a well-respected officer here. I'll give you a few days before doing anything here."

"Yes sir. Thank you, sir."

ORLÉANS

Stan was up early and getting dressed when the doctor first arrived. "Good morning, Mr. Parker. I see you're ready to go."

"Yes, sir, big day today. Need to get after it."

"The reports from last evening says you slept well. No signs of fatigue or problems from yesterday's trauma?"

"No sir. But I guess I need to check into replacing the tree," Stan joked trying to ease his mind and the growing tension in the room.

"Yes, that would probably be a good idea. You need to stop doing that. Kind of hard on your body and the tree. I'll put your release through in a little while. Take care of yourself."

"Thank you. Doctor Beaudry, I'm expecting a telephone call any time now. I need to be on the road immediately after that, so I would appreciate your getting me out of here as soon as possible. It is an emergency."

"Yes, of course. And you, Mr. Miller. How are you this morning? Pulse is back down to 75 beats per minute. How about your back? Sleep okay?"

"Not really. Lots on my mind. Hard to sleep with the cast and collar, but I guess I'll get used to it. The valium seemed to help a little. No trouble breathing. My neck and shoulders are still sore."

"That is to be expected. There will be a nurse around in a little while to take you to rehab and work on your neck. Take it easy in there; you don't have to try to fix everything today. I know how you Americans are, especially you military types," he said with a smile. "Gentlemen, have a nice day … drive carefully."

Jacques passed the doctor on the way out. "Bonjour, any news yet?"

"Not yet," Stan confirmed. "We're still expecting a call this morning. Sleep okay, Jacques?"

"No, not at all. I was worried about all of this, so I called Marie and told her about Renee being kidnapped. That was a big mistake. I think I dissuaded her from calling the police, and convinced her to let you handle it, Stan, but I'm not sure. She going to talk to her priest and ask for his prayers."

* * *

Renee woke to a morning of doubt and fear.

She stared at the cigarette smoke-infused ceiling of her hotel-prison-cell and wondered what would become of them today. Her eyes wandered to the light fixture in the ceiling's center. The small incandescent bulb barely lit the room, but just enough to paint her pale alabaster skin with a sickening jaundiced color. She looked toward the other bed. Rafael and Miguel were still asleep. Behind her, it was now Sebastian's turn to guard the threesome.

Rousseau was gone. *But where?* she wondered. She thought about last night's exchange between Sebastian and Rousseau. *Sebastian, just before you came to Ormes, you passed an air force base in Bricy.*

Yes, what of it?

Were helicopters there or just fixed wing?

Both, why?

I thought we could heist one of the choppers and …

No, Daryl, we don't have time and it would be too dangerous. All we need is to have the Air Force after us. We'll just get in and out by car.

Did Rousseau convince him to steal one after all? Is that where he is now? she wondered.

With their hands tied and mouths taped shut the three disheveled prisoners' lives were now dependent on the honor of proven criminals.

Why would they release us? Renee asked herself. *Once they have the scroll, it's over. They'll just leave us to die, or worse, shoot us and be gone.*

Flushed with anger, her skin color morphed into a reddish hue that grew in intensity. *Wait, I can be tracked by my cellphone,* she thought. She began to squirm on the bed, rolling back and forth and kicking the headboard to get Sebastian's attention.

He came to her and ripped the tape from her mouth. "What is it?"

"I have to use the toilet."

"Okay, just a minute," he said, loosening the torn bed sheets binding her hands.

"Go."

She sat up and ran her fingers through her hair in an attempt to untangle the bird's nest now claiming her scalp. She reached for her purse as she passed the chamber's dresser.

"Leave it," Sebastian ordered.

"I need it," Renee pleaded. "You know … it's my time ..."

"Oh, all right. But be quick about it."

Renee entered the bathroom. She turned on her cellphone. Flushing the toilet after its use, she turned on the lavatory water for an extended time and went to work. *The sound will ease Sebastian's feeble mind*, she thought. She silenced the ring tone, shut off the vibration command, verified the tracking function was operable, and returned her phone to a hidden compartment within her purse.

Confident in her decision to act, she looked into the mirror to see a bruised left cheek from her bully's rough treatment during the sleepless night. As she washed her face and hands and ran a comb through her hair, she thought, *Asherah, be with me. Sebastian will soon be out of my life once and for all.*

She heard the hotel door open and the sound of the traffic passing by. She wondered, *Did Sebastian leave? Do I have a chance to escape?* She reentered the room to see Rousseau standing in the doorway holding a paper bag.

"Coffee?" he asked.

"Yes, I guess," she said, seeing her chance for escape vanish.

"Renee, wake the Tuguías," Sebastian ordered.

Rafael stirred as Renee shook his arm and loosened the straps binding his hands and legs. His brother did not.

"Miguel … Miguel … Miguel," Renee said, her voice rising in intensity with each call. "He's not breathing … he's … he's dead."

Rafael sat up and ripped the tape from his mouth. "You son of a bitch. You killed him, just as if you had stuck a knife into his heart," Rafael yelled as he rushed Sebastian. Rousseau reached out and stopped him, throwing him back on the bed.

Rafael sat once more, holding his head in his hands, weeping.

"Old man, the same fate awaits you if you do not cooperate with me," Sebastian said with no sense of remorse or apology. "Now go and use the toilet. It's going to be a long time before you will be able to again."

CHAPTER 36

ORLÉANS, FRANCE

"Hello, Andy, Katz here."

"Have you heard anything yet?" Andy anxiously asked imagining the day ahead.

"Yes, he just called with instructions."

"Hold on, Amir, I'll put you on speaker. Stan, Jacques and Debra are all here with me now. Amir, I'm confined to the hospital for a few days. Stan's in charge now. Call his cellphone in the future."

"Yes, I will. I have the number. As I was saying, Sebastian just called with instructions for us to deliver the scroll to the Grand Cimetière d'Orléans, near the train station at Fleur-les-Aubrais, Barrière Saint-Marc to be exact. Apparently, there's a memorial to the French soldiers who died in the First World War in the northeast part of the cemetery. We're supposed to leave it at the memorial at precisely two this afternoon. Nagar, Hassan and Wolff are heading there now to check out the location."

"Got it. Thanks," Stan said.

"Okay, Jacques, let's go. Sebastian will be there in a little less than three hours. Let's take both cars. We may need them."

"I know it well," Jacques said proudly. "My grandfather is buried there."

"I'm going too," Debra announced as she stood and steeled herself for what was to come.

"I don't think that's …"

Debra cut him off, remembering how he tried to dissuade Jacques. "Jacques has one car, and I have the other. If you want to go with me, fine. If not, stay here with Andy. I have at least one score to settle with that bastard."

"Let's go then," Stan said, realizing how determined she was.

Moments later, Stan popped the truck and brought the stored weapons to the back seat. Jacques led in his Citroën; Debra and Stan followed in her rental. They arrived at the Orléans water plant of Lyonnaise des Eaux near the cemetery's south entrance twenty minutes later. Jacques parked his car in the parking lot and joined the others. They circled the perimeter of the twelve-acre-oval-shaped cemetery. Four openings punctured the nine-foot-high stone perimeter wall, allowing pedestrians to enter through the wrought iron gates. Two gates were permanently sealed allowing automobiles to pass through only the south and west gates. Returning to their starting point, they entered the south gate of the oval's long axis. To their right, a caretaker's time-worn, French Renaissance styled home greeted them. A second home on the left mirrored the first to present a symmetrical southern entry.

Arriving and stopping at the memorial Stan said, "We're here. This is it."

"Give me a moment, will you, please?" Jacques asked getting out of the car. Thirty yards away, down a ten-foot-wide gravel path, stood a monument dedicated to the French soldiers who gave their lives in service to their country. Jacques walked past the words "*À Nos Morts* 1914-1918" chiseled into the modest stone pediment of the memorial to a field of hundreds of grave sites, each marked by a single white cross. He stopped and bowed his head in front of one of them. The ground plaque read, 'Sous-Lieutenant André Gaston, April 25, 1881-August 10, 1918.'

Jacques did not know his grandfather. Family stories told of a deeply religious man of Gnostic tradition. He married a woman of Armenian descent who was deported from Istanbul in 1915. He left his wife and young son in the winter of 1917 to defend his country and all that was good in the world, and to fight against the evil of the invading German armies. Sous-Lieutenant Gaston and his comrades in the French 1st Army joined the British 4th Army, the Canadians, and Australians to advance toward their German enemy in the Battle of Amiens.

It was at this point in the war to end all war that the allies' tactics changed. They no longer took up defensive positions of trenched warfare to protect their towns. They had to be on offense.

At Amiens there were no bombardments that preceded the attack. It was silent. It was deceptive. They held the element of surprise. The Germans were unprepared and greatly outnumbered. It was the turning point in the war. There Sous-Lieutenant Gaston lost his life on August 10, 1918 defending the railway between Paris and Amiens. Family lore suggested he did so knowing full well he protected the fifth and six sites along the Path of Initiation – La Cathédrale Notre-Dame de Paris and La Cathédrale Notre-Dame d'Amiens – and the Gnostic secrets they held.

Jacques now stood before his grandfather's grave promising to honor his memory by what he was about to do. He turned and walked back to Debra's waiting vehicle.

"Thank you," Jacques said, opening the door to the car and a new world of violence.

Straight ahead of them was a third house, one that once guarded the north entrance to the cemetery, and now stood above the gate in vacant disrepair.

Turning to Debra, Stan asked, "What do you think?"

"It seems to me they only have two options to secure the scroll," she said. "One – they will enter the west gate and exit to the south or vice versa or, two – they will not bring an automobile into the walled enclosure at all. I'm guessing the latter."

"Also, the train station is just north of here. They may try to get rid of the car and escape by train." Jacques added.

"That makes a lot of sense. Okay, Jacques, why don't you wait in your car and watch the south gate in case they enter from either direction? Debra and I will cover the one at the north in case they head to the train station. Don't follow them inside, Jacques. Give them time to exit."

Debra nodded in agreement.

Stan continued, "If they head north, I'll call you and you do the same if they enter or exit from the south. Keep your cellphone handy. Agree?"

"Yes, of course. Whatever you say."

Debra immediately reached behind her for the carbine, remembering her days of military service in the Golan Heights with the Women's Corps.

"Ever fired a weapon like that?" Stan asked.

She did not answer. The incredulous look on her face from her two years of combat said enough. She handed Stan the second Glock and magazines.

"Here, take this to defend yourself, if you need to," Stan said, handing Jacques Andy's handgun. Ever fire a Glock before? I just learned myself."

Jacques's eyebrows raised as he whispered the word, "No."

"Jacques, this is a magazine," Stan said as he began the instructions given by Andy just days before. "You have seventeen rounds in it. Insert the magazine into the handle of the gun, like so. Move the slide to the rear to engage the first bullet. It has three safeties to prevent an accidental firing. By squeezing this lever, when you pull the trigger, you will release the external safety and automatically release the two internal ones. Do not point it at anyone unless you are prepared to use it. Understand?"

"Oui!" Jacques said with a resolve to be rid of Sebastian.

"Here's an extra magazine, just in case. Release the spent magazine here and insert the new one."

"One final thing," Debra said. "We've got to give them time to feel comfortable that their plan has worked and to reveal the location of Renee and the Tuguías before we act. So don't do anything until Stan and I give you the go ahead. We'll just follow them until we hear something. Okay, we have an hour and fifty-five minutes. Let's stake out our positions."

SARAN

Sebastian draped a blanket over Miguel's lifeless body, retied Rafael's hands, taped his mouth, and laid him in the other bed. "Sorry to leave you like this old man, but if all goes well someone will be along before you have to use the toilet again."

Holding Renee's left arm and a gun to her back, they closed the door on Miguel and Rafael. Rousseau waited in his rental car as the pair walked to Miguel's Citroën. Sebastian tossed Renee's purse on the rear seat, popped the trunk, and commanded, "Get in."

Rousseau led the way. He returned his rental car and joined Sebastian. They turned east onto Rue de Joie and crossed the viaduct above the train tracks. "I think this road is aptly named," Sebastian said through a smile.

"Our road of joy is just ahead."

Without warning, a beeping sound came from Stan's cellphone as Renee's tracking device came within range. The Citroën stopped at the north gate to the cemetery at 1:40. "Rousseau? What the hell is Rousseau doing with … oh, that explains … that son of a bitch," Stan said to himself.

Renee was not visible. "I don't see her. Where is she?" Debra asked.

"The bastard must have her locked in the trunk," Stan growled.

Sebastian got out and entered the cemetery's northern portal. Rousseau drove on, heading south along the oval's perimeter road. Debra and Stan watched from the parking lot across the street as Sebastian broke into the vacant building and climbed the stairs to the second floor.

"Sebastian and his partner are here," Stan called to Jacques. "Be on the lookout for a white Citroën sedan. It's heading your way."

Jacques reported to Stan and Debra, "Got it. The Israelis just entered the southern gate."

Rousseau spoke to Sebastian a moment later, "The Israelis are here – coming at you from the south."

Sebastian responded to Rousseau, "Yeah, got them," his binoculars now fixed on the familiar black-bullet-riddled Mercedes approaching him from the south. "Get ready. Pick me up at the north gate when they leave."

"Will do," Rousseau confirmed as he moved his car closer to the pick-up point.

Seeing Rousseau's car move into position, Stan said, "Jacques, we'll follow the Citroën when it leaves. I'll let you know when. We'll take the lead when you get here. Follow me but keep a safe distance. Don't let him spot you."

"Got it," Jacques confirmed.

Sebastian watched his foes approach the monument. The man who shot him drove. Yossi Wolff emerged from the rear and carried a leather case toward the monument. "Get ready, Daryl. We're about to score."

Yossi Wolff's training had instilled a sense of commitment and pride in his job. He was a member of an elite group of Israeli professionals who placed their country above their own lives. He and his escorts did not give up easily, but this time they were ordered to do just that. Feeling an unfamiliar since of defeat, Wolff placed the scroll near the head of the reclining soldier and retreated through the west gate and out of sight.

Nagar and Hassan continued on to the chartered plane at Paris-Orly awaiting their return to Israel. Yossi Wolff remained behind and traveled to

Albi in search of the woman he once cared about – Noelle Martine.

"Okay, go," Sebastian ordered.

From his hunting blind of the cemetery's vacant building, Sebastian hurried toward the monument, retrieved the leather case and raced back to the north gate. Rousseau waited his arrival. He popped the truck and tossed the scroll to Renee.

"Here, take care of this for me," he sarcastically said. His smile and moving lips confirmed Stan's suspicion that Renee was held hostage in the trunk. Sebastian slammed the trunk lid shut and ran to the driver's side. "Daryl, move over. I'll drive."

The Citroën turned left in the direction of La Gare des Aubris-Orléans. "Let's go, Jacques. I have to hang up in case he calls me. I'll call you back," Stan said.

The pair followed at a safe distance with Jacques close behind.

CHAPTER 37

ALBI, FRANCE

A knock on the door of Father Pierre Dubois's library startled the priest deep in study.

"Yes?" he asked.

Noelle opened the door and answered, "It's Marie Gaston, Father."

Noelle lingered out of sight a moment as Marie entered. Marie was not only a faithful member of his parish, but also a good friend to the priest. As a member of the Dames of Malta, she had spent many years helping children, the homeless, handicapped and other disenfranchised citizens in the Archdiocese of Toulouse and its subordinate Archdiocese of Albi.

"Bonjour, Marie," he said rising to greet his unanticipated guest. "What is the matter? Are you crying, my dear?

"Yes, Father, it's Renee," she said.

Hearing the name Renee, Noelle continued to eavesdrop on their conversation.

"Jacques called me last night. Somehow she is entangled with Sebastian once again … I don't know how … I don't know why, but nevertheless she is."

"I'm sorry you're so upset, my dear. Please have a seat. Can I get you something … some water, perhaps? Don't worry so, Marie. Sebastian has been one of my most faithful parishioners. He speaks of her often with such fondness. I'm sure everything will be fine."

"No. No, thank you. I don't need anything. I think Sebastian has you fooled, Father. Jacques said he kidnapped Renee and said something about an ancient scroll. I haven't heard anything from him all day. It's late and I'm worried sick. Father, I don't know what to do. I just laid there all night … tossing and turning, not able to sleep. They won't involve the police. They just want to take care of it themselves."

"Who are 'they', my dear? Take care of what?"

"Jacques and friends of Renee. He was frightened, but said Renee was strong and courageous and said I should not worry. I don't know what they're planning, but I'm frightened for them as well. Father, did Sebastian ever tell you anything about an ancient scroll?"

"He never discussed it with me outside of the confessional and I'm bound under penalty of excommunication to protect its sanctity."

"So he did say something," Marie said.

"I didn't say that, my dear. Marie, things will be okay. Have faith in God, my dear. Why don't you pray with me?"

CHAPTER 38

FLEURY-LES-AUBRAIS, FRANCE

"Parker?" Sebastian asked.

"Yeah, where are you?" he asked with Sebastian fully in sight.

"You can find Rafael and Miguel in Saran, Le Motel Orléans-Nord, Room 105. Miguel died during the night. I don't know why. I have Renee with me, so don't do anything stupid. I will call you later when I let her go."

"Damn it. I knew it. He has her with him," Stan said.

Stan saw Sebastian driving Miguel's stolen Citroën. Rousseau was on his right. Renee could not be seen. They turned on to Rue La Martine and headed north toward the train station of Aubris-Orléans.

Stan called back. "Jacques, looks like you were right … looks like they're planning to escape by train. They still have Renee. They have her locked in the trunk – I know it!"

Two large parking garages connected by a center helix came into view as they approached. To their left were two exit ramps from the building on ground level. The blue signage to the right, marked with the letter 'P', indicated their point of entry. They descended down an entry ramp and vanished from sight.

Stan thought about Miguel's earlier comment at St. Croix, *once a candidate's spirit resulted in him gaining sufficient strength and moral conviction to represent good against evil, he was considered a warrior and knighted.*

He thought about Renee being trapped in the trunk of the car and realized he had no choice. *Warrior or not, I cannot turn back now.*

"Jacques, once they enter the helix there will be no escape. When I think they're vulnerable, I'm going to make a play for them. Hang back and cover me."

"Got it."

Sebastian exited the helix on the third floor and drove to the north side of the packed garage. He made a wide swing to the left and cut the wheel hard to the right, but had to back up in order to position the car directly in front of the narrow parking space.

Stan and Debra emerged from the helix unseen. This was the moment he had waited for. He switched off the deployment of the car's airbag.

"I'm going to ram them. Hang on."

"Wait, I'm getting out," Debra commanded.

She opened her door, slung the carbine over her shoulder and raced to position herself on the west side of the garage.

Sebastian's eyes focused on the car to his left and small space he was about to enter unaware of Stan' presence. Stan stomped the gas pedal to the floor. The car leapt forward. The smell of burning rubber concealed the stench of the petroleum-laden air surrounding him. Rousseau caught sight of the car charging directly toward him and scrambled to get off three rounds into Stan's windshield. Stan swerved in both directions. Each bullet missed hitting him. Glass shattered around him. With accelerating speed and careful not to come anywhere the trunk, Stan locked his elbows and slammed into the passenger's side of the car. The ten-year-old Citroën slid to the left absorbing the blow of the impact. The front door was crushed. Rousseau's bloody face lay against the dashboard, unconscious.

Renee felt the impact of the crash, as her body was hurled into the side of her black surroundings. Renee cradled the leather case, as if holding a doll, to comfort her terror. She had no idea what was going on outside but feared she may be left to die inside of a steel sarcophagus. Panic overcame her. She had to get out … somehow.

The crash pushed the front half of the Citroën into the Audi on its left. Sebastian flung himself into the back seat to escape. Suddenly semi-automatic gunfire erupted from the carbine pinning him down inside the Citroën. He opened the left rear door ever so slightly and fired a handgun in the direction of the carbine's burst. Debra recoiled permitting him a split second to exit the vehicle. Renee's cellphone and the contents of her purse spilled to the ground as he exited. He ignored the screams and pounding coming from the trunk as he darted from the car. Sebastian dropped to the deck and rolled to avoid the bullets spraying around him and continued firing in Debra's direction.

The momentary silence of Debra's magazine exchange emboldened Sebastian to expose himself. He jumped up and hid behind a minivan when the carbine stopped echoing off the concrete walls surrounding them. He unloaded four quick rounds in Stan's direction.

Debra had not seen Jacques approaching him from the east, until now. She pushed in another magazine but did not fire as he approached in anger – his temper pushing him toward resolution.

Standing erect like the steely, frozen figure of an unfeeling robot, Jacques sighted down the barrel of the loaned Glock and fired repeatedly in the direction of his long-time nemesis. Blood spurted from Sebastian's leg – a leg that once had scored many goals for Le Lycée Lapérouse. "That's for my lifeless grandchild!"

The once famous football star from Albi now screamed and scrambled for cover. Jacques walked closer with a fearless and deliberate stride. He fired once again. Sebastian fell to the ground clutching his chest. "That's for Renee, you bastard!"

Stan ran to Jacques' side. "Give me the gun, Jacques."

"But …" Jacques protested.

Stan grabbed a handkerchief from his pocket. "Just give it to me," he repeated. He wiped down the handle Jacques once clutched.

Leaning against the bumper of the minivan, Sebastian pushed himself up and stood in a pool of blood. He fired once more and missed Stan shot back, striking him in the forehead with the same caliber bullet that was lodged in his chest and leg. Sebastian recoiled toward the rear and crumpled to the floor, dead.

Stan and Jacques raced to the rear of the Citroën. Stan climbed through the cab to reach for the key fob lying on the console and tossed it to Jacques. With trembling hands, Jacques popped the truck lid.

"Papa!" exclaimed Renee as she shielded her eyes from the bright light. She threw her left arm around her crying father; her right arm still clinging to the scroll.

"Thank you, Papa, thank you," she said, now beginning to cry.

Jacques lifted her from her prison and gently lowered her to the ground.

Stan picked up Renee's cellphone from the ground, gave it to Debra and said, "Here, call Andy. I'm sure he's out of his mind with worry."

Stan gently hugged Renee's thin, battered frame. "I love you so much. Thank you," she whispered wrapping her arms around his neck in a full embrace.

As she turned to make the call, Debra saw Sebastian lying in a pool of blood. "I guess it's over," she said as the reality of what had just happened began to sink in.

"No, not yet. I want you three to leave right now. I'll wait here for the police and take the hit," Stan said slamming the trunk lid close.

"But what will happen to you? Shouldn't I stay to explain the kidnapping?" Renee asked.

"Don't worry. I'll be fine. I'll call Bertrand. He was the police officer who investigated the crash in Artenay. He knows me and Andy, about Sebastian and the ambush. I'll explain the kidnaping and where the hostages are. I'll be fine. Don't worry. Okay?"

"I'd better stay," Debra said. "How else are you going to explain the carbine holes in the walls? None of the bullets actually struck him. We can say I jumped out of the car to create a diversion to allow you time to be in position to defend yourself should he attack you again. After all there's evidence that they shot at you already."

"Who are you?" Stan asked. "French Literature at the Sorbonne, really? Thanks. It makes sense for you to stay."

"I did spend a little time in the Israeli Army, don't forget. And I spent a lot of time praying while on patrol … maybe unknown to me Asherah was listening then. Seems like she's been listening today as well. 'Vengeance is mine; I will repay, saith the Lord.' Well guess what? I guess they can now be considered equal partners."

"Don't be too long," Renee said. She gathered her belongings from the ground and stuffed them into her purse.

"Jacques, take Renee back to the hospital, then take the scroll on to Albi. We'll join you there in a few days when Andy gets released. We'll figure out what to do with it then."

"Certainly. Thank you both so much for saving my little girl. God be with you," Jacques said as tears streamed down his face.

Stan waved goodbye, then placed the phone call. "Officer Bertrand, this is Stan Parker, Special Agent Miller's friend. The man who Andy and I pursued in Artenay is dead and here with me now. Daryl Rousseau, the policeman who was with us in Artenay, turned out to be his accomplice. He's also here now. He's alive, but unconscious. He'll need an ambulance. We're on the third floor of the garage next to La Gare des Aubris-Orléans. I'll wait for you to arrive. You'll find their hostages in Saran at Le Motel Orléans-Nord, Room 105. I think one of them may be dead. I'll explain everything when you get here."

Bertrand removed the phone from his ear in surprised affirmation. "Rousseau, I knew it. I guess I'm ready to accuse your precious Capitaine Rousseau now Général Dupont, you effete son of a bitch!" Bertrand exclaimed.

He turned his attention back to his phone. "Okay, I'll notify the Fleury-les-Aubrais police and send one of our guys to the hotel. We'll be there in ten minutes. If they arrive before us, don't try to explain. Just tell them I'm on my way. Out."

* * *

"How's my main man doing?" Stan asked.

"Hey, Stan, what took you so long? We've been worried you might have a problem with the police. Renee's been here for a while. Debra caught a taxi and arrived about an hour and a half ago. She told us all about it. I'm really proud of you, my friend!"

"Thank you," Stan said puffing out his chest and smiling. "Yeah, I had to catch a cab as well."

Debra shook her head with astonishment. "Well, Mr. Machismo has emerged from his professorial duties," she said with loving laughter. *But you know, I guess I'll let him get away with it ... I think he's earned it,* she thought.

"Bertrand explained yesterday's ambush to the local police of Fleury-les-Aubrais when they arrived. Since they are both sectors of the Police Nationale, they let Saran claim jurisdiction and continue dealing with the opened file. Bertrand took me back to police headquarters in Saran to answer a few questions. And, yes, I could not have done it without Debra and Jacques," Stan added, embarrassed by his obvious oversight.

"I think we finally have closure. I convinced Bertrand since we had been burned by Rousseau, and therefore the Police Nationale – Andy and I did not know who we could trust. He bought the story of Debra's help for the diversion and reluctantly chose to believe we had no choice, but to try to apprehend Sebastian on our own."

"He completely understood I had to use aggressive, deadly force, when I pointed out the bullet holes and shattered glass from Rousseau's gun in Debra's windshield. By the time Bertrand arrived, Rousseau was dead. Bertrand wrote the whole thing off as self-defense. I think mostly he was just so happy about getting to rub Rousseau's nose in Dupont's face nothing else much mattered. They impounded Debra's rental. We'll need to report that to the agency and work out the details. But the case is closed and as far as the police are concerned we're free to leave the country. Renee, I assume your father is on his way to Albi?"

"Yes, he sure is. I've never seen him as proud or happy as he was on our ride to the hospital. He couldn't stop talking about you and Debra and how you two … to quote him now … 'saved my little girl,' " Renee said. "He's expecting us all in a couple of days. I called him to tell him Andy will be released on the day after tomorrow. What about Rafael and Miguel?"

"Bertrand said they found them in the motel room, asked Rafael a few questions, got him something to eat and drink, and then had an officer drive him to Paris for a flight back to Santiago de Compostela. The coroner picked up his brother at the same time. He determined Miguel died from lack of oxygen due to his lung cancer. Of course, it was exacerbated by the gag."

"Get some rest, old friend. I'm going to take Renee and Debra out to have the most wonderful meal of their lives! I'm sure we can find a bottle or three of Gerard Bertrand Coteaux du Languedoc and a juicy, medium-rare Boeuf au Poivre with a side of matchstick potatoes somewhere in Orléans. Should we sneak one in the hospital for you when we return, maybe with a side of béarnaise sauce?"

CHAPTER 39

ALBI, FRANCE

Fräulein Müller's thoughts were on Sebastian and the evening they spent together less than two weeks before. He was so virile, so handsome and such a rising star within the Order her mentor, Fra' Schmidt, nobly led. Now, he was on some kind of mission with Colonel Sordi. She was so proud of him and couldn't wait to see him again after it was over. She knew it would win him further acclaim within the Order and her increased stature being by his side. Fra' Schmidt would relent and allow them to go public with their affections. She knew it.

The telephone ringing shattered the silence of her memories and aspirations and back to the job at hand. "Good morning," Erma said. "Sovereign Military Order of Malta, Fra' Schmidt's Office, how may I help you?"

"Hello, my name is Father Pierre Dubois. I'm a priest and a brother in the Order. Benito Sordi told me I may be able to reach him there from time to time."

"Yes, Father, he is often here, but not at this time. I understand he is out of the country … in France, I believe. Would you like to speak with Fra' Schmidt?"

"No … no, thank you … not now."

"Would you like me to leave a message for Colonel Sordi?

"No, I'll call back another time. Thank you. Goodbye."

A veil of horror descended from the heavens as Dubois thought about Marie's visit on the prior day and Sordi's telephone call from a week and a half ago. *He really didn't do anything crazy, did he?* Dubois asked himself. He placed another call, this time to Rousseau.

"Bonjour, Service de Protection des Hautes Personnalités."

"Bonjour, my name is Pierre Dubois. Do you have an officer by the name of Daryl Rousseau working in the department?"

"Oui. Capitaine Daryl Rousseau."

"May I speak with him please?"

"No, I'm sorry. He's not available. He is on assignment."

"Thank you. Goodbye."

Dubois picked up the Friday morning edition of *Le Figaro* from his desk and raced through its pages. On the back of the first section an unnoticed headline jumped off the page – *Five Men Die in a Brutal Attack Near Orléans.* Shocked, he began to read aloud. "Two Italians, Benito Sordi and Alberto Moretti, were killed yesterday along with three officers from the Police Nationale in a gangland shooting north of Orléans. The names of the police officers were not released pending notification of their next of kin. Officers at the scene say two of the assailants fled the scene after a barrage of gunfire. The reason for the shooting is unknown at this time, but officials …"

"My God, what have they done?" Dubois asked aloud.

Noelle overheard his cry. She knew, but did not answer. A phone call from Yossi earlier in the day told her about yesterday's near fatal attack on him and his countrymen, the shameful order for him to give up the scroll, and not wanting to return to Israel under these conditions. His call made her realize she wanted more from life than the Church could offer. Father Dubois' seeming duplicity and Yossi's desire to renew their prior relationship now sealed her fate.

CHAPTER 40

EDINBURGH, SCOTLAND

Yesterday had been life altering for a man with few remaining years. Rafael was an emotional wreck when he was dropped off at Charles de Gaulle Airport. He could not go back to Compostela and resume his prior life. Not now.

He pondered his life's journey and what he had learned.

He knew that about the same time as Egyptians searched for divine truths along the Nile, Hindus and other eastern religions sought spiritual fulfillment by energy flowing through the seven chakras of the body. From the first chakra in the base of the spine keeping one safe and connected to the ground, to the seventh chakra in the head that reaches for the divine, all points of concentrated human energy needed to be connected, open and in balance to have fulfillment.

Similarly, the six Chakras of earth energy in Galicia and France and one in Scotland evolved from the locations of the seven planetary Druid oracles and points of spiritual growth of Druidism. These sites determined a path for ancient pilgrims to follow the stars to the end of the known world and their soul to continue toward the setting sun at the ocean west of Compostela.

Over hundreds of years they evolved from Druid oracles to Roman Temples, as Rome invaded England and captured Gaul, to Christian cathedrals, as France reclaimed its country. Roman Catholicism grew from these locations while repression of unorthodox beliefs in France and Spain caused the Cathars and Templars to go underground.

From Israel and Judah, the Hebrew faith evolved and expanded the Torah. The prophet Elijah's understanding of God was cast as a spiritual journey as well. What better way could be found for a pilgrim's spiritual growth than to recast Elijah's journey on a western path of Gnostic initiation to the mystical locations? And what better way could this be done than for the Templars to leave the style of the Romanesque period of Santiago de Compostela and build the Kingdom of God in the new sacred geometry of the Gothic cathedrals.

Rafael had been connected to this and the Path of Initiation through France for years. What could he now take from it?

He called Renee and found she was safe. Her father was safe as well she said and he had the scroll. Rafael knew Jacques could be trusted.

He did not return home. Rafael spent the night in Paris and caught a morning flight to Edinburgh.

He had sought the courage and strength to renew his life three separate times during the emotional roller-coaster of his first fifty-four years. Rosslyn Chapel called to him once again.

He had journeyed from Compostela – the beginning, the base chakra of spiritual energy, to Rosslyn – the end, the Crown Chakra, whose opening was essential to divine understanding, healing and inner peace.

Rafael felt despondent and alone in war-torn Spain when his good friend Jacob neared his bar mitzvah and moved to Israel. On the path he found strength to look at something larger than himself.

Miguel moved to Chartres thirteen years later. He was alone once more and had difficulty coping with the reinstated Jesuits and Opus Dei technocrats of the Franco Regime. Again, he looked within himself on El Camiño de las Estrellas to find a changing new world order of the 1960's where non-violent change, peace, and justice were beginning to be embraced.

Sixteen years after that, Mitterrand's political victory in France gave him hope for the future of Spain. The path led him to visit Miguel and enjoy a different spiritual experience. The elation Miguel felt as a part of a new world order was palpable. Franco had died seven years before. Spain was changing. There was hope for his friends in the Basque region of Spain.

Now, at age eighty-four he found himself at Rosslyn for the fourth time. He was alone once more.

He knew the mystical healing power of Rosslyn. At the Crown Chakra, the pilgrim opened his conscious mind to Sophia, the Gnostic goddess of wisdom, and what lay beyond. He overcame his fear of death and channeled his spiritual energy to reach the source of life. Never had this been more meaningful than it was today.

Rafael entered the intimate room of Gnostic teachings captured in stone. The many carvings of the Green Man, an ancient Celtic god of nature peering out from surrounding leaves; the fallen angel, Lucifer, hanging upside down and bound with rope; the Dance of Death revealing the spiritualism of life and death's pending victory; the carved stars of the vaulted ceiling representing the Milky Way and uniting the pillars of Portugal and Scotland. These and other carvings intertwined in a frosting-like-skin to cover the late Gothic structure that honored the Knights Templar.

The Apprentice Pillar drew him closer. His fingers caressed the twisting motion of the second Solomonic pillar. It was the end of his life's journey. He returned to a front pew and closed his eyes.

He had much to resolve as his world closed in on him. He drew into his inner world and reflected on the last two days. *My brother is dead. Three police officers are dead. The five assailants are dead. Dr. Parker and Even Nagar were shot. Special Agent Andrew Miller is recovering in a hospital bed from a near fatal car crash. And for what! For a six-year old's commitment to his father. For a 2,000-year-old scroll that may not be true! I wish I never had David translate the scroll in the first place.*

David Hitzig touched his shoulder and brought him back to the moment.

"Rafael," David said, "I'm here as you asked."

Rafael came out of his trance-like state and turned to greet his new friend and associate. "David, thank you for coming."

"You're welcome, but why am I here?"

"Look around you, son. The Templars have been misunderstood since being arrested by King Phillip. He painted them with the brush of being the

Pope's army and moved the Papacy to Avignon where he could control it. The Templars were not warriors acting on behalf of the Papacy. They did not care about saving a single individual's soul. Unlike the other knights of the crusades, they wanted to unite Christianity, Judaism and Islam in true Gnostic monotheism."

"Okay, I believe you. But that was almost seven hundred years ago. Why here? Why now?

"David, I have failed. I have come to Rosslyn once more to pay my debts to you and my brother and seek inner peace. Here is the €10,000 as agreed. Thank you for keeping silent. You can now tell the world about the scroll or don't tell, it's entirely up to you."

"What do you mean? Are you not going to make it public?"

"I don't know. I am not sure what to do. Do you want to bring it to the Israeli government? The only thing I can think about is avenging my brother's death. And the only one left is an American named George Wilson. Stan warned Miguel about him early in our mission. I later found out from Renee who he was, how he helped Sebastian and the part he played in this mess."

"No, I do not want to represent the scroll as being real to Israel or anyone. I have no idea whether it is or not. That's between you and your father. I just wanted to make sure if it were made public and if it were real, it would wind up with the other writings of that era. That's all."

"Well, that's good to know. That takes one option off the table."

"Let's get back to George," David said. "In the New Testament Paul is quoted as saying, 'Avenge not yourselves, but rather give place unto wrath: for it is written, Vengeance is mine; I will repay, saith the Lord.' Rafael, do you know what that means?

"Yes, God is the only one who can kill. He will avenge our transgressors. That's why I'm struggling now. He seems to be indiscriminately killing everyone around me."

"I wish that were true. But nowhere in the Torah does God ask people to let him kill on their behalf. Paul is taking a verse from Deuteronomy and twisting it to deal with the Romans. The Torah tells us 'Vengeance is mine, and recompense, for the time when their foot shall slip; for the day of their calamity is at hand, and their doom comes swiftly.' Do you know what *that* means?"

"No, actually I don't. That's the first I've heard the passage spoken this way."

"The passage suggests God will be vengeful to those who turn against him and worship another god. In this context, God is forecasting the Israelites will worship another god, Baal as it turned out, and forewarning them he will bring his destructive wrath if they do. It has nothing to do with a single person or even a few. He does not go about killing indiscriminately. He expects to work through people, not to do their work for them."

"So, if you want to kill George to avenge your brother – have at it. Don't expect God to do it for you. He also says, 'Thou shall not kill.' Kind of puts you in a box, doesn't it?"

* * *

"Father Dubois," Noelle said. "I have Rafael Tuguía on the phone. He's asking if you could arrange and attend a meeting with Jacques, Marie and Renee Gaston and himself on Sunday in your office after services."

CHAPTER 41

ROME, ITALY - AUGUST 13, 2012

The Lateran Basilica seemed even more intimidating than usual to Father Pierre Dubois as he walked on the cobbled streets toward the Baroque church and seat of the Roman Pontiff. He passed the Egyptian obelisk anchoring Lateran square that served as a reminder of Constantine's victories on behalf of Rome and the Church and entered the administrative offices of the Bishop of Rome.

Cardinal Ricci, Cardinal Vicar for His Holiness, greeted his guest with a glowing smile underscoring his affection for his protégé. "Ah, there you are my son," he said. "I was delighted to receive your call."

Dubois bowed his head and quietly said in an anticipated courtly manner, "Your Eminence."

"Please have a seat, Pierre. What may I do for you?"

"Your Eminence, shortly before his death, Bontio Sordi said I should contact you if anything should happen to him."

"Yes, I heard of the tragic event. What a pity to lose a man of his stature. Do you know how or why it happened?"

"I had no idea what he meant when he told me to contact you or that his death had occurred until one of my parishioners, a Marie Gaston, contacted me three days ago. When we met she told me about her daughter's horrific situation. Then I read about the killings in the paper and put two and two together.

She was so proud of her daughter's strength and courage in the face of such danger but was frightened she would come to a tragic end. She asked me if I knew anything about an ancient scroll her husband told her about. I did but could not divulge anything I knew because of the sanctity of the confessional. Earlier, another of my parishioners confessed that he spied on Marie's daughter and found her to be involved in a plot to reveal what he claimed was the true story of Jesus and Mary that still haunts Albi today."

"The story of Mary Magdalene being the rightful heir to the leadership of the Church rather than Peter?" the Cardinal asked.

"Yes, your Eminence. But how did you …?"

"It haunts everyone in the Vatican as well, my son," Ricci interrupted. "Were you aware of the scroll's existence?"

"Several days before Bontio's death, he told me of an ancient scroll that if revealed to the world would put an end to Catholicism and Christianity as we know it," Dubois said. "He told me if the Israelis verified its authenticity, they were prepared to purchase the scroll. They contracted to pay twenty-five million dollars to a Gnostic order of Mandaeans so they could return to the homeland in Iraq.

"He explained he planned to secure the scroll and turn it over to the Church and promised me his plan would not involve violence in any way. I believed him to be sincere and thanked him for his initiative on behalf of the Church.

"Your Eminence, I told Benito about the confession of my parishioner. I brought the scroll to Benito's attention. I was afraid of what its revelation might do. I now keep thinking all of this violence could have been avoided, were it not for me breaking my vows," Dubois concluded.

"You may be right my son; we will never know. But considering the alternative, I think you acted wisely and in the best interest of God and the Church. May Colonel Sordi's soul, and the souls of all the faithful departed, through the mercy of God rest in peace. Amen," Cardinal Ricci said making the sign of the cross. "Tell me, do the Israelis now have the scroll? What should we expect?"

"No, your Eminence. I have it secured in Albi. I was sent here by its owner, Rafael Tuguía, to speak to you about a possible solution. Yesterday, Rafael presided over a meeting with Marie Gaston, her husband Jacques, their daughter Renee and me. Jacques comes to his faith with a Gnostic heritage. Renee was the woman Rafael originally contacted to make the scroll public.

"Rafael presented his thoughts to the group and listened to each of them make their case from disparate points of view. Marie was an unquestioning advocate for turning it over to the Church. Jacques wanted it released for historical reasons and as he said, 'righting a terrible wrong' as you might expect. Renee wanted it released as well, but for another reason. The scroll speaks to the importance Jesus placed in women during his ministry.

"Your Eminence, Renee reminded me of Pope Gregory's homily in the late sixth century. He mistakenly and greatly disparaged Mary Magdalene by conflating John's story of her with the Mary whom Luke called a sinful woman. This remained unchecked for nearly 1,400 years until the Church finally corrected it just forty years ago. Renee argued the Church must do 'much, much more to correct a number of misconceptions about women found in the bible' and to continue her words, 'join the twenty-first century.' "

"Rafael wants nothing for himself. At the end of the meeting he said, 'As I see it I have only two options. I can either release its contents to the world letting the chips fall where they may or secure twenty-five million dollars in retribution from the Vatican to help the Mandaeans relocate.' "

"Retribution? He calls his extortion attempt – retribution?"

"Be that as it may, your Eminence, I don't think he's bluffing. Here are the wiring instructions to the Mandaeans' account in Iran and a copy of the translation I brought for you to read."

"Thank you, Pierre," Cardinal Ricci said as he took the instructions and the document David Hitzig had prepared and began reading.

Moments later he said, "Thank you for bringing this to me, Pierre. Asherah is of course troubling, but this passage about Mary Magdalene is devastating. It supports much of what is said about Peter rejecting her in the Gospel of Mary because she was a woman. I know that James and the Church of Jerusalem wanted to confine the teachings of Jesus within the community of the Torah. He and Paul argued about this. But listen to what he writes. We cannot allow it to be made public, no matter how untrue."

Lazarus, when you were spiritually dead Jesus returned to Bethany to awaken you. John the Baptizer's soul entered you that night and you were born again as John to lead our community.

Jesus chose Peter to tend to his flock, but he chose your sister, Mary, to lead our church and continue his life's work and you the incarnation of John, to assist her.

Simon Peter continued to doubt your and Mary's authority. He doubted that Mary was chosen to lead because she was a woman. When assembled he later asked us, did he really speak with a woman in private, without our knowledge? Should we all turn and listen to her? Did he prefer her to us? Mary wept at his remarks but Levi challenged him saying, if the Savior made her worthy, who are you to reject her? Surely the Savior knows her well. That is why he loved her more than us.

I implore you to remember the true stories of our ancestors and discount the ramblings of Saul of Taurus. It was Saul who stoned to death our Brother Stephen. It was Saul who attacked me on the Temple steps. Rome urged his repression of our Nazarene ways and teachings of ancient scriptures.

When Emperor Caligula placed his friend Herod Agrippa on the throne of Judah, Saul cast himself with his Roman name, Paul, to win Agrippa's favor. But I believe him to be the same man he once was. He preaches about the greatness of Jesus the Nazarene, but dismisses his life's work by seeking to make him a god in the likeness of Julius Caesar. Paul misrepresents our Nazarene ways in order to bring thousands of Gentiles to a new religion of his own making. As Paul continued to preach about the Savior as the messiah crucified by the Romans, Agrippa turned against him and us and threatens our entire existence. He executed James the Great, son of Zebedee. Simon Peter is now in prison. Surely others will follow. That is why you must leave Caesarea now while you still can.

Go into the world as John and proclaim the good news. Continue the Savior's teachings and protect your beloved sisters. Peace be with you.

"Pierre, I too have been complicit in this thing. Colonel Sordi came to me with much the same story as he presented to you. I told him if he and his friends were successful in retrieving the scroll for the Church, we would be able to arrange some compensation for their trouble in the same amount as the Israelis had offered. The money has been appropriated."

"Your Eminence?"

"Regrettably this forgery has been the basis of too much conjecture and bloodshed. It is a ruse designed to tear the fabric of the Church apart. The Colonel and the others were not thieves or killers, they were soldiers of Christ and now are martyrs in His name. I will make His Holiness aware of their martyrdom, Marie's devotion to the Church, and Rafael's proposal. By the time you get home I will have made my decision and call you."

* * *

Renee's joyful homecoming was quickly shattered by having to see Noelle once again. Renee was silent as she entered the church office for her family's meeting. Noelle's sad eyes looked in her friend's direction but her voice failed her. She greeted Marie, "Father Dubois and Rafael are ready for you. Please go in."

Rafael had reached a decision with their counsel. Marie and Jacques returned home. Renee joined Stan, Debra and Andy for dinner and explained what had transpired. The following evening, they joined Rafael, Marie and Jacques for dinner at Renee's childhood home.

Marie took great pains in preparing the meal to help bridge the divide that had occurred. The food was exceptional; the mood was tense.

"Mama, I don't understand how you could have wanted the scroll turned over to the Church," Renee said respectfully. "You know that they will bury it in the Vatican Archives, and it will be lost for all time."

Marie expected the question.

Renee continued, "After everything we've gone through to help Rafael and Miguel and the Mandaeans. Andy was almost killed in the accident and Stan, Debra and Papa could have been too."

"Renee, you above all people should remember our time in New York," Marie began. "Was the Statue of Liberty not conceived to embrace peace and justice? Was she not sickened by the wars and greed of men, as am I? That is why I did it … to end this ancient war once and for all. A war that is based on a 2,000-year-old myth. How much longer can we, as Christians, continue this fight one another … or the fight with Islam … or the fight with the Jewish people … or the fight with Asian mysticism … or whatever struggle tears God's children apart at any given moment? It has to stop … it has to stop! In the end it doesn't matter who's right or who's wrong. We're all right, we're all wrong."

"I think I understand," Stan offered, beginning to appreciate the point of view of his future mother-in-law. "But isn't there a higher purpose to be served here?"

"What do you mean?" Marie asked.

"I do not want to be indifferent about the truth."

The other guests remained silent.

"Nor do I, Stan, but who really knows what the truth is?" Marie continued to appeal to their better angels. "Renee, before your trip to Chartres, your father was frightened and concerned for your safety. Rafael, the day you visited Jacques to remind him of his Gnostic heritage and about Renee's connection to your mission, he told me everything you and David told him about the scroll – about Paul, about Mary Magdalene, and about Yahweh and Asherah. So, I have a question for you all. Was its God's and Asherah's shared vengeance that so many are dead, or could it be that the four of you are still alive because of Asherah's compassion? It doesn't matter whether Mary or Peter was chosen. What matters is you are all safe. The only harm that could come to you was if you kept the scroll and made it public."

As she continued her plea for her daughter's understanding and returned affection, a knock on the front door broke the tension in the room. Jacques answered it.

"Marie, it's Father Dubois," he said turning from him.

She wiped the tears from her eyes and composed herself before turning around. "Yes, Father, please come in. What can I do for you? Is there any news?"

"Marie, I'm sorry to interrupt your dinner, but I just returned from seeing Cardinal Ricci in Rome. He called a few moments ago to share his decision."

The room fell deadly quiet.

"Rafael, Cardinal Ricci sends the blessings of His Holiness. With the Pontiff's concurrence, the Cardinal has arranged for a wire transfer of twenty-five million dollars to the Mandaeans as you instructed. Cardinal

Ricci asked me to call tonight and tell him of your decision. If you choose to go forward, he will release the funds immediately, I will take possession of the scroll and return to Rome on the next available flight. It will take some time because the monetary transfer is so large and has to go through international channels. Cardinal Ricci was told they should expect the funds by the day's end tomorrow. I will wait for your confirmation that the funds have been credited before releasing the scroll."

Marie's guilt and thankfulness caused her to break down in tears.

"Thank you so much, Father," Rafael said. "Please proceed. This will mean everything to them, I am sure."

* * *

It did. The sum of twenty-five million dollars was transferred to the Mandaeans' bank account by the Vatican treasury. The following Sunday, Rafael was in Iran making a ceremonial presentation to Ganzeḇrā Nasisiyah, the High Priest of the Mandaeans, surrounded by the local priests – the Nasoreans.

* * *

Two weeks later, Rafael joined his father and his brother and was interred in a grave site near the Cathedral of St. James in Santiago de Compostela.

CHAPTER 42

WASHINGTON, DC - AUGUST 28, 2012

Dr. Malcomb Hedges, President of Georgetown University, opened the new academic year in the 464-year-old Jesuit school tradition of the Mass of the Holy Spirit. Healy Hall provided his stage set. Healy Lawn provided the setting for his congregation.

"Last year, on this day and in this city, America dedicated a memorial to Dr. Martin Luther King," he began. "We all recognize his words spoken on August 28th forty nine years ago, 'I have a dream that one day this nation will rise up and live out the true meaning of its creed: We hold these truths to be self-evident, that all men are created equal.'

"But he also left us, all of us, not only the African Americans among us, but all of us – men, women, boys and girls – with the challenge of moral leadership when he said, 'In the process of gaining our rightful place, we must not be guilty of wrongful deeds. Let us not seek to satisfy our thirst for freedom by drinking from the cup of bitterness and hatred. We must forever conduct our struggle on the high plane of dignity and discipline. We must not allow our creative protest to degenerate into physical violence. Again and again, we must rise to the majestic heights of meeting physical force with soul force.' That is the challenge that must also be the legacy of Georgetown University as we begin a new year. We must be ever vigilant to ..."

Renee's mind drifted from Dr. Hedges' remarks as she looked at Gaston Hall silhouetted against the clear blue sky. *This cool August day is the perfect way to begin my last semester,* she thought.

She reflected on King's words 'bitterness and hatred' and decided to let her resentment go. *Noelle was wrong to not tell me she was involved, but I need to take Dr. King's advice and let her know there are no hard feelings. Her loyalty to me in high school, and to my parents as Sebastian tried to drag them into his deranged world, and her heartfelt apology to me should be enough for me to forgive her. She had no idea of the disaster that was in front of us. This could have turned out so much worse.*

She took Stan's hand in hers, smiled and thought, *Mama also got it right. 'We must not allow our creative protest to degenerate into physical violence,' as Dr. King said. Somehow I lost sight of that. Gender equality will happen one day; it will just take more time and thoughtful leadership.*

* * *

George remained in his apartment. He did not feel like asking for God's blessing at the Mass of the Holy Spirit. He was depressed that he would not have Sebastian's financial backing to pursue his dream. He chose to turn his attention to the Republican Convention in Tampa for his spiritual fulfillment. A knock on his door interrupted the talking heads on TV.

"Who is it?" George asked.

"FBI. Open the door," Andy said.

"What the hell does Miller want now?" he said to himself.

He opened the door to see Special Agent Andrew Miller wearing a walking cast on his left leg to support his weight. Accompanying Miller were two plain clothes officers from the French Intelligence Agency. Andy grabbed George's shoulders and forcibly turned him around to cuff him. "George Wilson," he began, "I have a warrant for your arrest from the First District Court of Appeals obtained by the Office of International Affairs of the Justice Department. It has been issued in accordance with Chapter 209, Title 18 of the US Code – Crimes and Criminal Procedure for your extradition to France where you will stand trial. In pursuing extradition,

France charges you with the kidnapping of Renee Gaston, Miguel Tuguía and Rafael Tuguía; for the murders of Miguel Tuguía, Alberto Moretti, Guy Romano, Jean Durand, Leon Roux, Benito Sordi, Daryl Rousseau and Sebastian Philippe; and for the attempted murders of Yossi Wolff, Even Nagar, Gil Hassan, Stan Parker and Andrew Miller."

Andy read him his Miranda rights, then began to escort him from the room. "Oh, I almost forgot," he said turning off the TV and spotting George's journal. "Renee told me if I ever got the chance, this would be interesting reading."

* * *

"Hey, Stan, where are you? I've been trying to reach you for about an hour."

"I turned off my cellphone. Renee and I are just leaving the Mass of the Holy Spirit. Why, what's up?"

"I had a really good morning," Andy said. "Not only did two French Intelligence officers present me with the Médaille d'honneur, but also my transfer orders to the New York Field Office were approved!"

"Hey, Andy, congrats. That's great. I'm really excited for you, man! That's terrific."

"Yeah, the French Ministry made a special exception, and named me an honorary French policeman for our work on behalf of the French government. You and Debra should soon receive a commendation as well. Have you and Renee eaten lunch?"

"No, not yet, the Mass just ended. We were about to grab a bite."

"Why don't you both join me at Old Ebbitt. My treat. After this morning, I could use a well-prepared fillet, béarnaise and at least a couple of Dewars. I think you're going to find the news about my last official act with the DC office to your liking."

EPILOGUE

WASHINGTON, DC AND ELSEWHERE

To Renee's dismay, Republicans took control of the House with a thirty-three seat majority while Democrats retained control of the Senate in November 2012. A month later, Renee completed the requirements of the Master of Arts in Global, International and Comparative History. Two weeks later she became Mrs. Renee Gaston-Parker and took up permanent residence at their condo overlooking Oronoco Bay Park and the Potomac River. Neither George nor his red BMW convertible were anywhere in sight.

The Capitol dome restoration was completed in the same month as the 2016 Presidential candidate was elected. During the prior three years, interior paintings were cleaned and restored, over a thousand cracks were repaired and the building was repainted. Even with this accomplishment, the Architect of the Capitol, Stan Parker, lost his job to a new, Republican administration. Afterward, Stan became a full time professor at Georgetown University and opened a small architectural practice in Alexandria.

Of course, neither Stan nor Renee got their wish in the 2016 election. Renee's candidate, Hillary Clinton, who declared in a Beijing speech "women's rights are human rights", won the popular vote by nearly three million people, but lost the antiquated Electoral College vote.

That same year, history and black women also took a step backward, as the renovation of Chartres Cathedral brought with it the notion that the black Madonna should be painted with white features and makeup.

The day after the 2017 presidential inauguration, however, Renee began to see the light at the end of the tunnel with the Women's March. The march in Washington drew nearly a half-million people while nationwide over three million people participated in the single day event.

ABOUT THE AUTHOR

Architect Bill Blizzard's fascination with the construction of Gothic cathedrals led him down a path of theological inquiry. During a time when the only design tool was a compass and the only engineering knowledge came through trial and error, masons placed one stone on top of another and reached ever higher toward the heavens.

Blizzard has studied the works of many academicians and theologians including Dominic Crossan, Marcus Borg, Matthew Fox, Mary Starbird, Elaine Pagels and Karen Armstrong, among others for over two decades. Of particular note is the late Bishop John Shelby Spong. Among the many works of this prolific theologian is *The Sins of Scripture, Exposing the Bible's Text of Hate to Reveal the Love of God.* [7] In this book, Bishop Spong not only describes the negativity found in certain biblical text, but also discusses how they have caused societal harm from those who assume biblical authority to do evil in the name of God. In many ways, he suggests, we have unwittingly used the Bible to create a society and a world that may have been different had we read it through a Jewish lens and understood the context and times the texts were written.

SHARED VENGEANCE concerns itself with the text relating to the Bible and women. This is Bill's first novel.

NOTES

ACKNOWLEDGEMENTS

1. Reference for: *Rosslyn, Guardian of the Secrets of the Holy Grail,* Text © by Tim Wallace-Murphy and Marilyn Hopkins, 2000, First Published in Paperback by Element Books Ltd 2000, Element is a Trademark of HarperCollinsPublishers Limited.

FACT

2. Deerwester, Jayme (October 8, 2016) Reference for the quote from Nancy O'Dell, Co-Anchor Access Hollywood, *USA Today, "Nancy O'Dell breaks her silence on vulgar Donald Trump recording"*

CHAPTER 11

3. Spong, John Shelby, Episcopal Bishop, now deceased (2007), Reference for Joseph providing protection for Mary and Jesus, *Jesus for the Non-Religious, Recovering the Divine at the Heart of the Human,* p 29

4. Feather, Robert (2005) Reference to Akhenaten being the unnamed pharaoh in Genesis who promoted Joseph, *The Secret Initiation of Jesus at Qumran, The Essene Mysteries of Mysteries of John the Baptist,* p 87

5. Pickett, Lynn, (2003) Reference for the Ten Commandment being derived from the Egyptian Book of the Dead, *Mary Magdalene, Christianity's Hidden Goddess,* p 162

6. Wallace-Murphy, Tim and Hopkins, Marilyn (1999), Reference for the Renaissance in the Languedoc, *Rosslyn, Guardian of the Secretes of the Holy Grail,* .p 123

ABOUT THE AUTHOR

7. Reference for: *The Sins of Scripture, Exposing the Bible's Text of Hate to Reveal the Love of God,* Copyright © 2005 by John Shelby Spong, Harper Collins Publishers, New York, NY, 10022

www.ingramcontent.com/pod-product-compliance
Lightning Source LLC
Chambersburg PA
CBHW070810180626
46818CB00001B/194

9780578336084